SCHLOCK HOMES
The Complete Bagel Street Saga

By Robert L. Fish

GASLIGHT PUBLICATIONS

BLOOMINGTON, INDIANA · 1990

AUTHOR'S NOTE
The characters in this book are all real,
and any similarity to fictional characters is strictly coincidental

ISBN: 0-934468-16-8

Library of Congress Catalogue Card No.
84-73092

Printed in the United States of America

GASLIGHT PUBLICATIONS
626 North College Avenue
Bloomington, IN 47404

Contents

PUBLISHER'S PREFACE

THE STORY of the invention of Schlock Homes has been told many times and needs only brief mention here. Robert L. Fish (1912–1981), a civil engineer by profession, was sitting at home one Sunday afternoon in 1959 in Rio de Janeiro. There was nothing of interest on television; his wife and two daughters were out; he was alone and bored. To amuse himself, he sat down and wrote "The Adventure of the Ascot Tie." It was the first Schlock Homes misadventure and, thanks to the encouragement of Frederic Dannay (half of Ellery Queen), the beginning of a distinguished second career for Fish as a mystery writer. In time, he was to win no fewer than three Edgar Allan Poe Awards from the Mystery Writers of America.

To the general reader, Fish's best-known work is probably *Mute Witness* (1963), the book from which the movie *Bullitt* was adapted. To the mystery aficionado, he is best remembered for his two series protagonists, Kek Huuygens the smuggler and Captain José de Silva the Rio police detective. But to all, casual reader and hardcore collector, fan and professional alike, he will always be best loved for the exploits of the indefatigable Schlock Homes.

And that is no small statement to make regarding a man about whom the word "love" always comes first to mind. Robert Fish was genuinely loved by everyone who knew him. He was a short, stocky, gruff teddy bear who almost incongruously exuded tolerance, encouragement, and wondrously ad-lib humor. He never forgot a face or a dirty joke. He was a tenacious fighter for authors' rights. He served for many years as a hands-on member of the board of directors of the Mystery Writers of America and took a turn as its president. He showed a particular interest in new writers, and, after his death, the MWA established the annual Robert L. Fish Award for the best mystery short story by a beginning author. When he died of longstanding heart trouble in February 1981 – appropriately working at his desk, conceivably thinking out the plot of another Schlock Homes fiasco – there was an outpouring of sentiment that has probably never been equalled in the mystery world.

That world waited for the publication of the complete collected Schlock Homes cases. And waited. A chance conversation at a social function revealed that, for reasons even now unknown, no publisher had expressed interest in such a project. So it is that Gaslight Publications, a publisher of specialized, semi-scholarly monographs, finds itself in the happy position of offering, to aficionado and newcomer together, *Schlock Homes: The Complete Bagel Street Saga.*

Don't worry. You need not be a Sherlock Holmes expert in order to enjoy the Great Defective (though it helps). All that is expected is a taste for outlandish humor and a love for Sir Arthur Conan Doyle's original in any of his hundreds of incarnations. Robert L. Fish never would have demanded more from anyone.

SCHLOCK HOMES
The Complete Bagel Street Saga

The Adventure of
The Ascot Tie

IN going over my notes for the year '59, I find many cases in which the particular talents of my friend Mr. Schlock Homes either sharply reduced the labours of Scotland Yard or eliminated the necessity of their efforts altogether. There was, for example, the case of the Dissembling Musician who, before Homes brought him to justice, managed to take apart half of the instruments of the London Symphony Orchestra and cleverly hide them in various postal boxes throughout the city where they remained undiscovered until the dénouement of the case. Another example that comes readily to mind is the famous Mayfair Trunk Murder, which Homes laid at the door of Mr. Claude Mayfair, the zookeeper who had goaded one of his elephants into strangling a rival for Mrs. Mayfair's affection. And, of course, there was the well-publicized matter involving Miss Millicent Only, to whom Homes refers, even to this day, as the "Only Woman." But of all the cases which I find noted for this particular year, none demonstrates the devious nature of my friend's analytical reasoning powers so much as the case I find I have listed under the heading of *The Adventure of the Ascot Tie*.

It was a rather warm morning in the month of June in '59 when I appeared for breakfast in the dining room of our quarters at 221B Bagel Street. Mr. Schlock Homes had finished his meal and was fingering a telegram which he handed me as I seated myself at the table.

"Our ennui is about to end, Watney," said he, his excitement at the thought of a new case breaking through the normal calm of his voice.

"I am very happy to hear that, Homes," I replied in all sincerity, for the truth was I had begun to dread the long stretches of inactivity that often led my friend to needle both himself and me. Taking the proffered telegram from his outstretched hand, I read it carefully. "The lady seems terribly upset," I remarked, watching Homes all the while for his reaction.

"You noticed that also, Watney?" said Homes, smiling faintly.

"But, of course," I replied. "Her message reads, 'Dear Mr. Homes, I urgently request an audience with you this morning at 9 o'clock. I am terribly upset.' And it is signed Miss E. Wimpole."

He took the telegram from me and studied it with great care. "Typed on a

3

standard post-office form," he said thoughtfully, "by a standard post-office typewriter. In all probability by a post-office employee. Extremely interesting. However, I fear there is little more to be learned until our client presents herself."

At that moment a loud noise in the street below our open window claimed my attention, and as I glanced out I cried in great alarm, "Homes! It's a trap!"

"Rather a four-wheeler I should have judged," replied Homes languidly. "These various vehicles are readily identified by the tonal pitch of the hub-squeal. A trap, for example, is normally pitched in the key of F; a four-wheeler usually in B-flat. A hansom, of course, is always in G. However, I fear we must rest this discussion, for here, if I am not mistaken, is our client."

At that moment the page ushered into our rooms a young lady of normal beauty and of about twenty-five years of age. She was carefully dressed in the fashion of the day, and appeared quite distraught.

"Well, Miss Wimpole," said Homes, after she had been comfortably seated and had politely refused a kipper, "I am anxious to hear your story. Other than the fact that you are an addict of sidesaddle riding; have recently written a love letter; and stopped on your way here to visit a coal mine, I am afraid that I know little of your problem."

Miss Wimpole took this information with mouth agape. Even I, who am more or less familiar with his methods, was astonished.

"Really, Homes," I exclaimed. "This is too much! Pray explain."

"Quite simple, Watney," he replied, smiling. "There is a shiny spot on the outside of Miss Wimpole's skirt a bit over the exterior central part of the thigh, which is in the shape of a cut of pie with curved sides. This is the exact shape of the new type African saddle horn which is now so popular among enthusiasts of equestrianism. The third finger of her right hand has a stain of strawberry-coloured ink which is certainly not the type one would use for business or formal correspondence. And lastly, there is a smudge beneath her left eye which could only be coal dust. Since this is the month of June, we can eliminate the handling of coal for such seasonal purposes as storage or heating, and must therefore deduce her visit to a place where coal would reasonably be in evidence the year around—namely, a coal mine."

Miss Wimpole appeared quite confused by this exchange. "I was forced to leave the house in quite a hurry," she explained apologetically, "and I am afraid that I was not properly careful in applying my mascara. As for the jam on my finger, it is indeed strawberry," and she quickly licked it clean before we could remonstrate with her manners. She then contemplated her skirt ruefully. "These new maids," she said sadly, with a shake of her head. "They are so absentminded! The one we now have continues to leave the flatiron connected when she goes to answer the door!"

"Ah, yes," said Homes, after a moment of introspection. "Well; it was certain to have been one or the other. And now, young lady, if you should care to reveal to us the nature of your problem?" He noticed her glance in my direction and added reassuringly, "You may speak quite freely in Dr. Watney's presence. He is quite hard of hearing."

"Well, then, Mr. Homes," said she, leaning forward anxiously, "as you undoubtedly deduced from my telegram, my name is Elizabeth Wimpole, and I live with my uncle Jno. Wimpole in a small flat in Barrett Street. My uncle is an itinerant Egyptologist by trade, and for some time we have managed a fairly comfortable living through the itineraries he has supplied to people contemplating visits to Egypt. However, since the recent troubles there, his business has been very slow, and as a result he has become extremely moody, keeping to his own company during the day, and consorting with a very rough-looking group at the local in the evening.

"In order to understand the complete change in the man, it is necessary to understand the type of life we enjoyed when itinerant Egyptologists were in greater demand. Our home, while always modest, nonetheless was the meeting place for the intelligentsia. No less than three curators, an odd politician or two, and several writers on serious subjects counted themselves as friends of my uncle; and the head mummy-unwrapper at the British Museum often dropped by for tea and a friendly chat on common subjects.

"Today this has all changed. The type of person with whom my uncle is now consorting is extremely crude both in appearance and language, and while I hesitate to make accusations which may be solely based upon my imagination, I fear that several of these ruffians have even been considering making advances against my person, which I am certain my uncle would never have countenanced at an earlier day.

"While this situation has naturally worried me a bit, I should have passed it off without too much thought, except that yesterday a rather odd thing occurred. In the course of casually arranging my uncle's room, I chanced upon a telegram in a sealed envelope sewn to the inner surface of one of his shirts in a locked drawer. The nature of the message was so puzzling that I felt I needed outside assistance, and therefore made bold to call upon you." With this, she handed Homes a telegram form which she had drawn from her purse during her discourse.

Homes laid it upon the table and I stood over his shoulder as we both studied it. It read as follows: "WIMPY — WE HEIST THE ORIENTAL ICE SATURDAY. AMECHE OTHERS. HARDWARE NEEDLESS — THE FIX IS IN. WE RIG THE SPLIT FOR TUESDAY. JOE."

A curious change had come over Homes's face as he read this cryptic message. Without a word he turned to a shelf at his side and selected a heavy book bound in calfskin. Opening it, he silently studied several headings in the index and then, closing it, spoke quietly to our visitor.

"I wish to thank you for having brought me what promises to be a most interesting problem," he said, tilting his head forward politely. "I shall devote my entire time to the solution. However, I fear there is little I can tell you without further cogitation. If you will be so kind as to leave your address with Dr. Watney here, I am sure that we shall soon be in touch with you with good news."

When the young woman had been shown out, Homes turned to me in great excitement. "An extremely ingenious code, Watney," he chuckled, rubbing his hands together in glee. "As you know, I have written some sixteen monographs on cryptography, covering all phases of hidden and secret writings, from the Rosetta stone to my latest on the interpretation of instructions for assembling Yule toys. I believe I can honestly state, without false modesty, that there are few in the world who could hope to baffle me with a cipher or code. I shall be very much surprised, therefore, if I do not quickly arrive at the solution to this one. The difficulty, of course, lies in the fact that there are very few words employed, but as you know the only problems which interest me are the difficult ones. I fear this is going to be a five-pipe problem, so if you do not mind, Watney, handing down my smoking equipment before you leave, I shall get right to it!"

I reached behind me and furnished to him the set of five saffron pipes which had been the gift of a famous tobacconist to whom Homes had been of service: a case which I have already related in *The Adventure of the Five Orange Pipes.* By the time I left the room to get my medical bag he had already filled one and was sending clouds of smoke ceilingward, as he hunched over the telegram in fierce concentration.

I had a very busy day, and did not return to our rooms until late afternoon. Homes was pacing up and down the room in satisfaction. The five pipes were still smoking in various ashtrays about the room, but the frown of concentration had been replaced by the peaceful look Homes invariably employed when he saw daylight in a particularly complex problem.

"You have solved the code," I remarked, setting my bag upon the sideboard.

"You are getting to be quite a detective yourself, Watney," replied Schlock Homes with a smile. "Yes. It was devilishly clever, but in the end I solved it as I felt sure I would."

"I was never in doubt, Homes," I said warmly.

"Watney, you are good for me," answered my friend, clasping my hand gratefully. "Well, the solution is here. You will note the message carefully. It SAYS: 'WIMPY — WE HEIST THE ORIENTAL ICE SATURDAY. AMECHE OTHERS. HARDWARE NEEDLESS — THE FIX IS IN. WE RIG THE SPLIT FOR TUESDAY. JOE.' Now, disregarding the punctuation that separates this gibberish, I applied the various mathematical formulae which are standard in codifying, as well as several which have not been known to be in use for many years, but all to no avail.

"For some hours I confess to having been completely baffled. I even tested the telegram form for hidden writing, applying benzedrine hypochloric colloid solution to both surfaces, but other than an old shopping list which some post-office clerk had apparently written and then erased, there was nothing to be discovered.

"It was then that I recalled that Mr. Jno. Wimpole was acquainted with a mummy-unwrapper, and the possibility occurred to me that in the course of their many conversations, it was possible that the secret of ancient Egyptian secret writing had entered their discussions. Beginning again on this basis, I applied the system originally developed by Tutankhamen for the marking of palace laundry, and at once the thing began to make sense. Here, Watney; look at this!"

Bending over triumphantly he underlined the letter *W* in the word *Wimpy,* and then proceeded to underline the first letter of each alternate word, glancing at my startled face in satisfaction as he did so. The message now read: WHOS ON FIRST.

"Remarkable, Homes," I said dubiously; "but if you will forgive me, I find I am as much in the dark as before."

"Ah, Watney," said my friend, now laughing aloud. "When I first read this message, I also found myself baffled. But that was some hours ago, and I have not spent this time idly. I am now in possession of the major outline of the plot, and while it does not involve any serious crime, still it has been quite ingenious and clever. But there is nothing more to be done tonight. Pray send a telegram to our client advising her that we shall stop by and pick her up in a cab tomorrow morning at ten, and that we shall then proceed to the locale where the entire mystery shall be resolved."

"But, Homes!" I protested. "I do not understand this thing at all!"

"You shall, Watney; the first thing tomorrow," said Homes, still smiling broadly. "But no more for tonight. The Wreckers are at Albert Hall, I believe, and we just have time to change and get there if we are to enjoy the performance."

The following morning at ten o'clock sharp our hansom pulled up before a small building of flats in Barrett Street, and Miss Wimpole joined us. Both the young lady and myself looked askance at Homes, but he leaned forward imperturbably and said to the driver, "Ascot Park, if you please, cabby," and then leaned back smiling.

"Ascot Park?" I asked in astonishment. "The solution to our problem lies at a racing meet?"

"It does indeed, Watney," said Homes, obviously enjoying my mystification. Then he clapped me on the shoulder and said, "Pray forgive my very poor sense of humour, Watney; and you also, Miss Wimpole. I have practically solved the problem, and the solution does indeed lie at Ascot Park. Watney here knows how I love to mystify, but I shall satisfy your curiosity at once."

He leaned forward in thought, selecting his words. "When I first decoded the message and found myself with another message almost as curious as the first, namely, WHOS ON FIRST, I considered it quite carefully for some time. It could have been, of course, some reference to a person or commercial establishment named 'Whos' which was located on a First Avenue or Street. While I did not believe this to be true, it is in my nature to be thorough, and since New York is the only city to my knowledge with a First Avenue, I cabled my old friend Inspector LeStride, asking him to take steps. His reply in the negative eliminated this possibility, and I returned to my original thesis.

"Note carefully the last word, which is 'First.' This might, of course, have been an obscure reference to the Bible, in which it is promised that the last shall be first, but in perusing the original message I sensed no religious aura, and I am particularly sensitive to such emanations. No; instead I allowed myself to consider those cases in which it might be important to be first. I do not, of course, refer to queues or obstacles of that nature. The logical answer, naturally, is in wagering. The various means available to the Englishman of today to place a wager are extremely proscribed, and after checking the team standings and finding Nottingham still firmly in the lead, I turned to the racing news.

"And there I found, as I had honestly expected to find, that in the second race at Ascot today, the entry of the Abbott–Castle stables is a three-year-old filly named *Who's On First.*"

He turned to the young woman at his side. "My dear," said he, "I fear that your uncle is involved in a touting scheme and that the group with whom he has been meeting lately have been using the telegraph system to send advices regarding probable winners. This is, of course, frowned upon in most racing circles; but as I have so often stated, I am not of the official police, and therefore feel no responsibility for bringing people to their so-called justice over minor vices. I shall look forward, however, to the proof of my ratiocination at the track in a few moments."

"Oh, Mr. Schlock Homes," cried Miss Wimpole, clasping his hand in gratitude, "you have relieved my mind greatly. I have been so worried, especially since I have accidentally come across large sums of money hidden in obscure places in the house and feared that my uncle had become involved with some desperate characters engaged in nefarious practices. Now that I am cognizant of the nature of the enterprise, I can relax and may even replace at least a part of these sums with my conscience at rest, knowing that they were not gained through fearful means. But you must let me pay you for your efforts in this matter, Mr. Homes. Pray tell me what your fee is."

"No, Miss Wimpole," replied Homes with simple dignity. "If my theory is as good as I believe it to be, there shall be no question of payment. I shall take as payment the benefits of the information which you yourself were so kind as to bring to my attention."

Within a few minutes our hansom drew up at the ornate gate of the famous racing meet, and while Homes went to study the posted odds and speak with some of the bookmakers with whom he enjoyed acquaintance, I purchased the latest journal and retired to the stands to await his return. He was with me in a few moments, smiling broadly.

"It is even better than I had imagined, Watney!" said he. "The true genius of these people arouses my profoundest admiration. I note that in addition to *Who's On First* in the second race, this same Abbott–Castle stable has entered a horse named *What On Second* in the first race. And when I spoke to one of the track stewards just a moment ago, he informed me that because of rumours which have been flooding the steward's office – rumours apparently started by one of the hansom drivers at the gate – they propose to combine the two races. Now, at long last, the true nature of this ingenious plot finally emerges!"

"But what might that be, Homes?" I asked in bewilderment. "Can it be that the stewards are cognizant of the touting scheme and are using this means to combat it?"

"Your faith in track stewards is touching, Watney," said Homes dryly. "I am quite convinced that without the aid of one of their members, named Joseph, the entire scheme could not have been contemplated. No, no, Watney! The plan is far more intricate. These people know that if they go to a bookmaker with a bet on any one horse to win, the maximum odds which they can expect will be in the nature of five, or at most ten, to one. But think, Watney, think! Consider! What would the odds be against a *tie?*"

At once the devilish cleverness of the entire business burst upon my brain. "What do you propose to do, Homes?" I asked, searching his strong face for a clue.

"I have already done it, Watney," he replied calmly, and withdrew from his weskit five separate betting slips, each for the sum of £20, and each to be redeemed at the rate of 200 to 1 should the combined race end in a tie.

"Well, Watney," said Homes, when we were once again seated comfortably in our rooms in Bagel Street, "I can honestly state that to my mind this was one of my most successful cases – certainly from the financial standpoint. I feel that the ingenuity involved in codifying the betting information, while leaving out certain obvious factors, places our Mr. Wimpole and his associates in a special category of brilliance. We must be thankful that they have selected this relatively harmless means of breaching the law, and not something more nefarious. I certainly do not begrudge him his gains, although I must say that in seeing through their clever scheme, I feel quite justified in keeping mine."

Homes lit his pipe, and when it was pulling to his satisfaction, spoke again. "And now, Watney, we must search for another case to ward off boredom. Is there any crime news in that journal you are perusing which might prove to be of interest to us?"

"Only this," I said, folding the sheet in half and handing it to Homes with the indicated article on top. "Some three million pounds' worth of diamonds were stolen last night from the home of the Japanese ambassador. They were known as the Ogima Diamonds, and were considered the most valuable collection of their type in the world. The article states that the police believe it to be the work of a gang, but that otherwise they find themselves without a clue."

"Ah, really?" murmured Homes, his nostrils distended in a manner I had long since come to recognize as indicating intense interest. "May I see the article, Watney? Ah, yes! Ogima . . . Ogima . . . There is something faintly familiar . . ." He reached behind himself to the shelf where the reference books were kept and, drawing one out, opened it to the letter *O*.

"Ogima in basic Swahili means pencil-sharpener," he said, half to himself, "while the same word in ancient Mandarin referred to the type of pick used with the one-string guitar. No; I doubt if this is of much help. It would be far too subtle."

He returned the reference book to the shelf, and studied the article once again. Suddenly his faced cleared, and he leaned forward excitedly.

"Of course! You will note, Watney, that *Ogima* spelled backwards becomes *Amigo*. I shall be very much surprised if the answer to this problem does not lie somewhere south of the border. Your timetable, Watney, if you please."

The Adventure of
The Printer's Inc.

THE SUMMER OF '58 had been a rather quiet one. My friend, Mr. Schlock Homes, had returned from the Continent, where his success in disbanding a group of political fanatics given to ritual orgies had earned him the gratitude of both the British and Polish governments as well as the plaudits of the press on both sides of the Channel; a case I have already chronicled in *The Adventure of the Danzig Men*. Since his return there had been but several minor cases. For example, he had been able to uncover the defalcations of Lord Carstairs, with the result that this gentleman was forced to resign from all six of his exclusive clubs; a case I find detailed in my notes under the title of *The Adventure of the Dismembered Peer*. There had also been other inquiries of lesser interest; in general it had been a period of relative inactivity for Homes.

One evening in September we were returning home after dining in a small restaurant near our rooms at 221B Bagel Street. Our landlady, Mrs. Essex, had gone to visit a sick sister in Sussex, and our page was enjoying holidays, so that we found ourselves unattended for the first time in years, and living a bachelor's existence. To take any messages during our absence we had left a small lad named Finster Ismir, one of the street Arabs whom Homes employed from time to time for minor errands. As we arrived at our entrance, Homes greeted him cordially.

"And how are the Bagel Street Irregulars?" he queried kindly, smiling at the urchin.

"Oh, sir," replied the lad, "since Dr. Watney has been treating us, we are all quite regular once again."

Homes glanced at me approvingly and turned to enter the doorway when the street Arab spoke. "Begging your pardon, sir, but during your absence you have had a visitor. He was a man of middle age, well dressed, and he awaited your arrival in your rooms for over an hour. He has but recently left, having promised to return in a few minutes with a problem which he claims to be quite urgent."

Homes clapped the boy on the shoulder and after thanking him for his services, we mounted the steps to our rooms.

"Until our mysterious visitor returns," remarked Homes as we entered, "let us see what we can deduce from the evidence he must have left during his stay."

I glanced about the room and said, "Really, Homes; I fail to see any change since we left."

"It is not that you fail to see, Watney," replied my friend dryly, "but that you fail to observe. For example, here are the remains of a cigar with no tooth marks on the end, nor is it damply matted as is usual. Our visitor must therefore be a man without teeth and with very dry lips, a sign, as you must know from your medical experience, of incipient diabetes. Unfortunately, we have no time for further analysis, for here, unless I am mistaken, is our mysterious friend now."

The door opened to admit a large, bustling individual, who immediately pumped Homes's hand vigorously, and seating himself before us, fitted a cigar neatly into a holder and began to speak.

"Mr. Homes," he said, "I am being persecuted, and I am desperately in need of your help. My name is George Good, and I am —"

"You are a bookmaker," interrupted Homes smoothly. "Note the callus on the inside of the index finger of the right hand, Watney; it comes from holding the needle when sewing the binding into place. Note also the spot of yellow glue on the cuff; it is a sure indication of the trade. And when we are able to observe the hilt of a knife protruding from Mr. Good's pocket, a knife certainly employed for the cutting of pages, we can definitely conclude that Mr. Good is a bookmaker."

"You amaze me, Mr. Homes," said our visitor in awe. "I am indeed a bookmaker, and in the course of writing the many betting slips each day, I have developed this callus which you so cleverly noted. I carry the knife for protection, for mine is not the most peaceful of occupations. I apologize for the egg stain, but in all honesty I have been so disturbed of late that I scarcely know what I am doing, let alone what I am wearing."

"Tell us your problem," Homes said in a kindly manner. "At the moment I am between cases and can devote my full attention to it."

"Well, Mr. Homes," said the large man, leaning forward in his chair, "as I have stated, my name is George Good and I operate a small book which is known throughout the trade as the 'Good Book.' While it is not the largest of its kind, I have been able through the years to develop a small reputation, and my income from this endeavour is both steady and satisfactory.

"As you must know, in my profession there are many dishonest people, but I pride myself that I have been able to place myself on the same footing of respectability as my friends Amos Roggi and Job Weldon in keeping book-making a decent profession.

"I am here for the sake of these two friends as well as for myself, because today we are all being theatened. Of late, Mr. Homes, the dock area of London, which is where we all operate for the most part, has been flooded with leaflets of this nature." And he took three papers from his pocket and handed them to Homes.

I leaned over my friend's shoulder and we both perused them. The first read:

THE GOOD BOOK SAYS:
Gambling is a Deadly Sin!

Hear Professor Martin
Expound on the Evils of Gambling —
Place: Johnson's Warehouse —
Time: Every Night at 9 O'Clock
Directly after the Lecture there will be A
DEMONSTRATION

The other leaflets were quite similar, except that one began: THE BOOK OF AMOS SAYS: while the other began: THE BOOK OF JOB SAYS:. Otherwise the three were identical in text.

"Now, Mr. Homes," said our visitor earnestly, "you must believe me when I swear to you that I never said anything of the sort. Nor did my friends Amos or Job. You must realize that a canard of this description can be ruinous to our profession." The sincerity of his voice left no room for doubt as to the truthfulness of his statement. "My friends and I are prepared to pay any reasonable amount to have you trace this to its source and stop these fiends from jeopardizing our livelihood!"

Homes studied the leaflets with intense interest. There was a shadow of a frown in his eyes which indicated to me that there was something of a puzzling nature in the message which for the moment he could not fathom.

"Tell me, Mr. Good," said he finally, "have you any enemies?"

"Well, Mr. Homes," replied the bookmaker, "you must understand that in my business, as in all businesses, there are occasional disgruntled clients. It is true that I have been the object of several armed attacks, and I was once flung from a Thames riverboat after having been handcuffed and gagged, an occasion on which I consider myself fortunate to have escaped with only a dipping. At one time I also admit to having discovered an infernal machine attached to the brake pedal of my hansom, but since I seldom apply the brake, I was saved from any unpleasant accident." He paused, and then continued.

"However, an enemy in the sense of one who would deliberately threaten a man's livelihood is difficult to imagine."

"Well, Mr. Good," said Homes after considering this information, "if you will leave these interesting leaflets in my hands I shall get to work on the problem at once. Please leave your address with Dr. Watney here, and you may expect to hear from me within a very few days."

For some moments after our guest had taken his leave, Homes remained in a brown study, the offending papers held tautly in his strong, thin fingers. Finally he sighed heavily and arose.

"It is best to strike while the iron is hot, Watney," said he. "I suggest we attend tonight's lecture and see what we can learn. In a way it is a pity, as Crippen is singing tonight at Bow Street, and I had hoped we might attend. However, business before pleasure; so if you will excuse me for a few moments, I shall hurry into suitable raiment and we can be on our way!"

In a few minutes we were rattling along Old Holborn on our way to Limehouse. Homes, a veritable master of disguise, was dressed as a retired brewmaster, and was busily chewing on a small cake of yeast.

"Authenticity, Watney!" he exclaimed. "Authenticity! It is the secret of all successful disguise. But here we are in Limehouse. It is many years since I made my first visit to this quaint section of our great city, but I see it has changed but little."

We descended before a large warehouse, brilliantly illuminated by gas lamps, and made our way inside. We had apparently arrived too late for the lecture, for as we entered we could hear the fading sound of applause, and we were in time to notice a large man in the act of descending from the platform which had been raised at one end of the room. He was a startling figure, fully seven feet in height and weighing no less than twenty stone. His hair was of a deep orange shade, and as he descended the steps leading from the dais, I noticed that he limped badly. At sight of this strange figure, Homes gave a sharp cry and grasping my arm with a grip of iron, drew me back into the shadows along the wall.

"Watney!" he exclaimed, his voice tense with excitement, "that is certainly not a person named Martin! That is the most dangerous man in all London! It is Professor Marty, the one they call – with good reason – the Butcher!"

"But, Homes," I cried, "are you sure?"

"Watney, I never forget a face! You may recall that he was the master criminal who forged the papers in that quadruple paternity case of last year: the one you so aptly chronicled in *The Scion of the Four!* This case is becoming far more complex than I had originally contemplated. We must keep our eyes peeled, for the Professor is the cleverest criminal outside of prison today!"

Keeping well back in the shadows, we slowly circled the huge hall. Throughout its length, large tables covered with baize had been placed, and on one side of these tables men were busy shuffling cards and awaiting the audience to arrange themselves about the table to begin the play. The appointments of the hall were no less than luxurious: thick draperies of expensive silk hid the walls, while soft music came from an alcove where a small ensemble played quietly. I assumed that this was the demonstration mentioned in the leaflets, and said as much to Homes.

"It is probably much more of a demonstration than you imagine," was his strange reply. "Let us watch the play with care, for this is obviously a major operation on the part of Professor Marty. Note the draperies and the orchestra. Note the mahogany tables and the new green baize. Note the enormous size of the organization which is needed to handle the demonstration at all of the many tables."

"Not only that, Homes," I answered, "note also that all of the banknotes are new. The cashiers in the corner are changing everyone's money for new bills, and only new bills are allowed in play!"

"It is all part of the décor of luxury, Watney! The Professor does nothing on a small scale, and the use of new money is in keeping with the general beauty of the establishment here. Keep watching with the utmost care, for there must be an explanation for this extravagance on the part of one who values money above life itself! And make no mistake, Watney; this has cost the Professor a fortune! I find it difficult to believe that he has done all this simply for the purpose of embarrassing a small group of bookmakers!"

The play at the various tables was, by now, quite active and the hum of voices, together with the calls of the dealers, arose until there was a steady level of sound which was quite loud. Suddenly I was sure I had the answer.

"Homes! I've got it!" I cried. "This is nothing but a gambling house, and the leaflets were simply a means of enticing victims to this place. Let us call the authorities at once and have them take action!"

Homes shook his head sadly. "I wish it were that simple," said he, "but you vastly underestimate the diabolic cleverness of Professor Marty! During our stay here I have been observing the card play with exceptional care, and I have noted something which you evidently did not. *Each card in use is marked in such a manner that the dealer knows precisely the value of his opponent's hand.* No; Professor Marty has made sure that nobody can bring a charge of gambling against him, for he has eliminated the element of risk from the play!"

We remained silent, lost in contemplation of the fiendish intelligence against which we were pitted. At last Homes sighed heavily. "I fear there is little more to be learned on this visit, Watney," he said. "The answer must lie in those leaflets which Mr. Good has left in our possession. I suggest we return to our rooms, for I feel a comfortable chair and a few bars of Rubinoff will do more in aiding me to arrive at a solution to this problem than any further study we might make here."

Once again back in Bagel Street, Homes quickly changed to his dressing gown and bade me good night. "I shall stay up a bit more, if you do not mind, Watney," said he. "All problems are of interest to me, but any business involving Professor Marty is of particular interest. If you would not mind handing me those leaflets from the table before retiring, I shall get down to it!"

The following morning I entered our sitting-room to find the lamps still burning and Homes dozing in a chair, his hand still clutching the three sheets of paper. At my entrance he awoke, instantly alert, and arose to greet me.

"I believe I have come to the proper solution, Watney," said he, smiling genially. "I suggest we repair to the restaurant on the corner and enjoy a hearty repast, during which I shall explain my theory to you and ask for your reactions."

We were soon seated across from one another in a corner booth in the restaurant and the waiter had taken our order. Homes leaned back comfortably and reaching into his pocket produced the three leaflets, laying them on the table before us.

"Do you note anything out of the ordinary about these pages, Watney?" he inquired. "You do not? Well, when first I saw them it struck me that there was something missing, but at the moment I was unable to place my finger upon it. It was only last night upon our return from Johnson's Warehouse, when I had an opportunity to spend more time in the study of these documents, that I realized what it was.

"You have undoubtedly seen many leaflets in your time, Watney, as have we all, and there is always one mark on every leaflet or any printed matter, as far as that goes, which we see but we do not observe, since we see it but subconsciously. That is the seal of the Printer's Guild at the bottom of the sheet. It is always there; every folder announcing the sale of used traps, every journal which appears daily at our breakfast table, every concert announcement posted on a wall; they all have imprinted at the bottom of the page the small oval of the Guild. It is so obviously and everlastingly there that we never see it.

"And so we return to the case of these leaflets which Mr. Good brought to our attention. I did not consciously look for the mark since I felt I knew it was there. But when I studied them with the care they deserved, I noted that these marks were *not* there. And therein lies the solution to our problem."

"You mean . . . ?" I asked, astounded.

"Exactly! My old enemy Professor Marty is running an illicit printing establishment and earning great sums of money through his failure to pay proper Guild wages, or the dues which that organization requires."

"But the card room, Homes," I protested. "What reason could he possibly have for arranging such an elaborate establishment, and what possible connexion could there be between Johnson's Warehouse and an illegal printing plant?"

Homes smiled gently. "You may recall the noise involved in the cardplay once the so-called demonstration was in session. A printing press has many qualities, Watney, but silence is not one of them. To operate a printing press, one must be prepared for a certain amount of noise, and if this press is to be operated clandestinely, the noise obviously must be hidden. Where better to hide one noise than under a greater noise; the noise, for example, of the players as they place their wagers and follow the play?"

"Then you believe that this illicit press is being operated on the premises of Johnson's Warehouse?"

"If my theory is correct it must be! Either in an attic or in a basement." Homes leaned across the table confidently. "I have an idea as to how we can get Professor Marty himself to disclose the secret of the hiding place. It is a device I have found of use in the past, and I have no reason to doubt it will be successful once again. Tonight please see that your revolver is available, and we shall bring the case to a successful conclusion!"

Homes was unable to travel to Limehouse with me that evening as he had to stop and arrange for the various accoutrement necessary to his scheme. However, I had scarcely alighted from my hansom when he appeared at my side.

"Everything is arranged," he said in a low voice. "Pay close attention to your instructions! As soon as we are finished with this conversation, I should like you to enter and mingle with the others in a natural fashion. At precisely ten o'clock you will hear a cry of 'Fire!' as I throw these smoke bombs upon the floor. This cry will be repeated by many voices, for I have stationed the Bagel Street Regulars about the place. Your job is simply to keep an eye on the Professor during the resulting confusion. It is certain that he will go at once to the place where the press is concealed.

"A few moments after the initial cry, there will be a general retraction, and people will begin saying it was only a false alarm. At that point, my dear Watney, you will kindly leave the hall and join me at the corner of the street, where we will plan the next step in our campaign."

To this end I entered the hall and walked slowly from table to table, always keeping my eye on the huge figure that dominated the room from his position at the foot of the dais. At exactly ten o'clock there was a sudden commotion and great pillars of smoke arose as many voices took up the cry of "Fire!" The orange-haired giant sprang from his place and limped rapidly towards one corner of the large room while I watched every move that he made. At that moment voices were raised crying that the whole thing was a false alarm, and I watched until the Professor had returned to his place before leaving the hall and joining Homes on the street corner.

He grasped my hand in great excitement. "Did you watch him?" he cried.

"Certainly. As soon as the tumult arose, he left his position near the platform and hurried immediately to the southwest corner of the room."

"What was there?" Homes demanded.

"A fire extinguisher," I replied.

Homes smiled grimly. "A fire extinguisher!" he remarked softly, as if to himself. "Hanging on the wall! Pure genius! You see, Watney, one might lift aside the heavy draperies in search of a keyhole to a secret passage, but who would ever lift aside a fire extinguisher in such a search? We accept it so much that we scarcely note that it is not a part of the wall, but can readily be used as an agent of concealment.

"Well, Watney, this gaming establishment remains open until midnight, and I suggest that we give the Professor an extra hour before we attempt to find the secret hidden behind that fire extinguisher. You remembered to bring your revolver? Good! I never underestimate Professor Marty, and I should not like to see harm come to either of us."

We turned and began walking slowly up the street as Homes continued. "Fortunately I foresaw the possibility of our arriving at this point in our investigation, and have engaged a room across the street from the hall. There I have concealed a bull's-eye lantern as well as the other instruments necessary to gain entrance to the building. Let us wait out the hours there."

It was almost two o'clock in the morning before Homes gave the signal to move. He had been standing behind the curtain of the room watching the building across the way, and he finally turned.

"I believe it is safe now," he said, pulling on a pair of dark gloves. "Remember! No noise! Transfer your pistol to your right-hand pocket for easy accessibility, and do not hesitate to use it should the necessity arise!"

We stole across the street carefully, and Homes tackled the lock on the door while I kept a careful watch in the street against the possibility of a constable passing. A soft exclamation from Homes and I hurried up the steps to join him. A moment later we had entered the darkened room and softly closed the door behind us. Homes lifted the shutter of the bull's-eye lantern and directed the beam across the empty covered tables toward the corner I indicated.

"Come, Watney," he whispered, stealing forward quietly. "Lift away the extinguisher and let us see what is behind it."

I picked the heavy metal tube away from the wall, and Homes gave a grunt of satisfaction. Neatly placed beneath the bracket was a small keyhole, and Homes applied himself to it at once. A moment later a section of the wall swung smartly back, revealing a set of steps leading down to the cellar.

We quickly descended, stepping carefully on the wooden treads. A turn at the bottom of the steps allowed us to send the beam of the bull's-eye flickering over shelves of playing cards and stacks of new bank notes. But what was of greater interest to us was that there, in the center of the room, as Homes had so accurately predicted, stood a complete printing plant.

We were at breakfast the following morning in our rooms, for Mrs. Essex had returned, when a heavy step announced the arrival of a visitor. Before we could arise, the door burst open and in strode Professor Marty, shaking with rage.

"It was you, you foul busybody!" he cried. "Did you think for one moment that I did not recognize you the first time you stepped into Johnson's Warehouse? I have had you followed every minute since, and had my men not lost you while you were crossing the street last night, you would never have lived to uncover the secret of that cellar room!"

Homes smiled coldly. "Pray be seated, Professor," he said. "You are a man of intelligence, and should know when the game is up. Had you not called upon me, I had every intention of stopping by to speak with you, and even bringing Printing Guild officials with me. You are finished, Professor Marty, as you should have known you would be when first you chose Schlock Homes as an opponent!"

Professor Marty fell into a chair, his face twitching. "Homes," he rasped, "you are a devil! What do you want?"

"First," said Homes, laying the leaflets on the table, "you must guarantee to never again practice this filthy game of plagiarism! Through your un-authorized use of the good names of these men you have been responsible for much unhappiness. Second, I never want to see any product of your printing plant come to my attention without the mark of the Printer's Guild upon it!"

The Professor sat before us, a puzzled, broken man. "I have no choice," said he. "It shall be as you demand." He arose and limped dejectedly from the room.

Homes lit a cigar and leaned back relaxed. "I suggest, Watney, that you contact Mr. Good and inform him that neither he nor his friends will be troubled in the future.

"And now, Watney, what is new in the newspapers which might be used to occupy our talents for a while?"

"Very little, Homes," I replied, scanning the morning journal carefully. "Of course there is much publicity being given to the embarrassing position of the Government because of the large amount of counterfeit banknotes which recently has been flooding the city."

"Counterfeit money?" Homes mused. "It seems to strike a chord. Counterfeit money? Of course!" He suddenly burst into hearty laughter, as hilarious as ever I have seen him.

"No, Watney," said he, choking with laughter, "I fear that this is one case I shall not take!"

"But, Homes," I remonstrated, "why not?"

"The Professor!" he gasped, doubled over and wiping the tears from his eyes. "The Professor! You recall the stacks of new money in the warehouse? *These counterfeiters have victimized Professor Marty himself!* And much as I disagree with their métier, I cannot find it in my heart to pursue them!"

The Adventure of
The Adam Bomb

I HAD BEEN PURSUING an errand for my friend Mr. Schlock Homes in the small village of Elbow Twisting, Herts., when the fateful telegram arrived. I do not have it before me as I write but it is not necessary, since its tragic message is engraved upon my memory. It read: "MR. HOMES PASSED AWAY YESTERDAY. INTERMENT AT 4 P.M. PORTLAND CEMETERY," and was signed by our housekeeper, Mrs. Essex. It was in complete shock that I threw my few possessions into my bag and caught the first train for London. There I transferred to a hansom and proceeded directly to the cemetery, my mind a blank.

As we rattled through the dismal streets, I remembered that Homes had insisted upon doing research on a rare virus; so rare, he had informed me, that no known case of the disease had as yet been discovered. I had warned him of the dangers of such investigation, but he had passed it off with his usual disregard for either personal danger, or the advice of others, and had now apparently fallen victim to the very germ he had been seeking. It was with heavy heart that I descended at the cemetery, barely able to think coherently.

There was a large group gathered about the open casket, and I forced myself to step forward for a last look at the frozen profile I had known so well. His brother Criscroft came forward and grasped my hand wordlessly. In silence I stepped back and observed the crowd about the grave. There I could see many police agents whom Homes had assisted in past cases; many persons of high estate who owed a great deal to my dead friend for their present state of well-being; and included in the crowd I could also see the smirking faces of many criminals to whose downfall Homes had been dedicated. I could not help myself; tears formed in my eyes and fell unhindered to the ground. Feeling more alone than at any time in my life, I watched the undertaker's men bolt the cover into place and begin the sad task of lowering the casket into the waiting earth.

A sudden elbow in my ribs caused my attention to turn to a short, stocky figure at my side. He was a Cockney, poorly dressed, and with a long scarf wrapped about his neck, and a huge straggling mustache covering half of his face.

"Good riddance to bad rubbish! Eh, wot, Gov'nor?" said the vile apparition in a high whining voice, once again nudging me with his sharp elbow.

"Hold your foul tongue and be off with you, you miserable specimen!" I cried, brandishing my stick. "No finer person ever breathed the clean, sweet air of Putney, and I shall tolerate no word against his memory! Be off, I say, or you shall suffer the worse for it!"

"My, my, Watney, such devotion would better to have been deserved," came the voice of my friend Schlock Homes with a low chuckle. "No, do not look now, but meet me in fifteen minutes at the Uppin Arms in Jermyn Street!"

I could not help myself; I turned in astonishment but the small figure had disappeared and I was left with my mind awhirl, watching the coffin lowered into the cold grave.

I found my way to Jermyn Street after the funeral, but to this day I do not know how. It was difficult to believe that I had not been dreaming, for I had seen his body with my own eyes; yet the memory of that voice in my ear left me no choice. Afraid of what I might find, I pushed open the heavy door of the pub and entered into the gloom. The Cockney, still with his scarf, but lacking his grotesque mustache, confronted me from a corner booth, and his twinkling eyes could belong to nobody in this world except my old friend Schlock Homes!

"Homes!" I cried, sinking into the seat opposite as my legs weakened under me. "How is it possible? What is the reason for this macabre joke? Why have you given this terrible shock to all of your friends?"

"Only to you, I am afraid, Watney," replied Homes. "It was essential to a case I am engaged upon that I disappear, and ever since the time I disappeared in that tavern in Switzerland for several months, only a buried corpse could have satisfied my enemies. Both Criscroft and the police agents were aware of the scheme, and I believe I have made Mrs. Essex quite happy by allowing her to play a role in one of my cases. You, however, are too honest and open in your feelings, and any of my enemies, seeing your countenance, would have known at once it was a trick. I am indeed sorry, Watney, for the shock you have suffered today, but believe me, it was of vital necessity!"

"And your sending me to Elbow Twisting?"

"A part of the same plan, I am afraid. I had planned to die of a virulent disease, and I was sure that I could scarcely hope to deceive you on that score!"

"But the body, Homes! I saw it myself!"

"An excellent example of Madame Tussaud's art, Watney. They have owed me a favour since the time I foiled those two miscreants who concealed themselves on the premises for the purpose of robbing the safe during the night. You, yourself, chronicled the case in *The Adventure of the Waxed Pair.*"

"But your appearance, Homes! Your extra weight!"

"Only stuffing; actually, one of Mrs. Essex's pillows."

"And your height, Homes! You are fully a foot shorter!"

"Special shoes. But this involved procedure was not formulated either to demonstrate my ability at disguise, nor to needlessly cause you anguish, Watney. No, it was necessary as, if you will allow me, I shall explain at once."

We ordered drinks, and once they were before us, Homes leaned back and proceeded to explain the strange events of the past few weeks.

"You are, of course, acquainted with my brother Criscroft," said he, "and you know of his important position in the Home Office. You must also be familiar with the high regard in which I hold him, not only for his intelligence, but also for his almost infallible sense of prescience.

"Well, some three weeks ago, while you were out on a call, Criscroft appeared in our rooms in Bagel Street. He had not sent any previous notice of his coming, which in itself was highly unusual, and he was not his usual calm self. He wandered about the room making small talk, as if reluctant to state the purpose of his visit. I waited patiently for him to approach the subject, but he continued with his evasions.

"'You were familiar with the Brace–Partridge plans?' he asked, obviously making conversation.

"'Certainly; a lovely couple,' I replied. 'Unfortunately, I was unable to attend the nuptials.'

"'But you sent a fish slice?'

"'Of course. Halibut, I believe. However, I am sure that you did not remove yourself from your busy desk in Whitehall for the purpose of discussing London's social season with me. Pray tell me what is actually bothering you!'

"He threw himself into a chair and stared at me broodingly. 'If only I knew,' he replied. 'In truth I have nothing to go on but a feeling of foreboding, and I hate to interrupt your schedule with something which could well be only a wild-goose chase!'

"'Simply state the facts and let us proceed from there,' I said. 'You have never given me cause for complaint until now.'

"'Very well, then,' said he. 'The facts are these: Quite recently a person giving his name as Frederic Adam appeared at the War Office and claimed to have invented a new type infernal machine which he wished to patent under the name of the Adam Bomb. The War Office wanted more detailed information; he refused to disclose any of his secrets. They then offered him the use of the Sussex Proving Grounds for him to demonstrate his new invention, but he declined on the basis that the proving grounds were too small, and that the test would jeopardize near-by residents. Since the Sussex Proving Grounds are fully four acres in size, the War Office considered his excuse quite spurious, and sent him about his business.'

"'I should tend to agree with their action.'

"'I am not so sure. Well, a few days later a colleague of mine in the Explosives Section happened to mention the case to me in our club, not for action, but merely in idle conversation as demonstrating the type of annoyance they suffered at the hands of cranks. For some reason a feeling of foreboding seemed to overcome me, and I pressed him for all details of the man and their conversations, but other than the facts, which I have just stated, he was unable to be of further assistance.'

"'What did you do then?'

"'Actually, there was little that I could do officially. However, unofficially I began making inquiries into Mr. Frederic Adam's past, and while I could find nothing actionable in his activities, I did discover that while a student he had studied under Professor Marty, who, as we both know, is not only a brilliant scientist, but the most dangerous criminal in all England.'

"'Professor Marty, you say? You interest me deeply!'

"'I thought I should. Well, my investigation seemed to show that there had been no contact between them since Adam graduated University, but this in itself means nothing. Adam, it appears, had private means, and established a laboratory near Glasgow, where he pursued his researches, and from whence he travelled when he appeared at the War Office.'

"'And since that time?'

"'He has recently purchased an abandoned coal mine near Newcastle in Northumberland County and is even now moving his scientific equipment into it. It is heavily guarded, extensively fenced, and quite impossible to enter. Other than his previous acquaintance with Professor Marty, and this feeling of foreboding which I have, I admit to small basis for further investigation, but I cannot rid myself of the conviction that it is vital that we know what he is planning!'

"'And what do you wish me to do?'

"'I suggest that you attempt to gain entrance to this mine in one of your inimitable disguises. Since I know that you are under constant surveillance by the criminal element of London, you must first convince them that you have taken sick and succumbed to your illness. You will then be free to pursue your investigation without undue suspicion on their part.'

"We therefore decided on the plan which you are now witnessing. I am very sorry that it was necessary to include you among the victims of the deception, Watney, but the assurance of every scoundrel in England tonight that Schlock Homes is safely disposed of beneath six feet of earth owes much to your touching performance at the grave!"

"But, Homes," I inquired, "is this not basically a matter for the police? Can they not demand entrance to this mine and see what deviltry is afoot?"

He smiled at me pityingly. "The police," said he, "may serve to locate something of the size of an elephant, assuming the area of search were sufficiently proscribed; but in the first place, there is no evidence that Mr. Adam is engaged in anything nefarious, which would seriously complicate the possibility of obtaining search warrants. In the second place, I doubt if the police would be in a position to recognize a clue should they encounter one. No, Criscroft is right. I shall have to go down there myself and attempt to gain entrance to this mysterious mine in some fashion."

"And what is my role in all this?"

Homes leaned forward impressively. "This mine which Adam has purchased," said he, "is located at Seldom-on-Tyne, a suburb of Newcastle, in Northumberland County. We shall select a country inn on the river, sufficiently distant from the mine to avoid suspicion, but close enough to allow easy travel. There we shall share quarters, for I am certain to have errands for you to do. Besides, it is always well to have a friend in the vicinity when one is working underground."

"And our luggage?"

"All has been arranged. Even now your baggage and mine are awaiting us at King's Cross. Our reservations on the sleeper are being held at the ticket office. I suggest we dine at some small restaurant where my dishevelled appearance will not cause comment, and then, if you wish, we can pass the hours until train time in shilling seats at Queen's Hall, where the Minsk dancers are performing."

"I would like that!" I cried with enthusiasm. "I have always wanted to see the Russian Minsk dancers!"

"Actually," said Homes, "I believe these are the Harold Minsk dancers from the United States."

"But, Homes," I said in disappointment, "this is misrepresentation!"

"Yes," replied Homes thoughtfully, "I suppose you might call it a ballet ruse, but we do have the time to pass in some manner, and I understand that their talent is quite revealing."

The following morning I found myself ensconced in a fairly clean inn at Skeleton Quay, but a few miles from the heavily guarded mine. Homes had separated from me at the station, selecting to hire a ramshackle bicycle and pedalling off along the road ahead of my trap. I was amazed at his appearance; with his cap pushed back, his scarf waving in the breeze, his mustache rampant, and his shrill whistle, he appeared in all respects to be what he pretended to be, a Tyne-side worker on his way to the job.

It was evening when he came whistling up the stairs to our room and entered the door. As soon as it was closed, he quickly locked it and fell into a chair, laughing.

"There was little to it, Watney," he said. "I managed to combine the stupidity of a natural with the native cunning of the local folk, and this, plus my pure Geordie accent, did the job. They hired me at once! You are now looking at the new sweeper in the Adam mine."

"A sweeper?" I asked in amazement. "Certainly you could have obtained a better position than that!"

"I am not there to make a living," he remarked dryly, "and the sweeper, my dear Watney, is one person who has access to all parts of the installation. Also, in order not to interfere with the work, my duties require me to be in places when the other workers are having meals, which will allow for opportunities for observation which might otherwise be difficult.

"It is an interesting operation, and one which must have cost a pretty penny. Huge equipment is arriving constantly and being unpackaged. My duties take me to many parts of the mine, and I find it to be far more extensive than I should have imagined. I suggest, Watney, that tomorrow you take a trap into Newcastle and visit the local Coal Board for the purpose of obtaining a copy of the original survey of this mine. I am beginning to have a glimmer of the aim behind this tremendous imposture, and I shall need to be familiar with the terrain!"

When Homes had left the following morning on his bicycle, I arranged transportation and went into Newcastle. While the Coal Board would not permit the original drawing to leave the premises, there was no difficulty in arranging to trace the underground map comprising the various tunnels of the old abandoned mine. With the tracing safely concealed on my person, I returned to Skeleton Quay and spent the remainder of the day strolling along the river and admiring the fortitude of the brave people who could tolerate such a place.

The usual whistle announced the arrival of my friend, and once in the room I could tell from the excited gleam in his eyes that he was on the trail of some interesting discovery.

"We are getting warmer, Watney!" he exclaimed. "You have the underground map?"

"A tracing of it," I replied. "It is indeed extensive. Some of the tunnels cover many miles."

"Fine! Please spread it out on this table and allow me to study it!"

Taking a standard one-inch map from his jacket, he laid it side by side to my tracing, and began to pore over the two maps with the greatest of concentration. Finally he shoved them to one side and leaned back.

"I begin to see light, I believe, Watney. Let me tell you of an interesting discovery which I made today. During the lunch hour it is my duty to clean the offices while the staff are eating, and I naturally took the opportunity to make a thorough search of the desks and drawers, as well as of the papers lying about. I found them to be covered with many scientific symbols, and I knew that if the solution to our problem lay in decoding all of these, our task would be a difficult one indeed! However, there was one formula which was recurrent, appearing at the head of each sheet of paper, and I memorized it, rather than take the chance of having it discovered during the nightly search which all employees must endure on leaving the premises."

"And what is this formula, Homes?" I asked breathlessly.

He leaned over the table and scrawled on a piece of paper. I stared at the figures in bewilderment, for he had written: $E = Mc^2$!

"You believe that this strange formula might throw light on our problem?" I asked in amazement. "But it is so short that it barely permits of decoding!"

"True, but still it is the only formula repeated on all the papers, and must therefore be vital to our case. As to its lack of length, I have solved shorter. I once located the body of a murdered man with nothing more to go on than the single letter X which appeared mysteriously on a newspaper diagram of the scene of the killing."

He rubbed his hands together nervously, in that gesture which I well knew indicated a desire to be alone with an interesting problem. "And now, if you will excuse me, Watney," he said, "I shall get right to it while the events are fresh in my mind, for I feel that I have all of the necessary facts within my possession!"

The following morning I awoke to find Homes pacing the floor in smiling satisfaction, and he chuckled at my startled expression, for he was no longer in disguise.

"Yes, Watney," said he in high good humour, "the masquerade is over! The problem is solved! I am afraid that Mr. Adam will have to apply to the Labour Board for a new sweeper, although in truth I doubt if they will be in business long enough to require such services!"

"But, Homes," I exclaimed in awe, "do you mean that with the little information which you showed me last night you have managed to arrive at an answer to this mystery?"

"The importance of information is in direct relationship to our ability to interpret it," he replied. "Come to this table and allow me to show you the connexion between the facts which we were able to collect."

Spreading the one-inch district map upon the table, he placed the mine tracing over it and carefully oriented the two until they were properly superimposed.

"I began my cogitation," he said, "by considering the possible reasons Mr.

Adam might have for locating his so-called scientific experiment in a mine. In the papers which I perused during my search of the office, I recalled reading something about a 'mushroom cloud,' and mines, of course, because of the dampness and constant temperature, are ideal for the cultivation of mushrooms; but since I was—and am—convinced that these papers were spurious in intent, I disregarded this line of thought.

"I then considered what more logical reason he might have for this odd selection of location. Suddenly a possibility struck me! Mine tunnels, Watney, run for many miles underground, and are a perfect means of getting from one place to another without detection! I immediately began to trace the various tunnels, comparing their location with the surface objects under which they passed. And then I had it!" He placed a long tapering finger on one spot of the superimposed maps and continued. "Here, Watney, is the answer! Tunnel No. 5 runs in a north-easterly direction, passing beneath nothing more important than farm country and several small villages, until it reaches here, at which point, you will note, *it stops directly beneath Eastland Prison!*

"It was now quite obvious that the *E* of the formula stood for *Eastland,* and I therefore returned with even greater enthusiasm to the study of the remainder of these mysterious symbols: Mc^2! I attempted to rationalize the *M* for either miles or meters, or the *c* for either cubits or cells, but the answer refused to appear. It was only after many hours of pondering that I realized that I was being unnecessarily complex in my reasoning. The equal sign in the formula clearly indicated that the symbols were mathematical in nature, and I therefore reapplied my efforts to the problem, studying it from a purely mathematical approach. And then I finally saw it! Do you recall from your school days what the small 2 above the *c* stands for in mathematics, Watney?"

"The square, does it not?" I hazarded.

"It does indeed," said Homes, his eyes twinkling. "But is it not also called the *power?*"

And then, suddenly, I saw the answer. "McPowers!" I cried. "Angus McPowers, the Glasgow assassin!"

"Precisely! The man known in thieves' argot in Glasgow as the 'Scotch Cooler!' His execution at Eastland Prison is scheduled for next week, and his friends and criminal associates have sworn they would arrange his escape at all costs! In the mine, Watney, I also came across a large machine which was marked 'Cyclotron,' and which can only be an electrically operated cycle of some new scientific design intended to spirit this murderer beyond reach once they have tunnelled him to freedom! But I am afraid they did not plan on the interference of Schlock Homes when they designed this ingenious escape!"

"A brilliant tour de force, Homes!" I exclaimed, grasping his hand. "What will you plan to do now?"

"It is already done, Watney," he replied simply. "Early this morning I entered the mine in my sweeper's disguise and reversed the electrical connexions on their high-powered cycle. Then, upon my return here, I sent telegrams to both Criscroft and Scotland Yard advising them of the situation. Even now the watch on McPowers is being doubled, and the Adam gang are under twenty-four hour surveillance. McPowers will go to his Maker as the judge ordered—that I promise!"

The following morning, back once again in our quarters in Bagel Street, Homes entered the breakfast room just as I was finishing my perusal of the daily journal.

"Is there anything of interest in the headlines this morning?" he inquired genially, sitting down to his breakfast and drawing a napkin languidly into his lap.

"A rather curious disappearance in the north," I replied, reading further into the article.

Homes sat back in alarm, breakfast forgotten. "Do not tell me that despite all of my efforts the police have allowed McPowers to disappear!" he cried.

"Not exactly," I said, handing him the journal folded to the article. "It seems that sometime during the night the whole of Northumberland County disappeared."

"Northumberland County, eh?" said Homes, relaxing and accepting the newspaper. "Ah, well, at least there should be no need for us to become involved. Northumberland County is of sufficient size that even the police should be able to discover it!"

The Adventure of
The Spectacled Band

BETWEEN the years '55 and '57 the genius of my friend Mr. Schlock Homes came, in my estimation, to its highest fruition. The early struggle for recognition was long past, and his fine reputation now extended to many countries beyond England. His excellent work in America during the war years led to the capture of the largest receiver of stolen black-market war supplies, a case I find listed in my notes under the title of *The Adventure of the Barbed-Wire Fence*. In France he had been of signal service to the Parisian police in helping them apprehend the gang known as the "Kidnapping Cabbies," a case which was widely publicized on both sides of the Channel as *The Adventure of the Taxi-Drivers' Métier*.

But his work was not all abroad, for in England his efforts had often saved the face of Scotland Yard, and earned him the gratitude of the Government. In going over my notes for these years I find it difficult to select any single case as being representative of his mental alertness during this period, but possibly the one which best illustrates his extreme ability to see past the obvious to the hidden subtlety beyond, is the one which I find annotated under the title of *The Adventure of the Spectacled Band.*

It was in the early winter of '56 that I returned one afternoon to our rooms at 221B Bagel Street. I had had a hard day, and I found myself quite exhausted as I let myself into our quarters. Homes was napping on the couch in front of the fireplace and I did not disturb him, knowing that he had been working quite hard of late on a new monograph covering a study of alcohol fractionation. It was a gray day, with dark clouds heavy with their burden of snow, and I felt restless in the shadowy room. I had puttered about for some minutes when suddenly I heard the voice of my friend behind me.

"You are quite right, Watney," he chuckled. "Conscience is indeed a hard taskmaster!"

"It most certainly is!" I retorted with a touch of asperity; and then I stopped in amazement. "Homes! You have done it again! You have read my mind!"

"It was really not too difficult," said he with a broad smile, swinging his long legs to the floor and turning up the lamp. "I have been watching you since you entered the room. After removing your overcoat, you went immediately to the sideboard, from whence you removed a bottle of vodka and poured a generous portion into a glass. At that moment you glanced at your pocket watch and a look of remembrance cast itself over your features. It was only last evening, as I recall, that you were lecturing me on the dangers involved in partaking of alcohol before the hour of five, and promising that you would abstain from an earlier tot if I agreed to join you in this forebearance.

"Following this, you glanced surreptitiously in my direction, and then obviously made up your mind, for I saw you adjust the stem of your watch. You then moved to the clock on the mantelpiece and advanced the hands fifteen minutes. When this was accomplished, you returned to your liquor glass, but just as you were about to taste it, you shook your head sadly and poured it back into the bottle. It was at that point that I observed that conscience was a hard taskmaster!"

"An admirable reconstruction, Homes!" I replied with awe. "Actually, I had set my pocket watch with the mantel clock this morning, and only in the course of passing Big Ben today did I note that I was fifteen minutes slow, and I corrected my watch accordingly. I returned home at precisely five and began to mix myself a vodka martini when I remembered that our timepiece was incorrect. I verified my watch, winding it as I did so, and then proceeded to correct the mantel clock. When I returned to the business of making my martini, I thought that under the present political situation my choice of liquor might have an erroneous interpretation placed upon it, and my conscience did indeed bother me when I recalled our brave boys at Balaclava and myself about to partake of vodka! I therefore poured it back into the bottle and was about to open the Scotch when you spoke."

"The important thing," replied Homes with a twinkle, "is not so much the process as the result. Now that we have determined both the correct hour and drink, I suggest we waste no more time. A long drink for me, if you please, Watney, while I show you a curious message which reached me this afternoon!"

He flung a telegraph form across to me, and I paused to read it carefully. "MR. HOMES," it read, "I SHOULD LIKE TO VISIT YOU AT FIVE O'CLOCK TODAY TO BEG YOUR OPINION REGARDING THE STRANGE ACTIVITIES OF THE MYOPIC MOUNTAINEERS," and was simply signed Jabers Willson.

"The Myopic Mountaineers?" I asked in bewilderment. "Pray, who might they be?"

"I have no idea," replied Homes, chuckling genially, "but the name, you must admit, is intriguing. However, I imagine we are soon to be informed, for here, unless I am much mistaken, is our mysterious visitor now!"

The door was opened and our page ushered in a short, stocky man who accepted my offer of a whisky, and after seating himself opposite us, began at once to speak.

"Mr. Homes," he said, twisting his whisky glass nervously in his large hands, "I do not know if, in fact, I have any real basis for this visit, but now that I am here and you have been kind enough to give me your attention, I might as well tell you my story.

"I am a wholesale druggist by trade, and I specialize in the import and sale of narcotics to hospitals and medical men in private practice. At one time my business gave me a very fair profit, but since the recent development of the modern synthetic anesthetics, the demand for my products has steadily dropped, until today it appears that my large stocks of heroin, cocaine, and opium may actually result in a huge loss to me. With business so poor, I felt I had no real use for my main warehouse in Cheapside, and I therefore decided to lease it as a means of augmenting my greatly reduced income.

"You can well imagine my delight, therefore, when I was recently approached by a Mr. Murphey, who offered me a rental figure for my premises which was far beyond my wildest expectations."

Homes, who had been listening to this tale in complete engrossment, raised a hand in interruption. "What did you plan to do with your stocks of medical supplies?" he asked, his keen eyes watching Mr. Willson closely. "Did Mr. Murphey insist that you remove these, to allow him the full facility of the space?"

"On the contrary, Mr. Homes," the stocky man replied earnestly, "Mr. Murphey was most co-operative, and said that he would have no objection whatsoever to my storing them on the premises. I offered to remove them to another location, but Mr. Murphey would not hear of my being put to this inconvenience. I have a reinforced concrete vault in the basement which I have used from time to time for the storage of old papers and receipts, and I therefore placed my stocks of narcotics in this deposit. Mr. Murphey offered to take charge of the keys, but after all there are limits to the favours one can ask of a tenant, even the best natured, and as you can imagine I did not wish to lose this opportunity to rent the space at his high figure. Despite Mr. Murphey's kindhearted insistence I refused to burden him with the responsibility, and he finally accepted my refusal in the spirit in which it was offered. With this part of the business resolved, we quickly signed the necessary papers, and I left him in possession of the warehouse."

"It appears to me that you have made an excellent contract," remarked Homes, leaning back in his chair. "Pray tell me why you now feel you have cause to doubt it?"

"Well, Mr. Homes," replied our visitor unhappily, "as I said before, I am not sure that I do have cause to doubt it. However, allow me to continue with my story, for subsequent events have been strange indeed!

"Yesterday I had occasion to visit Cheapside, and being near the warehouse I thought I would drop in on Mr. Murphey and see if there was anything I might do as his landlord. Imagine my surprise when, as I neared the building, I heard the raucous sound of music coming from the interior — music referred to, I believe, as 'hillbilly.' Upon entering I found Mr. Murphey and three or four others seated near the basement steps, playing various loud instruments, and all wearing heavy dark glasses and dirty overalls. Mr. Murphey left his group to speak with me, and it seemed to me he was quite upset by my visit.

"I asked him in some amazement if he had paid me the high rental just to have a place for his musicians to rehearse, and he seemed to think for a while before answering. He finally responded by saying that he and his friends were all quite wealthy and they had decided to mount a club for underprivileged adults as a philanthropic gesture. Since they were also all amateur musicians, they planned to provide the music for the membership themselves. Seeing me stare at the heavy glasses and dirty overalls, he laughed gaily and said they were not as young as once they had been, and since they all wore glasses they had, in a moment of humour, decided to call themselves 'Murphey's Myopic Mountaineers,' and to dress accordingly."

Homes smiled grimly as the name in the telegram came into the conversation. "Tell me," he inquired with interest, "when you first met Mr. Murphey, was he wearing glasses? Or did he appear to require them?"

"No, Mr. Homes," said our visitor. "On the contrary. I know that people with poor eyesight usually have large pupils, but Mr. Murphey's pupils were extremely tiny, almost pinpoints, which leads me to believe his eyesight is better than normal.

"To continue, however; after returning home I thought over my strange encounter at the warehouse, and felt it exceedingly odd. I therefore determined to ask the advice of someone more familiar with these matters than myself, and for this reason requested an interview with you."

Homes arose and began pacing the floor in quick strides, rubbing his thin, strong hands together briskly, for we had allowed the fire to burn low and the room had become quite chilly.

"You did the right thing, Mr. Willson," he said, his eyes gleaming. "I find the facts you have given me quite unusual, and it seems very possible that Mr. Murphey and his musicians are planning some action which could well prove to be nefarious. It is too late today for further investigation, but be assured that tomorrow I shall devote my full time to its solution! Tell me, is there any point from which the interior of this warehouse can be observed in secrecy?"

"There is a skylight which can be reached from the building next door," Mr. Willson said, also rising.

"Fine! If you would care to leave your address with Dr. Watney, as well as directions for locating this warehouse in Cheapside, I hope to be in touch with you quite shortly with the answer to this most interesting problem!"

For some time after Mr. Willson had been ushered out, Homes sat before the fire, his eyes closed and his fingers tented in that pose I knew indicated furious thinking. Finally he opened his eyes and sprang to his feet.

"Well, Watney," he said briskly, "there is nothing that can be done on this case until tomorrow, so I believe I shall spend the evening in further work on the fractionation of the alcohols. Would you please hand me that flask at your side?"

"But which flask, Homes?" I asked in puzzlement, viewing the many bottles in confusion.

He leaned over and extracted one from beneath my eyes, frowning a bit. "By this time, Watney," he remarked in a slightly irritated voice, "you should know my methyls!"

The following morning, shortly after ten o'clock, found us standing precariously on the roof of the building in Cheapside, watching a very strange performance through the dirty skylight window. Below we could see an unfurnished room, empty except for four men dressed as Mr. Willson had described, who were busily playing loud music at the far end of the room. From time to time one would drop his instrument and disappear down the cellar steps, to be replaced by another who emerged from the same place. Suddenly Homes gripped my arm fiercely.

"Watney!" he ejaculated, his voice trembling with excitement. "Note the man who has just entered and taken his place in the front of the band! The one who is limping and has the orange-red hair! That is no Mr. Murphey; that is none other than Professor Marty, the most dangerous criminal in all London!"

"But Homes," I cried in dismay, "are you positive?"

"There can be no doubt! He is the only man in all England who plays the Burmese nose-flute left-handed! Come, Watney, there is work to be done! I fear that if the Professor is involved in this scheme, we have indeed tackled opponents worthy of our mettle!"

Tugging my arm, he led me from the roof to the stairway leading downward. Once in the street, he paused and considered the neighborhood carefully. The warehouse was located in the middle of the block, and was quite long and narrow. The shuttered façade fronted on a narrow street, while the back wall loomed over Cheapside Boulevard, a heavily travelled artery. Walking rapidly, Homes circled the block several times, and then slowly began to widen the circle of his investigation until we had covered four or five city blocks in all directions.

The area was largely commercial, with many office buildings and banks alternating with one another to crowd the area. After seriously contemplating the buildings that faced the various streets along our route, Homes once again patiently retraced his steps, but his attention now focused upon the pavements of the streets over which we strode. Completely mystified, I followed upon his heels, but in all truth I could see nothing out of the ordinary in the roadway he was studying so carefully. Finally he straightened his back and turned to me in great satisfaction.

"It is precisely as I had imagined!" he remarked triumphantly. "The greatest problem of necessity had to be ventilation, but in solving this problem, they were forced to disclose their whereabouts!" At the stupefaction of my expression, he burst into laughter.

"No, Watney," he chuckled, "I was not attempting to be mysterious, but only thinking aloud. I suggest that we repair to some restaurant in the vicinity for lunch, while I explain to you my theory of this odd case!"

Once we had been seated in a corner booth and the waiter had retired with our order, Homes leaned over the table and began to speak with that forceful manner which I knew meant he had seen light in our most puzzling problem.

"Let us take things in their order," said he. "It would be obvious to the most dense that where Professor Marty is concerned, some vicious plot against the public welfare is being hatched. I had already viewed with great suspicion this so-called Mr. Murphey as soon as Mr. Willson told us he had elected to call his musical group the Myopic Mountaineers, for you must admit that the name alone is highly suspicious!"

"Suspicious in what way, Homes?" I inquired.

"Why do they not call themselves the Four-Eyed Four?" replied my friend, his eyes gleaming. "Or the Fibromyosis Five? Or the Sarcoma Six? Or the Staphlycoma Seven? Or the Epicanthic Eight? No, no, Watney! The common practice of musical organizations is to include their number in their name! Certainly you have heard of 'City' Pound and his Twenty Shillings? Or Cesar Franc and his Ten Centimes? What possible conclusion can we come to, therefore, when the Professor purposely omits the number in his group? Only that he wishes to keep this number a secret!"

"But for what possible reason, Homes?" I cried.

"There can be but one; so that when visitors come into the warehouse, they are unable to discern that the group is not intact. In this fashion the Professor is able to maintain a group engaged in other activities, without anyone being the wiser!

"Think, Watney! In addition to avoiding the number involved, their name also cleverly excuses the use of both dirty overalls and dark glasses. Yet we have Mr. Willson's word that 'Mr. Murphey' has excellent eyesight, and from the poor illumination in the warehouse, we can assume that his companions are equally well-endowed. Why, then, the disguise? It is true that these glasses hide the face and make identification more difficult, yet the Professor made no attempt to avoid recognition when he first approached Mr. Willson. The answer is simplicity itself, Watney. It is not a disguise at all; the spectacles are simply safety glasses used to protect the eyes against welding flashes and dirt chips; and the overalls are simply overalls, and nothing more!"

"But, Homes," I objected. "What possible reason could the Professor have for this imposture?"

Homes's eyes narrowed. "Did you happen to note, Watney, during our recent excursion, that within the area of this warehouse there are a total of sixty-three banking houses? I am positive that the Professor selected Mr. Willson's warehouse for its proximity to these banks, and the loud music is merely to hide the sound of their digging! Each day, Watney, they are enlarging some tunnelling arrangement to reach the underground vaults of these banks!"

I stared at Homes in astonished admiration. Only a mind as sharp as his could have seen the subterfuge behind the Professor's devilish scheme and properly arrived at the true solution! "But, Homes," I said, recalling the beginning of our discourse, "what did you mean when you said the problem of necessity had to be ventilation?"

"Just that, Watney! It is obvious that a tunnel of the size required to connect all of these banking establishments with their working base at the warehouse would require ventilation. Ventilation shafts, of necessity, must come at least to street level, where they are visible. In our stroll about the neighborhood this morning, I carefully noted all possible air-vent outlets, and I am positive I have properly identified the ones they have installed!

"After midnight, the law requires the abatement of loud noises, including music, and they must perforce stop working on the tunnel at that hour. If my theory is correct, we can gain entrance to this tunnel by means of these air shafts, and once within their warren, I promise I shall put a stop to their vicious plot!"

"But, Homes," I admonished, "should we not inform the police?"

"It would be without purpose; the police cannot act before the fact. Their only recourse would be to place a watch over each bank vault in order to catch the miscreants in the act. We, being under no such compulsion, can abolish the entire scheme before it becomes operative, and save the police much work!

"Well, Watney, there seems to be little more to be done until the early hours of the morning. I suggest that we finish our repast and then return to Bagel Street where I can pursue my researches until that time. It will also be necessary for me to obtain certain materials to take with us, for I shall foil this foul scheme of the Professor's at all costs!"

It was after midnight when we left our quarters. Homes carried a small black bag with great care, and nestled it cautiously between his long legs as our hansom rattled through deserted streets across the great city. We descended a few hundred feet from the warehouse, and Homes waited until the cab had disappeared into the darkness before turning into Cheapside Boulevard and walking purposefully to a manhole cover neatly set into the pavement.

"Quickly, Watney!" he said, straining at the heavy iron lid. "It should be one of these!"

Without a word I knelt by his side and aided him in wrestling the awkward metal ring from its cumbersome base. A steel ladder disappeared into the murky darkness below, and with a quick glance in all directions to insure our privacy, Homes descended rapidly. I followed with caution, feeling my way into the blackness rung by rung, until I felt my companion's hand on my ankle, guiding my feet to the solid earth at the bottom. I could hear Homes's quick breathing, and his fumbling at the catch of the black bag. A moment later he had produced a bull's-eye lantern and was sweeping the shaft with a steady beam of light. Despite my faith in my friend's remarkable analytical reasoning power, I was forced to catch my breath in admiration, for as he had so accurately predicted, we were in a long tunnel that curved out of sight in both directions!

"Homes!" I whispered. "You were completely correct! This tunnel is of a size that could easily attain all of the banking establishments within a great area!"

"And we have come none too soon, Watney," he replied in a low, firm voice. "Note the finished state of their work—it is typical of the Professor to be fastidious in the details of his vile schemes. It is obvious that he must be almost ready for his coup. Note the completeness of their installation; they have even provided wagons to speed the work of looting the vaults. The only thing they failed to take into account was the existence of Schlock Homes, and this oversight shall cost them dearly! Watney, quickly, my black bag!"

I held the bull's-eye lantern while Homes neatly extracted two long sticks of explosive and attached them firmly to one of the wagons. As I watched in fascination he affixed a fuse to their caps and leading it some distance away, knelt and lighted the end.

"Away, Watney!" he whispered excitedly. "This fuse should take no more than two hours at the most to reach the charge, and I suggest we be well away when that occurs!"

We quickly made our way back as we had come, and once at the foot of the ladder, Homes covered the lantern, plunging us into darkness. I rapidly mounted the metal rungs of the ladder, hearing the heavy breathing of my friend behind me. Within minutes we had reseated the manhole cover firmly on its base, and hurried up the deserted street to a cab stand around the corner. Less than ten minutes after Homes had lighted the fuse that was to end the Professor's nefarious plan to rob most of London's banks, we were settled back in a hansom and rapidly covering the city on our way back to Bagel Street.

Because of our late hours and strenuous activities, it was well after the hour of noon when we arose. Homes entered the breakfast room just as I was sitting down to a belated lunch, but knowing his interest in current affairs, I opened the afternoon journal even before taking my first kipper and had noted the headlines by the time he was seated.

"Good afternoon, Watney," said he, seating himself and reaching for the kipper rack. "What news do you find in the journal which might prove to be of interest to us?"

"Well, Homes," I replied, studying the paper closely, "the first article which I see says that it appears that the consumption of drugs is rapidly increasing in London of late."

"Is that so?" he said, exhibiting but slight interest. "You might mention this fact to our Mr. Willson when you give him your account of our activities. If this is the case, it may well give him a market for his stock and partially compensate him for the undoubted loss of a well-paying tenant. But I am not interested in the commercial news, Watney; is there no crime which might claim our attention?"

"Well, there is this, Homes," I replied, studying another article closely. "It says here that service on the Cheapside Line of the London Underground Subway System was disrupted early this morning, and that the police feel that sabotage was undoubtedly involved."

"Sabotage!" cried Homes, leaning forward eagerly with flashing eyes. "To my mind, Watney, sabotage — next to the pilfering of coal — is the dirtiest of all crimes! I must offer my services to the authorities immediately! A telegram to Scotland Yard if you please, Watney!"

The Adventure of
The Stockbroker's Clark

THE YEAR '54 was one of exceptional activity for my friend Mr. Schlock Homes. During the early months of the year he had been busy across the Channel, for it was only through his efforts that the tulip crop of Holland was saved from being smuggled out of that country. This particular case, which earned for Homes the Hague Five-Star Man of Distinction award, was given wide publicity at the time, and I find the details recorded in my casebook as *The Adventure of the Dutch Bulb-Snatchers*. His return in the spring immediately found him involved in the odd problem of the footballer who was being kept against his will on a second-rate team, a case I find listed in my notes as *The Adventure of the B-Leaguered Goalkeeper*. It was also about this time that he was able to be of assistance to Sir Merivale Lodge's sister, Wisteria, and shortly thereafter he solved the puzzling problem of confused identities at Bedlam Hospital which later become known as *The Adventure of the Five Napoleons*.

When September arrived, therefore, both Homes and myself felt the need for rest, and arranged to leave our quarters at 221B Bagel Street for a well-deserved holiday at Watts, in Middlesex, planning to spend our hours in complete inactivity. But even in this quiet rustic retreat, repose was not to be permitted the great detective, for it was here that Homes was confronted with a challenge that gave him an opportunity to once again demonstrate his exceptional powers of reasoning, in solving the problem which I find in my notes under the title of *The Adventure of the Stockbroker's Clark*.

We had no sooner settled in our rooms at the Watts New Hotel, when a series of loud, jarring explosions drew us in haste to the window, where we were in time to observe one of the new horseless carriages grind to a halt at the hotel doorway. The driver emerged, and after studying the swinging sign above the entrance, disappeared from our view into the building. The expression of distaste on Homes's face clearly indicated his opinion of the mechanical monster in the road below, and with a sad shake of his head he prepared to reseat himself, when a sharp rap came at the door, and our host the innkeeper ushered in a large, florid gentleman who threw off his goggles and duster and, uninvited, flung himself into a chair before us.

"You like my new Clark–4?" he asked, laughing a bit too loudly. "Best foreign motorcar on the market; it cost a pretty packet, but what of it, I say! Money's to take and to spend, and I take it easily, so I spend it easily!" He paused as my friend eyed him in icy silence, and then continued, although his geniality appeared a bit more forced than formerly.

"Well, Mr. Homes, I finally wormed your present address here out of your housekeeper, Mrs. Essex, although I admit I had to make up quite a story since she stupidly refused a bribe. However, I promise you won't suffer for it financially! I'm a generous man, though people deny it, but I insist on receiving fair values for my brass!

"Now, Mr. Homes, I have a pretty problem for you to solve, but before I propound it, I understand that you pride yourself on your ability to deduce a person's occupation from their appearance, and I would like to wager that you can't guess mine!" Leaning back negligently, he lit a huge cigar, and allowed the match box to dangle loosely from one hand.

Knowing Homes's dislike for ostentation and braggadocio, I fully expected my friend to eject our unpleasant visitor forthwith, but to my great surprise he studied the man before him dispassionately for several minutes before answering.

"From the soft condition of your hands, and your apparent prosperity," remarked Homes at last, his cold eye roving over the seated figure as he spoke, "I should judge you to be engaged in commerce of some sort, most probably in the retail end. I note the match box you hold advertises the Chez One-Hoss, a well-known night club in Hertford, not far from here, and one which is largely frequented by the more successful agrarians of that area, so I would deduce that the items you handle are primarily intended for the use of farmers.

"Your right trouser leg exhibits two marks, one being greasy and deriving, I should imagine, from contact with a thin metal hoop which was some ten inches from the floor; the other showing marks of wood powder which I can readily recognize as birch, and which appears approximately four inches higher on your trouser leg.

"The items you sell, therefore, are manufactured of both wood and metal, and come in two distinct sizes: one being ten inches in height and the other fourteen inches in height. Since a metal watering bucket is exactly ten inches high, rimmed with a hoop, while the standard butter tub or bucket used by the dairy farmers of this neighborhood is exactly fourteen inches high and made of birch, I should say it is fairly easy to deduce your occupation. You, sir, are undoubtedly the operator of a bucket shop!"

"Well, now, Mr. Homes," said our visitor, chuckling heartily, "I guess that with your reputation you can afford a miss now and then, and you were certainly bowled clean on me! These marks on my trouser leg are the result of my fixing my Clark–4 myself, for I don't allow any fool of a mechanic to tamper with my machine, no, sir! An operator of a bucket shop! Ha! Ha! You couldn't be further off! As a matter of fact I happen to be a stockbroker, and it is in connexion with this that I wish to employ your services.

"My name, Mr. Homes, is Jonathan Fast, and I operate the largest brokerage firm devoted exclusively to the sale of stocks and bonds to small investors in the entire Empire. I had an associate who called himself Peter

Luce—although I always knew his name had been Anglicized from Pietro Lucciani—but he proved to be too soft in his dealings with clients. I was therefore forced to squeeze—that is to say, buy him out, although I still retain his name in the firm, out of respect for his memory, as well as the many friends he had among the poor.

"Since my firm specializes in dealing with the uninitiate in the investment business, we are often approached by people who are either illiterate, or uneducated, or both; but we never refuse an order no matter how small, and always push our firm's motto, which is: 'Don't Hide Your Money In A Shoe: That's Obtuse – We Will Handle It For You: Fast & Luce.'

"As a result of this policy, which I might mention has been singularly successful throughout the years, we are accustomed to receive messages and orders from all parts of the world, and many are so poorly written that at times it becomes quite difficult to decipher them. However, since one never knows today who can or cannot afford to dabble in stocks, we go to extraordinary lengths to properly interpret all messages, even employing translators when necessary.

"Today, however, I received a communication which is in plain English, but which frankly I am unable to understand. Our experts at the office have done their best to interpret it but without success. Knowing your reputation for solving puzzles of this nature, I therefore went to some trouble to locate you, and I should like you to decipher this for me as quickly as possible."

He withdrew from his pocket a wrinkled sheet of paper and laid it on the table before us. It was printed in crude block letters on a torn and dirty sheet of wrapping paper, and I reproduce it below for the reader:

At the appearance of this strange letter, Homes's boredom disappeared at once. Handling the wrinkled missive with the greatest of care, he bore it to the window and studied it carefully in the fading afternoon light. Then, to my amazement, he bent his head over the paper and carefully smelled it! Then, nodding his head as if at the verification of some private conclusion, he turned to our visitor.

"The envelope!" he demanded, his voice tight with hidden excitement. "Do you still have the envelope?"

"There was no envelope. The message was slipped under the door of my office precisely as you see it."

Homes took this information with barely concealed disappointment, but when he again turned to face our visitor he was once again his old, calm self. "Well, Mr. Fast," he said shortly, "if I may retain this paper for a few days, I have no doubt but that I shall be able to decipher it. It promises to be a most interesting problem, and since I am supposedly on holiday, I see no reason not to give it my full attention. I imagine that your firm is in the London Directory, and as soon as I have news, I shall be in touch with you."

"Very well, Mr. Homes," replied our visitor, collecting his driving equipment and consulting a heavy pocket watch, "but don't waste any more time on it than is absolutely necessary. Sometimes we have found that the crudest messages have resulted in the greatest profit—that is, the greatest opportunity for us to be of service to our clients!"

When a new series of loud explosions indicated to us that the Clark-4 and its owner had left the hotel doorstep, Homes carefully covered the torn paper with a clean piece of glass to protect it against any possible damage, and then, relaxing in an arm chair, lighted his pipe. A slight frown crossed his brow as he turned to me.

"A most disagreeable character, Watney," he remarked, puffing slowly. "Common politeness forced me to listen to his story, and I fully intended to show him to the door as soon as, in all decency, I could; but once he produced that badly scrawled message on that quite odorous paper, I'm afraid I was lost! I can only hope that the secret it contains does not work to the advantage of our Mr. Fast, for I cannot recall a previous client who struck me so poorly!

"However, Watney, it never does to tackle a new case in the evening. Morning wakens the brain as well as the body, you know, and I therefore suggest that we relax tonight and come fresh to this problem on the morrow. The Watts Town Hall has a program of Polish folk dances this evening; I understand they begin with 'Five Minuets' of Latis Knuze, and finish with the famous 'Oy Gavotte.' Should we wish to attend the performance, Watney, I suggest we leave at once, for the country does not keep our city hours, you know!"

The following morning, well rested by ten hours' sleep in the fresh Middlesex air and fortified by a huge country breakfast, Homes lighted a cigarette and withdrew the mysterious paper from beneath the glass.

"Well, Watney," he said, his eyes twinkling, "I should like to have your opinion of this strange billet-doux. What are you able to deduce from a study of it?"

I took the crumpled sheet from his hand and scanned it closely, attempting to adopt the studious mien of my friend when he was involved in the analysis of some abstruse problem, although in truth I could see little there to give us any important lead.

"Well, Homes," I answered slowly, "it is clear that this was written by a person of great personal slovenliness, for you will note that in handling it he was careless enough to leave his handprint, and a dirty one at that. The poverty of the writer is also apparent from the fact that he delivered it in person rather than spend thruppence on a postal stamp. However, the significance of the intended message, I must confess, completely eludes me!"

Homes laughed and retrieved the note from my outstretched fingers. "Not bad, Watney," he chuckled, "but I was requesting information regarding the message itself, for this also eludes me at the moment. As to the writer, that worthy is fairly easily described, I should have said; for it should be obvious to the most dense that this note was written by a midget suffering from amnesia, who lives in Soho and most probably in Greek Street, and who is involved, or at least has some connexion with the publishing trade."

I stared at my friend in complete astonishment, for I could see nothing in the torn sheet which could possibly lead to this startling conclusion. "Homes!" I ejaculated, "how can you possibly arrive at these statements on the basis of this paper?"

"Later, Watney," he replied, arising with a smile and removing his dressing gown. "At the moment I am not prepared to satisfy your curiosity, for my own has only been whetted until now. I fear I must interrupt my holiday and travel down to town, for it is there that the answer lies. If you will be so kind, Watney, as to arrange a trap to take me into the station, I shall change and be ready in a moment."

I had the trap at the door as he descended from our rooms, and I fear that my astonishment caused me to gape, for he was dressed in old clothes of solid black, with white shirt and string tie, and he had adopted the straggling mustache and black velour hat of the Bohemian.

"Strangers to Soho, Watney, do not garner information easily," said he, smiling broadly at my puzzlement. "One must appear to be of the neighbourhood in order to elicit relevant data from the denizens of that romantic district. I shall plan to return on the 5:12, should you care to meet me, and we can spend the evening discussing my findings."

I passed the balance of the day exploring the historical inns and well-equipped public houses of the little town, but still I managed to be on hand at the station when Homes's train came puffing to a halt alongside the rustic platform. I fully expected my friend to descend with that broad smile which I knew indicated the successful conclusion to a particularly involved problem, but when the train ground to a halt, Homes stepped down with a worried frown on his face, and scarcely acknowledged my greeting.

"I am afraid that my efforts today were not crowned with success," said he bitterly as our trap bore us to the hotel. "It appears that I shall have to decipher the cryptic message after all, and with no help from the writer!"

"You were able to locate him?"

"Oh, that was no problem! I located him easily enough! But he denies having written the thing—a further proof, if one were needed, of his amnesia, but certainly of no particular aid to us in solving the problem. No, I fear that further study of that mysterious paper is indicated!"

When we had finished with our dinner, therefore, Homes pulled his chair to the table and began brooding over the cryptic note, his briar filling the room with clouds of smoke. Knowing his dislike of interruption in moments like this, I buried myself in a book, but a few seconds later Homes slammed his hand on the table and arose.

"It is useless, Watney," he said in great disgust. "I am too tired to concentrate. I suggest a good night's rest, after which I can tackle this again in the morning, fresh and alert!" And bidding me goodnight, he stalked off to his bedroom.

The morning, however, brought no improvement, for I entered our sitting room to find Homes staring dejectedly out of the window, his long thin body drooping with weariness, and his usually sparkling eyes dull and unseeing.

"Homes!" I cried in alarm, worried by his appearance. "What is the trouble?"

"It was the incident of the dog in the night!" he replied bitterly.

"The dog in the night?" I asked in bewilderment. "But the dog barked all night!"

"Precisely," he said, his voice heavy with exhaustion. "As a result I didn't get a wink of sleep! However, in the course of being kept awake, I did get some glimmer of possible purposes behind this mysterious message, and since I know I shall not rest until it is solved, I shall return to the city today and follow several new leads. Possibly I can snatch a few moments of rest on the train, for my day shall be heavily proscribed. I shall return on the 5:12 unless I telegraph you otherwise."

It was mid-afternoon, and I was lounging at the door of the public room of the hotel, waiting to see if their opening hours were in strict accordance with the law, when a uniformed messenger handed me a telegram from Homes. I ripped it open eagerly and read: "MEET ME SIX TONIGHT AT CRASHING BOAR PUB IN FLEET STREET. CASE SOLVED. BRING NOTE. HOMES."

The Crashing Boar Pub in Fleet Street stood well back from the pavement in a little mews running between two huge printing plants, and I arrived a few minutes late to find my friend Schlock Homes ensconced at a corner table partaking of a whisky. He called the waiter over and ordered a similar drink for me while I seated myself opposite and handed him the torn sheet of paper. Verifying it, he tucked it into his weskit pocket and leaned back smiling. I have never ceased to be amazed at the recuperative powers of Homes, especially when he has reached the successful conclusion of a case, for looking at his bright eyes one could never guess that he had spent two full days without sleep in pursuit of the answer to this most puzzling problem.

"Well, Watney," said he, smiling broadly, "the answer was before my eyes from the beginning, but I was too much of a fool to see it. I have been developing a tendency lately to search for obscure and hidden meanings in the most direct things, and as a result I often waste time before coming back to the correct path.

"This case is a perfect example. As you so cleverly noted when you first saw the note, the message was obviously written by a person of slovenly habits, as witness the handprint left by a dirty hand. But what you failed to note was the size of the hand; clearly it was too small to be that of an adult, and yet a child could not have been responsible for the written words. *Ergo,* it was written by an adult with a hand the size of a child's; in other words, by a midget! The fact that he failed to sign his missive could not have been the result of oversight, since the laborious forming of the block letters showed that he had put much effort into the composition. The only possible reason which I can deduce for this failure to append his name, is that at the moment he was unable to recall it – a classic example of amnesia, and not as unusual as we might like to think.

"When I was first handed the note, I was struck by the rather pungent odour that arose from the paper, and being somewhat of an expert on strange odours, I was able to immediately identify it as being of Parmesan cheese, used for the greatest part in the cooking of Sicilian pizza and encountered to my knowledge only in the Italian restaurants in Soho, and most probably in Greek Street itself!"

"But, Homes," I interjected, "how were you able to deduce the connexion with the publishing trade?"

"The handprint, Watney! It was not ordinary dirt from the street; the most casual examination would have shown it to be printer's ink. Shortly before inadvertently leaving that mark upon the paper, the writer had handled fresh newsprint, and some of the ink had come off on his hands."

"A masterful analysis, Homes!" I exclaimed in admiration, grasping his hand across the table. "Once you have explained it, it all seems so clear and obvious. But the meaning of the message itself – how were you able to decipher that?"

"Quite by accident, as a matter of fact, Watney. Once I had arrived at a description of the writer, I came at once to Greek Street and began interviewing various residents. In short order I found myself directed to a corner newsstand where I encountered the owner, a midget, busily handling journals, which explained the dirty hands. He denied completely having written the message, which was the final proof of my identification, for it confirmed conclusively his amnesia. Being unable to shake his story, however, I was forced to return to Watts unsuccessful.

"Today I returned determined to revive the failing memory of that poor man, bringing with me for the purpose a small battery-operated hand buzzer, which I stopped and obtained in a fun shop in Shaftesbury Avenue, for it is a well-known principle that sudden shock works wonders in these cases. I was about to offer my hand, in which I had concealed this mechanism, when I chanced to note a magazine for sale on display there. The magazine was called *Time.* At once the entire affair became crystal clear!"

Taking the torn sheet from his pocket, Homes spread it on the table before me. "'Your Time Is Running Out,' it reads," said he, "and it means exactly what it says! I immediately taxed our small newsdealer with selling subscriptions to magazines as a sideline, and he freely admitted that he did, indeed, augment his income in this fashion. He continued, however, to forcibly deny that he had reminded Mr. Fast that his subscription was running out, so I once again offered him my hand, as if in leave-taking. Unfortunately, the fun shop seems to have mounted the buzzer in the inverted position, and I am afraid that my reactions caused him some suspicion, for he threatened to call a policeman unless I left at once.

"However, his admission was not essential, for I knew now the truth of the matter. As you know, my conviction is that when you have eliminated the impossible, whatever remains, however improbable, must be the truth!"

"Marvelous, Homes!" I cried enthusiastically. "What do you intend to do now?"

Homes shrugged indifferently. "Actually, nothing," he said, yawning deeply. "There is no need for action that I can see. Obviously the message does not affect Mr. Fast either adversely or otherwise, and if this obnoxious boor is so careless as to allow a magazine subscription to pass the renewal date, I do not consider it my duty to so advise him. However, if you feel that our responsibility to a client demands an explanation, you might drop him a line in the morning explaining the steps we have taken and the results of our investigation.

"But now, Watney, we have interrupted our rest long enough with this minor matter. I suggest that since the hour is late, we pass the night in our own beds in Bagel Street, and return to Middlesex tomorrow to continue our holidays!"

The following morning we caught an early train back to our sylvan lodgings in Watts, and as the train passed through the beautiful Middlesex scenery, I unfolded the journal I had purchased in Euston Station and carefully scanned the news. Suddenly an article claimed my attention and I began to delve into it with increasing interest.

"Something in our line, Watney?" came the relaxed voice of my companion. "I see that you appear to be quite impressed by whatever you are reading."

"Nothing criminal; no, Homes," I replied, folding the paper to the article and handing it to him. "But I fear there will be no need for us to give Mr. Fast a report on his query. It appears that as he was cranking his new Clark–4 yesterday, it gave an explosion more violent than usual, and as yet the police have been unable to properly separate the tangled parts of Mr. Fast and his motorcar."

"It was bound to happen sooner or later," said Homes, taking the paper from my hand and reading further into the article. "While I hold no brief for Mr. Fast, who was patently offensive, still I would be derelict in my duty if I did not express my views on these gasoline-driven monstrosities that are rapidly threatening us all with monoxide poisoning, explosions, and other ills!

"A letter to *The Times,* if you will, Watney!"

The Adventure of
The Missing Cheyne-Stroke

THE ACTIVITIES of my friend Mr. Schlock Homes in the year '56 furnished me with many cases of sufficient interest to record in my journal. Among my notes I find reference to the odd problem of the elderly egg candler whose partner, Homes was able to conclusively prove, had deliberately attempted to induce blindness in the old man for the purpose of being free to juggle the company books. His method was fiendishly ingenious: He kept introducing crates of hardboiled eggs for the old man's inspection, and only the sharp perspicacity of my friend foiled the nefarious plot. My casebook also records the name of the American barque *John D. Carr,* whose disappearance was a fortnight's sensation, until Homes was able to accurately predict its exact location—in drydock—from a simple mathematical calculation and the word of the steersman that he had lashed the wheel before going over the side—a case I have already chronicled in *The Adventure of the Locked Rhumb.* However, of all the cases noted for that year, none in my estimation demonstrates the accuracy of my friend's prognostication, nor the expansiveness of his imagination, as much as the case which became famous as *The Adventure of the Missing Cheyne-Stroke.*

It was a beautiful afternoon in June, and I was lounging at the open window of our quarters at 221B Bagel Street, enjoying the rare sunshine and resting my leg which still ached at times from an old Jezbel wound suffered in the battle of Piccidilli. Schlock Homes, an ardent chemist, had busied himself with his new Gilbert set, and an air of contentment combined with the odours of his experiment wafted through the room.

Our pleasant idyll was suddenly broken, however, by the urgent sound of footsteps in the hall, and a moment later a knock at the door announced a visitor. He was a huge young man, carelessly dressed in sport clothing, and he filled the doorway, breathing heavily from his climb up the steep staircase.

"Mr. Schlock Homes?" he inquired, glancing anxiously at my friend. "A mutual friend was kind enough to give me your address, and I hurried here as quickly as possible!"

Homes waved him to a chair and the young man flung himself into it. "Mr. Homes, there is no one else in England who can help us in this crucial hour! Charlie Charles is missing, and there is no stroke like him on the river! Miss Tompkins keeps crabbing; Cox couldn't keep time with a metronome; and Miss Judd, to put it plainly, is a feathering idiot! Unless you are able to find Charles before tomorrow morning, I fear we are lost!"

Homes listened to this passionate outburst in amused silence, and when the young man had finished, he remarked with a smile, "I am afraid that I am the one who is lost, sir. Who is Charles Charles?"

The young man contemplated us in amazement. "Certainly you must have heard of Charles!" he exclaimed. "He took both his Black and Blue in sculling, and is the amateur oars champion of all England!"

"Possibly it would be well if you began at the beginning and told us all," said Homes, leaning back comfortably. "I would deduce that you are referring to some species of sport, and I fear that neither Dr. Watney nor myself is an expert in that field. These names and terms which you are using are quite unfamiliar to me."

"Well, Mr. Homes," said the young man, leaning forward earnestly, "it seems hard to believe that you have not heard of the great Charlie Charles, but I shall attempt to clarify my remarks. My name is Legion, John Legion, and I am the rowing coach at Cheyne College in Lincs, at the little village of Clapham. Tomorrow morning the International Mixed-Foursome College Rowing Championship is being held here in London, and sculling squads from all over the world have gathered for this competition. Each team is comprised of two men and two women and we, as well as the other visiting teams, have been assigned dormitory space as the guests of Putney University. Each athlete has his or her private room to insure the necessary privacy and rest before tomorrow's important event.

"Charles Charles is our forward-left-stroke, and until this morning I would have wagered a week's wages on Cheyne to win tomorrow. This noon, however, I went to his room to speak with him and found it deserted; a further search indicated that he was not on campus and had not been seen. I have searched in all possible places, but I have been unable to uncover any trace of his presence! If you are unable to locate Charles before the race tomorrow, I fear we shall lose!"

Homes's eyes glittered with interest. "You have but the one sculling team?"

"Yes, just the one."

"And only one forward-left-stroke?"

"Again yes, just the one."

"And this is the one who is missing?"

"Yes, this one."

"Singular," said Homes thoughtfully. "Quite singular! However, I fear that we can solve little here. Let us repair to the campus of Putney University and see what can be learned from a study of the actual scene. If, as you say, the race is to be held tomorrow, we shall have need for prompt action, indeed!"

A few moments sufficed for Homes to change from his dressing-gown to more suitable habiliments, and minutes later we were rattling along the banks of the Thames in Mr. Legion's trap while the young coach gave us more details on the sport of shell racing and the eminent reputation of the missing stroke, Charles Charles. Homes sat silent, his eyes closed, but I knew he was absorbing every word of the conversation and storing it in his colossal memory for future reference.

We turned from the Embankment, coming in on Kew, and shortly thereafter came upon the Putney campus. The dormitories assigned to the various rowing teams were huge blocks of buildings, facing upon a large quadrangle of well-kept greenery. The entrance to each building had been hung with slogans and banners, each announcing support of a different team. Across the ornately carved doorway at which our trap halted, a huge pennant waved, reading: "Clapham! Here comes Charlie!" Mr. Legion eyed this sadly, but without comment led us through the shadowed entrance to the room which had been assigned to the famous left-stroke.

A scene of utter chaos confronted us. Bedclothes were strewn about the floor; a battered portable typewriter leaned drunkenly against a chair leg; books and papers were scattered over the desk; socks lay under the bed; and neckties hung from the chandelier. At sight of this disorder, Homes's eye brightened, and I knew from his manner that his interest in this strange case had been actively aroused.

"Charles seems to have put up a brave struggle," he said, surveying the destruction piercingly. "With your permission I shall properly examine the room, for it is more than possible that the answer to this strange disappearance lies here!"

For the next thirty minutes the great detective searched the room with that attention to detail which had often rewarded him with success in the past. With fierce concentration he studied the closet, removed some of the socks in order to peer beneath the bed, and even explored back of the doors. One drawer of the dresser exhibited an unusually large collection of timepieces, including many wrist watches and pocket watches; a second drawer was filled with dirty laundry; while a third seemed to be the repository for old letters and clippings. Suddenly Homes stiffened to attention, and drew from beneath these papers a heart-shaped piece of coloured tinsel which I immediately recognized as an old Valentine. Scanning it carefully, he finally folded it neatly and placed it in his waistcoat pocket, after which he returned to his search with even greater energy. A sigh of satisfaction indicated to me that he had discovered something further of interest, and he arose from his perusal of the cluttered wastebasket clutching a crumpled sheet of typing paper. Placing it in his pocket with the Valentine, he gave the room a final searching glance, and then led the way to the open quadrangle.

"One final question and I believe I shall have all I can hope to garner here," he said, fixing Mr. Legion with a thoughtful glance. "Can you tell me what course of study Mr. Charles was following at Cheyne College?"

"He was a Typing major, Mr. Homes," replied the young coach, obviously puzzled by this seemingly irrelevant question. "But I fail to see what possible connexion this could have with his disappearance."

"It may be of the greatest importance," Homes replied seriously, "or, of course, it may not. There being little more to be learned here, with your permission we shall return to our quarters and study our findings in greater detail. Yes, yes, Mr. Legion! I am fully aware of the urgency of the matter, and I suggest you drop by at eight this evening, when I hope to have some news for you!"

On the drive back Homes sat forward, chuckling and rubbing his hands, a sure sign that he had seen some light in this most confusing case. "A brilliant boy, this Charles Charles!" said he, "for despite the obvious confusion of his last minutes in that room, he still managed to leave sufficient clues to point a clear trail to his captors. It is our duty to properly interpret the signs he has left, and we must not fail him in this!"

We descended at Bagel Street and Homes fixed himself a long drink immediately upon our entrance, and then sank into his favourite chair, spreading the crumpled paper and the folded Valentine before him.

"An hour of solitude, if you please, Watney," he remarked, his warm smile robbing the words of any rejection. "I am sure that the complete answer to this puzzle is before me, if only I can grasp it!"

I retired to the window seat once again, although I was bursting with questions regarding the two papers on the table. But knowing Homes and his love of mystery, I bided my silence and watched the long shadows of evening settle over the huge city. I must have dozed a bit, for suddenly the firm grip of my friend's hand on my shoulder brought me from my reverie with a start.

"Watney!" he cried in great excitement, "I have it! You must send a telegram to Legion at once! When he comes tonight I wish him to bring the room assignment plan for all of the teams with him, as well as the names of the occupants. This is most important."

"But, Homes!" I said in vexation, "I fail to understand how you were able to deduce anything at all from the little you found in that room!"

"Later, Watney," said he, smiling at my puzzlement. "All shall be clear before the night is finished. We have a busy evening in store for us, I fear, so if you do not mind I shall relax a bit before our visitor arrives, with a few moments of Venuti. My violin, if you please, Watney!"

At eight o'clock sharp Mr. Legion appeared, and while he was as consumed with curiosity as myself, he said nothing but placed the assignment list on the table and drew up a chair alongside Homes and myself. Homes immediately fell to studying the list with great care, whistling a minor Shostakovich harmonium concerto to himself as he did so. He seemed to be searching for a particular item, and after at least a minute of full concentration the whistle abruptly ceased and a bright smile lit his countenance. I knew at once that he had found the information he had been seeking.

"The case is solved!" he announced complacently, leaning back and enjoying the effect this pronouncement made upon us. "With any luck Charles Charles will be back in his own room before midnight! Allow me to begin at the beginning and show you the steps in the solution.

"It was evident as soon as we saw Charles's room that he had been removed against his will. My only hope was that he had been able to leave behind a clue as to his assailants before being kidnapped. He is an extremely clever boy, that Charles, and should go far in life; for despite the pressure of those last few moments he managed to leave not one, but two, distinct signs pointing to his captors, probably feeling that if we missed one, we would scarcely miss two. The first clue was in this paper which he crumpled and flung into the wastebasket, where it avoided all eyes but mine." And Homes handed to us the sheet which he had retrieved from the basket and had guarded so carefully.

It was a standard sheet of typing paper and had repeated upon it one sentence, typed at least thirty times. It read: *Now Is The Time For All Good Men To Come To The Aid Of The Party.* When we had a chance to study it sufficiently, Homes returned it to the table and continued.

"Had Charles been a student ot political science, I might well have passed this by as being a part of his study, but since we know he was majoring in another subject—namely, Typing—its significance increases sharply. I realize that there is a ball tonight for the visiting teams, but he could not have been referring to this party, since it was obvious that his paper was written much earlier. It can therefore only be a message."

"But, Homes," I interrupted, "what can it intend to convey?"

"Think, Watney! In this International Competition tomorrow, there must be many teams from behind the Iron Curtain. Charles, by referring to the Party is telling us who his captors are! I admit I am surprised that they adopted a method so lacking in subtlety but time, I imagine, was running out. These Governments, which we will not mention by name, will do anything to win a sporting event!"

"Of course!" cried Mr. Legion, striking his fist upon his knee. "Now I understand! It was not the first attempt, Mr. Homes. Just yesterday one of the members of an Iron Curtain team falsely accused Charles of having stolen his watch. The facts are quite innocent: Charlie has taken up amateur magic as a hobby and as yet is not too adept at it. He can make things disappear, but he still has trouble at times in bringing them back. His first efforts being unsuccessful led these people to call for the police, but when, after a further try he was able to produce the watch, they were forced to drop their ridiculous charge. Now I can see that it was only a means of preventing him from competing in the race!"

Homes nodded. "Had they known, as I do," said he, "that Charles is the possessor of some fifty watches they would have realized the idiocy of such a charge, for Charles—of all people—has no need for another timepiece. However, to return to our exposition, we now are familiar with the group who arranged the kidnapping. It now remains to show you the exact person involved, and the place where he is being held prisoner!"

Taking the folded Valentine from the table, he opened it to the scrawled message within and passed it to us to read. Written in a bold hand it said:

Roses are red,
Violets are blue;
Sugar is sweet,
And so are you.

"The fact of finding a Valentine in June, when everyone knows that the Saint's day is always commemorated in February, made it plain to me that it was planted there, necessarily as a purpose of leaving a message. Note the words well, for they are Charles's means of directing us to the place of incarceration selected for him. In studying the room assignments of the various teams I paid small attention to the Iron Curtain countries, for they are too intelligent to hide him in their own quarters. No, for this I was certain that they would employ the services of sympathizers, and I therefore searched among teams coming from countries who have long exhibited jealousy of all things British. And then I found, as I had truly expected to find, that the Vassar team from the American colonies had the following people — "

His thin, strong finger pointed to the list before us, and we read:

VASSAR TEAM:
John (Muscles) O'Grady	Room 196
Marybelle (Honey) Ross	Room 211
Thomas (Bull) Jones	Room 243
Ming Toy (Sugar) Epstein	Room 216

Both Legion and myself stared at Homes in complete puzzlement, for we could see no connexion between this list and the Valentine message. Homes saw our expression and could not repress a laugh.

"Re-read the Valentine message phonetically," said he with a deep smile, "taking alternate lines and see what you have. *Ross is a red;* violets are blue; *Sugar's suite;* and so forth. Yes, my friends, that is the answer! Mr. Charles is being held against his will in Room 216, in the dormitory assigned to Vassar. The feminine members of the team were the sympathizers who fell in with the foul plan; I should have suspected a woman immediately, for Charles was too smart to fall victim to a man. However, the native chivalry of the British sportsman would have demanded that he allow a female entrance to his quarters without involved checking! We must rescue him tonight if he is to race tomorrow. Heaven knows what these fiends might have done to him in his incarceration!"

"But, Homes!" I cried. "Is this not a matter for the police?"

Homes shook his head. "We have a duty to England in this, her hour of need, not to involve her in international incidents, Watney," he replied, his voice reproachful at my lack of understanding. "No, during the dance tonight they may well feel safe enough to leave him unguarded, for they have no idea that Schlock Homes is on their trail! We must spirit him away before they know he is gone, and guard him until the race!"

"But, Mr. Homes," interrupted Legion, his strong young face alit at the prospect of action, "how will we gain entrance? The door is sure to be locked, and we cannot break in without exciting suspicion."

"I happen to be familiar with all types of latching devices," replied Homes confidently. "My reputation in this field has reached a point, I believe, where one seldom thinks of Bagel Street without thinking of locks! It will be small trouble to adapt a standard picklock to our purpose. Watney, my welding equipment!"

"You wish the blanched solder?"

"No, no! The silver braze! There, that should do the trick! Now, gentlemen, the plan shall be as follows: You, Mr. Legion, shall stay below in the entry to see that we are not followed. Watney, you and I shall make our way to Room 216 and see if we can manage to spirit Charles away without raising an alarm. Should we have need of your physical prowess, Mr. Legion, be sure we will call out! And now, gentlemen, if you are ready I suggest we waste no further time!"

Within an hour we were once again on the Putney campus and Legion melted into the shadows as Homes and I slipped silently into the darkened building. Across the quadrangle music and laughter came from the hall where the crew members were enjoying their party, but all was still and desolate in our sector. Legion had furnished us with the layout of the building and we were able to make our way to Room 216 without the necessity of showing a light. As I waited breathlessly, Homes crept to the door, picklock in hand,

and pressed his ear to the panel. When no sound came to him, he silently tried the handle, and to his amazement the door swung open.

"The fools did not even lock it!" he whispered. "Come, Watney, with care!"

A crumpled figure lurched half erect from a chair in one corner, and then collapsed once more, muttering incoherently. "You were certainly gone long enough, baby doll," babbled this apparition. "Did you bring the other bottle?"

"Delirious, poor devil!" exclaimed Homes in a low voice. "Quickly, Watney, your medical skill is urgently required!"

I instantly took charge of the boy, checking for pulse and respiration, but as I bent over him the true cause of his suffering immediately became apparent. "We must get him back to his room!" I cried. "Have Mr. Legion arrange for black coffee at once! These devils have plied him with alcohol, and he is in sad shape!"

It was some thirty minutes later before I had the boy sitting up amid the dishevelment of his own room. He was pale and silent, but the worst effects of his drugging had passed.

"Do not attempt to speak, Mr. Charles," said Homes in a warm voice. "You have been the victim of an attempt at kidnapping, but thanks to your cleverness in leaving those messages, and Mr. Legion's promptness in calling me into the case, we were able to locate you and rescue you in time. I wish to congratulate you on keeping your head as you have done, and to tell you that England is proud of you! Go out tomorrow and win that race, for that will be the biggest blow against your captors and their alien philosophy!"

"Thank you very much, Mr. Homes," replied the lad, attempting to speak calmly, although memory of his past ordeal forced bitterness into his voice. "And now, if you will forgive me, I must get my rest."

He embraced us both with a warmth that was surprising from one in his weakened condition, and immediately turned to his bed. Homes and I walked quickly into the night, while Legion prepared to mount guard over his star until the actual moment of the race.

The following day, exhausted by the events of the previous evening, both Homes and myself slept late, and it was therefore well into the afternoon when I came into the dining room. Homes appeared a moment later, yawning deeply, but by that time I had already folded the journal to the sporting section and was reading the racing results. Homes merely lifted an eyebrow in interrogation, and I smiled back at him.

"Yes, Cheyne, of Lincs, representing England, did indeed win the mixed foursome sculling championship, and the teams have already dispersed to their respective homelands," I said, folding the paper with a smile and handing it to him. "And in my estimation the thanks for this brave deed should go as much to you as to Charles!"

Homes shrugged modestly. "Where our great country is involved," said he, "there is no question, nor can there ever be, of thanks. I am happy that we were able to settle the problem so peacefully; and in my humble opinion the greatest share of the credit should go to that brilliant lad, who is a credit to England!

"But that case is finished now, Watney, and although we have need for new horizons, I feel we have honestly earned ourselves a day's rest. So no crime news at the moment, if you please. Rather, I suggest we pass the time at an afternoon concert at Robert Hall. There is a gas-pipe organ solo today which I should sorely hate to miss. We may, however, be late; what time do you have, Watney?"

I searched my pockets without success for several moments. "I am afraid I must have dropped my timepiece during last night's events," I answered a bit shamefacedly. "Do you not have the correct hour?"

"My watch is also missing," replied Homes. "In the excitement of rescuing that poor chap last night, I fear I must have lost it without noting. However, surely one of the visiting Vassar team must have encountered our watches this morning; yet you tell me they have disbanded and left without attempting to contact us! We shall have to notify the authorities at once!"

"But, Homes," I protested, remembering his words, "is there not the possibility of an international incident occurring over this?"

"Kidnapping is one thing," he replied coldly, his voice tinged with anger, "but the failure to report and return lost property is quite another! A telegram to my brother Criscroft at the Home Office, if you please, Watney!"

The Adventure of
The Artist's Mottle

"CRIME, WATNEY," remarked my friend Mr. Schlock Homes, laying aside the financial section of the journal and reaching for his Yellowbole and shag, "is the contrived and exhibited manifestation of the subconscious negation of theosophistic impregnation and authoritative influence. It has the added disadvantage, of course, of being illegal, which so often forces its perpetrators into opposition to the law."

We were seated comfortably before a roaring fire in our quarters in 221B Bagel Street on a blustery afternoon in late March of '60. The whipping wind blasted our windows with that late, cold rain of a dying winter, and the calm peace of our living room, in such sharp contrast to the bitter weather without, may have been responsible for the sudden philosophical attitude of the great detective.

"True," I agreed, marvelling as always at the concise manner in which Homes could bring his intellect to bear on a point of view. "A further disadvantage, of course, is that crime does not pay."

Homes puffed strongly, sending clouds of smoke about the room. "I have heard that statement many times," he observed, frowning fiercely at the leaping flames, "but never from criminals, although one might reasonably assume they would be in the best position to comment. It may be true that crime does not pay; but then what does, these days?"

There was a note of bitterness in his voice that I had never heard before, and I sat up in alarm. Homes and I never discussed his financial position, and I had always assumed he had sufficient income to indulge his passion for deduction.

"If you are short, Homes . . ." I began, reaching for my wallet.

He shook his head. "A temporary thing, Watney, but I appreciate your kind offer. No, I took a flyer in De Diamonds Consolidated Beer, but it seems that recently some villain slipped into their headquarters and watered the stock. It was, of course, quite undrinkable after that, and it appears that my losses may be substantial." He shrugged his shoulders ruefully. "Coming at a time when lucrative cases are few, I fear I shall be reduced to accepting even minor commissions such as this," and he handed me a telegraph form which he drew from his dressing gown pocket.

"HOMES OLD BEAN OLD SOCK," it read, "HATE TO BOTHER YOU AND ALL THAT BUT I'M OFF ON ANOTHER OF THESE BLASTED SAFARIS AND I HATE TO LEAVE THE OLD MANOR WITHOUT HAVING SOMEONE KEEP AN EYE ON THE OLD BELONGINGS YOU KNOW, SO I'D APPRECIATE IT A BASINFUL IF YOU COULD MANAGE TO DROP IN AND SEE THAT THE PORT IS STILL IN THE CELLAR AND THAT NOBODY STEALS THE FAMILY SILVER AND ALL THAT, BECAUSE OF COURSE THE ESTATE IS ENTAILED AND I HATE ARGUMENTS WITH TRUSTEES WHICH YOU CAN UNDERSTAND OF COURSE, SINCE THEY ALWAYS GET SO FUSSY, BUT IT SEEMS THE PATER LOADED THE OLD MANSE WITH VALUABLES AND OBJETS D'ART AND TO TELL YOU THE TRUTH I DON'T EVEN KNOW IF THE JUNK IS INSURED, SO YOUR BEAGLE EYE WOULD BE GREATLY APPRECIATED AND PAID FOR OF COURSE AT YOUR USUAL RATES WHATEVER THEY ARE; THE KEY, OF COURSE YOU'LL WANT TO KNOW WHERE THE KEY IS, NOW JUST WHERE THE DEVIL IS IT — OH YES, IT'S WITH THE LAWYER CHAPPIES OF COURSE, JUST TELL THEM I SAID YOU COULD HAVE IT, SO PIP-PIP AND WIPE YOUR FEET BEFORE YOU GO IN AND BEST OF EVERYTHING."

"But, Homes," I cried, turning the message over and scanning the back, "this carries no name! How are you able to even determine who your client is?"

Homes smiled at my puzzlement. "The lack of a signature is in itself a signature," he replied cryptically. "You have obviously failed to note, Watney, that the message is exactly two hundred words in length, and therefore carries the standard two-hundred-word rate. To have signed the message would have taken it out of this special rate category and made it subject to a thruppenny-ha'penny surcharge. Only a person with arithmetical training raised by Scottish standards could have been so precise, so it is easy to deduce that Sir Angus McGrogger is the author. I have been through to his advocates and am already in possession of the key which you may note he mentions in passing.

"If you are free in the morning, Watney, I should like the pleasure of your company, since the entire business is bound to be boring. The manor is located at Yulebe, Surrey, so if you would be kind enough to consult your ABC timetable, we can schedule an early start, and return before dark. I am quite anxious to be here tomorrow, for they are hanging those four felons at Pentonville, and you know my passion for strung quartets!"

And so, in this innocent fashion, began the case which I find filed in my notes as *The Adventure of the Artist's Mottle.* Little did we know that gloomy afternoon as we riffled through the timetable, that because of this simple house inspection Homes's abilities for deduction would be challenged to their utmost, or that because of his decision to accept this commission his financial problems would be resolved. At the moment our only problem seemed to be in interpreting the timetable.

"There is a train that runs on even days that fall on odd dates," I said, tracing the minute hieroglyphics with my finger, "and on odd days that fall on even dates, but unfortunately it is a military express from Southampton direct to Yulebe, and only stops in London to discharge arms. Besides, it has the notation M−W−F listed above, which I frankly do not understand."

"Milk, Wine, Food," replied Homes curtly, reading the list over my shoulder. "It has a combination restaurant car and bar, is all. Here is one on the Tewksbury Line that goes to Hoolbe, Surrey, which is within kissing distance of Yulebe, and from there we might possibly get a buss."

"But that one is annotated T−T−S. What can that mean, Homes?"

"Most probably, Tewksbury Temperance Society, indicating that on that train the bar is closed. You will note, Watney, that much thought has gone into the preparation of this schedule, for the trains that go on weekdays other than Sunday, run only on alternate afternoons, except in August. Had I the time, I am positive that I could solve this particular code, but wishing to return as quickly as possible, I suggest you arrange a hansom for us tomorrow!"

The following morning, therefore, found us racing through the lovely Surrey landscape, with Homes leaning back negligently humming a Bartok tympany concerto, while I studiously noted the various public houses along our route to clearly mark our return. It was a most pleasant journey and before we knew it we had entered the environs of Yulebe and moments later were rolling up the carriageway of the McGrogger domain. The house lay well back in a well-ordered garden; a tall thin edifice of medium squatness, neatly combining neo-antique architecture with old-modern. With a sigh of resignation, Homes descended from the carriage and we made our way up the marble steps to the ornate entrance.

"You might check the cellar and wine stocks, Watney," said Homes, pocketing the key and eyeing the rococo hallway with faint distaste. "I shall make an inspection of the upper rooms in the meanwhile. There seems to be no visible sign of forced entry, so I should judge that a few hours at the most should see us through."

In accordance with these instructions, I descended immediately to the lower levels of the mansion, finding myself upon arrival in a huge subterranean gallery lined on both sides with bottle racks which were filled from floor to arched roof. I had time to inspect but two bottles and was busily engaged in removing the foil from a third when a faint cry made me pause and listen intently. There could be no doubt: Homes was calling me, and even the thinness of his voice muffled by the heavy floor above could not disguise the excitement of his tone. I hurried up the cellar steps and dashed along the hallway, pausing only to arm myself with a stout cane from the umbrella stand should my friend have need of physical help. But when I arrived at the room from whence his voice was issuing I found Homes quite alone, albeit his previous ennui had completely disappeared. He was striding up and down the room in great agitation, and his firm step and glistening eye told me at once that he had unwittingly come upon a crime that gripped his imagination.

"Watney!" he cried at sight of me; "it is well that we came and came when we did! What say you of this dark deed?" And he swept his thin, strong hands about him as he spoke.

I looked about me in befuddlement, for in all honesty I could note nothing out of the ordinary. The room in which we found ourselves had apparently been transformed into an art gallery, and a large plaque mounted upon the oaken door announced that the room contained the McGroggor Abstract Art Collection. The walls themselves were completely covered with paintings, but it was not until Homes spoke again that I realized the cause of his perturbation.

"Vandalism!" he cried, his pointing finger shaking with the strength of his emotion. "Despicable vandalism!"

It was then that I saw the truth of his statement, for the canvases were a nightmare. Some were crisscrossed with bars of paint; triangles and circles had been smeared haphazardly across others; one had been brushed with a dull base and spattered with little blue and pink dots; while several others exhibited splashes of colour of the most atrocious hues.

"Homes!" I ejaculated, struck with horror at this vile deed. "This is appalling! What do you plan to do?"

"Do?" Homes thundered, his strong voice resolute with fury. "I shall trace this fiend to the ends of the earth and see that he receives his just desserts!

I shall not rest until I bring him to justice! Watney, in our carriage you will find my kit. Please bring it at once while I begin my search for clues!"

A moment later Homes was on his hands and knees, his magnifying glass in hand, as he peered intently at the heavy nap of the Oriental rug. A moment later he was studying the windows, after which he turned to me in deep disgust.

"The window catches are open!" he announced with a frown, shrugging his shoulders. "Anyone could have entered and left at will. However, even the most astute criminal must leave some sign of his passing, and I pride myself that few are better at noting and interpreting these signs than Schlock Homes! I suggest you return to your chores below, Watney, for I shall be some time here!"

It was fully an hour before I returned to the upper level. I had been unable to completely finish my inspection of the McGrogger wine stocks, but I flatter myself that I had no need for shame at my progress. I entered the gallery to find Homes sunk in thought in a deep chair which he had drawn up to front the defaced paintings.

"We progress, Watney," he remarked, his gaze still fixed upon the canvases before him. "A picture of this vandal begins to form."

"But, how, Homes?" I protested, bewildered. "I see nothing here to give any indication whatsoever as to the person responsible for this outrage!"

Homes smiled grimly. "Yet there are many clues here, Watney. It is quite obvious, for example, that the man who defaced these priceless paintings is of medium height; a Latin whose origins most probably were in Spain. I should judge that he has probably dabbled in art and been disappointed with the results. He is in excellent physical shape, and without doubt was once an athlete. He is also, without question, quite bald."

"Really, Homes!" I exclaimed. "This is plainly impossible! This time you are pulling my leg!"

"By no means, my dear Watney! In good time you shall know all, but actually the facts I have revealed speak for themselves. Unfortunately, I fear that this information by itself is insufficient for us to properly identify our culprit. There must be more; there must be more!" And springing to his feet, Homes began restlessly pacing before the ruined canvases, his bony hands locked behind him, his sharp features twisted in fierce concentration. I waited patiently, until with a sad shake of his head he turned to me with a sigh of defeat.

"I fear there is little more to be learned here at this time, Watney," he said. "Let us return to London and Bagel Street. There are inquiries to be put in motion, and possibly the fresh air on our return will stimulate some further thought!"

During our drive back to London, Homes remained hunched in one corner of the carriage, his eyes closed, and his fingers tented in that pose that has always indicated to me his desire to be left alone with a problem. He did not speak until our cab had turned into Bagel Street and pulled up at our doorway.

"It occurs to me, Watney," he said as we descended and made our way up the stairs to our rooms, "that it would be of the greatest value in identifying our criminal were we able to determine if he were right- or left-handed. In addition to the other facts which we now possess, it could well be the factor to conclusively pinpoint our man."

"But, Homes," I protested, "how is it possible to determine this?"

"By copying his method, Watney. Of course! By copying his method!" At the thought all signs of dejection slipped from my friend's face, and as he slipped into his dressing gown he was his old enthusiastic self once again.

"Watney, certainly we must have an old piece of canvas about the apartment. If you would please manage to locate one, we shall get right to it!"

I rummaged through our closets until I uncovered a bit of torn schooner-sail that I had long intended to repair, but as I delivered it to Homes, another thought struck me.

"One problem, Homes," I said. "We have no paints, or colours of any nature."

"For our purpose we have no need for formal oils. If you would be so kind as to ask Mrs. Essex for the use of her cupboard, I am sure we can unearth sufficient materials for our experiment!"

I returned in a few minutes with catsup, a bottle of mustard, some clothes-blueing, a dish of egg white, some old ravioli sauce, and a small jar of chutney mixed with curried chives. Homes had stretched the piece of sail tautly across the fireplace and was smoothing the edges down with an old clothes brush.

"Excellent!" said he in high spirits as I laid my booty upon the sideboard. Now, Watney, my plan is as follows: Using these makeshift colours I shall cover one part of the canvas in the same furious manner as the vandal, using solely my right hand. The balance I shall treat in similar fashion, but using only my left hand. Expert examination of the result could well determine if dexterity can be proven through this method. I suggest you stand well back, Watney, for I note you are wearing your new tweed!"

The next few moments were a blur as Homes, his enthusiasm aroused to fever pitch, attacked the canvas from all angles. Within a very short time he stood panting breathlessly over the finished product, which bore but a superficial resemblance to the vandalized paintings in the McGrogger manor. Homes carefully wiped his hands on his dressing gown and, falling back to my side of the room, studied the smeared sail in silent contemplation for several minutes. Finally he nodded his head in satisfaction.

"Right-handed, I should definitely state," he remarked. "We shall of course require the opinion of one more versed in art, and to this end I suggest, Watney, that you take this down at once to old Mr. Braigis at Crusty's Gallery for his conclusions. I shall continue with other lines of investigation while you are gone, for I am determined to bring this vandal to justice posthaste!" As I left the room Homes was reaching to the bookshelf at his side for a reference volume, and immediately became so engrossed that he barely nodded his farewell.

When I returned from Crusty's Gallery, Homes interrupted his reading only long enough to cock an eyebrow at me in interrogation. I explained that old Mr. Braigis had been out, but that I had left the canvas, requesting a telephoned opinion upon the morrow.

"No matter," said Homes, in that insufferably superior manner he so often adopted when the successful conclusion of a case was approaching. "I believe I am well on the trail of the miscreant, and so if you will favour me with continued silence, Watney, I shall continue my researches!" He buried himself once again in the reference book, and when I finally retired he was still too engrossed to even acknowledge my goodnight.

The following morning I awoke a bit disgruntled at the cavalier treatment Homes had accorded me the previous evening, but as soon as I reached the breakfast room, the warm smile of my friend across the table soon dispelled my black mood. He refused to discuss the case until my appetite had been satisfied, but as I lit my first after-breakfast pipe, he turned to me with a glint of humour in his fine eyes.

"Are you still angry with me?" he inquired.

"Really, Homes!" I replied, smiling despite myself. "At times you are quite impossible!"

"Like the solution to this mystery?" he asked, smiling broadly. "Really, Watney, you should know me well enough by now to forgive my bad manners when I am at a partial loss for the solution to a problem! However, this condition, I am pleased to state, no longer prevails. Come, I have a cab awaiting us and as we drive out to McGrogger's Manor I shall subtly ask your forgiveness by explaining this most interesting case!"

"But, Homes," I cried, "if you know who the miscreant is, should you not first take steps to see to his apprehension?"

The smile faded for a moment from Homes's visage. "Unfortunately I fear it is too late," he replied. "I have made inquiries and it appears that he is beyond our jurisdiction. However, I believe I can guarantee Sir Angus that he will never vandalize another painting in England!"

Once we were seated in our hansom and rolling swiftly along the broad avenue leading to the Great North Road, Homes carefully lighted a cigar and began to speak.

"You will recall, my dear Watney, that on our recent visit to McGrogger Manor I stated certain particulars regarding our miscreant. That he was an athlete was immediately evident: many of his colours were obviously not applied either by palette knife or brush—they could only have been thrown. The lack of overtoss—or slop, as it is known in art circles—on either frame or wall indicated the excellence of his aim; a sure sign of the trained athlete. This lack of overtoss also provided me with the basis for deducing his height; a taller or shorter man would have tended to splash, due to the changed angle of incidence. The perfect impingement could only have resulted if the height of the throwing arm were equal to the distance from the floor to the centre of the canvas.

"The temperament which could lead a man to deface paintings in what must surely have been a fit of pique at his own deficiencies, could only be Latin. His selection of colour indicated that his subconscious had led him to the hues most familiar in his youth. The predominance of the reds and oranges, coupled with the already demonstrated Latin background, clearly indicated a person raised in Spain."

"But, Homes," I objected, "why must it have been a painter at all? Could it not have been simply a passing vagabond?"

Homes shook his head decisively. "The normal vandal tends to slash, rather than to daub. Only a person trained to some extent in art would consider that overpainting a picture actually represents greater destruction than cutting the canvas."

As I nodded agreement at this astute observation, Homes continued. "His excellent physical condition I deduced from the fact that he was able to vandalize these pictures in a period of time which of necessity must have been proscribed, for he could never be certain when someone might enter. Even smearing one small bit of sail caused me to become breathless, so that the overpainting of so many in a brief time must certainly have called for the utmost in physical endurance!"

"True," I said, fascinated by this dissertation. "But how could you possibly have concluded that he was bald?"

"Quite easily, my dear Watney! Certainly a man of the background and temperament which we have described, faced with the imagined need for destroying a large number of paintings in the minimum of time, would be led to tear his hair; yet the most minute examination of the carpet nap failed to reveal the slightest sign of ruptured follicle. Our only conclusion must be that he lacked the wherewithal!"

"And with this you were able to identify him?"

"With this and his right-handedness," replied Homes, smiling modestly. "He is a frustrated painter named Passo Picablo, and the answer I have received from the Continental police indicates that he must have made good his escape. The Sûreté informs me that he is definitely known to be in Paris!"

"But are you positive, Homes?" I asked anxiously. "Your evidence is, after all, largely circumstantial."

"There can be no doubt. I have brought with me a book which makes reference to the early life of this vandal, and once we have the damaged pictures before us, I am sure that I can convince you of the correctness of my analysis. But here we are at McGrogger's Manor. Come, Watney, allow me to complete this exposition where it began – in the gallery!"

Leading me quickly along the hall, Homes opened the door to the exhibit room, and we passed within. The tragically mutilated pictures faced us as we entered, and Homes paused dramatically before the canvas spangled with the blue and pink dots.

"The final proof, Watney!" he cried, pointing to the picture.

"You mean these blue and pink dots?" I replied, much puzzled.

"That was his secret, Watney! You see, they are not dots. They are *periods!*"

"But what is the difference between a dot and a period, Homes?" I asked, now completely befuddled.

"In all honesty I am not enough of an art connoisseur to know," said Homes earnestly, "but there can be no question that these are periods, and not dots! Nor can there be any question that they identify our culprit without possibility of error! Read this!"

He thrust the book beneath my eyes, and as I read, my admiration for the analytical powers of my friend rose to new heights. A clearly marked passage left no room for doubt, for it read: "Passo Picablo is best known, and can most readily be identified, by his blue and pink periods!"

The following morning Homes appeared at our breakfast table as I was in the act of opening our morning mail. He seated himself opposite me, and as he reached for a rasher of bacon he inquired genially, "Is there anything in the morning post which might be of interest to two idle investigators this fine morning?"

"A letter from Crusty's Gallery," I replied, reading further into the missive.

"Now that the case is closed," remarked Homes, helping himself to the remains of the chutney and chives, "their opinion is hardly of importance."

"I am not so sure," I said, handing him a cheque that had been enclosed. "Old Mr. Braigis is offering three hundred guineas for the canvas I left there yesterday. He further states that in his expert opinion your controlled feeling for orderly chaos, particularly as exhibited in the threnody of selective contemporary media, offers you a great future. What do you suppose he means, Homes?"

"There is undoubtedly a mystery here," replied Schlock Homes, fingering the cheque thoughtfully, "but at the moment I do not believe I am inclined to delve into the matter too deeply!"

The Adventure of
The Double-Bogey Man

A PERUSAL of my notes for the year '42, made in September of that year and accounting the many cases in which I had engaged with my friend Mr. Schlock Homes, gave me as rude a shock as ever I have suffered. It was in February of '42 that I had begun the study of a new method of speedwriting, feeling that a facility in this science might well aid me in both quickly and accurately annotating our adventures. Unfortunately, a sharp increase in my medical practice, possibly caused by a section of slippery pavement near our rooms at 221B Bagel Street, left me little time for my studies, and I came back to my casebook to find I was unable to translate my own hieroglyphics. In desperation I took my Pitman notebook to a famous expert, but when he announced that it was all Gregg to him, I found myself without recourse.

Even Homes, with his vast background of cipherology and cryptology, was able to be of small help. He did manage to decipher one title as *The Sound of the Basketballs,* but since we could recall no case involving sports that year, we were unable to go further. These many adventures are therefore lost to posterity, and I bitterly hold myself to blame for their loss.

October, however, brought a case of such national importance that it dwarfed all work Homes had previously done that year, for beyond furnishing him with an opportunity to once again demonstrate his remarkable ability to analyze distortions in their proper perspective, it also gave him a chance to serve his country as few men have been able to serve her. In my notes, now meticulously kept in neat English, I find the case listed as *The Adventure of the Double-Bogey Man.*

I had returned from carefully sprinkling powdered wax on the offending section of pavement, in the hope that this might resolve its slippery condition, to find that in my absence Homes's brother Criscroft had arrived and was ensconced together with my friend on the sofa before the blazing fireplace. As I entered, they were engaged in a favourite game of theirs, and as always I stood back in reverent silence as they matched their remarkable wits in analytical reasoning. Their subject appeared to be an old-fashioned tintype of a mustached gentleman dressed in the clothing of yesteryear, stiffly seated in a bower of artificial flowers, his bowler held woodenly before him, and his frozen face reflecting the ordeal of the portraiture.

"An ex-student of the Icelandic languages, dedicated to the growing of rubber plants," Criscroft suggested, eyeing the discoloured photograph closely.

"Colour blind and left-handed," returned Homes languidly, as I held my breath in admiration.

"A one-time trampoline acrobat, adept at playing the twelve-toned gas-organ," observed Criscroft.

"A victim of the hashish habit," Homes said, smiling. "Went before the mast at an early age, and has travelled widely in Kew."

"The son of a Northumbrian bell ringer," offered Criscroft. Then, turning and noting my presence, he held up his hand. "But enough of this, Schlock. Watney has arrived and we can get down to the real reason for my visit. Put Father's picture away now, and let me tell you why I left the Home Office in such troubled times, and hurried here as quickly as possible. We are in serious need of your help!"

Once I had placed drinks in their hands and Homes had lit a cubeb, Criscroft proceeded to lay his problem before us.

"As you are probably aware," he said, "we have recently allowed some of our former colonies to join us in confronting the present unpleasantness emanating from Berlin. The representative of the former American colonies is a certain General Issac Kennebunk, Esquire, and in confidence I may tell you that it appears this gentleman will be selected to assume the duties of Chief of Staff of our combined Allied forces." He cleared his throat and leaned forward impressively. "With this fact in mind, you can readily understand our perturbation when I inform you that, as of yesterday, General Kennebunk is missing!"

"Missing?" I cried in alarm, springing to my feet. "Missing what?"

"General Kennebunk *himself* is missing," said Criscroft heavily. "Since yesterday morning when he left a War Council meeting to return to his rooms, he has neither been seen nor heard of. Suffice to say that the General is knowledgeable of all our secret strategy. Should he have fallen into the hands of our enemies or their sympathizers, it could prove to be quite embarrassing for us."

"And you wish me to locate him," stated Homes positively, rubbing his hands together in that gesture that I well knew indicated both extreme interest and poor circulation.

"Precisely. Needless to say, as quickly as possible."

"Then permit me a few questions. First, where was the General in digs?"

"The War Department arranged a suite for him at an old inn, The Bedposts, in Bolling Alley."

"He stayed there alone?"

"Except for his military aide, a certain Major Anguish McAnguish, who temporarily was sharing his quarters."

"And the Major?"

"He has also not been seen since the disappearance, but as you can well imagine our principal interest is in General Kennebunk."

"Naturally. And what steps have been taken so far?"

Criscroft arose and stood with his back to the fire, his hands clenched behind him, his face ashen with the strain of his great problem and overwhelming responsibility. "The War Department brought in the military police at once, in the person of a former police agent named Flaherty, whom I believe you know. As soon as the Home Office was notified we insisted on taking the assignment out of his hands and contacting you. The War Department was most enthusiastic in this regard; however, they still wish to also retain Flaherty, although they admit you are the possessor of the sharpest analytical brain in England today."

"Flaherty will get them nowhere," replied Homes seriously, although it was plain to see that the compliment had pleased him. "I assume, then, that I have a free hand. The rooms are under guard?"

"I have seen to it that they were immediately sealed, and that guards were posted. Orders have been issued to allow only you and Watney permission to enter."

"Fine!" said Homes, rising and removing his dressing gown. "In that case let us proceed there at once. One moment while I don suitable raiment and we shall be on our way!"

Criscroft's hansom deposited us at the mouth of Bolling Alley, and the Home Office specialist leaned over from his seat to grasp his brother's hand gratefully. Then with a wave, he drove off and we turned down the narrow lane in the direction of the famous old inn.

Our credentials gave us immediate access to the floor that had housed the missing officer, and after ascertaining from the rigid soldier on duty that there had been no visitors, we unlocked the door and passed within. At first view there was certainly nothing to indicate the forceful removal of the General. The beds were neatly made up, the furniture properly placed and but recently dusted, and the late autumn sun passing the white starched curtains gave the apartment a cheerful air. Homes paused in the doorway a moment, his piercing eyes sweeping the scene closely; then, closing the door firmly behind us, he began his search.

The dresser drawers gave no clue of anything untoward. The articles of clothing therein were neatly arranged and concealed nothing. Homes dropped to his knees to search beneath the bed, but other than some regulation Army boots, and a pair of what appeared to be spiked mountain-climbing shoes, the space was bare. Stepping to the closet, Homes stared at the rows of uniforms neatly arranged upon the rack; then, with sudden resolve he pushed them to one side and probed beyond. I heard a low cry of triumph from my friend, and knew he had discovered his first clue. With gleaming eyes he withdrew oddly shaped sticks, several oversized white pellets, and some tiny wooden pins. Handling these objects with extreme care, he laid his find upon the bedspread with great delicacy and then stepped back to contemplate them, showing inordinate interest.

"Homes!" I cried in amazement, reaching for these odd objects, "what can these be?"

"Take care!" he advised, grasping my arm and drawing me back. "It's more than possible that these are strange weapons, and it would not do to destroy ourselves before our investigation has fairly begun! Let us leave them for a moment and continue our search!"

The very cleanliness of the room seemed to mitigate against finding more; the wastebasket was empty, the desk top cleared of all but essentials. Opening the desk drawer, Homes withdrew a blank white writing pad and was about to replace it when his keen eyes noted faint markings on its surface. Carrying it swiftly to the window he held it horizontally at eye level against the light.

"Quickly, Watney!" he exclaimed in great excitement. "We have something! My bag!"

Dusting charcoal over the empty sheet, he blew it gently until it settled in the crevices left by the pressure of the quill upon the previous page, and a message appeared as if by magic. Homes placed his find carefully upon the desk, and I bent over his shoulder to read the missive with him.

"*Mammy*," it said (or Manny; the inscription was not too clear): "*Only time for nine today; back up to fifty-six! Started off four, but I won't talk about the rest. The trouble is still my right hand, and the result is the old hook! Talk about the bogey-man; the double-bogey man has me!*"

This perplexing message was simply signed with the initials of the missing colonial officer: I.K.,E. I raised my eyes from this strange paper to find Homes with such a fierce look of concentration upon his lean face that I forbade speaking. At long last he looked at me frowningly, his mind returning from the far places of his thoughts.

"We must return to Bagel Street at once, Watney!" he said, his voice taut with urgency. "I believe I begin to see a pattern in this business, and if I should prove to be correct, we must waste no time if we are to save this General Kennebunk!"

"But, Homes," I cried, "do you mean that the answer lies in decoding this cryptic message?"

"This is no code, Watney, although there is no doubt that it contains a hidden message. Come, we have much to do!" Folding the paper with great care, he thrust it into his weskit and turned to the door.

"But these objects," I said. "Shall I take them with us?"

"No," he replied, staring at them with great loathing. "They will always be here should we require them, but I believe I already know their foul purpose. Come!"

We locked the door behind us, and passing the key to the guard, hurried to the street. A passing cab picked us up at once, and throughout our journey Homes leaned forward anxiously as if in this manner he could hasten our passage. While the cab was slowing down before our quarters Homes thrust the fare into the cabbie's hand and sprang to the pavement even before the horses had fairly stopped. I hurried up the stairs behind him, anxious to be of immediate assistance.

"First, Watney," he said, turning up the lamp and hurriedly pulling his chair closer to the table, "if you would be so kind as to hand me the Debretts, we can get started!"

I placed the tome in his hand and he slid his strong finger down the alphabetical list rapidly. "McAnguish, McAnguish," he muttered as he noted each line. "Ah, here we are! Anguish McAnguish, 224 Edgeware Mews, Hyde Park 6–24 . . . No, no, Watney! This is the telephone list! The Debretts, please!"

I replaced the volume, blushing slightly, and he fell to studying it while I watched his face for some clue as to his thoughts. He scribbled some data on a pad and handed the book back. "And now the World's Atlas, Watney, if you please." He looked up as he spoke, and noting the look of befuddlement on my face, smiled and spoke in a kindly tone.

"No, Watney, this time I am not attempting to mystify. In time you shall know all. It is simply that every minute may count, and there is no time at present for explanations. So if you will excuse me, I shall get on with my work!"

I waited as he flung the Atlas open, and then, seeing that he had already forgotten my presence in his interest in the maps before him, I quietly left and went to my room.

I awoke to find the first faint strands of dawn feathering the windowpane, and even as I wondered what had aroused me so early, I felt again the urgent pressure of Homes's hand upon my arm.

"Come, Watney," he said in a low voice, "our train leaves in thirty minutes. I have a cab waiting and you must hurry if we are not to miss our connexion. Get dressed quickly and I shall meet you below."

His footsteps diminished as he left the room and I groped for my Oxford bags with mind awhirl, sleep fighting to once again assume control. I entered our sitting room to find that Homes had already descended, and even as I picked up my overcoat I noted that the table was still covered with many volumes from Homes's vast reference library, and that the lamp was still lighted. It was evident that my friend had passed the night at work. I was turning down the lamp when a faint cry from below caused me to instantly slip into my coat and hurry down the steps.

Homes was already seated in the cab, and even as I came running up he gave the driver instructions to start, his strong hand pulling me into the moving vehicle. "Forgive me, Watney," he chuckled as we rattled off towards Euston Station. "The complete answer came to me but a short while ago, and I still had to telegraph Flaherty to meet us with some of his agents at the train. I also had to arrange our passage on the Ayr Express and see that a cab was waiting to take us to the station. I'm afraid that I left the problem of awakening you until the last."

"And the answer lies in Scotland?" I asked.

"It does indeed," replied my friend, smiling. Then, leaning forward, he cried, "Tuppence extra, driver, if we do not miss our train!"

We came clattering into Euston Station at a terrific clip and Homes had me by the hand, dragging me from the swaying vehicle while it was still moving smartly. We ran down the deserted platform, peering into the compartments of the steaming train, and then, as the cars began to move, Homes flung open a door and sprang aboard, pulling me behind him. I had scarcely time to catch my breath when we passed beneath the first tunnel, and Homes then seated himself comfortably in the first smoking compartment we passed.

"Flaherty and his men are aboard," he said, reaching into his pocket for his briar. "I noticed him in the car behind as we came along the platform. With any luck at all, we should have this case finished by nightfall!"

"But I do not understand any of this, Homes!" I cried perplexedly. "I have seen all that you have seen, and none of it makes any sense to me at all! Do you mean you have deduced the General's whereabouts, and the plot behind his disappearance, simply from the little data of which I am cognizant?"

"Little data?" he replied in honest surprise. "Little data? Actually, Watney, I have never had a case before so replete with data! Allow me to demonstrate!"

He drew the folded paper containing the cryptic message from his weskit pocket and placed it upon the small table beneath the train window. I moved to the other side of the compartment in order to face him, and he began his explanation.

"First, Watney," he said, smoothing the sheet so that I could once again read the scrawled words, "listen carefully to what the General says. He begins by saying, 'only time for nine,' a common colloquialism meaning quite clearly that he has only time for a few words. He follows this up with 'up to fifty-six' and the words 'off four.' What can these words possibly indicate? Only one thing—they are directions! The most positive directions that exist, Watney—*latitude and longitude!* Up fifty-six. Off four. Obviously fifty-six degrees north latitude, and four degrees west longitude!

"Do we have anything to support this supposition? What else does he say? He says, 'the trouble is my right hand.' And who is his right hand? *Major Anguish McAnguish!* And Debretts gives the home seat of the McAnguish family as Carnoustie in Scotland, *at exactly this latitude and longitude!*"

Homes leaned back, puffing furiously upon his briar. "Let us go a bit further," he said, as I sat wide-eyed at this brilliant exposition. "The General next states, 'the result is the old hook.' I do not know if you are familiar with the slang speech of America, Watney, but the 'old hook' means that he is being pressured into something which is, to say the very least, extremely distasteful to him. And he finished by saying, 'the double-bogey man has me!' We all know what the bogey man is; it relates to demonology and the superstitions of our childhoods. And the double-bogey man can only be twice as terrifying in the imagination of this poor chap!

"On this basis, let us restate the message the General might have written if he had been permitted freedom and had not been forced to conceal his meaning from his enemies. He would have said: 'Just time for a brief note. I must go back to Carnoustie, because McAnguish is blackmailing me. There I shall be forced to undergo an experience which is too terrible to contemplate!'"

My friend stared at me broodingly. "And I am sure that I know just what this terrible experience will be, Watney! Pagan rites!"

I sat up in alarm. "Pagan rites, Homes?"

"There can be no doubt. Remember the bogey man, Watney! I do not know if you are familiar with Voodoo or any of the other pagan religions based upon sorcery, but human sacrifice often plays a part in the ceremonies, and very often human sacrifice using the most primitive of weapons! You recall, I am sure, the war clubs and the wooden darts which we discovered in the rooms of the General, which are also, I might point out, the rooms of our Major Anguish McAnguish!"

Homes leaned back once again and eyed me grimly. "Remember, Watney, our Aryan enemy has made Paganism its official religion. And Scotland has many Nationalists who are not out of sympathy with these enemies. There can be no doubt that somewhere on the heaths of Carnoustie this rite is either in progress or being prepared! I can only hope that we are in time to rescue this General from these fiends before it is too late, for it is quite evident who the victim of this sacrifice is to be!"

"How horrible, Homes! And it is for this reason that you brought along Flaherty and his men?"

"Precisely. There may well be fisticuffs or other violence, and besides, we have no official position in this, particularly across the border in Scotland. However, grim as the situation may be, it is certain that we shall be of small use if we do not rest before our arrival. I would suggest twenty winks while we can, for we are certain to be quite busy before the day is over!"

I awoke to find Homes in whispered conference with a heavy-set gentleman whose pocket sagged under the weight of a truncheon, and who could be none other than the police agent Flaherty.

"I understand, Mr. Homes," this person was saying respectfully. "It shall be as you say."

"You have a photograph of this colonial officer?"

"I do, Mr. Homes. He is a balding gentleman much given to wearing colourful knickerbockers and rather dashing shirts when off duty, and I am sure I shall have no trouble recognizing him."

"Good. Then we are ready. I have studied a one-inch map of the area, and I am convinced that there is but one heath sufficiently large and isolated as to be suitable for their nefarious purpose. The officials of the train have agreed to stop close by this heath to allow us to descend and deploy. Come, Watney, on your feet! I feel the brakes being applied at this very moment!"

Seconds later we found ourselves beside the railway track while the Ayr Express slowly gathered speed again. In addition to Homes and myself, Flaherty was accompanied by three large men, all similarly attired, and all weighted down by their truncheons. At a cautious signal from Homes, we crossed the tracks and advanced, spreading out in a widening curve, fanning across the heath.

The section of heath we fronted was well landscaped, with numbered flags, probably marking watering holes, spaced about. We advancing slowly when, of a sudden, there was a sharp whistle in our ears and a white stone flew past to disappear in the distance. "It's a trap, Homes!" I cried, flinging him into a nearby sand-filled depression and desperately covering him with my body.

"I believe in Scotland they call these ditches 'bunkers'," he replied, rising and dusting himself off carefully. "Come, men, we must be close!"

He leaned over the edge of the depression, studying the landscape with Flaherty beside him. Suddenly the police agent stiffened, and peering into the distance pointed his finger excitedly. "It's him, Mr. Homes!" he cried. "I don't know how you ever deduced it, but as always you were right! And he is surrounded by three others, all of whom are armed with heavy clubs! But wait!" The police agent turned to Homes with a bewildered air. "He, too, is armed!"

"It is as I feared," said Homes, watching the four men approach. "Either hypnotism or drugs, both quite common in this type of affair! In his present condition the poor man may even struggle, but at least we have discovered him before they could put their odious plan into practice! Come, men, let us spread out and surround them!"

"I'm sorry, Mr. Homes," said Flaherty, placing his hand on Homes's arm. "My instructions are very clear. You have found him, and a very fine piece of work it was, but it is my duty to effect the rescue. You must go back to London and take no part in this."

"Nonsense!" Homes cried, incensed. "Come, men!"

"No, Mr. Homes," Flaherty replied quite firmly. "The instructions come from the Home Office itself. You are far too valuable to risk in an operation such as this. But fear not; I promise you I shall get him safely away from these culprits, and this whether he struggle or not!"

"Do not fail, then," Homes replied sternly. "England depends upon you! Come, Watney, we have but forty minutes if we are to catch the next train south!"

I had opened the morning journal and was engrossed in attempting to open my eggs and turn the pages simultaneously, when Homes entered the breakfast room and seated himself opposite me.

"I believe you are wasting your time, Watney," he remarked genially. "I have already been informed by Criscroft that the General is back in London, and I seriously doubt that the censors would allow an account of yesterday's proceedings to reach the public columns."

"I am not so sure, Homes," I replied, noting a small article buried in one corner. "It is true that no great details of the affair appear, but it does say that because of a nerve-wracking experience that he underwent yesterday, General Isaac Kennebunk, Esquire, is under doctors' orders to take a few days' rest."

"I can well imagine how nerve-wracking it must have been," said Homes, his eyes warm with sympathy. "However, I would judge that several days engaged in one of our pleasant English sports could well erase this terrible memory. I believe I shall suggest this to the Home Office. A letter to my brother Criscroft if you please, Watney!"

The Adventure of
The Lost Prince

IT was a bright Thursday morning in May, in the year of '48. I had come into the breakfast room of our quarters at 221B Bagel Street to find my friend Mr. Schlock Homes in the process of lighting his after-breakfast hookah, a gift from the Sultan of Swatt, the former Bey Beruit. After exchanging our usual morning courtesies I sat down to eat, selecting one of the journals from a pile by the desk and perusing it intently as I attacked my first kipper. A moment later my thoughts were disrupted.

"I should not even think of the tweed, my dear Watney," Homes remarked, a mischievous smile lighting his face.

"On the contrary," I replied absently, and then looked up in startled amazement. "Really, Homes! I fail to see . . ."

"Precisely, Watney," my friend interjected. "And yet it is neither mind-reading nor legerdemain. You have a set method of attacking your *Daily Times*. You begin by reading the headlines of the extreme right-hand article; your eye then travels to the left-hand article, and you finally concentrate on the centre article. The right-hand article in today's *Daily Times* deals with a red-petrol case, which held no interest for you. On the left you found a column head concerning a state visit of an African potentate and his retinue who are here for conferences and to enjoy the theatre season. When this proved of no interest to you, you continued to the centre. Here you read that a stock merger was to be effected, and your eyebrows lifted in interest. As you continued further into the article, a smile appeared on your face. Obviously this merger will affect your holdings, small as they are, and you wondered at this point if you might afford some small extravagance. Your eye then travelled speculatively to the wardrobe chest. I recall that a few days ago we paused at a window in Regent Street and you commented upon a tweed suit you saw displayed there. Therefore my remark."

"It does seem simple when you explain it," I admitted, my original annoyance abating a bit. "Actually, however, this is the *Herald Press* in my hand, and I have been reading—with pleasure, I admit—an article on the advantages of passing one's holidays on our lovely English rivers. I had more or less decided on the Tweed, and was wondering if my wardrobe still contained the straw floater I won on Boat Race night in '14, when you spoke."

Homes smiled in congratulation at my adroit escape from his trap, and returned to his hookah.

"Incidentally," I added smugly, matching Homes's smile, "I see that you have another case coming up, which should be a lucrative one. The person coming to see you should be here very soon, if he is not already overdue."

"Excellent, Watney! You are improving! It would be interesting to learn the reasons for your statement."

I shifted in my seat, imitating the pedantic tones of my colleague. "You have preceded me to breakfast, which indicates to me that you have an appointment, obviously an early one. Your selection of costume indicates that the person is an important one, since you often receive your brother Criscroft and others in your dressing gown. Hence a lucrative case."

"But why a case at all, my dear Watney?" asked Homes, his eyes twinkling. "Certainly in our many adventures we have made sufficient acquaintances, many of high station, so that one might be calling for no reason other than to extend his regards."

"That was the simplest of all deductions," I answered dryly. "To be frank, your good humour this morning is a welcome change from the irritability that has had you in its grip for the past fortnight. Only a new case could have wrought this change in your nature."

Homes laughed aloud in pure enjoyment. "Actually," he said, copying my tones with a faithfulness that was characteristic of his great histrionic ability, "I had a dentist's appointment this morning and dressed accordingly. Then, one-half hour ago, I received a telegram cancelling it, as my dentist himself has been taken severely with the toothache. Hence, as you say, my good humour."

To hide my chagrin I ate another kipper. Homes arose and laid his arm in a kindly fashion across my shoulders. "At least, Watney," he said, smiling in a friendly style, "we are free of other appointments today. Possibly we can spend the afternoon at the concert hall. Joshua Lowfitz and his Trumpeters are doing the *Waltz* of Jericho, and I understand their performance brings the house down."

"I should really enjoy that, Homes!" I cried, rising to my feet. But our plans for a musical afternoon were not to be realized, for at that moment there came the sound of a carriage wheel scraping against the kerb and we looked out of the window to see a heavily veiled woman descend and enter our doorway. A moment later our page ushered in our visitor, who was followed by a liveried footman carrying a small bundle.

"Mr. Schlock Homes?" The voice was musical, but taut with suppressed emotion.

Homes bowed slightly, moving his hand in a gentlemanly gesture towards a chair. The veiled woman seated herself gingerly on the very edge as she spoke.

"Mr. Homes, believe me when I say that the secrecy of any of your past endeavours is as nothing to the confidential nature of the case which I now bring you. Because of the eminent position of the family which I represent, even the little information I am able to give you must be treated with the utmost circumspection." She paused as if seeking further words, and then with a muffled sob she fumbled in her reticule and withdrew an envelope which she handed to Homes.

He removed from the envelope a wrinkled sheet of paper, perusing it quickly, his eyes glittering with scarcely suppressed excitement. I passed to his side and read the message over his shoulder. It was printed in crudely formed letters, and read:

> No sens lookin under the bed or wistlin. We got him. If you wanna see him agin put eleven millun quid in a shu-box. Give it to the cooks boy he nose wat to do with it. Dont tell the busies or you wont never see him no more.
>
> (sined) The Gang
> Ps. if you cant rase that much you kin put in less but dont go
>   under five quid or you rely wont see him no more.
> Pss. better put in some toffies too it can't do no harm.

Homes was breathing heavily with excitement as he finished the strange note. He folded the wrinkled paper carefully and laid it upon the desk before turning back to our distrait guest.

"Can you give me a description?" he asked softly.

There was another muffled sob from behind the veil. "He is eight years old," she said, "with long silky hair, black eyes, and the cutest pointed ears! And his nose is all speckled."

"And the family wants him back?" I asked in amazement.

"Desperately," she answered simply. She turned back to Homes. "When he was taken they also took his little blanket. However, I brought with me the little blanket that was his father's when he was small. I did not know if it would help, but they are identical and I felt I should bring anything that might prove to be of use." She took the bundle from the footman and placed it in Homes's hands. His eyes lit up as he saw the word "Rex" embroidered in gold thread in one corner.

"Of course!" he muttered audibly. "I should have recognized the crest on the carriage! It is Prince..."

"Hush!" commanded the veiled figure. "No names!" She rose to her feet and passed to the door. "I am sure there is no need to remind you, Mr. Homes, that time is of the essence!"

"I swear I shall not rest until I resolve this," Homes promised fervently. "If your Ladyship could pass at this same hour tomorrow, I hope to have some definite news for you."

"Oh, pray heaven that you shall!" came the muffled reply, and with no further word she passed through the door, to be followed immediately by the silent, liveried servant.

As soon as the sound of the carriage had died away in Bagel Street, Homes fell into a chair and began studying the note with fierce concentration. I stood behind him and also re-read it, but it provoked no startling ideas.

"Do you suspect it of being in code, Homes?" I asked, watching his frowning features carefully.

"No, no, Watney!" he replied impatiently. "It is precisely what it purports to be: a note demanding ransom. Still, a fairly clear picture of the writer begins to emerge from his note."

I studied the crumpled paper in his hand once again. "But I see nothing in it to give any clue whatsoever as to its author," I objected.

Homes laughed shortly. Do you not? Really, Watney, there are times when I despair of you! Certainly it should be evident to all that the writer of this note comes from a tropical climate, is visiting London for the first time, and is a great admirer of George Bernard Shaw!"

"Now really, Homes!" I cried. "This is a serious case! You gain nothing by levity at a time like this!"

"Oh, I am quite serious! In time you shall know all, Watney, but at the moment there is little time to lose!" He sprang from his chair, beginning to undo his cravat. "It is essential that I go out for a few hours. If you would be so kind as to arrange a hansom for me, I shall hurry and change into more suitable vestments!"

"But, Homes," I said, studying his neat clothing with surprise, "there is nothing wrong with your costume."

He smiled enigmatically without answering and disappeared into his room. I sent our page out to flag down a passing cab, and he managed to have one waiting at our portal when Homes emerged from his room once again. I gaped in astonishment; for had it not been for the familiar grin of my old friend, I should have been forced to swear that I was facing the famous actress Diana Dors.

"Homes!" I cried in astonishment.

"Later, Watney," he chuckled, and with the supreme artistry that marked every detail of his incredible impersonations, he rearranged his features and minced from the room.

It was dusk before Homes returned. His high heels tapped quickly up the steps and once in the room, he removed his spike-heeled shoes, slipped off his blonde wig, and flung himself into a chair.

"It is as I suspected!" he said heavily. "An inside job! However, I have the miscreants located, and tonight we shall see an end to their foul scheme! I suggest, Watney, that you make a visit to Mrs. Essex's domain and arrange a bite of supper, for we must go out again tonight. And you had also better arrange a bull's-eye lantern and take along your pistol, for I know not what deviltry we may encounter!"

"You mean . . ." I began.

"Yes!" he said. "Our case is nearly finished. Tonight I hope to effect the rescue. But now, if you will call upon Mrs. Essex, I suggest we satisfy the inner man, for I have gone without lunch and we have a long night ahead of us!"

He refused to speak further until our supper had been placed upon the table, and then the only words he offered were a subdued request for the salt. It was not until our supper was represented by a pile of soiled dishes that Homes leaned back and sought solace from his hookah. Another person might have appeared ridiculous sitting there in a low-cut gown sucking on a curved pipe, but Homes appeared quite natural.

"Well, Homes," I said, leaning back in surfeit, "if we have the time, I would certainly appreciate an explanation of this very odd affair."

"Certainly, Watney," he replied, his eyes twinkling. "Actually, we have almost an hour before we must leave." He laid aside his hookah, adjusted the strap of his gown, and reaching for the note which he had left upon the desk, opened it and handed it to me.

"There are several things which are evident from this note, Watney. First, you may note that they request eleven million pounds to be placed in a shoebox. It should have been apparent to you at first glance that this amount of money, even in the maximum of denomination, represents a volume far too great for even the largest of shoeboxes. Hence the deduction that the writer was unfamiliar with shoeboxes, and therefore, with shoes. The only conclusion one can logically draw is that he comes from a tropical climate where shoes are not a necessity.

"Then, too, you will note his instructions to pass the money to one of Cook's boys. It is evident that the writer of this note did not realize that

Thomas Cook have eleven branches in London, or he would have been more specific. That this fact was unknown to him forces one to the conclusion that this is his first visit to London."

"But his admiration for George Bernard Shaw?" I cried.

"That was the simplest of all the deductions," Homes replied. "Surely you must have noted in studying the message that it was written in reformed English!"

I sat in silent admiration of this masterful exposition. "But even knowing all this, Homes," I finally said, "I fail to see how you were able to locate the miscreants."

Homes reached over and took the *Daily Times* from the pile in the corner, tapping it with one finger. "You have a short memory, Watney," he said, smiling briefly. "Do you not recall that just this morning I mentioned an article regarding the visit of an African prime minister and his retinue? In that group there are bound to be some who are visiting London for the first time; moreover, they come from a climate where shoes are unnecessary. And among other things, they came to enjoy the theatre season. I would wager that Shaw was their first choice!"

"And from this you deduced an inside job?"

Homes nodded. "They are guests at the Palace," he said. "I know it is difficult to pass the Palace guards at any time. Certainly trying to take a small boy past who might be recognized, or who might attract attention by screaming, is quite impossible. No, Watney, there can be no doubt. He is being held in the Palace itself."

"In their quarters?"

Homes shook his head. "I do not believe so. With the constant passage of upstairs maids and housekeepers, it would be extremely foolhardy. I should imagine, rather, that they have him locked in one of the unused basement rooms; possibly in one of the coal cellars, since in this weather they would be rarely visited."

He arose and, stepping into his high-heeled shoes, adjusted his blonde wig. "But it is getting on to the hour for our departure. I suggest you arrange the accoutrements, Watney, for we must be on our way!"

Moments later we were seated in a cab heading in the direction of the Palace. I had slipped the bull's-eye lantern under my cape, and my pistol was concealed in my weskit pocket.

"But are you familiar with the room arrangement at the Palace?" I asked as our cab clattered over the cobbled pavement along Piccadilly. "Have you ever been in the Palace?"

"I spent the afternoon there," replied my friend simply. "The guard allowed me, as a returning celebrity, to visit my humble old aunt, who I convinced him is housekeeper in charge of the royal linens. And I explained, as I left, that I would be coming back tonight with an aged uncle to have one last chat with Aunt Liz before sailing for the colonies." He turned to me seriously. "In the course of searching for the powder room I was able to make sufficient search of the premises to determine the location of the basement area. When we arrive, I suggest you to allow me to do the talking, as I made, I believe, quite an impression upon the guard!"

Our hansom drew up to a back entrance of the great, ornate Palace, and within seconds Homes was engaged in a giggling conversation with the uniformed figure at the gate. Moments later we found ourselves inside, in a long, empty corridor.

"This way, Watney!" Homes whispered in great excitement, once the outer door had closed upon us. He drew me by the hand to a staircase in one corner, leading downward. Once on the steps he removed his shoes, tucked them in his purse, and slipped silently ahead of me. The lower level was dark, and I handed him the lantern. Removing the cover he sent the light flickering over a series of cellar doors, each one labelled with the name of a different preserve. We made our way silently along the narrow passageway, and Homes paused at each door listening intently. Suddenly he raised his hand for complete silence and turned to me with triumphant satisfaction in every line of his face.

"In here, Watney!" he whispered. "Where it says 'Peaches!' Come! We must break it down!"

Making as little noise as possible we placed our shoulders to the door and heaved with all our strength. The door sprang open with a clatter that we feared might bring our adversaries down upon us, but apparently the heavy floors and thick walls of the Palace had been built for such an eventuality, for they contained the sound and there was no outcry. Homes immediately swung the lantern about the small room and there in one corner, as he had so accurately predicted, was the figure of a small boy huddling back in terror on a pile of empty jars. At his feet was a dog who came bounding up, licking our hands.

"There, there!" said Homes soothingly, drawing the terrified boy to his ample breast. "It is all right! We are friends." He stroked the boy's hair as I inspected the young lad. It was true that his ears were slightly pointed, but the smear of peach jelly across his face prevented us from noting the speckles on his nose. The small figure clung to Homes, weeping copiously.

"I assure you there is nothing to fear, Your Highness," Homes said in a kindly voice, still stroking the sobbing boy. "Come, let us take you to your suite. I am sure that no further attempt will be made against your person."

He led us from the darkened cellar, up the curving stairway to the corridor above. The little dog followed behind faithfully, trying to lick our heels. Once in the upper reaches, however, the boy made a sudden twisting motion, and with a low cry broke away and dashed down the corridor and out of sight. I began at once to follow, but Homes laid a restraining hand upon my arm.

"No, Watney. Let him go his way alone," he said, a happy smile creasing his face. "There has been sadness in this house tonight, and it will be a nice surprise for their Majesties!"

He turned to the rear door, with the little dog following us and whimpering softly.

"But what shall we do with the dog, Homes?" I queried.

He paused in deep thought. "Why, Watney," he finally said, "I have long felt that we have the need of a mascot. Let us take him home with us, in memory of a case where we have been able to serve our country!"

I lifted the little creature, placing him under my cape for warmth, and we made our way back to the street. A few whispered words and a muffled slap and we were back in our cab, rolling across London in the direction of Bagel Street.

Although our activities the previous evening had consumed many hours normally devoted to sleep, the following morning found us both neatly dressed and at breakfast at eight o'clock, prepared to welcome the veiled emissary from the Palace. Our little mascot lay quietly at our feet while Homes fed him scraps from the table. At the sound of the carriage below, the great detective quickly arose and opened the door to our quarters, and before anyone could stop him our little mascot had sprung outside and was racing down the steps.

"After him, Homes!" I cried, jumping to my feet.

"Not now!" Homes cried. "We cannot keep a messenger from Her Majesty waiting! It is a shame, but there is nothing that we can do!"

There was a commotion in the street and moments later the door was flung open and the lady from the carriage, her veil now tossed back from her radiant face, stood in the doorway, our mascot clutched in her arms.

"Thank you, Madam," I said, reaching forward. "These streets are most dangerous with the traffic of countless vehicles."

But she paid me no heed. "Mr. Homes!" she cried. "You have done it! You have found him!" She clasped his hand in hers in profound gratitude, lifting shining eyes to his.

"It was really nothing," Homes said modestly, although the sparkle of satisfaction gleamed in his eyes.

She pressed a signet ring firmly into his hand. "This is in gratefulness from an appreciative country," she said, and without another word she turned and left our quarters.

"Homes!" I cried. "She has inadvertently taken our mascot!"

"It matters not," said Homes, his eyes still lifted in dreamy speculation to the empty doorway. "Actually, the Palace is probably a better place for him with their countless forests." His eyes fell again to his hand.

The mark of the signet ring is still there, and Homes often looks at it in silent contemplation on those long evenings when we sit about the fireplace and recall his most successful case.

The Adventure of
The Counterfeit Sovereign

It was a gray, windy day in mid-April of '51 when I returned from my medical rounds and climbed the stairs to our rooms at 221B Bagel Street to find my friend Mr. Schlock Homes bending excitedly over an impressive array of test tubes, retorts, and similar chemical apparatus. Knowing his dislike of being disturbed while engaged in his researches, I quietly found myself a seat to one side and watched with interest as his fingers reached for a bit of litmus paper.

"You have arrived at a crucial moment, Watney!" said he, his keen eyes glittering. "If this litmus paper remains blue, all is well. If it turns red—then I am afraid we shall have to depend upon store-bought whisky for our afternoon libations!"

He turned back to his task and a moment later lifted his head in triumph, the still-azure strip dripping onto the carpet. Rinsing his hands, he dried them carefully on his dressing gown and flung himself into a chair.

"And none too soon!" he added in a pleased tone, "for we are to receive a distinguished guest shortly, and I fear that in my preoccupation with my last case I have allowed our liquor stocks to reduce themselves to a bit of Mrs. Essex's cooking sherry, and nothing more."

"A distinguished guest, Homes?" I asked, mystified.

In lieu of answering, he handed me a telegraph form and watched me closely as I read it. It was a request for an audience with Homes, and I noted automatically that the hour for the appointment was nearly upon us. The form was signed quite simply: Wilhelm Hans Wolfgang Herman Adolph von Saxe-Homburg, Grand Duke of Kitzle-Farbstein, King of Belgravia.

There was something faintly familiar in the signature and I looked up to see Homes nodding at me, as, in his inexplicable fashion, he answered my unspoken thoughts.

"Yes," he said, smiling. "It is the same. You may recall that I was fortunate enough to be of service to His Majesty before, in the matter of those incriminating letters I was able to recover from Polly Ad..." He paused. "But no names!"

His eye fell upon the mantel clock and he sprang to his feet. "I must dress!" he exclaimed. "If you would be so kind as to handle the conventions, Watney, I shall be back in a moment!"

He had no more than disappeared when the sound of a four-in-hand drawing up to the kerb could be heard, and a moment later the heavy tread of boots came tramping up the stairs. The door was flung open and I found myself facing a man fully seven feet in height, dressed in regal mink slashed with sable. The rich brocade of his ruffled silk shirt front was pinned at the throat by a large royal crest carved from a single opal, while his astrakhan-trimmed boots were banded by small emeralds embedded in the rich leather. Across the broad chest ran a diagonal swath of marten carrying a veritable host of medals. But the most surprising feature of his appearance was the thin strip of black that hid the upper portion of his face, although it could scarcely conceal the famous Kitzle-Farbstein nose.

"Your Majesty..." I began, overwhelmed by the royal presence, but before I could continue, he raised a large gloved hand imperiously.

"Please!" he said in a deep, rich voice with but the faintest trace of accent. "I come here incognito! To everyone I must be plain Mr. Kitzle for this brief period." He paused, peering at me with difficulty through the narrow slits of his mask. "But you are not Homes!"

His hand flew to the jeweled dagger at his hip, but I was saved the embarrassing necessity of defending myself by the drawling voice of my friend from the doorway.

"No, Mr. Kitzle," said Homes, advancing further into the room. "This is my old friend Dr. Watney, and whatever you have to say may be said freely in his presence, as he is remarkably inattentive."

The gloved hand fell away from the dagger and I found myself breathing normally once again. Homes waved our guest graciously to a seat and sank into one opposite while I repaired to the retort and began mixing drinks.

"You must forgive me," said His Majesty apologetically. "I have recently had the strangest adventure, and I still find myself a bit unnerved. It is precisely for this reason, Mr. Homes, that I requested an interview, for I should appreciate your views on the entire matter."

Homes leaned forward politely. "As always, Mr. Kitzle," he replied, "I am at your complete service. Please favour us with the details."

"Well, Mr. Homes," said our visitor, sitting forward and accepting a drink, "as you know, I am addicted to fox-hunting, not—as so many of your countrymen—for the sport, but because I have found that a good fox-fur makes up into an extraordinarily handsome cravat. In any event, yesterday, as I was riding to the hunt this particular fox disappeared over a low wall of an enclosed estate and I therefore reined my horse and followed on foot. To my amazement the grounds, although quite extensive, were heavily populated with people all dressed in white fencing jackets, and all wandering about quite aimlessly. I might mention that their tailor was extremely careless, for it appeared that the sleeves of all of these garments had all been sewn shut at the cuff... but I digress.

"I stopped several and asked them if they had seen a small brown fox with beady eyes and a general air of fright, but they all merely shook their heads vaguely and continued their wandering about. Not being accustomed to this cavalier treatment, I was about to remonstrate with one of them when there came the distant toll of a bell, and they all turned their footsteps in the direction of a huge house which I then noticed for the first time.

"Determined not to leave without notice of my fox, I followed. At the head of the lawn were a set of steps leading to a portal marked 'The Sanitarium,' but as I approached I found my way barred by a large, burly individual who placed his hand roughly on my arm and began to interrogate me thoroughly.

" 'You!' he said. 'Why aren't you in your jacket?'

" 'Unhand me!' I demanded. 'I am the King of Belgravia!'

" 'Of course!' this person agreed, still gripping me tightly. 'Who said no? But what I want to know is, how did you get out this morning without your white jacket?'

"Well, Mr. Homes, of course it would be quite gauche to wear a white jacket for fox-hunting, and for a moment I was inclined to so advise this uncouth person, but his crudeness led me to feel unobligated to explain. I therefore removed his hand from my sleeve by striking him unconscious, and as I turned away to once again seek my fox, a small person with spiky white hair, a broken nose, and a curious scar running from ear to ear, and also dressed in the same white jacket with sewn sleeves, came up and spoke to me . . ." He paused, eyeing Homes curiously. "You spoke?"

"No, no!" Homes cried. He was now leaning forward most intently, his eyes gleaming. "Pray continue!"

"In any event, then, this man with the spiky white hair said to me, 'Pick Windsor; or Napoleon! I am the King of Belgravia!'

"Well, Mr. Homes, naturally I was startled, but before I could clarify the situation, my fox darted out of some bushes where it had been hiding, and streaked down the driveway. I followed at once, but unfortunately the estate on that side borders the Great West Road and I lost the animal—a bit unsportingly, I think—to a small lad on a bicycle. As I returned to my horse it occurred to me that there was something unusual in my adventure, and I thought at once of seeking your advice."

Homes's eyes shone with excitement. He placed his drink to one side with a shudder and leaned back in his chair, tenting his fingers in concentration. For several moments he maintained silence, but when he finally spoke it was on a subject so far removed from the matter on hand that even I, used as I am to the peregrinations of his brain, was surprised.

"Mr. Kitzle, who handles the hiring of your kitchen staff?"

The King of Belgravia lifted his eyebrows at this unexpected query, but did not hesitate to answer. "My Prime Minister, Baron Meiterlunk."

"Ah!" said Homes, nodding his head in satisfaction. He eyed our royal guest keenly. "And would I be wrong in suggesting that of late you and the Baron have not been seeing eye-to-eye on many questions, and that the Baron at this precise moment is in London?"

The King's jaw fell open, disclosing diamond-studded teeth. "Why, yes!"

he exclaimed in utter amazement. "Although how you were able to deduce this I cannot imagine, as these are facts known only to myself!"

Homes smiled faintly but refused to explain, remaining instead in a brown study that lasted for several more minutes. At long last he rose to his feet with a sigh.

"I fear the affair is more complicated than it appears on the surface," he said thoughtfully. "However, Your Majesty may be assured that I shall tackle the problem at once. If Your Highness would be so kind as to leave the exact location of this estate with Dr. Watney here . . ."

"Of course. And thank you very much for your attention, Mr. Homes." His Majesty arose and bowed gratefully. "I shall await your reports with great eagerness."

Once our distinguished guest had taken his leave, Homes flung himself back into his chair and reached for his whisky glass with a dubious look at the murky contents.

"A dirty business I fear, Watney," he said, finally returning his eyes to mine. "The outlines of this dastardly plot against His Majesty are fairly easy to perceive, but the exact details remain obscure. And also, the best means of foiling the plot."

"But, Homes!" I cried, "I do not understand this at all. What plot is this of which you speak?"

"The plot against His Majesty, of course," Homes returned equably.

"But I heard nothing here today that would indicate any plot against His Highness!"

"You heard, but you failed to properly interpret what you heard," Homes replied obliquely. "However, it appears to be too late to take any steps today. You have our old fencing jackets? Then if you would be so kind as to bother Mrs. Essex for the loan of her sewing basket, we had best prepare for the morrow!"

"Her sewing basket, Homes?"

He turned back to his retort, frowning thoughtfully and paying no heed to my bewildered question. "And, Watney, if you will, while you are up you might hand me a bit of charred oak. I have just noticed that it was not a piece of litmus paper I used this afternoon, after all; but rather a thruppenny-ha'penny return slip for passage on the Hammersmith omnibus!"

The following morning Homes had me up at seven, and after a hurried breakfast of curried kippers led me swiftly down the steps to a trap he had engaged earlier. The chill of the morning was acute, and the fog that was so normal over Whitehall had not as yet burned away, so that our heavy quilted fencing jackets proved a welcome protection against the sharpness of the morning air. Homes gave our destination to the driver, and then leaned back frowning.

The questions that had boiled within me since the previous evening now erupted, but they fell upon deaf ears. "A dastardly affair, Watney," was my companion's only comment on the long drive, after which he lapsed into a silence which did not invite interruption. I therefore leaned back and reviewed in detail our conversation of the previous day, but try as I might I could find nothing there to justify the look of introspection that Homes was wearing.

We drew up at the estate at approximately the same place His Majesty had described as the point where he had tethered his horse. Requesting the driver to wait, Homes led the way over the low stone wall and into the cover afforded by a clump of bushes that margined the area. At that hour there were but few other jacketed figures in sight, but our luck was in for one of them was a short man with spiky white hair, a broken nose, and a scar that traversed his face completely. This one was idling his time away by pointing his sewn coat sleeve in various directions and saying "Bang!" At the sight of this strange figure Homes was seized by uncontrollable excitement and drew me deeper into the obscurity of the brush.

"Watney!" he whispered in great agitation. "I feared there was something familiar in the description His Majesty gave yesterday of his impersonator! That 'Bang!' has revived my memory! That is none other than Colonel Moron, the finest shot in all Europe, and the second most dangerous man in all of England!"

"But, Homes," I objected, "did you not tell me that Colonel Moron . . ."

"Exactly! I had thought him safely incarcerated, but it appears that he is free once again! This development must be given considerable thought!" He leaned against a bush in fierce concentration, his strong, thin fingers biting hard on my arm, and once again I was thankful for the protection of the fencing jacket. When at last he straightened up there was a light in his eye that boded ill for some miscreant.

"Of course!" he said, almost to himself, and turned to me. "Colonel Moron must wait. At the moment it is more important that we see the inside of the house. Come!"

We waited until the small man with spiky hair had wandered out of earshot, and then emerged from the bushes and walked quickly across the grass towards the large house that dominated one end of the estate. There seemed to be no one in attendance at the entrance, and without a word Homes swung open the door and stepped within. I followed closely and we found ourselves in a deserted passage, from one end of which came the clatter of pots and pans. Motioning me to maintain silence, Homes led the way down the passage and we peered in at the doorway.

It was a huge kitchen with eight or nine cooks busily preparing food. Homes turned to me, chuckling in pleased satisfaction. "I was sure of it, Watney!" he said. "It is the final proof!" But at that moment a large man wearing a chef's cap firmly set upon his head turned and noted our presence for the first time.

"You!" he cried fiercely. "Why are you snooping in this kitchen like some Schlock Homes?"

Both the smile on my friend's face, and his lazy drawl, indicated to me that he had indeed found the solution to the problem, and no longer felt the need for subterfuge. "Because," he replied coolly, "I *am* Schlock Homes!"

"Sure you are," returned the other. "And I am Pierre of the Ritz!" But when we put forward our hands to accept this introduction, the large man turned away abruptly and called over his shoulder, "Come, come, now! It's still two hours until lunch!"

"You must forgive him," Homes explained as we left the house and crossed the grounds. "All great chefs are temperamental, and I have heard of this Pierre. However, it is of small importance. I see the entire scheme now, as well as the means of foiling it!"

"But, Homes. . ." I began.

"Explanations must wait, Watney. We must return to Bagel Street as quickly as possible, for I must send a message to my brother Criscroft asking him to intercede with the authorities!" He hurried me across the wall and moments later we were clattering over the cobblestones of the Great West Road heading back to the city.

Once in the cab I could contain myself no longer. "Really, Homes!" I cried in exasperation. "This is too much! You speak of plots and solutions; I do not understand any of this! Why do you insist on all this secrecy? Do you not trust me?"

Homes laughed and laid his arm affectionately about my shoulder. When he chose to exert his great charm it was difficult to remain angry with him. "No, no, Watney," he said, chuckling. "The truth is that only at 'The Sanitarium' did I see the plan with all of its ramifications, plus the ideal means of thwarting it. Tell me, what is your opinion of the establishment we have just left?"

"Well," I said, mollified by this request for my help, "it is obviously the home of a very wealthy man, for the grounds are quite extensive and well cared for."

"And the large number of persons in evidence?"

"Relatives?" I hazarded.

"But if they were relatives," Homes pointed out, "how do you account for their clothing?"

"Hand-me-downs?" I suggested.

"No, Watney," he replied, serious once again. "There can only be one explanation that explains the uniformity of the white jackets and the huge kitchen which we saw."

"And that is . . . ?"

"The place is obviously a restaurant! As you should know, it is the modern custom to name roadhouses in such a manner as to attract customers, and the name 'The Sanitarium' is ideal for this purpose. The name comes from the

Latin and suggests cleanliness, which is the prime concern of people eating out. And in line with this same custom, it is also quite common to dress the waiters in keeping with the décor; hence the white jackets, which also suggest cleanliness."

"But the sewn cuffs, Homes!" I cried. "How do you explain those?"

"Quite simple, Watney! A further extension of the sanitary theme and the final proof of my deduction. Obviously to keep their fingers out of the soup!"

I leaned back, amazed at the way Homes could bring clarity out of confusion. Once it had been explained, of course, it appeared quite simple, but I realized the gifts with which my friend was endowed, to be able to cut so cleanly through the fog of misleading facts. Then another thought struck me.

"But, Homes," I said. "You spoke of a plot. . . ."

"Precisely, Watney! As soon as His Majesty described the white jackets I thought of a restaurant. The story of someone impersonating him brought up the possibility of a plot in connexion with this restaurant. It was for this reason that I inquired if Baron Meiterlunk handled the hiring of the servants, and if he were in London. Seeing Colonel Moron in person confirmed my suspicions, for it was then apparent that Meiterlunk planned on smuggling an assassin into the palace in the guise of a waiter!"

I nodded at the certainty of Homes's theory, but then my face fell. "But how can you stop the plot, Homes?" I asked in discouragement.

Homes leaned forward, his fine eyes fixed seriously upon mine. "It is apparent that Colonel Moron, in the short time since his escape, cannot have completed his training as a waiter," he said calmly. "Baron Meiterlunk is too much of a realist to attempt to place a person disguised as a servant on the palace staff unless he were completely trained in his duties. If we are able to prevent Colonel Moron from completing his training, the plot is bound to fall through!"

"But might not Meiterlunk find another instrument, then, for his scheme?" I objected. "A buxom upstairs maid, for example?"

Homes shook his head decisively. "You underestimate the Baron, my dear Watney. Once he finds himself foiled he will soon make it his business to discover who was responsible. And once he knows it was Schlock Homes who put an end to his dastardly scheme, he will realize the hopelessness of his position and never try again. No, you may be sure that the Grand Duke of Kitzle-Farbstein, King of Belgravia, is safe. Baron Meiterlunk will return to Belgravia without his assassin, and be content to be Prime Minister and nothing more!"

Our cab rolled up to our door and I managed to pay the driver despite the sewn sleeves of my jacket, and then followed Homes up the stairs. Once within the privacy of our chambers, Homes flung off the restricting jacket and reached for the Iranian wagon-lit* in which he kept his tobacco.

---

* Persian sleeper, of course!

"And now, Watney," he said, once his briar was going to his satisfaction, "the wire to Criscroft that shall scotch this nefarious plot once and for all!"

As he dictated to me, my mind reared at the sheer brilliance of his scheme. It was now certain that Colonel Moron would never complete his training as a waiter, for Homes was arranging to have "The Sanitarium" deprived of its food-dispensing license!

It was several days before the fruits of Homes's efforts on behalf of the King of Belgravia became apparent. I had come in to a late breakfast of kippered curry to find Homes deep in his newspaper, and with a smile of triumph he handed it across to me, the article he had been perusing uppermost.

It detailed an account of the return to Belgravia of its Prime Minister, Baron Meiterlunk, and noted that he returned alone. The King was remaining for a few days for the poule-shooting at Sandringham. Having already praised Homes for his coup several times, I felt it best to give his ego a rest, and for that reason pretended interest in another article, but his keen eyes immediately noted my defection.

"You have noted something of interest to us?" he asked, alert at once.

I could not keep up the pretense. "No, Homes," I replied, a bit ashamed of my subterfuge. "Actually, it is nothing but a tragic story of a food riot in some insane asylum."

"Poor souls!" said Homes softly, displaying that humanity that never ceased to surprise me. "I wish I could help!" He looked up, laying aside his pipe.

"Do you know, Watney," he added, his fine eyes serious, "whenever I read of places of that nature, I cannot but think: 'There, but for the grace of God, goes Schlock Homes . . . !' "

The Adventure of

The Snared Drummer

IT was rare indeed that my friend Mr. Schlock Homes forsook the sanctuary of our quarters at 221B Bagel Street for the social life that swirled through the London of our day. There was one occasion, however, when he always made an appearance in public: the annual dinner of the Crones, the women's auxiliary of the Actor's Club. While I have never questioned this complete reversal of his normal tendency towards seclusion, I have always suspected that it was largely due to the fact that the only women with whom Homes felt at ease were the Crones.

The dinner in the spring of '52 was a great success. As was customary the guests furnished the entertainment, and Homes had given his celebrated imitations of William Gillette and Basil Rathbone and had been received as always with enthusiasm. Now, with the entertainment finished and dinner past, the party broke up into small groups that formed islands in the vast hall, discussing the various items of interest of the day. I was standing at Homes's side, attempting to properly diagnose the exact proportions of gin and vermouth in the punch bowl, when a small agitated man scurried up and clutched my friend's arm.

"Mr. Homes!" he said in a quiet voice that nonetheless carried a note of desperation. "I am in serious difficulty. I have a problem which only you, I am afraid, can solve. I am sure that you do not remember me, but I have been fortunate enough to have met you in the past."

"Certainly," replied Homes with a friendly smile. "You are Mr. Frederic Highe, as I recall, and you are a producer of musical extravaganzas. As to where we met before, it is not as great a problem as you suppose. As a matter of fact, we were introduced earlier this evening."

"So we were!" exclaimed Mr. Highe in astonishment, amazed as were so many when, for the first time, they fronted evidence of my friend's remarkable memory. "Well, Mr. Homes, I find myself in desperate straits indeed! I would appreciate it very much if you could find it in your power to come to my assistance."

"Of course!" Homes replied warmly, drawing our new acquaintance to one side. "Just what is your problem?"

The small man glanced over his shoulder furtively. "Not here, Mr. Homes!" he whispered nervously. "Not here! If you could come to the theatre tomorrow at eleven, I shall explain everything!"

He looked about once more, his sharp eyes darting about the assembled throng in search of potential eavesdroppers. "I have rented the Castle in King's Row, where I am rehearsing *The Ruins of Astolot*. Do not fail me, for the love of God!" Without another word our new-found friend detached himself from our side and with one last appealing glance at Homes, melted into the crowd about us.

"A new case, do you suppose, Watney?" Homes asked, frowning in calculation.

"I beg your pardon, Homes?" I asked. "I'm afraid my curiosity regarding this exact blend..."

He sighed deeply as he answered his own question. "It could only be, I suppose," he said thoughtfully. "He has never heard me sing!"

At exactly eleven o'clock the following morning, Homes dismissed our hansom at the entrance to the deserted Castle Theatre, and we made our way through the unattended door to the darkness within. In the distance we could see the lighted stage, with our friend Mr. Highe speaking with another man on its empty expanse, but before we could move down the deserted aisle, a shadowy figure suddenly barred our way.

"Here, now," he said fretfully. "No admittance, gents!"

"But we are here to see Mr. Highe at his own behest," Homes explained quietly.

"He's pretty busy," said the other, scratching his head. "He's casting *The Ruins,* you know. However, if he is expecting you, please seat yourselves until he is free."

We edged our way to the front row and silently slid into two empty seats while the conversation on the lighted stage continued. Mr. Highe was speaking to another man seated at a table with a paper before him, and a pencil in his hand.

"Do you have sufficient bowmen?"

The other ran a finger down his list, nodded, and made a mark against one of the items.

"Enough halberd carriers? Musketeers? Pikemen?"

Those were dutifully checked off and the man once again nodded.

"How are you fixed for blades?" But before the other could complete his examination on this point, Mr. Highe noticed our presence in the auditorium and came hurrying down the steps at one corner of the stage.

"Mr. Homes!" he cried in embarrassment. "They should have informed me of your arrival. Please forgive me for having made you wait, but if you will be kind enough to come with me I shall explain everything!"

He led us immediately to his office, and once the door was closed fell into a chair, his face white and strained. Homes and I settled ourselves on a divan against the wall as our friend leaned forward in obvious agitation.

"Mr. Homes," he said, twisting his fingers nervously, "I am in a terrible position! We are planning to open *The Ruins of Astolot* in less than two weeks, and our principal tympanist has disappeared! He is absolutely vital to the production, for he is the only one who knows the score!"

"Disappeared?" Homes asked, his voice alive with interest.

"Completely! I have checked his rooming house, the local police precinct, and the four closest bars, and he has not been seen for over three days. He could not be visiting friends for he has been in England but two weeks and is acquainted with no one. It is essential that he be located at once!"

Homes absorbed this information in silence, his broad, scholarly forehead creased in a frown of concentration.

"What is his name?"

"Richard I. Porter."

"And his description?"

"He is a man in his middle thirties, approximately six feet tall, with a tanned complexion, light-browning hair, and weighing, I should judge, in the neighbourhood of thirteen stone."

Homes nodded. "And you say he has been here but two weeks?"

"Yes. He is an American who came here under contract to me for this one production."

"And he left no note?"

Mr. Highe shook his head sadly. "Nothing. Nor any explanation in any form whatsoever. The only thing we found in his dressing room was a clipping from an American journal, and hoping that you might find it of use, I took the liberty of saving it."

He produced from his pocket a torn piece of newsprint, long and narrow, and handed it to Homes. The great detective took it from the outstretched fingers and leaned forward to study it. I leaned over his shoulder; it was apparently a column devoted to the type of tattling which has become so popular, and carried the byline of a certain Hilda Harper. One item had been heavily encircled with dark pencil, and read:

> Dig Those Crazy Dues Dept.: The T-men are going to nail some of those musical tax-dodgers. One square from Local 802 crossed the pond to lay low, but they have him boxed. Better kick in March 15th or find a better 'ole, pal!

The gibberish made no sense to me at all, but I was amazed at the change wrought in my friend Schlock Homes. His eyes glittered with interest as they raced across the printed lines; his hands tightened convulsively on the fragile paper as he came to the end. He quickly read it a second time, his excitement mounting, and then fell back in deep thought, his thin, strong fingers tapping against the article.

"Homes!" I cried. "Is it a code? Have you solved it so soon?"

"It is no code, Watney," he replied slowly. "Would that it were!" He rose to his feet, clutching the column of newsprint in his hand. "Mr. Highe, this promises to be a most interesting investigation. If you will allow me to retain possession of this paper, I shall begin work at once!"

"Of course, Mr. Homes," replied the producer, also arising. "I saved it solely for your use. Take it and pray heaven it aids you in solving this mysterious disappearance."

Homes smiled enigmatically. "I fear that 'disappearance' may not be the proper word," he said. "However, sir, I hope to have more definite information for you tomorrow."

"The sooner the better, Mr. Homes," said the producer fervently. "Is there anything I can do?"

"Yes," replied Homes, his jaw tightening as he considered his answer. "I would suggest you begin to immediately instruct another tympanist in the vagaries of your score!"

In our hansom back to Bagel Street, I attempted to draw Homes out on the cryptic meaning of his last statement, as well as on his interpretation of the odd case, but he remained silent and preoccupied, refusing to take any of the bait I extended. As we approached our destination he suddenly leaned forward and paid our driver so that we were free to spring from the cab as soon as it wheeled itself to a halt before our door.

No sooner were we within our quarters than he flung himself into a chair still clutching the newspaper article tightly in one hand, and scowling at it fiercely.

"It is here!" he said, almost to himself. "I am sure of it!"

"But, Homes!" I exclaimed. "What is there? It appears to me to be the purest of nonsense."

"No, no, Watney. Far from it. Most of the message is crystal clear; it lacks but a shade to be complete."

I stared at my friend in astonishment. "Really, Homes," I said slowly, "I can find no meaning whatsoever in those strange words."

"No? And yet, Watney, there is no attempt to disguise the message. It is extremely clear—tragically clear, I might say. It states without equivocation that a group of hoodlums from the London slums have decided to do away with our tympanist. Their reference to the place where they intend to perpetrate this foul deed is all that puzzles me at the moment. . . ." His voice faded as he studied the paper with renewed vigour. "Of course! What a fool I am! Quickly, Watney, the London Directory!"

In haste I pulled the required volume from our shelf of reference books and handed it to Homes. He ran his finger rapidly down the various listings of the book, and then with a bound he was once again on his feet and turning in the direction of the door.

"I shall return as quickly as possible, Watney," he said, his eyes shining as always at the thought of action. "Should I be late I suggest you prepare a bull's-eye lantern and see to the priming of your pistol, for if I am correct in my analysis of this strange affair we shall be busy tonight, and it will not be pleasant business!"

It was quite late in the evening when my friend reappeared. Mrs. Essex, our housekeeper, had laid on a sumptuous tea of roasted Brussels sprouts, and Homes grasped one hungrily, munching on it as he spoke.

"You have the lantern and the pistol?" he inquired. "Good!" His face fell as he added, "I am afraid that we are too late to save Mr. Porter, but at least we shall be able to locate his body and convince our client of the uselessness of awaiting his return."

"His body, Homes?" I cried in dismay. "You mean . . . ?"

He nodded his head sadly. "Yes, Watney, it is almost certain that Mr. Porter is no longer among the living. But at least I know where they have concealed his remains, and it is there that we shall repair once it becomes dark."

"But, Homes!" I cried in puzzlement, "I do not see how you were able to locate Mr. Porter simply from the cryptic references in that newspaper!"

Homes finished the last of the toasted Brussels sprouts, and wiping his lips, dropped into a chair. He lit an Armenian, and once it was drawing to his satisfaction, withdrew the clipping and presented it to me.

"You will note this message, Watney," he said in that slightly superior manner he always adopted when explaining the solution to one of his cases. "The T-men, of course, can only be teddy boys grown to manhood. And made no less vicious, I warrant, by their added years. Their exact reason for eliminating Mr. Porter is still obscure, although the motive was obviously revenge, since you will note their use of the word 'dues.'

"The references to death and burial are too frequent to avoid. 'Nail,' 'boxed,' 'the better hole,' and particularly the reference to the infamous Ides of March. No, Watney, the message was quite clear on these points. It was determining the place where this foul crime was to occur that presented the only problem."

"And how did you solve this, Homes?" I asked, all attention.

He tapped the newspaper clipping with his finger. "It is all right here, Watney! You will note that the message reads: 'One square from Local 802' – that is to say, one city block from public house No. 802. Across a pond! This afternoon I found pub 802 in the licensing listings of the London Directory, and when I left your company I went to investigate. A square from this public house is Hyde Park, and across the pond there, there is but one edifice." His cool eyes stared at me somberly. "It is an undertaking establishment, Watney!"

I caught my breath at the masterful manner in which Homes had managed to see light in this most puzzling of cases. But then my face fell. "That is all very well, Homes," I said, "but how are we to prove your theory to the satisfaction of our client?"

"It is for this reason that I requested you to prepare a bull's-eye lantern," he replied. "Tonight we shall break into this evil house and there I am sure we shall find the remains of Mr. Porter, for they will scarcely have had time to dispose of his cadaver." He rose to his feet, pocketing the newspaper article. "I believe it is sufficiently dark now, Watney. Come, let us be on our way!"

In a very short time we were rattling along High Holborn in the direction of Marble Arch. Homes was carrying the lantern well concealed beneath his cape, while I took charge of the primed pistol. At the corner of Hyde Park

Road, Homes directed our driver to turn in the direction of Knightsbridge, but before we had proceeded very far my companion had the driver stop the cab and we descended.

"We shall proceed on foot, Watney," he said quietly as the cab rolled away. "It would not do to blatantly announce our arrival."

We crossed the darkened park in silence, carefully avoiding the strolling lovers and political orators, until we found ourselves at the edge of the pond. This we quickly skirted, taking every precaution not to fall in, and moments later found ourselves before a silent, deserted building. The black windows that stared down on us would have struck fear into the soul of a lesser man, but Schlock Homes, once on the scent, was beyond fear.

"Watch the path!" he commanded, and immediately tackled the huge door with his set of picklocks. Moments later he called to me softly, and I hurried to join him, passing into the building at his side. Once within, he quietly closed the door behind us and lifted the cover from the bull's-eye lantern, flashing the beam to all corners of the room.

We were within an area that apparently served as a combination chapel and meeting hall, for wooden folding chairs were stacked neatly against the wall, and a lectern was pushed to one side. The keen eyes of my friend noted each detail revealed in the uncompromising circle of light cast by the lantern, and suddenly I heard him catch his breath. The light had traversed one wall and was now fixed upon two doors set side by side. Homes smiled in satisfaction at the sight, for they were clearly marked "Hymns" and "Hearse."

"The one obviously goes to the organ loft," he said. "It is the other we want. Come!"

He led the way quickly to the right-hand door and we passed into a narrow hallway that appeared to serve many rooms. With silent tread Homes went from door to door, trying each one, until I felt him pause decisively, his hand frozen on the knob.

"The final proof, Watney!" he whispered in great excitement. "Note the wreath!"

I crowded behind him and peered into the scene revealed by the bull's-eye lantern. There, on plain wooden trestles, lay a coffin, and above it a horseshoe-shaped wreath of flowers was suspended. Homes flashed the beam across the satin band spanning the two sides of the floral arch, and my admiration for my friend's analytical powers rose to new heights. Now there could be no doubt but that the body of Richard I. Porter lay within the casket—for his initials were clearly printed on the satin band!

The following morning, having sent a report to our client on the special black-bordered telegraph forms that Homes reserves for such occasions, I returned to our sitting room to find my friend having his first after-breakfast pipe. As was my wont, I sat down and riffled through the journals in search of some item which might prove challenging to the reasoning powers of the great detective. I was reading the *Old Statesman* when I must have stiffened, for the voice of Homes broke into my cogitations.

"You have found something which might prove to be of interest to us, Watney?" he asked genially.

"In all honesty I really do not know," I replied, studying the article more closely. "Frankly, the wording is completely unintelligible to me. It appears to be in some form of cryptology, or code."

"Code?" His interest immediately fired, Homes laid aside his pipe and reached eagerly for the folded sheet which I handed to him. He leaned forward and began to read aloud:

> "One American practitioner of percussion instruments who eschewed the burden of juridical assessments on his emoluments, is rumoured to have traversed the Atlantic in search of haven. His dissembling, however, is purposeless, since the personages charged with pecuniary aggregation by the American Authorities are cognizant of his locative situation."

Homes grasped the paper in feverish excitement, his eyes glittering as always at the challenge of a new problem.

"Watney!" he cried. "It is undoubtedly a code; it could be nothing else! Quickly, my monograph on Common Codes and their Cures, if you please!"

The Adventure of
The Final Problem

IT was in the fateful year of '62 that I first began to notice the effects of the many years of devoted sacrifice and profound mental effort on my friend Mr. Schlock Homes. Aggravated by the lingering effects of those early days when he was a Coke addict, and brought to a climax by his more recent habit of filter tips, the signs were all too plainly noticeable. It was with heavy heart that I advised Homes that unless he saw fit to take a complete rest from his labours, I should not care to speak for the results.

I had first noted his looking seedy in early May of that year, and had attributed it at the time to an increase in his consumption of pomegranates. When this was replaced in his diet with watermelon and no improvement ensued, I knew there was no choice left but to plan a complete cessation of his efforts, and the passing of at least the summer in absolute relaxation on the Continent.

To this end, therefore, we packed our bags early in June of '62 and departed our quarters at 221B Bagel Street for our European holidays. In line with my strict admonition, Homes left all elements pertaining to his profession behind, taking with him only the barest minimum of clothing and, of course, his beloved violin. The newly formed Flying Squad of Scotland Yard, led by Inspector "Hansom" East himself, escorted us from our rooms to Victoria Station, and Homes was quite touched by this mark of esteem.

We passed an idyllic month on the Costa Brava, at a little town just north of Cape Ouf-de-Grasse. In this time Homes's appearance improved greatly; his weight rose to ten stone and the old sparkle returned to his eyes. Although at first he seemed to evidence signs of restlessness at his enforced idleness, in time he proved to be an ideal patient, whiling away his hours in the healthy sunlight that flooded the sidewalk cafés, and even playing his violin for the musical connoisseurs who frequented those places. Nor, oddly enough, did he seem to lack for funds. Although we had left London with proscribed purses he appeared to be in excellent financial shape, even going so far as to augment his meagre wardrobe with a new hat, a very fine white cane, and a quite attractive pair of dark glasses.

But even the Costa Brava in time began to pall. The appreciation — I assume he meant "musical" — of his listeners, Homes said, was dropping, and for this reason I readily fell in with his suggestion that we continue along the Riviera to what Homes called, in his literary manner, "new hunting grounds." The following morning, therefore, found us up and out of the hotel before dawn, and Homes demonstrated his vastly improved physical condition by sliding from our room, even burdened by our bags, on a rope placed there, apparently, for that purpose. Minutes later we were driving our trap smartly along the lovely winding road that skirts the blue Mediterranean.

But the pleasant relaxation of our holiday was not to continue, for in the picturesque principality of Monaco, fortune contrived to involve Homes in a case which I record here with heavy hand. We had arrived in the early afternoon and immediately set about finding quarters. Cheap rooms, however, were not to be had, and in the end we were forced to accept a suite in a major hotel at a quite disgraceful rate. Homes, however, waved the cost aside, and once our bags had been deposited there, picked up his violin and announced his intention of inspecting the local sidewalk cafés. I attempted to point out to him that it was quite late in the day, and that the beneficial rays of the sun would shortly disappear, but he was adamant.

We had threaded our way through the densest part of the throng before the Chez Guavara when of a sudden a hand shot out of the crowd, reaching up from a table to grasp Homes's coat sleeve. A voice cried out in pleased surprise.

"Mr. Homes! And Doctor Watney! How fortunate to have encountered you in this fashion! We have been searching all through Europe for you!"

We turned to find ourselves facing none other than Inspector "Hansom" East, whom we had thought safely in England. He drew us hastily into two idle seats at his table and with a swift glance about, leaned forward and spoke in a confidential low voice.

"Mr. Homes, the Flying Squad at this moment is engaged in checking every village along the Corniche for you! Although you are not aware of it, your brother Criscroft in the Home Office has arranged that my services be placed at the disposal of the authorities here in an effort to resolve a problem of dire consequence. And only you can help me find the answer!"

Homes looked at the eager face confronting us with a slight frown.

"I shall be honest with you, Inspector," he said slowly. "I have more or less decided to abandon detection for all time. This holiday has opened my eyes to far greater possibilities for, shall we say, a richer life."

I am afraid that my mouth gaped at these words. The Inspector's face fell.

"Mr. Homes," he said fervently, "it is vital that you aid us, at least in this one case. England has given her word to Monaco that this affair will be clarified, and it would look poor indeed for the British Lion were we to fail!"

Homes's eyebrows went up. "Very well, then," said he with small enthusiasm. "In that case it appears I have little choice. Pray favour us with the details."

The Inspector sighed with relief. "I knew you would not let us down, Mr. Homes! Well, then, the story is this: As you know, the Casino here at Monte Carlo is the principal source of revenue for the country, and it is to the interest of the Western powers that Monaco remain free and solvent. We are, therefore, most interested in the continued success of the Casino. Yet, Mr. Homes, all this is in grave jeopardy today!"

Despite his air of indifference I could sense a quickening of interest in my friend at these words. He leaned forward. "In which way?" he inquired quietly.

"Hansom" East glanced about secretively to make certain we were not being overheard. "Mr. Homes, of late there have been a mysterious series of rapping and chipping sounds from somewhere beneath the floor at night in the Casino. These frightening noises are clearly audible in the gaming rooms. The Directors have attempted to explain them to the players as merely the rumblings of an incipient earthquake in the neighbourhood, but it is doubtful if these thin excuses can serve for very long." He bent closer, wringing his hands.

"Mr. Homes, there is every indication that the Casino is haunted! I need not describe to you how disastrous it would be if this fact were to be disclosed. Gamblers being notoriously superstitious, the gaming tables could lose their customers within a week, and the entire country fall into bankruptcy! The blow to the Western powers in that event would be incalculable!"

Homes received this information with narrowed eyes as his brilliant mind encompassed the problem in all its ramifications. "You have investigated the possibility of human agency?"

The Inspector shook his head. "The Casino employees flatly refused to do so, and frankly, I have been so busy searching for you that I have not had the time. However, I believe you can rule out this likelihood; it is hard to conceive of a person so unpatriotic as to threaten our national security for any urge so minor as that of frightening people. No, Mr. Homes, only some supernatural phenomenon can explain this mysterious affair!"

"Your logic appears unimpeachable," Homes admitted, and pushed himself to his feet. "However, I suggest we repair to the Casino itself, where we will be better able to test the validity of your theory."

To this end we left the café, with Holmes still grasping his violin tightly. Our trap being the closest, the three of us entered and I handled the reins as the Inspector gave directions. Homes leaned back, his fingers tented, his broad forehead wrinkled in concentration. Within minutes we were entering the curved driveway and drawing up before the broad marble stairway leading to the gambling salon where, as the Inspector had so clearly explained, the freedom and liberty of us all was being protected. The Inspector began to usher us into the building, but Homes desisted.

"If you do not mind, Inspector," he said, "I should prefer to begin my inspection with the grounds. If you would be so kind as to explain my presence to the Directors, I shall meet you later in the office and we can discuss my findings."

"Very well, Mr. Homes," the Inspector agreed. "And may fortune attend your search!"

As soon as the Inspector had disappeared within, Homes began to circle the huge building, his sharp eyes noting each crevice and cranny in the walls. Suddenly he stopped short and grasped my arm tightly.

"There, Watney!" he whispered in great excitement. "Do you see it?"

"See what, Homes?" I whispered back, and then cleared my throat. "See what, Homes?"

"That hidden door!" he exclaimed, and hurried forward. Sure enough, there was a small portal obscured by the tall bushes that edged our path. Bending to it with a picklock in hand, Homes soon had it open and we crept within.

We faced a dusky passage lighted only by a series of small bulbs which were operated, as Homes correctly deduced, by a small switch beside the entrance. Motioning me to silence, the great detective edged slowly forward. A sharp turn in the passage brought us face to face with a second door, and once again Homes applied himself to the lock. Moments later the portal had surrendered to Homes's mastery and we passed within.

We were in a room that had, apparently, once served as some type of storeroom. Abandoned accoutrement of gambling were scattered about and moldy sofas and hassocks filled one wall. Against a second wall there was propped diagonally the upper portion of a wooden bunkbed, which had been wrenched from its mating part and leaned almost vertically against the plaster. The mattress had been removed from this affair, and the many wooden bedslats formed a ladder-like arrangement. The remainder of the broken bed was scattered about the floor. Homes's eyes raised to the ceiling; a hole had been started just above the bed, and bits of chipped concrete lay about on the floor where they had fallen.

For fully five minutes Homes studied this scene, his keen eyes examining every bit of the small room, but particularly the broken bed leaning upright against the wall. When at last he turned to me, his face – to my utter astonishment – was contorted with pity.

"Poor chap!" he murmured. His fine eyes came up to mine, compassion flooding them. "Let this be a lesson to you, Watney, even as it has been to me. When the Inspector expounded his theory of a supernatural agency at work, I could find no hole in it. And yet, here before us, is the proof that the agency was human indeed. But in sad shape, poor chap!"

"But, Homes," I exclaimed, "I do not understand this at all. I see nothing to indicate human occupation here, and I certainly do not comprehend your reiteration of the phrase 'poor chap'!"

"No, Watney?" He smiled sadly. "And yet it is all here for us to see. The man who made those sounds in the night had no thought of disturbing those above; he was merely seeking to alleviate his own distress, for he suffers great physical misfortune. Not only does he endure the torture of a serious back ailment, but it is also obvious that he is a victim of asthma. This, plus his greatly straitened circumstances, it seems to me, merit my calling him 'poor chap'." He turned to study the ragged hole begun in the ceiling. "There is but one further point to check in order to prove everything, but there can be little doubt."

"But, Homes . . . !" I began. My friend, however, was paying no attention. Instead, he had whipped out a pad and pencil and was busy making measurements in the room and marking them down. When he was finished he grasped his violin and strode down the passageway, noting the number of paces he had made and their direction. When he had finished he added this information to his notes, thrust the pad into his weskit pocket, and turned to me.

"Come, Watney," he said, "let us visit the office and check the location of that hole in the ceiling. Unless I am greatly mistaken, we will find it was intended to break into a fresh-air duct."

The Inspector was sitting with two of the Directors when we entered the large office. At sight of Homes he sprang to his feet, but Homes waved him to silence with a strong hand. "Gentlemen," he asked, "would it be possible for you to furnish me with the architectural plans for this building?"

The Directors were obviously puzzled by this request, but one of them immediately withdrew the plans from a drawer and handed them over. The tall detective spread them out upon a desk and began making rapid measurements. His strong, thin finger came down upon a spot.

"Gentlemen," he said in quiet satisfaction. "Am I correct in assuming that these lines indicate an air duct?"

The Directors bent over the table. "That is the vault you have your finger on," one replied.

Homes's face fell, but only for an instant, as his genius considered this new fact. "Tell me, gentlemen," he said softly, "is the vault *air conditioned?*"

"Why, yes, it is, Mr. Homes," the Director replied, surprised.

The Inspector leaned forward anxiously. "Have you found something, Mr. Homes?"

There was a moment's silence before my friend answered. "Gentlemen," he said at last, "I can guarantee you the cessation of the noises which have been frightening your clients. But it will cost you ten thousand francs, and you must ask no questions."

The Inspector's face lighted up. "Mr. Homes, you are wonderful! The money is no problem. But how . . . ?"

"No questions!" Homes said sternly. He accepted the packet of notes handed him by one of the Directors and bowed slightly. "Thank you, gentlemen. And now, good day. Come, Watney."

He waved away the enthusiastic thanks of the three men and led me out of the building. I started toward our trap, but Homes's firm hand turned me from my path in the direction of the small portal hidden in the thick bushes. I pulled back violently.

"What now, Homes!" I cried in exasperation. "You may go your way alone! I have been patient with your mystification, for I know this is your conceit, but when you accept money for aiding your country, I will have no part of it!"

"No, no, Watney," he said softly. "You do not understand. The money is not for me; it is for the poor soul who has been forced to bury his misery in that tiny warren! Come, we must wait for him. As we do so, I shall explain everything."

We drew back into the heavier of the thick bushes where our presence could not be noted, while still affording vision of the small door. Homes turned to me.

"The answer to this entire problem lay in that broken bunkbed, Watney," he said softly. "Mute though it be, it spoke volumes. As soon as I saw it I began to cast about for reasons, not only for its condition, but also for its position almost up-ended against the wall. And then suddenly the pieces fell into place, and I saw the only combination of circumstances that could account for all the facts."

His voice saddened. "That the hapless fellow was in straitened circumstances was evident. You know the difficulty we had in finding a hotel room, and had our purse been less full we might have been reduced, as this poor man was, to seek clandestine lodgings where we would. That the unhappy soul suffered from a back injury was evident from the fact that he had eschewed the softer sofas and had, in fact, even removed the mattress to leave the hard support of the bedslats. As you know from your medical knowledge, Watney, only a hard surface such as this would serve to give him any small modicum of relief."

"True," I admitted, entranced as always when Homes explained his remarkable deductions. "But, Homes, how could you know that he also suffered from asthma?"

"By the position of the bed, Watney! Very nearly upright! I am sure that you yourself have often recommended this position to sufferers. And when I saw the attempt at making a hole in the ceiling, and learned that it led to a source of cool, fresh air, my case was complete." He smiled. "With this ten thousand francs, however, I am sure the poor chap can arrange more comfortable quarters and need no longer unwittingly frighten the Casino clientele."

I clasped his hand, ashamed of my previous doubts. "Homes, forgive me!"

"Hush!" he commanded. At first I thought it was only an exhibition of his modesty, but then I saw he was peering intently through the darkness. "Here he comes!"

A figure was approaching, staying well into the shadows. It paused before the small door to glance backwards. Homes's hand tightened on my arm.

"It is Professor Marty!" he whispered, and shook his head sadly. "There, Watney, is the proof that crime does not pay, for the Professor must have gained millions in his years as the leading criminal of all Europe, yet he is reduced to this sad end!"

"What do you intend to do, Homes?" I whispered back.

"Despite our differences in the past, I cannot help but feel pity for one in his sad circumstances," Homes replied warmly. "It is obvious that he no longer represents a threat to society. I shall therefore give him the money and wish him Godspeed."

He stepped from the bushes, confronting the crouching figure at the door.

"Professor!" he called in a kindly voice. "All is known! Please accept..." But before he could finish, the tall red-haired man had whirled about wildly and was dashing around the building.

"After him!" Homes cried. "In his desperate condition there is no telling what measures he may take!"

Without loosening his grip upon his violin case, he dashed for the front of the building with me in hot pursuit. A carriage was disappearing through the curved entrance to the grounds. Without a pause Homes flung himself into our trap, grasping my hand and pulling me into the moving vehicle even as he cracked the whip over our startled steed.

"He cannot have gotten far!" cried he, leaning over our horse and snapping the whip in his ears. "The road is but one, and with any luck we shall overtake him in minutes!"

We fled up the rocky, winding road, our horse straining at the bit, his hooves pounding the pavement wildly. I huddled in one corner attempting to catch my breath while Homes, like some figure from mythology, leaned over the frightened beast cracking his whip madly in its ears. Beyond the sharp cliff at our side the rocks fell sheer to the dashing waves below.

We curved with the road, our wheels scraping loudly against the low stone wall that bordered the drive and held us back from the precipitous drop to the sea. Suddenly Homes was straining wildly at the reins, pulling our terrified horse to a panting stop.

"The Professor!" he cried, pointing to a trap skewed to a stop in the road before us. "He has a flat wheel! Now is the time to give him the money!"

He sprang down and hurried forward, but the figure kneeling at the wheelhub was equally as quick, remarkable considering his many physical infirmities. Before Homes could reach him, he had come to his feet, reached within his carriage, and a second later was confronting my friend with a long sword in his hand.

"Homes, you are a devil!" he gasped. "How did you know?"

"The broken bunkbed," Homes replied calmly. "Come, Professor . . ."

"Then you shall die!" cried the wrathful figure. "You shall not live to reveal me as the man who broke the bunk at Monte Carlo!" And with no further word he sprang forward, his sword weaving dangerously in the still night air.

But he had not counted upon the lightning reactions of Schlock Homes! With a leap Homes was at our trap, had snatched open his violin case, and was reaching within. For one horrified moment I feared he meant to defend himself with his beloved Amati, but then I saw he had withdrawn the hardened ash bow and was springing back into the roadway to defend himself with it against the crazed Professor.

"You misunderstand, Professor!" Homes called sharply, but the whistling blade of the other almost cut off his words. There was nothing for it but to defend himself. "Stand back, Watney," he cried to me. "I can handle this. I merely mean to disarm the poor fellow!"

Would that I had words to describe that fearsome duel! Homes with nothing more than the slim horsehair-strung bit of ash, tipped by dainty ivory; while the Professor was armed with the latest type of buttonless foil! Back and forth they swayed, their breath loud and rasping in the night. And then, so quickly that the eye could scarcely follow, Homes flicked his wooden weapon hard against the guard of the other's foil, and with a sudden twist sent it flying from his hand and spinning over the edge of the precipice. The Professor gave a gasp of dismay and lunged forward in a frantic effort to recover his lost blade, and before we knew it he was teetering on the very brink, waving his arms madly in an effort to save his equilibrium.

We both sprang forward to help, but it was too late! With a hoarse shriek that still echoes in my ears to this day, the huge red-haired figure lost his balance and fell into the abyss. His fearsome screams diminished as he fell— then sudden silence held as we stood above, frozen with horror. I turned at once to my friend.

"Are you all right, Homes?" I asked anxiously, and then paused in astonishment, for there were tears in his eyes. "Homes? What is it? You must not blame yourself, for you did everything in your power to help the poor man."

"No, no, Watney," he began, but I continued, hoping to ease the pain etched on his fine face.

"Also," I added, "the sounds at night in the Casino will now cease, and that is all that really matters. You have preserved our English way of life, and that is no small thing."

"You do not understand, Watney!" he said with a tragic catch in his voice. "Not that! This!" And he held before my sight the battered remains of the weapon with which he had defended himself so valorously. The long shaft of wood was badly scarred and twisted from the violence of the struggle, and the white horsehair strands were completely severed and fluttering helplessly in the air.

Suddenly I saw the devastating truth. "Homes!" I cried aghast. "You mean . . . ?"

"Yes, Watney," he sobbed, the tears now coursing freely down the crevices of his face. "It was my last bow!"

It is painful to continue, but continue I must! Even as I watched, Homes walked brokenly to the low parapet that separated the road from the boiling chasm and with a sobbing curse flung the tattered bow from him with violence. Alas! Worn by struggle, the muscles of his fine body betrayed him; the impetus twisted him sharply against the low wall, and before my very eyes, my friend—the dearest friend a man could have—disappeared into the churning void below!

I cannot go on! Schlock Homes is no more! I could not even bring myself to peer over the edge of that treacherous hill which had claimed his life! True, he had died in saving his country, and at the conclusion of his most brilliant case, but his loss shall shadow my steps throughout my days!

With faltering steps and brain awhirl I made my way back to our hotel and thence to England, carrying with me—as I shall forever—the memory of the finest and wisest man I have ever known. And if, some night in the desolate quietude of our rooms at 221B Bagel Street, I seem to sense once again his presence, or seem to hear once again his soft voice, I shall know the truth of that immortal line by the great poet Stevenson:

Homes is the haunter, home from the hill . . .

The Return of
Schlock Homes

IT was with bitter thoughts that I trudged down the broad stone staircase of St. Barts that late afternoon of a cool September day in '62 and turned my steps in the direction of the modest quarters I had—so long ago, it seemed!—shared with my dear friend Mr. Schlock Homes. The day had gone quite badly: the cardiectomy I had performed that morning had seemed successful and yet the patient had inexplicably died. Far worse, the pretty young nurse I has asked to commiserate with me by sharing an afternoon libation had curtly refused my offer.

It was in a black mood indeed, therefore, that I tramped through the streets, recalling in my memory the last time I had seen Homes, and the vivid scene of that struggle on the rocky cliffs of the Corniche—Professor Marty armed with gleaming sword, and my friend with only a fragile bit of ashwood, and the hungry rocks below reaching up through the angry surf! And then, when the Professor had lost his balance and gone over the edge, that horrible moment when Homes, his last bow ruined, had gone to fling it to the waves and had also fallen to his death!

Schlock Homes no more!

Even after these many weeks it still seemed impossible. With a deep sigh that owed, perhaps, almost as much to the memory of my friend as to that of the young nurse, I turned at last into Bagel Street, came to our rooms at Number 221B, and clumped up the shadowy stairway.

The room was darkening with the growing evening, but sufficient light still remained for me to make my way to the bookshelf and remove my address-book without the necessity of turning up the lamp. I was in the process of tearing out the page with the young nurse's name on it, ripping it angrily into shreds and flinging the pieces from me, when a sudden sound gave me pause. Had I not been positive of Mrs. Essex's intense dislike of felines, I could have sworn that a cat was mewing in the room.

Turning, I searched the gloom of one corner, and there, to my utter consternation, sprawled a lanky figure idly drawing a bow across the strings of a violin and producing what was, even to my untutored ear, a reasonable facsimile of Zetzenbull's *Suite Sioux*. So grave was the shock that I am afraid my mouth fell open.

"Homes!" I cried, my knees weakening.

"Watney," replied my friend with a dry chuckle, "your mouth is open." He laid aside his instrument and drew himself lazily to his feet. "In addition, you are littering the floor."

"Homes!" I repeated, my eyes widened in shock. "You are alive! How is it possible?"

He eyed me thoughtfully. "When I was so careless as to fall over the parapet in Monaco," he replied after a pause, "I was fortunate in selecting a spot where some night fishermen were preparing to spread their nets for drying, pulling them taut before fastening them down. Professor Marty had already managed to free himself from the cords and was scuttling off down the beach when I arrived. Needless to say, a second tangling of their nets did little to soothe the fishermen, and by the time I could assuage their anger and climb back to the road, you had already disappeared. Upon arrival at the hotel I found you had taken my effects with you, and I was therefore forced to remain in Europe, although I was not particularly averse to so remaining."

"And what brings about your return now, Homes?"

The great detective smiled at me. "What brings about your haste to tear pages from that small morocco notebook, if questions of motives are being asked? You enter the room and immediately repair to the bookcase, take down your address-book, and violently rip out the pages. The only possible conclusion one can draw from your actions is that you are in dire need of the binding. Taking into consideration the season, one can only conclude that you have decided to go hunting and require elbow-patches for your hunting-jacket."

"Homes!" I repeated once again. "You have not changed!" I stared at him carefully. "But what brings you back to London? And are you here to stay?"

My friend walked over and raised the lamp, bringing into sharp focus his familiar and beloved profile.

"Why, as to that, Watney," he replied easily, "only time can tell. Actually, the need of an old friend was communicated to me and I felt it necessary, in his cause, to return."

"Homes!" I said, overwhelmed with emotion at his statement.

"Lord Epsworth," he continued, much as if I had not spoken. "Surely you remember him?"

"Of course," I replied. Lord Epsworth was an old friend of ours whose eccentricity for having all neighbours at a minimum distance of three miles from his estate had brought this measure to be known in those parts as the Epsworth League. "Just what is causing his Lordship concern?"

Homes smiled gravely. "Later," he said quietly. His keen eyes surveyed me. "You appear a bit under the weather, Watney. If you are free to join me in this case I should be much delighted. I suggest that the fresh air of the Highlands may be just the prescription you require for the obvious disappointment of missing your hunting."

"I should like that, Homes!" I cried.

"Good. Then I suggest you pack without delay, for in anticipation of your acceptance I have booked us space on the Glasgow Express which leaves Euston within the hour."

I went to my room and began throwing clothes into my old campaign bag, the young nurse now forgotten. The thought of Homes's return, and his request for my help on a case, was like wine to me. Feeling better by the moment, I joined Homes in the living room and we descended together to take a hansom to the station.

We arrived in good time, and once seated in our compartment Homes lit a Bulgarian and leaned back, flicking ashes on the floor. I smiled at the well-remembered gesture.

"This is like old times, Homes," I remarked warmly. "It has been some time since a case has taken us above the Scottish border."

"It has indeed," he conceded. "The last time was when we were so fortunate as to prevent warfare among some of the eminent Scottish families, when their tempers got the better of their judgment."

I nodded, recalling the case well. In my notes it still remains waiting to be delineated, bearing the title of *The Adventure of the Steamed Clans.*

"Well do I remember, Homes," I said, and then leaned forward. "But enough of these memories. If you don't mind, please favour me with the details of Lord Epsworth's problem."

A frown crossed my friend's face. He reached forward, crushing his cigarette out against the carriage window-sill, and turned to me in all seriousness.

"The facts are these, Watney. As you know, Lord Epsworth is the owner of a famous pig, known to all fanciers as the Duchess of Bloatings, and winner of countless medals and ribbons. Well, to be blunt, the Duchess of Bloatings is missing. Upon learning of his loss, Lord Epsworth immediately instituted a search, and even managed to engage the services of a wandering band of gypsies he had allowed to camp on his grounds, as the Duchess of Bloatings seemed particularly partial to the refuse their campsite offered.

"But all to no avail. When, as of last evening, no sign of the missing animal had been noted, he thought to advise the local constabulary, who in turn made contact with Scotland Yard, who got in touch with the Sûreté-Générale, who managed to locate me. It is for the purpose of finding the missing prize-winning pig that we are traveling north."

I nodded my head in understanding. "Tell me, Homes, do you have any theories on the matter?"

"None," he replied honestly. "Until we are upon the actual scene, I fear there is little to do. I suggest we dine and then have the attendant make up our beds. My trip from the Continent was quite tiring, and we shall have need for clear heads tomorrow!"

The following morning we engaged a trap at the station and drove through
the sparkling Scottish sunlight to Bloatings, the home of Lord Epsworth and
—until recently—his prize pig as well. We found his Lordship puttering in
the garden, using an old wood-shafted putterer of a type long out of style
below the border. At sight of the two of us he dropped the club and hurried
forward, peering at us queryingly through his thick spectacles.

"Homes!" he cried at last in recognition. "You have come!" He paused.
"But why?"

"The Duchess of Bloatings," Homes replied imperturbably.

"A beautiful animal," his Lordship stated, nodding his head. But then his
face fell and he added sadly, "But she is missing."

"I know," Homes said gently. "You asked me to investigate."

"I did? That's right, I did, didn't I? Come, let us repair to the study and I
shall give you all the details of this foul kidnapping!" He paused uncertainly,
staring about. "Now, where is the study?"

Homes, as usual, was able to supply the answer to the question, and
moments later we found ourselves seated in the vast library and being served
coffee.

"And now, Lord Epsworth," Homes said calmly, putting down his cup,
"the details, if you please."

"Of course," his Lordship said, smiling agreeably. "The details . . . of what,
Homes?"

"The loss of your pig," Homes reminded him.

"Oh! Yes! Well, it seems that about two evenings ago—or it may have been
three—or was it four?—the trainer, Jerkins, went to feed the Duchess and she
wasn't there. Most unusual, I assure you. She was often late for shows, and
occasionally for fairs, but never for meals. Jerkins looked about, of course, but
he failed to spot her. Eventually he told me, and I also looked for her, but to
tell the truth I'm rather nearsighted. Actually," his Lordship said sadly, "we
never did find her."

Homes nodded thoughtfully. "Is there any possibility she may have merely
wandered away?"

"The Duchess?" His Lordship shook his head. "She weighed over twenty-
two stone. Normally she had trouble standing, let alone wandering."

"I see. Tell me, your Lordship, do you recall anything out of the ordinary
that may have occurred that evening? Or any unusual sound that might lend
itself as some sort of clue?"

Lord Epsworth thought deeply for several moments. "Possibly the word
'unusual' is too strong," he said at last, "particularly since it happened every
day. But I do seem to recall the cook's children singing one of their little
nursery rhymes. I had quite a time understanding Jerkins at first, the little
ones made so much noise!"

A sudden gleam appeared in my friend's eyes. "Nursery rhyme?" he asked softly. "Very interesting! From the mouths of babes, you know, Lord Epsworth. . . . Can you recall exactly which nursery rhyme they were singing?"

Lord Epsworth frowned. "Let me see. . ." Suddenly he looked up, his eyes bright. "By Jove, Homes, you are amazing! Now that I remember, they were singing some song about pig-stealing!"

"Ah!" Homes said in satisfaction. "And where might I find these children?"

Lord Epsworth's face fell. "In London, I'm afraid. They are off on a holiday to their home in the section of Stepney." His face cleared as one mystery, at least, was resolved for him. "So that's why it's been so quiet here lately!"

Homes disregarded this. "Then we shall have to solve the case without their help," said he, and springing to his feet he began to pace before the library shelves, peering intently at the titles facing him.

Suddenly he withdrew a book and began to study its contents. When he turned to us there was a smile of satisfaction upon his face.

"Can this be the nursery rhyme the children were singing, your Lordship?" he inquired, and began reading aloud:

> " 'Tom, Tom, the piper's son
> Stole a pig and away he run.' "

Lord Epsworth sat up, astounded. "Homes, you are a genius! How you do it I'll never know! That was it exactly!"

"But in what way does it help us, Homes?" I asked, confused by the entire affair.

"That we have yet to determine," replied my friend evenly. He replaced the book on the shelf and turned to Lord Epsworth. "We had best get to work. I shall want a word with Jerkins and a look about. As soon as I have news for you, I shall be back."

"Do that," said his Lordship heartily, and then paused. "And when you are speaking with Jerkins, ask him if he's seen the Duchess of Bloatings about anywhere, will you?"

Without further conversation we left the library and made our way towards the sties that constituted Jerkins' domain. Until now I had held my tongue, but I thought I saw the solution to the mystery and could not refrain from voicing it.

"You know Lord Epsworth as well as I do, Homes," I said simply. "In my opinion he did not lose his pig, he merely misplaced her!"

Homes shook his head. "The thought had also occurred to me, Watney, but a twenty-two-stone pig is difficult to misplace. Besides, you are forgetting the nursery rhyme."

"I fail to see what a nursery rhyme could possibly have to do with it," I replied with some exasperation.

"You shall," he answered cryptically, and turned into the pen area.

Jerkins was there, mournfully cleaning the empty pen of his lost champion, but try as he would to help us, the poor fellow had no useful ideas on the subject, although he did recall the children singing that evening.

Homes dismissed the man and turned, studying the surrounding countryside carefully. In the distance the camp of the gypsies could be seen, and with a brief nod in my direction, Homes started off across the moors with the camp as his destination.

The camp was typical, consisting of ornately painted charabancs drawn in a rude circle about a campfire from which the odor of a succulent barbecue could be discerned. At our approach a tall, swarthy fellow rose from the group beside the fire and made his way hastily towards us, meeting us beyond the circle of the charabancs.

"Yes?" he asked truculently. "What do you want here?"

"Please forgive our intrusion," Homes said placatingly. "We are investigating the disappearance of his Lordship's prize pig and we thought it possible that you might have noticed some strangers in the vicinity the night of the event."

The dark-faced man opposite us shook his head. "I have been asked before and I have answered!" he said with some anger. "Do you doubt the word of Tomás, King of the Gypsies?"

Homes hastened to reassure him, and with the man glowering at us threateningly we withdrew and headed back in the direction of the main house, although the delicious odour of the meal cooking over the spit made me realize we had scarcely eaten that day.

"You were exceptionally polite to that crude fellow, Homes," I said.

Homes nodded. "You must remember that the gypsies were at their meal," he replied. "It would have been the worst possible form to interrupt them. Besides, I am beginning to get a solution to this puzzling affair, and my time would be better spent in pursuing it."

While he spoke we found we had returned to the pen area, and Homes fell silent, dropping into a brown study, staring about him with a blank expression which might have misled others, but which I recognized as his normal expression when his great brain was busy with an abstruse problem.

I could hear him muttering to himself, and suddenly I realized that he was softly repeating the children's nursery rhyme to himself. With a puzzled shake of his head he was about to leave when his eye happened to chance upon a mark in the dust at his feet, and instantly he was a changed man. With a muffled cry he fell to his knees and stared in fascination at the smudge.

"Homes!" I cried. "What is it?"

Without deigning to answer he reached into his pocket and withdrew his magnifying glass, bending closer to whatever had caught his eye. I could see his thin figure stiffen in barely concealed excitement as he read some significance in what appeared to me to be a mere smudge in the dust. Suddenly he looked up, his eyes gleaming in a manner I well knew.

"This mark!" he cried. "Do you see it?"

I bent closer, but again I could make nothing of the slight smudge before us.

"What is it, Homes?" I asked, mystified. "Certainly it is not a footprint!"

"But it is!" he exclaimed. "It is! Not, it is true, from a conventional boot – but a footprint nonetheless! As you know, I have made an extensive study of the wooden shapes and forms upon which various Indian tribes mould their moccasins, for each tribe uses a different form. And I tell you, without any doubt, that this mark was made by a moccasin formed on the last of the Mohicans!"

"Indians, Homes?" I cried. "American Indians? Here in Scotland?"

But my friend was paying me no heed. Once again I could hear him muttering the nursery rhyme, almost as an incantation, while his eyes stared fixedly at the smudge before him. At last he nodded briskly and rose to his feet.

"Of course!" he said softly to himself. "I am a fool! It was all there before me!" He turned to me, his fine dark eyes brooding. "I am afraid we must be the bearers of sad tidings to his Lordship. The Duchess of Bloatings is gone forever. By this time she is undoubtedly aboard a sailing ship bound for the American colonies, stolen by the savages of the Chesapeake region!"

"But, Homes!" I cried. "Certainly you did not come to this conclusion on the basis of that single smudge in the dust?"

"That was but the final proof," he replied. "Remember the nursery rhyme. And the fact that the cook's children come from Stepney!"

"Really, Homes!" I said with irritation. "You speak in riddles! What brings you to this bizarre conclusion?"

"Later you shall know all," he said grimly. "At the moment we must break the bad news to his Lordship. It will be hard for him to accept, but at least he will not suffer the pangs of uncertainty, not knowing what has happened to his pet pig. At least he will not spend his days in vain hope, waiting endlessly for one that will never return."

Turning, he led the way from the sties, and we went back to the garden. There we found Lord Epsworth, and Homes gave him the sad news. His Lordship took it as well as could be expected, even going so far as to thank Homes for his efforts. As he took leave of us he wrung Homes's hand.

"It was good to see you, Homes," he said as we climbed into our trap. "Thank you for coming." He stared up at us through his thick spectacles. "And if you see the Duchess of Bloatings along the road on your way to the station, would you mind pointing her back this way?"

Once in our compartment in the train I could contain myself no longer. "All right, Homes," I said shortly. "You have been mysterious long enough. Please explain yourself and your rather odd conclusions regarding this case."

"Of course," my friend replied, turning to me with a faint smile. "I should have thought by now you would have seen the answer for yourself, for it was surely simple enough."

He leaned back, lit a Trichinosis, and began his explanation in that pedantic manner I had long since learned to accept.

"The Indian footprint was but the final step in the proof, Watney. The nursery rhyme was the first and most important, and by itself should have given me all the information I required to solve the problem.

"Let us examine the words those children were singing. They went: *Tom, Tom, the piper's son,* and so on. Certainly there can be no doubt of the Indian connotation: What other groups use tom-toms? I saw this fact fairly early, but still the question remained: Which Indians? There are, as you know, many different tribes scattered along the coast of the American colonies.

"The answer, of course, was easily discernible once I remembered that the cook's children were from Stepney, born within the sound of Bow Bells, and therefore Cockney. *Piper,* of course, is the Cockney pronunciation of 'paper,' and the *Sun* is a paper published in the village of Baltimore. The discovery of the Mohican moccasin-print merely confirmed what I had long suspected — that this tribe was far more nomadic than their history records."

I stared at my friend in awe. "Homes," I exclaimed with admiration, "the time you spent away from London and from your profession has not dulled your analytical ability in the slightest!" A sudden thought occurred to me. "But how were these savages able to spirit the beast all the way to the coast without its making an outcry of some sort?"

"Most probably through the use of one of their many herbs," Homes replied thoughtfully. "The fact that the miscreants were able to silence the Duchess — that by itself should have led me to suspect the native cunning of the American." A faint smile crossed his fine features. "Possibly this very fact should be put to use. If you will allow me to suggest a title for this adventure, Watney, should you ever put it to paper, I would suggest The Adventure of the Disgruntled Pig."

I shook my head. "No, Homes," I replied affectionately. "This case, which leads me to hope you will return permanently to Bagel Street and to your profession, can only be titled *The Return of Schlock Homes!*"

It was the following week, and Homes had fallen easily into his old routine, when I came into the breakfast room one morning just as our page was delivering a large package to my friend, who was seated at table smoking his first after-breakfast pipe.

Homes waved me to a seat while he broke the seal of the bundle and extracted a large pig-skin portmanteau. With raised eyebrows he read the accompanying message and then passed it across the table for my perusal.

Dear Mr. Homes (the message read): *Lord Epsworth has told me of your solution to the mysterious disappearance of the Duchess of Bloatings, and in congratulations may I offer this token of my appreciation.*

The letter was signed: *Tomás, King of the Gypsies.*

"This is rather odd, Homes," I said, staring at the letter.

"I'm not so sure," Homes replied thoughtfully. "Had I not been on the scene, it is possible that suspicion might have fallen upon the poor gypsy." His warm eyes came up to mine. "Do you know, Watney, at times the pleasure of saving the innocent can be even greater than the satisfaction of punishing the guilty."

"Amen to that," I said, and reached for the kippers.

The Adventure of
The Big Plunger

To my friend Mr. Schlock Homes, inactivity was the deadliest foe with which he was ever forced to grapple. At those times, when interesting cases were not forthcoming, he would lie slumped in his chair before the fireplace in our quarters at 221B Bagel Street, his eyes dull and unseeing, lighting one Armenian from another and allowing them to burn out in his fingers. I had warned him many times that the scars would remain, but when Homes was in one of his moods it was most difficult to reason with him.

I was most strongly reminded of this characteristic of his quite recently when, in the course of groping blindly beneath my lowboy in search of a missing tuppence, I chanced upon an old folio of my notes which had been lost lo, these many years! I immediately squatted back upon my heels to peruse it, the years and my tuppence instantly forgotten. And there, in my own scrabbled hand, I read the delineation of the early cases in which Homes and I had been involved.

One such period of inactivity, it appeared, had occurred in the year '29, and had been all the worse for having followed upon the solution of a problem which had been exceptionally challenging. At the request of the Moroccan Government, Homes had spent the summer in North Africa tracing down an illicit cinema theatre which had been inciting the natives to revolt through the presentation of inflammatory films.

With his usual brilliant display of genius, Homes had eventually managed to trace the plot to an ex-German adventurer known as "Sahara" Bernhardt; the illegal theatre—called "The Desert Fox"—he had personally located and destroyed. Naturally, after such excitement, the dullness of a damp London autumn lay particularly heavy upon him, especially since there seemed to be no immediate clientele for his exceptional analytical powers.

On this particular day, however – a gray, rainy afternoon in October, as I recall – I returned from my medical rounds to find Homes a changed man. Where I had left him dull-eyed and bored, I returned to find him pacing the floor in barely concealed excitement, his eyes alive and dancing once again. At sight of me he smiled his old smile and extended a telegraph form in my direction.

"A message from my brother Criscroft, Watney!" he exclaimed. "He has urgent need of my services. At last my ennui shall end!"

I nodded in delighted satisfaction. Criscroft Homes, whose position in the Foreign Office was a bit difficult to define, was not only Homes's sole relative, but also by far his favourite. Many a time we had visited him at his club, where he usually sat alone contemplating his naval responsibilities or some other weighty military problem. For him to request aid of Homes was a sure indication of an interesting problem.

I reached for the telegraph form, but before I could take it there came the sound of footsteps upon the stairs, and a moment later Criscroft himself had entered the room, crossed it to shake our hands fervently, and in almost the same motion flung himself into a chair by the fireplace, frowning at us both. A moment later he spoke.

"I hope you are free, Schlock," said he heavily, and leaned forward as if the comfort of his accommodation were somehow alien to the seriousness of his mission.

"Free? I have never been more free!" Homes dropped into a chair across from his brother and looked at him with gleaming eyes. "What is the problem?"

For several moments Criscroft did not answer. He cast his eyes towards the sideboard as if searching for words. I hastened to prepare libations even as I covertly studied the two men. I could not help but note, as I muddled the mixtures, the startling resemblance between the two brothers despite their great differences in height, weight, colouring, facial features, and general appearance. In silence I served them and then retired to one side to listen.

For a moment Criscroft fingered his drink in thoughtful quietude and then, quaffing deeply, set his glass reluctantly to one side.

"Are you acquainted with Lord Fynch-fframis?" he asked at last.

"The noted financier? Only by name," Homes replied.

"I am afraid you will never know him in any other manner," Criscroft said sadly. "He is dead, and a certain Silas Weatherbeaten, an American, is being held in custody at Bow Street on suspicion of his murder."

"Weatherbeaten? The American financial genius?"

"None other. And, I might mention, the colonial denies any part in the sinister affair. His Embassy has been around to us, and we are put in the position where we must either prove his complicity or release him at once. Needless to say, relations between our great country and theirs could become strained were we to make a mistake in this matter, and for this reason I wish to enlist your aid."

"Give me the details," Homes said simply.

"Of course. Well, the story is this: Lord Fynch-fframis either fell, jumped, or was pushed from his offices on top of the Exchange this morning at 9:45. At the time of the unfortunate occurrence, the only one present with him in his office was this same Silas Weatherbeaten. The American's story is that the two men had been talking when Fynch-fframis walked to the stock ticker in one corner, after which he gasped, turned pale, wiped his forehead and then with no further ado flung himself headlong through the window."

"The stock ticker? What is that?" asked Homes.

"I have no idea. I am merely repeating Weatherbeaten's words."

"No matter. It can scarcely concern us where the man walked just prior to the plunge. Pray continue."

"Well, Schlock, since there were no other witnesses, we have only Weatherbeaten's story to go on. Scotland Yard has been unable to uncover any history of previous enmity between the two men, but on the other hand they have also been unable to establish the slightest reason for Fynch-fframis to take his own life. As you can well imagine, the situation leaves us in the Foreign Office in a serious dilemma."

"I understand. And that's all you have to give me?"

"All except this." Criscroft paused to delve into a pocket, sorted through the conglomeration he extracted, and finally came up with a thin slip of paper. "When Lord Fynch-fframis was picked up, he was found to be clutching this strip of paper. To the best of our knowledge it represents a code, but a code so devilishly complicated that to this moment Department M5 has had no success at all in solving it."

At these words Homes's eyes glittered feverishly and he reached forward with eagerness, taking the slip from his brother's fingers and bending forward to peruse it intently. At the frown that appeared on his face I stepped behind him and read the puzzling message over his shoulder. It was neatly printed on a thin strip of yellowish paper and I reproduce the mysterious hieroglyphics for the reader's inspection.

> ... T–T 7½ ... AllAf 44
> ... AlRs 12 ... G&F 11
> ... T–T 7 ... AllAf 43 ...
> AlRs 11½ ... G&F 10⅝
> ... T–T 6⅝ ... AllAf 42
> ... AlRs 11 ... G&F 10
> ... T–T 6½ ...

"Well?" The harshness of Criscroft's voice betrayed his anxiety. "Can you make anything of it?"

Homes remained in a brown study, his eyes scanning the strange message. Then he raised his head slowly, a curious expression on his face. "At the moment, no," he said slowly. "It bears no resemblance to any other code or cipher I have ever seen."

Criscroft drew himself to his feet and stared down at his brother. "I am sure you have solved more difficult ones, Schlock," he said at last. "You are aware of the urgency of this matter. Should you require me, I shall be available at any time. A messenger can reach me at my club."

"Good." Homes came to his feet, extending his hand. "Be sure I shall get right to it!"

Once Criscroft had left the premises, Homes fell back into his chair, staring at the mysterious message with a fierce scowl upon his face, while I studied it over his shoulder. Suddenly a possible solution occurred to me.

"Homes!" I cried. "These odd figures could well represent street addresses! 'T-T' could stand for Tottenham Towers, and 'G&F' might well be the corner of Grantham and Frobisher Streets."

He shook his head slowly, his eyes never leaving the message. "I doubt it, Watney. I am familiar with Tottenham Towers, and as far as I know the apartment numbers run evenly. I cannot recall any Apartment 7½."

I attempted to bring to mind the numbering system at the famous Towers, but to no avail. Homes turned to his shelf of reference volumes and, selecting one, swiftly became lost in its pages. I waited patiently until, some moments later, he flung it from him with a barely concealed curse.

"Useless!" he muttered, almost in anger, and returned once again to his fruitless study of the flimsy slip of paper. At length he raised his eyes to me.

"I fear my recent spell of inactivity has dulled my brain, Watney," he said sadly.

"Never!" I protested as loyally as I could.

Despite his preoccupation, a faint twinkle had come into his fine eyes. "Or possibly it is simply that I am no longer used to labour," he said. "If labour is the answer, however, time can handle that." And drawing his chair to the table he began the series of permutations necessary to decoding the thin strip.

Dinnertime came, but Homes worked on. Our housekeeper, Mrs. Essex, was on holiday and I suggested that Homes join me at a nearby restaurant, but he refused. And when I left to eat, it was to leave him still at it, frozen in his chair, his eyes poring intently over the thin yellow slip, and his thin fingers racing across the scratch-sheets...

I dined leisurely, knowing that when Homes was involved in a problem he did not particularly appreciate my presence. I had a brandy and cigar and then walked slowly back to our quarters. I mounted the staircase and entered the room to find Homes in conference with a ragged street urchin. The lad, of mixed Chinese-Israeli parentage, was known as Matzo-Tung and was the leader of the Bagel Street Regulars.

Together with Homes the boy was bent over a large street-map of the city, and as I entered both raised their eyes to me. I was shocked by the haggard expression on Homes's face; it was apparent that he had not paused for refreshment since I had left.

"Good evening," I said brightly, attempting to instill some cheer in the atmosphere. "Are you any forrader?"

Homes shook his head dispiritedly. "No, Watney," he said wearily. "I am reduced to clutching at straws. I have exhausted all other possibilities and am compelled to accept your suggestion that these strange hieroglyphics refer to street addresses indeed. The Bagel Street Regulars will check them out for me. Should this last lead be barren, I fear I shall be forced to confess failure!" With a sigh he turned to the young ragamuffin.

"Your instructions are clear?"

"Raht, Guv'nor."

"One lad to each address," Homes said sternly, "and the name of the tenant back here as quickly as possible."

"Raht, Gov'nor," said the lad and moved to the door.

"And mind the stairs," I said absently as he reached for the knob.

"The apples? I'll take 'em cheesy, Guv'nor."

He started to turn the knob, then paused with an odd expression on his face, and I saw that he was staring over my shoulder at Homes. I turned and to my amazement I saw that my friend was waving his hands frantically, his face distorted. I hurried to his side.

"Homes!" I cried anxiously. "Are you all right?"

"All right? I am a fool! What a fool I am! You, lad! Forget your errand! And here's a shilling for your trouble!"

Homes turned to me; all traces of weariness fled from his face, as the puzzled street urchin took the coin and slipped down the steps. "Watney! One moment while I change to proper clothing and we are off to visit my brother. How stupid I have been!"

And with no further comment he dashed from the room, removing his dressing-gown as he went.

I waited in mystified silence until, a few moments later, he emerged from his room straightening his weskit, and a second later I found myself being propelled down the stairway. Homes waved a passing hansom to the curb and hustled me inside.

"Homes!" I cried, tugging my arm free and straightening the fabric. "You have discovered the answer to this problem?"

"I have indeed!" My friend leaned back and patted his coat pocket where the mysterious strip of paper now lay. His eyes gleamed. "But I do not apologize for my delay, for it followed none of the normal, or even abnormal, rules of cryptography. And why?" His eyes twinkled. "Because it was never meant to be a code!"

Before I could ask an explanation of this strange statement, his eyes went to his time-piece and then to the man on the box. "Driver! A shilling bonus if you have us in Curzon Street in eight minutes!"

We came flying down Park Lane and turned precariously into Curzon Street with squealing wheel hubs, and seconds later the driver was hauling desperately upon the reins as we approached the club of which Criscroft Homes was a member. Homes was on the pavement before we had come to a halt, had paid the driver, and was pulling me impatiently up the broad stone steps of the club.

He brushed past the doorman, nodded distantly to the cloakroom attendant, and turned into the library, where, in one corner, Criscroft sat moodily. At the commotion our entrance provoked, he came to his feet and hurried forward as quietly as he could.

"Schlock," he said in a low whisper, obviously torn between the club rules for silence and his necessity for our information. He glanced about. "Not here. Come!"

He drew us hastily from the room, led us through a series of narrow corridors, until we found the kitchen. There he ensconced us on hard chairs, seated himself, and spoke in a normal tone of voice.

"Sorry," he said quietly, and then added in more anxious tones, "Do you bring me the news I have been awaiting? Are you able to help me resolve my desperate dilemma?"

"I am," Homes replied with quiet triumph. He leaned forward, narrowly avoiding a scalding teapot. "There is but one bit of information I require in order to complete my case. Am I correct in assuming that Lord Fynch-fframis originally came from common stock? That he was, as a matter of fact, born within the decibel range of the Bow Bells?"

We both stared at him in amazement.

"That is true," Criscroft said at last, staring hard at his brother. "Although how you ever managed to deduce it remains a mystery to me! It was knowledge that was kept secret even from Debrett's. I only obtained the true facts myself less than an hour ago." He leaned forward, a querying frown upon his face. "But how can this information possibly aid you?"

Homes smiled. "You shall soon see." His smile faded, to be replaced with a most serious expression. "The important thing is that you may now, with a clear conscience, free Mr. Silas Weatherbeaten. He was but an innocent spectator to this tragic affair."

Criscroft's eyes widened. "You can prove this?"

"I can." Without further ado, Homes reached into his pocket and produced the mysterious strip of paper. Brushing aside some crumbs, he spread it out upon a nearby bread-board. His strong, thin fingers pointed to the words, while his tone assumed that degree of pedantic superiority which was so usual with him when he was explaining the successful solution to one of his cases.

"When first I saw this queer admixture of letters and numerals," said he, his eyes fixed upon us both intently, "I attempted to solve it through the standard methods of cryptology, as well as through the application of certain mathematical formulae which I have been fortunate enough to develop personally. All my efforts—I can now freely admit—were without success. Then, in desperation, I was about to send young Matzo-Tung out on what would have proven to be a futile quest, when he happened to use a phrase that immediately clarified the entire affair to me. A moment's thought and the picture was clear!"

"But, Homes," I protested, "I heard every word the young lad spoke, and I can see nothing in his words that could possibly aid in the solution of this problem."

"Watney, you hear with your ears rather than with your intelligence," Homes replied cryptically. "Do you not recall the young boy saying, 'The apples? I'll take 'em cheesy, Guv'nor'?" His mimicry was remarkable as he duplicated exactly the heavy Cockney accent of the street urchin.

I stared at him in amazement. "But how could that possibly help, Homes?"

"He was using Cockney rhyming slang, Watney!"

"Cockney rhyming slang?"

"Precisely!" He laughed at my blank expression. "I can see that you are not familiar with the Cockney, Watney. He chooses many ways in which to express himself, and the most famous, of course, is his rhyming slang. In order to state a word, he chooses a phrase of which the final word rhymes with the word he is attempting to express. For example, the Cockney will say 'storm and strife' when he wishes to say 'wife.' And many of them, with time, have come to even leave off the last part of the phrase, so that 'storm' becomes 'wife'."

I stared at him. His eyes twinkled.

"Yes, Watney! Take our little ragamuffin this evening, for instance. Apples, of course, is from the Cockney phrase of 'apples and pears,' which means 'stairs.' 'Cheesy' means 'easy.' He was simply assuring you that he would go down the steps with care."

His face sobered. "The moment he spoke I saw all. The mysterious message became crystal clear. Come, let me demonstrate."

His fingers slid along the lines of the strange message.

"'T–T' can only be 'Tit-for-Tat'—or 'hat.' 'AllAf' is 'All Afloat'—or 'coat.' 'AlRs' is the famous 'Almond Rocks' that the Cockney uses to refer to his socks. And 'G&F' can only be 'Greens-and-Fruits' with which he designates his boots."

"Hat?" I asked, completely mystified. "Coat? Socks? Boots?"

"Exactly!"

"But the numbers, Homes," I said in bewilderment. "What significance can they possibly have?"

"Sizes, of course," Homes replied quietly.

We stared at him, considering his startling deduction. At last Criscroft cleared his throat and spoke. "But, Schlock—the numbers are continually decreasing."

"Precisely! And that is the answer!" The great detective's eyes gleamed; his deep voice became even deeper. "*The poor man was wasting away!* In all probability from some incurable disease. He was not wiping his brow when Weatherbeaten saw him this morning; he was undoubtedly trying to check the progress of his dread condition. And when he saw that it had not abated, but had even increased in tempo, he knew there was truly no hope for him, and that death was to be preferred to waiting until he was, quite literally, a shadow of his former self."

Words failed both Criscroft and myself at this remarkable demonstration of Homes's extraordinary reasoning powers. Impulsively I thrust out my hand in heartfelt congratulations.

"Magnificent, Homes!" I exclaimed, overcome with admiration.

Criscroft arose with shining eyes and placed his arms about his younger brother's shoulders in a demonstration of affection quite rare for a Foreign Office personality.

"Schlock, you may well have saved England another *cause célèbre*," said he solemnly, and brushed the hint of a tear from his cheek.

Homes shook his head modestly. "Do not thank me," he said quietly. "Thank the Bagel Street Regulars or even Lord Fynch-fframis himself. It was his unconscious reversion to his childhood language when faced with a crisis that solved this case, not me."

"Nonsense!" Criscroft replied roundly. He cast his eyes about. "This calls for a drink. Cook!"

The following morning I was in the process of simultaneously attempting to reach for my Brussels sprouts juice and open the morning journal when Homes entered our breakfast room. He nodded to me pleasantly and drew up a chair.

Knowing my friend's desire for the news as quickly as possible, I forewent my vegetable tonic and spread the newspaper to its fullest. Black ink in profusion sprang to my eye; it took a second or two until the full import of the startling headlines registered upon my brain.

Homes had been reaching indolently for his napkin; at the sight of the horrified expression upon my face he paused, considering me wonderingly.

"Something that might be of interest to us, Watney?" he queried.

"Homes!" I cried, unfolding the journal further, and then doubling it to present him with the scarelines. "Look! The stock market has crashed!"

For a moment he hesitated, and then, after careful consideration, he completed the manoeuvre of placing his napkin in his lap. His fine eyes were warm with sympathy as he replied.

"Well," said he softly, "there is one consolation. At least poor Lord Fynch-fframis was spared the added pain of seeing his life's savings swept away in the holocaust."

I stared at him, a wave of admiration for his understanding flooding me. "True," I said, and turned the page.

The Adventure of
The Widow's Weeds

TWO CASES of exceptional interest occupied the time and talents of my friend Mr. Schlock Homes during the middle months of the year '63. The first, which I find recorded in my casebook under the heading of *Inland Revenue vs. S.H.*, deals with a personage of such stature that revelation of his identity could only be embarrassing and would serve no good purpose. The second, however, which I find in my notes entitled *The Adventure of the Widow's Weeds*, cogently demonstrates, I believe, the devious paths of Homes's ingenuity when applied to his famed analytical method of reasoning.

It began one pleasant Friday morning in early June when I came into the breakfast room of our quarters at 221B Bagel Street to find Homes rubbing his hands with ghlee, an Indian ointment he found efficacious for the treatment of his recurrent attacks of itching. At the sight of me he wiped his hands carefully on the draperies and beckoned me to join him at the window, where he pointed interestedly to the street below.

"There, Watney," said he with a twinkle in his eye; "let us test your powers of observation. What do you make of that poor creature?"

I stared downwards, following the direction indicated by his finger. On the sidewalk, shuffling along in an uncertain manner and pausing every few moments to peer hesitatingly at the house numerals, was a small figure who, from her braided hair, I correctly deduced to be a woman. I looked up at Homes queryingly.

"I'm afraid I am not at my best before breakfast, Homes," I said, temporizing. His expression of expectation did not change in the least. With a shrug of defeat I returned my gaze to the figure below.

"I suppose," I said after more fruitless study, "that you have deduced she is searching out our number and is coming here to visit you. Although," I added in complete honesty, "if this be the case, I must confess to complete ignorance as to how you reached your conclusion."

Homes laughed delightedly and placed an arm about my shoulders.

"Really, Watney," he said with pretended regret, "I'm rather ashamed of my failure as a teacher. Take another look below. Here is a woman who shuffles along on feet far shorter than normal for her height, who wears trousers instead of the customary skirt, who carries her hands across her body and inserts them into the opposite sleeves of her jacket, whose complexion is almond-coloured, and whose eyes are slanted. Certainly there is but one conclusion that can be drawn from these observations."

"I *am* sorry, Homes," I said contritely, "but I really do need breakfast before tackling this sort of thing. What conclusion should I be drawing that I am not?"

"Obviously, that it is *you* she is seeking, and not myself. The pain of those poor truncated feet is evident from her shuffling gait; her tendency to try to warm her hands, even on a day that promises such heat as this one, is a common symptom of anemia. The almond complexion — as I am sure you will recall once you have had your first kipper — is a sure indication of liver ailment; while the slanted eyes, obviously caused by prolonged squinting, comes from poor eyesight and undoubtedly results in painful headaches." He shook his head. "No, Watney, this woman is seeking medical aid, not the aid of a detective."

I stared at my friend, open-mouthed with admiration. "It all becomes so clear and simple once you have explained it, Homes," I said in amazement, and then paused, frowning. "But, then, how do you explain the trousers?"

"Ah, Watney," he exclaimed, "that is the final proof! Any woman who dresses in such a hurry as to inadvertently put on her husband's trousers, and then having discovered the fact, does not take the time to correct the error, can only be driven by a need for haste more common to those seeking medical aid than to those soliciting advice."

He looked down to the street again and then smiled at me triumphantly, for the woman was, indeed, turning in at our street door. A few moments later, our page had opened the door of our quarters and was ushering in an attractive Chinese woman of middle age who bent her head politely in my direction.

"Mr. Homes?" she inquired.

"I'm Mr. Homes," I said, stepping forward. "I mean, I am Dr. Homes — or rather, I am Dr. Watney. If you will just wait until I get my medical kit, I shall be happy to attend to you."

She paid no further attention to me, turning instead to my friend.

"Mr. Homes? I have a problem which is of such an odd and unusual nature that I believe only a man of your extraordinary talents can solve it."

Her English, to my surprise, was quite adequate and even made more charming by the slight accent. Homes acknowledged the compliment with a slight nod, then with a languid wave of his hand he indicated that she make herself more comfortable. She seated herself gingerly on the edge of a chair while Homes dropped into one opposite and continued to study her through half-closed lids.

"Pray continue," said he. "If I can be of assistance, be assured I shall be. What is the nature of this odd and unusual problem?"

"Mr. Homes," she said earnestly, leaning forward a bit without removing her hands from her jacket sleeves, "I am a widow. Until recently my husband and myself ran a small tobacco-shop in Limehouse where we catered in the main to the upper-form students at the nearby academies, plus a few sailors who dropped in from the docks from time to time. We even furnished a small room on the premises where the students could smoke, since of course it is against the regulations for them to do so in their dormitories.

"And then, Mr. Homes, about a month ago my husband died. Needless to say, it was a terrible blow, but the philosophy of my race is that life must go on. I therefore arranged for the services of a fellow Chinese to help me in the shop. He has proven more than worth his wage and keep, even adding a new cigarette to our line which he makes himself at night in order to keep our costs at a minimum, and the sale of which has surpassed our greatest expectations. Nor is he lacking in commercial instinct; he advises our clientele that his new cigarette is 'Mary-Juana,' two feminine names undoubtedly selected to appeal not only to the British, but also to the many Spanish-speaking Lascars who frequent the docks. And to appeal further to the sailing trade, he has named them—"

She paused and frowned in an embarrassed manner. "But I digress—please forgive me." She leaned forward again. "Mr. Homes, with our increased custom one would think my problems at an end, but in truth they are just beginning. For the past two weeks—ever since I employed this man—there has been nothing but trouble."

Homes raised a quizzical eyebrow. "Trouble?"

"Yes." She nodded her head sadly. "The students, who have always been most tractable in the past, are now quite the opposite, singing or fighting at the slightest excuse, and even becoming destructive, scratching their initials on the walls of the smoking-room with whatever instrument is available. One even attempted the feat with a banana and became quite belligerent when he failed to obtain legible results."

I could not help but interrupt.

"It appears to me, Madame," I said a bit stiffly, "that you require the services of the official police, rather than those of a private investigator."

She raised her eyes to mine. "At one time," she said softly, "not fully recognizing the problem, I thought the same, and even mentioned it to my helper. But he was quite horrified at the suggestion and insisted that Mr. Homes would be more suitable to our problem." She turned her head to my friend once again. "You see, Mr. Homes, he has heard of you."

Homes disregarded the flattery, continuing to stare at her over his tented fingers. "You state that at one time you did not recognize the problem fully. I assume, therefore, that you do now."

"I do, but it is difficult to put into proper words. To me there can be no doubt but that my late husband's spirit is causing this havoc, that he is expressing his disfavour because I did not carry on his enterprise alone." She withdrew a petite hand from her jacket sleeve and raised it to forestall disagreement. "I know you English do not believe in ancient superstitions, but it is an integral part of our honourable doctrines. I am convinced that it is my late husband's spirit which is inflaming the students in their present ways. Obviously, the police would be of no help in this matter."

She hesitated a moment and then forced herself to continue, her eyes boring into those of my friend.

"Mr. Homes, I know that what I am about to ask is not easily understood, but I am desperate. Will you attempt to placate the spirit of my dead husband and persuade it to leave us in peace?"

I stared at her in amazement, fully expecting Homes to terminate the interview quickly and send the poor woman on her way; but to my surprise he failed to do so. Instead, he sprang to his feet and began to pace the floor rapidly, his hands locked behind him and a fierce look of concentration on his hawk-like features. At last he paused, turned, and nodded his head.

"I shall give the matter my undivided attention, Madame," he said. "If you will leave the address of your shop with Dr. Watney here, I promise you an answer in the very near future."

She rose, smiling tremulously at her unexpected good fortune, and pressed an already prepared slip of paper into my hand. Before I had a chance to suggest that my medical services were now available, she had closed the door behind her and disappeared down the steps. I shook my head at my friend in disappointment.

"Really, Homes," I said chidingly, "I am ashamed of you! Why do you promise such nonsense as placating the spirit of a dead man? Your failure can only lead to further disillusionment for that poor suffering soul!"

Homes stared at me calmly. "You noticed that, despite her obvious infirmities, she still insisted upon discussing her problem?"

"Of course I noticed it," I said a bit warmly.

"Then they must play a role of such importance that we are forced to respect her desires."

"But still, Homes," I said, "to promise to placate a dead man's spirit!"

"I promised her an answer to her problem, Watney, nothing more. Tell me, do you believe in superstition?"

"Of course not," I replied disdainfully.

"Nor do I. The fact that the trouble started with the advent of this excellent assistant, therefore, must only be coincidental, and the answer must therefore lie elsewhere." He withdrew his time-piece and glanced at it. "A trip

to the tobacco-shop after lunch is indicated, I think. A pity, though—
I had hoped to hear that programme of religious music at Albert Hall this
afternoon."

"Religious music, Homes?" I asked curiously.

"Yes. The *Suite Sistine* is being sung there today. By the Beadles, of
course." He shrugged. "Ah, well, duty before pleasure..."

I was quite busy that afternoon myself, having scheduled a trepanning
operation to relieve a hemorrhage—a bloody bore, I might mention—and it
was therefore quite late when I returned to Bagel Street and let myself into
our rooms.

To my surprise Homes had not yet returned, but thinking it quite possible
that he had managed to finish in time for the concert, I turned up the lamp
and prepared to await his return with a bit of research. No sooner had I taken
down the proper volume and opened it to the section on malpractice,
however, than I heard the sound of feet coming wearily up the staircase, and
a moment later Homes had come into the room and dropped heavily into
an easy chair.

One look at his drawn face and I moved to the sideboard and began to
prepare a drink.

"No luck, Homes?" I said.

"Nothing of any importance," he replied in a discouraged tone of voice. "I
did manage to have a fast walk-around of the two main academies in the area,
Twitchly and St. Pothers, and I also, of course, visited the tobacco-shop.
Oddly enough, none of the students was present, which was equally surprising to our client, and I was therefore unable to interview any of the little—"
He leaned over, accepted the proffered drink, then leaned back once again.
"However, I did see the damage they had wrought in the smoking-room, and I
must say the British schoolboy has improved greatly in imagination since my
days at Wreeking."

"Improved, Homes?" I asked, mystified.

He chuckled. "Have you ever attempted to write your initials using a
banana as a stylograph, Watney?" he inquired.

I shook my head. "I'm afraid it is scarcely an improvement to brag about,"
I said tartly. "In my days at Barbour College it would not have been considered
cricket to destroy the property of others."

"Destroy? I thought it rather an improvement. The original wallpaper—"

"Still," I insisted, "I'm afraid in my day we would not have considered it
cricket. Or at leasy not *very* cricket."

"You may be right," Homes admitted lazily, eyeing his drink. "But times
change, Watney. Today—"

He paused abruptly, and then sat up so suddenly that for a moment I thought his libation would be spilled in my lap. "Watney!" he cried. "You have it! Of course! Of course!"

"I have what, Homes?" I asked in bewilderment.

"The answer! The answer to it all!" He sprang to his feet, setting his drink impatiently to one side. "The evening journal, Watney! Where is it?"

"On the table," I replied, completely puzzled. "But I do not understand, Homes. I have the answer to what?"

But Homes was paying small heed to my query. In two strides he had reached the table and turned on the gas-lamp high above it. His hands found the journal, and he began turning the pages rapidly. Having at last found the section he wanted, he spread it open and began to run his hand rapidly down one of the columns. And then his rigid finger froze against a printed line and he turned to me triumphantly.

"Of course! I was a fool — and a forgetful fool at that. Particularly in view of the date!"

"The date?" I asked, now completely confused. "What has the date got to do with it?"

"As much as the reason why there were no students in the tobacco-shop today!" he replied cryptically. "Come, Watney! Explanations can wait! At the moment the most important thing is to relieve the poor woman's mind without delay."

With no further word he sprang for the door and was down the stairway in moments, rushing out to the kerb to wave wildly at a passing hansom cab. By the time I had managed to recover my wits sufficiently to follow, he had a jehu drawn up to the kerb and was bounding into his vehicle. His hand reached backwards, dragging me along, pulling me into the swaying carriage. As I recovered my balance, he fell back against the leather seat, his eyes gleaming excitedly.

"I only pray that we are not too late, Watney!" he exclaimed. "She must close that smoking-room at once, and hereafter keep it closed."

"But why, Homes?" I cried.

"Because all the trouble up to now was only leading to the culmination tonight! And why? Because we have been concerning ourselves with the wrong coincidence!"

I grasped his arm angrily. "Enough of these enigmatic statements, Homes," I said. "Pray explain yourself at once."

He disengaged himself from my grip and smiled at me faintly.

"Since the source of my enlightenment was a statement you made yourself, Watney, I should think explanations are unnecessary," he said, and then laughed aloud at the fierce expression on my face. "All right, then, you shall know all." His face became serious once again.

"To begin with, as a result of investigating the wrong coincidence, we were attempting to correlate the arrival of a new assistant at the shop with the troubles encountered there, whereas we should have attempted to correlate the troubles with the date."

"The date?" I asked, still mystified.

"Precisely. When you mentioned the word 'cricket,' and then were so kind as to repeat it, I suddenly realized that in all probability there was a serious rivalry between the students of the two schools, and a check of the journal indicated that tomorrow St. Pothers and Twitchly play for the Limehouse championship. And if the championship game is tomorrow, Watney, what has preceded it?"

"Examination week!" I exclaimed.

"Exactly. Well do I remember my own undergraduate days and the tensions that build up prior to final examination day. Combine this with the rivalry of the two top teams in the league, then put students from each of the two schools together in a small room at this particular time, and serious altercation is bound to ensue."

"But if examination day has passed," I objected, "why is it essential that the room be closed tonight?"

"Because of the game tomorrow! With the students freed of scholastic worries and intent upon building up spirit for the contest, the danger is even greater than before. No, Watney, the room *must* be closed at once. I only hope that we arrive at the shop before the students finish their supper and converge upon it."

"True," I admitted, and then frowned. "But why, then, should she keep the room closed *after* tonight? Surely the danger will pass once this evening is over, and besides, the students will be leaving for their holidays immediately following the game."

"They will, but within a few brief months they will return, and the ending of each half-term would only see a repetition of these unpleasant incidents. No, I shall tell her that her husband's spirit will only be placated by the permanent closing of the smoking-room. I shall tell her that her husband's untoward interference was not owing to her having acquired a new assistant, but because in his new state he has become convinced that academy students are too young to indulge in tobacco. In this fashion I shall resolve her immediate problem, and at the same time satisfy her superstitions."

I stared at my friend with admiration. "An excellent solution, Homes!" I exclaimed, and then paused. "But will not the loss of custom cause her to suffer financially?"

He shook his head. "If what the lady said is true, their new cigarette should develop sufficient trade with the sailors to compensate her for the loss of the students."

"I am proud of you, Homes," I said sincerely. "Never have I seen a case resolved with results so beneficial to so many."

"Thanks to you, Watney, and your inspired use of the word 'cricket.' I only hope we arrive in time, and that I have not overlooked anything."

The following morning, having finished my breakfast, I drew the morning journal to me and lit up one of the new cigarettes which our Chinese friend had been kind enough to present to us in gratitude for Homes's solution to the case. However, I found the taste far too acrid for my palate, and I was in the process of crushing it out when Homes entered the room. He noted my uneconomical gesture with raised eyebrows and seated himself across from me with a faint smile.

"The new cigarette is not to your liking, Watney?" he inquired.

"I'm afraid not," I replied, and proffered him the packet. "Possibly you might care for them."

He shook his head as he idly took the packet from my hand. "No, I'm too accustomed to my Mesopotamians," he replied, studying the outer wrapping. Then suddenly his eyes narrowed and he stared at me with a fierce frown.

"Watney! Is there any report in the journal of trouble in Limehouse last night?"

I hurriedly turned the pages of the journal and then stopped as my eye caught the heading of an article. "Why, yes, Homes," I said, marvelling as always at his uncanny ability to anticipate these things. "A riot at the docks, actually."

He slammed one hand down against the table-top. "I am a fool! She began to tell us the name of these new cigarettes and then stopped. I should have insisted upon knowing!"

I reached over and picked up the packet, staring at it. "But I do not understand, Homes," I said, puzzled.

He leaned over the table, his eyes burning with excitement.

"No? Do you not realize, Watney, that this name is an insult to every nautical man operating under steam, since it indicates that he is only fit to handle sail?"

Comprehension dawned on me. "Of course! And it is also a word commonly used to denote a midshipman, the bane of every honest sailor's existence."

"Precisely. We must telegraph her at once."

With a nod of agreement I reached for my pad of telegram forms, and under Homes's dictation I hastily scribbled the vital message. It read:

"Madame: You must immediately cease to call your new cigarettes Reefers."

The Adventure of
The Perforated Ulster

A HIATUS in cases of any serious consequence during the early months of the year '66 allowed my friend Mr. Schlock Homes an opportunity for some well-needed rest, as well as a chance to indulge in a few of his many hobbies. I recall in particular how diligently he practised his prestidigitation in preparation for the annual Magicians' Meet; but I am saddened to relate that when it finally was held, poor Homes was found wanding.

The same period, however, permitted me to bring some order to my voluminous notes, and it is well that I did so, for two cases which I had planned on ultimately relating turned out to be nothing of the sort. Homes had been writing a treatise on the mating-dance of the *ondatra bibethecus,* and I had somehow mistakenly incorporated his notes in my case-book as *The Adventure of the Muskrat Ritual.* An even greater embarrassment was narrowly avoided when I discovered a long series of correspondence covering an unpaid bill of Homes's to a doctor at a local hospital, which I had erroneously filed as *The Adventure of the Patient Resident.*

Time, however, permitted the correction of these errors, and it was with a feeling of growing ennui that I came into the breakfast room of our quarters of 221B Bagel Street one bright morning in April to find Homes already ensconced at the table, his creamed kipper already finished, and lighting his first after-meal Bulgarian. He smiled brightly as I entered, and I noticed a telegraph form fluttering from his thin fingers.

"Ah, Watney!" said he, his eyes sparkling. "It appears our inactivity is about to end. My brother Criscroft has telegraphed that he intends to drop by this morning, and as you are well aware, such visits in the past have invariably led to the most interesting of problems. I trust this occasion will prove no exception."

"But he offers no clue?" I inquired, sitting down and drawing my napkin under my chin.

"He says—but never mind. Here, unless I am greatly mistaken, is Criscroft himself."

He turned towards the door, and a moment later our page had ushered in Homes's illustrious brother. With a brusque refusal of a kipper, Criscroft flung himself into a chair and stared at us broodingly.

"Schlock," he said at last, his voice heavy with worry, "I know that in the past I have often brought you problems affecting the well-being of our country; but believe me when I say that never before has one of our basic institutions been faced with so dire a threat!"

Homes leaned forward, his voice deeply sympathetic. "As you well know," he said sincerely, "I am always at your service. Pray, how can I be of assistance?"

Criscroft shook his head in misery. "I greatly fear," he said in a tone heavy with dread, "that we have a case of pilfering at our club."

Homes's eyebrows lifted slightly. "But, certainly," he said with a frown, "a simple case of pilfering should not upset you to this degree. Any club might have an unfortunate member who temporarily finds his needs greater than his means."

Criscroft's face had fallen – if possible – even lower during this discourse. "You do not understand," he said, his voice almost breaking. "It is far more serious than that. Our club has *not* been pilfered. The pilfering, I fear, was done for the *benefit* of our club!"

Homes's frown deepened. He tented his fingers and stared across the ridge-pole of his knuckles into his brother's tortured eyes.

"You mean — ?"

"Exactly! Were it to be bruited about that our financial status was so precarious that such assistance was necessary to maintain us, the mere rumour might easily shatter the confidence of the public in this staunchest of all our national institutions!"

"And you think — ?"

"Indubitably! Were people to begin doubting the solidity of our British clubs, there is no predicting to what dark ends these suspicions might lead!"

"And you suspect — ?"

"Definitely! It is obvious that the perpetrator of this foul deed is not doing it out of idle whim, nor would he take so drastic a step out of mere personal spite."

"And you conclude — ?"

"Precisely! He is therefore acting under the orders of some group dedicated to the destruction of our system. Undoubtedly a foreign group, since no Englishman, however treasonous, would be so subversive as to attack the institution of the British club!" A look of peace replaced the agonized expression on his face. "You cannot know how good it is, Schlock, to benefit from your analysis. And I am convinced you are right!"

"Thank you," Homes replied modestly, and leaned forward again. "Pray favour us with the details."

"Of course," Criscroft agreed. "Well, as you may or may not know, I have recently assumed the chairmanship of our club's House Committee, and in this capacity I have the responsibility for the operation of the bar and kitchen. I have therefore taken, of late, to inspecting the culinary premises at odd hours, in order to see how the steward is handling his duties."

He paused a moment to collect his thoughts, and then continued: "Well, about a week ago, on one of my periodic tours of the kitchen, I chanced to note a new coffee percolator. I said nothing at the time, but I later made it my business to go back over the Committee minutes, and I found no recommendation for the purchase of this percolator, nor, in fact, any appropriation by the Finance Committee for its acquisition."

"And you considered this odd?"

"Extremely odd, particularly since few of our members are addicted to the bean, considering it quite rightly a colonial affectation. However, I continued to maintain my own counsel, awaiting further developments. And then, just the other evening, in checking the bar equipment for our annual Walpurgis Night Dinner—Lord Walpurgis is our oldest member and therefore annually feted—I was amazed to discover a new cocktail shaker."

"A cocktail shaker?" Homes's eyebrows shot up.

Criscroft smiled grimly. "You also note the foreign touch, eh? As we all know, a cocktail shaker tends to bruise whisky, and no true Englishman would think of employing one."

"Certainly not!" Homes exclaimed indignantly. His voice became probing. "And I assume that again there had been neither recommendation nor appropriation for its purchase?"

"Neither. I knew then, of course, that the matter was far more serious than a simple error in judgment, and I felt it vital to seek your aid."

"And well that you did so! What is the name of this steward?"

"Sean O'Callahan."

A thoughtful frown crossed the lean face of my friend. "Not an English name," he said slowly.

"Now that you mention it, it does sound foreign," Criscroft replied, and then looked troubled. "It is my hope that Sean is only an innocent dupe in the scheme. He is the fifteenth generation of O'Callahans to serve in that position at our club, and I should hate to think of him as a traitor."

"Still," Homes continued, his eyes glittering, "I assume you investigated him."

"To the limited extent of our ability. I have had four men from the Foreign Office on his trail for the past twenty-four hours, have had his telephone tapped, and have even had secret microphones concealed in his attic bedroom at the club. Unfortunately, the A.I.C. men who installed them apparently did the job backwards, so I fear they have been less than effective. He can hear us, but we cannot hear him. However, since the building is an old one, and fairly well inhabited by mice, I doubt if he ascribes too much importance to the additional sounds of our conversation."

Homes came to his feet, striding up and down the room, his hands clasped tightly behind him. "So to date you have been unable to earth anything? I mean, able to unearth nothing?"

"Only this," said Criscroft, reaching into a pocket and producing a small, thin pamphlet. "In the manner of the Purloined Letter it was cleverly concealed by simply leaving it on top of his dresser, which I must admit is quite suspicious in itself. However, I doubt if you will find it of much use. Our code experts claim it is beyond their ability to solve."

He handed the small brochure to Homes, who instantly dropped back into his chair to peruse it. I came to stand behind my friend while he examined the publication, and I reproduce its cover below for the benefit of such readers who are still with us.

Homes studied the cover for several moments and then slowly riffled the pages; the small booklet opened almost by itself to a page which illustrated a variety of cocktail shakers. He then turned several more pages, noting the detailed and colourful drawings and photographs of the items therein, and then shut the pamphlet with a dark frown upon his face.

"Schlock!" Criscroft cried, noting his brother's expression. "What is it?"

Homes turned a worried face in his direction.

"You can see the extreme care that has gone into the preparation of this booklet," Homes said heavily. "Certainly they would not have gone to this trouble just to embarrass your one club. I suggest the plot is far more sinister, and that in all probability they have infiltrated many more, if not, actually, all the clubs of London!"

Criscroft paled. "No!"

"I fear so. However, the game is early on, and there still may be time to scotch their nefarious plot." He shook his head and stared at the pamphlet once again. "There can be little doubt that this plan is costing them a pretty penny. It would undoubtedly, therefore, help to know the source of their finances."

"Raffle tickets?" I suggested helpfully.

He shook his head a trifle impatiently. "No, no, Watney! A plan this costly would not depend upon anything as uncertain as the proceeds of a raffle. Besides, what would they use as a prize? They are already using all standard items as part of their scheme."

Homes came to his feet. "No, the answer must lie, at least in part, with this steward Sean O'Callahan. If you will permit me to change to more suitable raiment, I should like to study this situation at first hand."

For a moment Criscroft looked a trifle upset. "You are not a member, of course," he began, and then shrugged. "If worse comes to worst, I shall just have to tell them you are my brother."

The Anathema Club, of which Criscroft had the honour to be a member, was an ancient and sturdy edifice located on the edge of Interdit Park, and as I entered the hallowed precincts I felt, as always, a touch of pride in just being British, as well as a wave of fury at the miscreants who dared to jeopardize all that the club stood for with their foul scheme.

Criscroft led the way to the pantry and then excused himself, leaving Homes and me to our own devices. With the briefest of glances about the tiled kitchen, Homes made his way to the small attic room which served the steward as a bed-chamber. O'Callahan, it appeared, was out shopping, but two A.I.C. men were there, pretending to dust the furniture, and Homes nodded to them distantly before beginning his search.

From my position near the doorway I watched as he bent to peer beneath the bed, examined the closet and its contents carefully, studied the dresser drawers in great detail, and then walked over to pick up an open envelope which lay on top of a small desk in the corner. One of the A.I.C. men interrupted his task, moving closer.

"It's only the morning post," said he with a faint sneer. "We've already gone through it. There is nothing of importance there, Mr. Homes."

Homes acknowledged the statement with a cool nod, but still proceeded to raise the flap of the envelope and withdraw the note contained therein. A small rectangle of greenish-coloured paper fluttered to the desk as he unfolded the brief note and perused it. His eyes widened as he scanned the lines, and then went instantly to the small bit that had fallen free. It was obvious that only the greatest of efforts prevented him from exclaiming aloud.

"Homes!" I cried. "What is it?"

With a warning glance in the direction of the two A.I.C. men, he shook his head meaningfully at me, and then quite casually slipped both the note and the small bit of greenish paper into his pocket.

"I don't believe there is anything more for us here, Watney," he said, winking at me. "I suggest we return to Bagel Street and take up our investigation in more comfortable surroundings." And he winked at me again.

"Homes!" I exclaimed. "You have something in your eye! Permit me——"

"Later," he said savagely, and strode through the doorway.

It was only as our hansom was rattling across the cobblestones of Upper Regent Street that he allowed himself to relax. "'There is nothing of importance there, Mr. Homes'!" he said with biting mimicry. "The fools! An obvious clue under their noses, and all they can think to say is: 'There is nothing of importance there, Mr. Homes'!"

"But, Homes," I said, staring at him anxiously, "what was there of importance?"

"Only this!" he replied, and thrust the note in my direction. I took it and perused it rapidly; its message was quite succinct. *Sir* (it read): *When last you visited my establishment, you forgot the enclosed.* And it was signed, *The Butcher.* I looked up queryingly.

"But, Homes," I said, "I see nothing of importance here."

"Then you are ready to join the Metropolitan Police and the A.I.C.," he replied acidly. His hand came out to retrieve the note. "The Butcher! That can only be Professor Marty, the most dangerous criminal in all England, and a man who earned the appellation of The Butcher for all too obvious reasons! And you may be sure, Watney, that where Professor Marty is involved, we are dealing with a foe worthy of our mettle!"

"And that little bit of greenish paper that was enclosed?"

"That?" Homes smiled grimly. "Only the answer, I am sure, to the major problem of this entire case – that of their finances!"

"But I do not understand any of this, Homes!" I exclaimed.

"Later," he said, and leaned forward. "Here we are in Bagel Street, and we have much to do if this problem is to be resolved in time."

He thrust a coin at our cabbie and hustled me to the pavement even before our hansom had stopped. I followed him up the stairway to our rooms, to find him already dragging two reference volumes from their shelf; he carried them to the table and turned up the lamp. His next move was to carefully remove the small bit of coloured paper from his pocket and place it gently upon the desk top, after which he bent down and began to pore over the opened books, each one page by page. I came to stand beside him, staring down at the small rectangle, and then reached out to pick it up.

"Why, Homes," I exclaimed in disappointment, "it is only a postage stamp. Perforated, I see, and from Ulster Premiums——"

"*Only* a postage stamp, Watney?" He looked at me askance, and then closed the two reference books with a slap. "Do you realize how rare this stamp is? Not only do Stanley Gibbons and Scott fail to list it, but they fail to list any issue marked Premium for any country at all! And pray note the superb mint condition, with the original gum intact, which adds immeasurably to its value! Why, this stamp must be worth a fortune! Five or six of them, released at judicious times on the philatelic market, could easily furnish the funds these miscreants require for their infernal plot."

"But, Homes," I protested, "who could possibly be behind this scheme? Certainly the Professor would not do it out of sheer malice; he must be employed by some group. Who could they possibly be?"

"Ah," said Homes, clasping his hands behind his back and beginning to stride the room. "That is the question! That and, of course, the best way to foil them." He paused a moment, frowning. "As to the people behind this dastardly plot, I am sure the answer lies in that pamphlet, if only I am clever enough to solve it." A grim smile crossed his lips. "As to the best means of stopping these culprits, I believe I already see a rift in that loot." His eyes came up. "Would you do me a favour, Watney?"

"Gladly, Homes," I replied warmly.

"Then I should like you to visit my brother at his club and arrange for me to secure a list of all club stewards in the city of London. And haste, I might mention, is of the essence."

"You may count on me, Homes," I began, but he had already fallen back into his chair and was reaching for the small brochure. It was obvious that he had already forgotten my presence. Pausing only long enough to have lunch, I set about my errand.

It was upon my return, as I was mounting the stairs, that I heard a sharp sound that sent me dashing up the remaining steps to burst through the door. It was only Homes smiting himself on the forehead.

"Of course," he muttered bitterly. "I am a fool! The answer was staring me in the face all along!"

"Homes!" I exclaimed, hurrying forward. "What is it?"

"Look," said he, and pointed a quivering finger at the sheet of paper he had been covering with his calculations. "Note this: if you take the letters in the name 'Professor Marty' and if you eliminate all duplication of letters, you will find you have, respectively, the following: P, R, O, F, E, S, M, A, T and Y. Placing them in alphabetical order, they then come out: A, E, F, M, O, P, R, S, T and Y."

He stared at me calculatingly, his eyes bright with excitement. "Now, Watney, if we assign a numerical value to these letters, with A as 1 and Z as 26, then note how they come out!" His fingers hastily marked the numbers down; he looked up triumphantly. "Watney, they come out 1, 5, 6, 13, 18, 19, 20, and 25!"

"Indubitably, Homes," I agreed doubtfully, and stared at him.

He smiled at my puzzled expression. "Let us now apply these numbers to the pages of this pamphlet," he said gently, "and see what items they refer to." His thin fingers began to turn the pages. "Ah, here we are! Page 1 deals with Upright Pianos; page 5 with Tapestries. Page 6 lists various Hassocks; page 13, Eggbeaters; and page 15, Rotisseries. Page 16 illustrates Ermines;

page 18, Bicycles; page 19, Emeralds; page 20, with a variety of Lamps, while page 25 fittingly closes our solution by showing Shovels!"

"Really, Homes," I said worriedly. "You should eat at more regular intervals—"

He waved this aside. "*The initials of these items, Watney!* They spell *UP THE REBELS!*" He tossed his quill aside and came to his feet. "I knew that name Sean O'Callahan had a foreign ring! I shall be greatly surprised if, upon investigation, we do not find it to be of Irish origin! I should have realized from the word Ulster that such a possibility existed!"

He nodded his head in conviction. "Think, Watney! Tomorrow is the fiftieth anniversary of the Easter Sunday uprising, and what better revenge could they ask than to attack Britain at its most vital spot?—the sanctity of the British club!"

I clasped his hand. "Homes, you have done it again! Only you could have solved the mystery of the brochure in the manner in which you did!" My face fell. "But even knowing this, how are we to stop this vile and despicable scheme?"

"Ah, Watney," he replied, "that is already attended to. You have a list of the stewards?"

"I do," I said with complete honesty, and handed it over.

"Then to work!" said he, and drew from his desk drawer huge sheets of identical stamps. "I shall stuff these into envelopes, and then you shall address them to the list of stewards."

He noted my baffled expression and laughed, albeit ruefully. "A pity, Watney, but there was no other way! While you were visiting Criscroft I was not idle. A friend of mine who is a printer hastily arranged for the printing of these perfect facsimiles."

"But, Homes!" I objected. "If one stamp is so valuable, will not this great number allow them even vaster funds for their foul designs?"

"Ah, Watney," he replied, shaking his head sadly. "It is easily seen that you know nothing of philately. Where one stamp is a great rarity, and worth a fortune, tens of thousands of that same stamp render the entire issue worthless. No, Watney, you may be assured that when these thousands of stamps enter into circulation, the entire scheme will fail!" He patted me on the head and then turned to his desk. "And now to work!"

It was several mornings later that I entered the breakfast room of our quarters, picked up the newspaper, and was just beginning to go through the columns in search of some crime report which might serve as a spring-board to Homes's analytical ability, when my friend came into the room and seated himself opposite me.

"Ah, Watney," said he, spearing a curry, "do you find anything of interest for two idle investigators in your perusal of the news?"

"Very little, Homes," I replied, scanning the leaders. "I do note a case of bankruptcy at some Coupon Trading Company—whatever they are—but such crimes are probably best left to the solicitors."

"I agree," he said, reaching for the cream.

"Although," I added, reading further, "I do note that the president of the company blames his misfortunes on something he calls forgery."

"Forgery?" Holmes sat erect. "A dire crime, Watney! And one which no true Englishman will warrant! A note to the authorities offering my services, if you please!"

POSTSCRIPT:

Criscroft Homes was kind enough to help me prepare this particular adventure for publication, and in the course of proof-reading the cover of the infamous brochure for Ulster Premiums he suddenly paused with a frown.

"I note, Watney," said he, looking up at me, "that further along in this tale you make the statement that only Schlock could have solved this case in the *manner* in which he did."

"That's true," I admitted. "Why?"

He pointed to the booklet cover. "Because," he said, smiling at me proudly, "you were quite correct!"

I am always pleased to be the recipient of a compliment, especially one coming from Criscroft, although in this case I have no idea of why he so flattered me.

DR. W.

The Adventure of
The Missing Three-Quarters

MY NOTES for the early part of the year '65 contain several instances of more than passing interest for those who follow the adventures of my friend Mr. Schlock Homes. There was, for example, his brilliant solution to the mysterious gunning down of a retired boilermaker, a case which I find listed as *The Adventure of the Shot and the Bier;* and there is also reference to the intriguing business of the hitchhiking young actress, noted in my journal as *The Adventure of the Ingénue's Thumb.*

It was not, however, until the month of June that a problem of major import came his way, allowing him full scope for his feats of analytical legerdemain, as well as once again permitting him to be of service to his country. In my case-book I find the curious affair noted as *The Adventure of the Missing Three-Quarters.*

It was early afternoon and I had returned to our quarters at 221B Bagel Street; I had been in the midst of a most interesting tracheotomy when I discovered I had somehow forgotten my sutures at home. I went to my room and obtained them, and was passing the sitting-room when I chanced to peer in to find Homes bending absorbedly over his laboratory bench. At the sight of me his face lit up with an excited smile.

"Ah, Watney!" said he with pleasure. "You are just in time! The olives, if you please."

I hastened to comply, and a moment later found myself with a dry martini in my hand and a napkin on my lap. Homes decanted a beaker of the solution into another glass and seated himself across from me. There was a strange look in his eye, a sure sign that this had not been his first laboratory experiment of the day.

"Watney," he said, studying the concoction in his hand, "are you busy this afternoon?"

"Nothing that cannot wait," I replied. "Why do you ask?"

He frowned at his drink for several moments. When at last he spoke, however, it was not to answer my query, but rather to pose a second question of his own.

"Tell me, Watney," he asked slowly, "what do the words 'leg of mutton sleeves,' and 'ruffled hemline,' and 'belt in the back' mean to you?"

I paused, considering his question, and then set my drink aside, tenting my fingers in that pose I had often seen my friend adopt when applying his brain in similar situations.

"Well," I said thoughtfully, "leg of mutton sleeves would undoubtedly be warm, although I should also expect them to be quite greasy. Hemline, of course, is the small village in Germany where the Pied Piper appeared, and after the loss of the children it is scarcely surprising to hear that the village is ruffled. As for belt in the back—" I hesitated a moment and then gave up. "I'm afraid I do not know, Homes," I admitted, "but I must say it sounds a bit cowardly."

To my surprise he did not smile at my failure to define the last phrase. Instead his frown increased and he shook his head.

"To tell you the truth," he said slowly, "I also do not know. However, to satisfy your curiosity regarding these strange words, they were contained in a rather garbled message I received from my brother Criscroft this morning. He further stated that he would stop by after lunch, so possibly we shall soon have clarification." He sat up, his frown disappearing. "Ah! Even sooner than I expected, for here, if I am not mistaken, is Criscroft now."

There was the tramp of footsteps on the stairway; a moment later the door swung back and Criscroft was framed in the opening. He refused my offer of a drink almost curtly, a sure sign of his perturbation, and then flung himself in a chair, regarding the two of us in brooding silence for several moments before he spoke.

"Schlock," he said at last, his voice fraught with worry, "a major crisis has arisen, and I fear I must once again ask your help."

"Of course," Homes said, leaning forward, his eyes warm with sympathy. "How can I be of aid?"

Criscroft continued to frown darkly. "Plans are missing," he said heavily. "Vital plans. If they are not recovered before evening, I fear England shall suffer greatly!"

Homes studied his brother's rigid features and then nodded. "Tell me all."

"Yes." Criscroft came to his feet and began striding the room, his hands clasped tightly behind his back. After several turns up and down he came back to stand before us, staring at the rug fiercely, putting his thoughts in order.

"Yes," he repeated, and brought his eyes up. "Well, the situation is this. As you may or may not know, Britain is suffering gravely from a serious lack of exports, and every means for alleviating the situation has been considered. The Queen's Council on Economic Affairs has determined that priority in the recovery plan shall be given to placing England in first position in the world of fashion." His hand came up abruptly, forestalling interruption. "Do not take the matter lightly! France owes much of its economic strength to women's styles, and we are determined that this rich lode of foreign exchange shall not remain untapped.

"To this end, therefore, the Council has arranged a contest in which designers from every country have been asked to submit their designs. To ensure that fairness prevails, and to reduce the possibility of information leaking out, no sketches or pictures of any kind have been permitted. The designs are being submitted in the form of simple patterns, and the same group of dressmakers—under international supervision—will fabricate all the gowns."

"So far," Homes said with a slight frown, "I see little to disturb you to this degree." His voice became chiding. "Surely you have faith in this country's designers being easily able to dominate a contest of this—or any other—sort?"

"You do not know the whole unhappy story. Pray allow me to continue. Well, we selected as our entrant a most promising young talent. His name is Donald Orr—head of D. Orr & Company—and in order to free him completely from other preoccupations during the contest, we arranged for him to do his work at Medicinal Manor, the town home of the Earl of Wintergreen. He—" Criscroft paused and eyed Homes sharply. "You spoke?"

"No, no. It is only that I am familiar with Medicinal Manor; the Earl is an old friend of mine. I have been fortunate enough to enjoy the cuisine there several times; Jenny, his cook, is undoubtedly the finest in all London. But I digress—pray forgive me, and continue."

"Ah! Well, possibly your knowledge of the premises will be of some usefulness. We shall see. To go on, then: Orr completed his work early this morning and then hid his patterns before he left the Manor for a brief walk. Unfortunately, he has spent some time recently in the American colonies, and he apparently forgot his 'Look Right, Look Left,' because when he stepped from a kerb on his way back, he was struck by a dray, and even now is in St. Barts in a bad state."

I sat up in alarm. "If I can be of any assistance—"

"No, no! He is in competent hands; a nurse's aide is caring for him. The thing is, he is unconscious, and the only words he spoke before he lapsed into his unconscious condition were to say he had hidden the plans in the kitchen. Those phrases I sent you this morning were found on a slip of paper in his pocket. Needless to say, we have searched the culinary area thoroughly, but without success. The Earl was not informed of the purpose of Orr's visit, and therefore can be of no aid. Frankly, unless you can help, we are lost!"

Criscroft's voice sank even lower.

"The contest ends tonight, and the dressmakers will work until dawn in order to present the gowns early tomorrow morning. If we are unable to locate the patterns by six o'clock this evening, England will have initiated a contest in which it will not even have an entrant! You can easily imagine the shame of it!"

Homes peaked his fingers and closed his eyes as he considered the complex problem. At last he opened them, looking up and speaking thoughtfully.

"To attempt to solve the code contained in those garbled phrases," said he, "would undoubtedly take more time than we have at our disposal. No; our only hope is to once again search the kitchen at the Manor, but this time to do it with more intelligence." He came to his feet swiftly. "If you will allow me time to dress suitably, I shall join you at once."

Criscroft shook his head sadly. "Much as I should like to accompany you, and vital as this case is, I fear it cannot be. Today is our weekly whist at the club." His eyes came up, stern and demanding. "But remember this, Schlock —England's future is in your hands!"

"I shall not forget!" Homes promised in a ringing voice, and then swung about, perplexed. "Now, what was I looking for a minute ago? Ah, yes. My deerstalker!"

It was less than an hour later that our hansom cab deposited us at the door of Medicinal Manor in Payne Square. Homes paid the cabby and we mounted the steps; the pull-cord was finally answered by Rhett, the old butler. His wizened face broke into a smile of delight as he recognized my companion.

"Mr. Homes, sir! It's good to see you again! Come in, come in."

"Hello, Rhett," Homes said genially, and followed the bent figure into the cavernous hallway, with me close at his heels. "Is your master at home?"

The old retainer's smile disappeared as he closed the door and turned to face us. He shook his head sadly. "I'm afraid not, Mr. Homes. He has taken the children off for the day, to take their minds from the troubles, poor tykes. I fear you have come at a bad time, sir."

"Troubles? Bad time?" Homes inquired sharply. "How is that?"

Old Rhett spread his veined hands apologetically. "Well, sir, first there was that tragic affair of that young gentleman, Mr. Orr, going out and stepping beneath a horse, and shortly thereafter Jenny went sneaking from the kitchen with something under her apron—undoubtedly food—and locked herself in her room, refusing to open the door."

Homes frowned. "Jenny? Locked herself in her room?"

"Yes, sir. Undoubtedly a fit of temper caused by too many guests. However, I have been given instructions by the gentlemen from the Home Office to give you the run of the house, so—" His gnarled hand waved gently towards the interior of the house. "If you require me for anything, sir, you have only to ring."

"Thank you, Rhett," Homes said in a kindly voice, and led me in the direction of the kitchen. On our way he paused a moment outside of the cook's room, but the only sound to be heard from within was a faint whirring, as of some kind of machine. With a shrug at the inexplicable sounds made by women in a temper, Homes continued down the passage.

The vast kitchen was strangely empty without the presence of Jenny, and Homes stared about silently for several moments, his sharp eyes taking in the two huge wood ranges, the ice-chest, as well as the coffee-grinder in one corner.

"Well, Watney," he said thoughtfully at last, "we have little time. We had best get right to it."

He began his search with the ovens, and then considered the other modern appliances; all proved empty of anything useful to his purpose. He then attacked the cupboards, going through them carefully, after which he moved to the drawers. Each was withdrawn, peered into intently, and then replaced. The closets followed, and when these had also been inspected without yielding any clue, Homes stepped back, frowning blackly.

"If Mr. Orr said he hid them in the kitchen," he muttered, almost to himself, "then he hid them in the kitchen! He would have no reason to lie. We must be overlooking something."

"But what, Homes?" I asked in bewilderment.

"I do not know!" he replied savagely, and then bent, as a last resort, to look beneath the sink. The rubbish bin there was filled to capacity; there was a sudden startled gasp from my companion, and then he swiftly reached out to pick something from the top of the bin. He arose with a strange light in his eye. I moved closer; he was holding a plain card-board tube about twelve inches in length and approximately one inch in diameter.

"But, Homes!" I cried. "What is it? Why are you studying it so intently?"

"Later, Watney," he exclaimed, and in two strides had returned to the cupboard counter, staring down at it with a gleam in his eye. I followed his glance, but all I could note were some crumbs and a knife lying back against a bread-board. Homes was nodding to himself in satisfaction; his whole attitude clearly demonstrated that he had discovered some valuable clue overlooked by the previous searchers.

"Of course!" he muttered to himself. "I am a fool! I should have seen it at once!"

"Seen what, Homes?" I asked, puzzled by the entire affair.

"There is no time now," he said, turning to me swiftly. "Ring for the butler at once."

Completely mystified, I hastened to follow his orders, and a moment later old Rhett had shuffled into the room. Homes moved forward, his eyes gleaming. "You say his Lordship has taken the children off for the afternoon. Did he perchance take them for a picnic tea in Hempstead Heath?"

"Why, yes, Mr. Homes," said the butler in utter amazement, "although how you knew it, I cannot imagine!"

"No matter," Homes said in triumph, and leaned closer. "What part of the heath would he be most likely to visit? Come, man, think! Time is of the essence!"

"His Lordship usually favours the Poet's Corner—" Rhett began in his quavering voice, but Homes had already disengaged himself and was moving quickly and purposefully towards the front of the house.

He trotted rapidly down the steps with me at his heels and flagged down the first hansom that appeared, jumping into it and pulling me after. "Hempstead Heath, driver!" he cried urgently. "The Poet's Corner! And hurry!"

We came clattering up through Swiss Cottage in the direction of Golder's Green while I hung on desperately to the sides of the swaying vehicle and tried to make sense out of what was happening. Homes was leaning forward eagerly, his hair whipping about his face, as if in this way to somehow hasten our passage. The mysterious card-board tube was clutched fiercely in one hand.

"Homes!" I cried. "Pray explain! This whole thing is completely confusing."

"Is it?" he asked over his shoulder, and then leaned back, coming into the greater protection of the cab. He turned to me with a wide smile on his face. "We have ample time before we arrive at the heath, so allow me to give you a brief lesson in logic."

He raised the card-board tube, using it to tick off his points against the fingers of his other hand.

"One: we know the patterns were hidden in the kitchen. Two: they are not there now. The only possible conclusion to be reached is that they have been removed. But, excepting for the children, only two people have left the house — Mr. Donald Orr and his Lordship. Certainly there is no reason to suspect Mr. Orr, which only leaves us his Lordship. Therefore it was he who removed them."

I sat up in alarm. "The Earl of Wintergreen a traitor?"

"No, no, Watney! Remember that his Lordship was not familiar with the purpose of Mr. Orr's presence in his home, nor of the contest. True, he removed the patterns, but he did it inadvertently."

"Inadvertently?" I exclaimed.

"Precisely! You may recall the crumbs on the cupboard counter. Certainly Jenny, before locking herself in her room for some unknown reason, would not have left her kitchen in such a state of disarray. She is far too well-trained for that. Therefore, somebody used it after her. Since it could only have been his Lordship, and since he was taking the children out, it was fairly easy to deduce a picnic tea. Hempstead Heath being the closest park, it was logical to assume he had taken them there."

I shook my head in admiration. "It is so clear when you explain it, Homes," I said, and then frowned. "But you have still said nothing of the missing patterns."

He raised the thin card-board tube he had been holding so tightly. "This, Watney, is an empty container for a roll of waxed paper. When his Lordship discovered he was out of waxed paper in which to wrap his sandwiches, he quite naturally searched for a substitute, and found the patterns. Being unaware of their true importance — "

I stared at him, aghast. "Homes! You mean — ?"

"Exactly! Let us pray we are not too late!" He bent forward again as our cab swerved wildly into the heath and raced along the winding dirt road that led to the Poet's Corner. Suddenly Homes raised himself, peering forward excitedly. "That carriage!" he cried. "It is Wintergreen's — he is leaving!"

Our driver leaned down from his box, shouting tensely. The spirit of the chase had undoubtedly entered him as well. "Shall I go after him, sir?"

"No, no!" Homes cried. "Stop here! And wait for us!" He flung a coin in the direction of our jehu and dragged me from the cab even before it had fully stopped. "Watney! Quickly, before the wind snatches them away! The sandwich-wrappers!"

We rushed about, picking up the pieces of paper and smoothing them out, attempting to get them all, and then at last paused, panting, when the last visible one had been rescued. Homes's sharp eyes scanned the landscape, but as far as we could see, none of the wrappers had escaped us. With the precious pieces of paper held tightly, my friend ran back to the hansom and entered. I climbed wearily in behind him and fell against the seat, fighting for my breath. The driver instantly whipped up his horses, heading for the City.

"And now, Homes?" I asked, when at last I was able to speak.

"Now?" he responded, leaning back with a triumphant smile on his face. "Now we shall deliver these patterns to Criscroft at his club, after which our obligation will have been fulfilled. It has been a pretty problem, and I believe this evening I shall relax from it with a few bars of Hershey on the violin. If you wish you may turn the pages."

"I should like that, Homes," I exclaimed warmly, "but I really do think I should return to the hospital. The chap I left there this morning has been remarkably patient, but still — "

It was well past the hour of noon when, exhausted by our efforts of the previous day, I entered the breakfast room to find Homes already there before me, the afternoon newspaper at his elbow, attacking his first kipper with Vigor, a new sauce he found to his liking. At the sight of me he glanced up from his journal, and then nodded as he answered the unspoken question in my eyes.

"Yes, Watney," he said gently, with a smile on his lips. "Our efforts of yesterday were crowned with success. Look for yourself."

He reached across the table, placing the folded journal on my plate; I seated myself and drew it to me. There was a picture on the front page; the headline above it read: ENGLAND WINS FASHION CONTEST, while below it, in smaller letters, was the caption: *Miniskirt Is Born!*

I frowned in puzzlement at the strange words, glanced at the picture, and then raised dazed eyes to my companion.

"Homes! Do you suppose — ?"

He returned my horrified look equably. "It did occur to me last evening that possibly the Earl and the children had not eaten all their sandwiches, but had taken some home. However" — he shrugged — "one should never quarrel with success." His smile dismissed the discussion. "And now, Watney, since you have the journal in hand, what other news do you find that might be of interest to us?"

I glanced at the prize-winning costume once again, and then hastily turned the page, running my eye down the columns, searching. Suddenly my eyebrows shot up.

"Homes!" I exclaimed. "Indeed there is! His Lordship, the Earl of Wintergreen, has asked assistance in locating his missing cook!"

Homes sat up in alarm. "Jenny has disappeared?"

"Yes," I said, and read further into the article. "It says here that when last seen, she was wearing a dress with puffed sleeves, a pleated skirt, and with a sash behind."

"With that description there should be no trouble in locating her," Homes said thoughtfully, and laid aside his napkin. "A telegram to his Lordship offering my services, if you will, Watney!"

The Adventure of the
Disappearance of Whistler's Mother

IT was seldom, indeed, that the successful conclusion of a case left my friend Mr. Schlock Homes dissatisfied and unhappy; but one such affair did occur in the latter part of '66, and I relate the case to demonstrate how the best intentions of the finest of men can at times lead to unwanted results.

The months preceding this particular affair had been busy ones, and reference to my case-book for that period reveals numerous examples in which his analytical genius was given full opportunity for expression. There was, for example, his brilliant solution to the strange affair of the American baseball manager who went berserk, which I find noted as *The Adventure of the Twisted Lip;* and shortly thereafter his attention was drawn to the mysterious curse placed upon the south forty of a local grange owned by a prominent manufacturer of stomach drugs. I am sure my readers will recognize the case, which I later delineated as *The Adventure of the Bane in the Lower Tract.*

One might reasonably have imagined, this being so, that when at long last a dropping off of activity afforded my friend a well-needed chance for rest he would have been pleased; but such was not the case. Boredom was always distasteful to Homes, and I was not surprised, therefore, to return to our quarters at 221B Bagel Street one late, blustery afternoon in October to find my friend, hands thrust deep into the pockets of his dressing-gown, sprawled out in a chair before the fireplace, glowering fiercely into the flames.

Nor did he greet me in his customary manner, but came to his feet at my entrance and moved to the window restlessly, scowling down at the pavement.

I set aside my bag, removed my greatcoat and bowler, and was just turning to the sideboard when a sharp ejaculation caused me to swing about and contemplate Homes. He was leaning forward, staring down at the street in sudden excitement, his entire attitude expressing inordinate interest.

"Homes!" I exclaimed. "What is it?"

"Come here, Watney," said he, and drew the curtains further apart as I obediently hurried to his side. His thin finger pointed downward, quivering with excitement. "What do you make of that poor fellow there? Harrowed, is he not?"

My glance followed the direction of his finger. The figure to which Homes was referring was dashing madly from one side of the street to the other, studying the numerals of the houses in obvious agitation. Despite the dank chill of the day he wore neither cape nor beaver; his hair was tousled, his weskit awry, and his manner extremely disturbed.

"Harrowed?" I repeated wonderingly, watching the eccentric path woven by the man below. "In my opinion, medically speaking, he appears not so much harrowed as ploughed."

"No matter," Homes replied with barely concealed triumph. "The important fact is that he is coming to visit us, for you will note he has paused before our doorstep, and even now is entering. And here, if I am not mistaken, is our visitor now."

Homes was, as usual, correct, for there was the sound of footsteps pounding loudly on the stairs, and a moment later the door burst open. The dishevelled man stood panting upon the threshold, casting his eyes about wildly until they lit on Homes.

"Schlock 'Omes!" he cried in a thick French accent. "Thank *le bon Dieu* I 'ave found you in!"

At closer sight of our visitor, Homes's eyes widened in sudden recognition. He hurried forward, taking our perturbed guest by the arm and leading him to an easy chair beside the fireplace.

"Duping!" he cried. "My Lord, man, what is the trouble? What brings you to London? And in this sorry state?" He turned to me, his eyes glowing. "Watney, this is none other than my old friend from Paris, Monsieur C. Septembre Duping! You may recall that back in '41 I was able to be of some slight assistance to him in that sinister business of the simian with the inclination for strangling women and stuffing them up chimneys."

"Of course," I replied warmly, my eyes fixed upon our famous visitor with admiration. "As I recall, I even recorded the case in my notes as *The Adventure of the Monk's Habit*."

"Precisely," Homes agreed, and swung back to our guest, dropping into a chair across from him and leaning forward sympathetically. "Septembre, pray tell us what is bothering you."

The man seated facing him took a deep breath and then nodded. The warmth of the room after the raw weather outdoors had obviously done much to relax him, as well as the fact that I had hastened to furnish him with a whisky, taking one myself to keep him company.

"Yais," he said heavily, and raised troubled eyes to my friend's face. "'Omes, a terrible thing 'as 'appened. I know you are too *occupé* to come to Paris, but I still wished for ze benefit of your analytical brain."

"Of course," Homes replied warmly. "What is the problem?"

Our guest laid aside his empty glass and hesitated a moment, as if to emphasize the extreme gravity of the matter. What at last he spoke, the very quietness of his tone impressed us with his seriousness. "'Omes," he said slowly, "*Whistler's Mother 'as been stolen!*"

If he had expected any great reaction from Homes, he was surely disappointed, for other than a slight narrowing of his eyes, caused by a puff of smoke from the fireplace, my friend's face remained impassive. "Ah? Most interesting. Pray continue."

"Yais." Duping sighed deeply and then plunged ahead. "Well, ze facts are zese. *Hier,* at ze Louvre, zey 'ave a *réception* for a new painter 'oo is visiting Paris, and to make ze affair properly impressive, zey arrange it in ze form of a musical *soirée,* calling ze program "Ello, Dali.' I mention zis fact only to explain why zere was so unusual-large a crowd zere; how you say, *normalment* at zis hour ze Louvre is quite empty. Well, to make a long story *court,* at nine o'clock, when ze *musicale* is start, Whistler's Mother is zere, where she 'as been for years. At ten o'clock, when everybody leave—" He spread his hands. "Gone! Wizout a clue!"

Homes nodded, his eyes fixed on the other's unhappy expression. "I see."

"Yais. Well, I imagine you will want ze description." Our visitor thought a moment, assembling the data in his mind, and then continued. "A black background, and gray. 'Er size, in your English measurements, *approximativement* five-foot-four by four-foot-nine. As you can well understand, a 'eavy frame, of course. What else? Ah, yais—ze age. About ninety-five years, I believe." He shook his head sadly. "Let us 'ope she is in good condition when returned, and not damaged or smashed."

Homes nodded and sprang to his feet, beginning to pace the room, his thin hands clasped tightly behind his back. After several turns he came to stand before our guest, staring down with a frown on his face. "And has a reward been offered?"

Duping shrugged. "Money is no object, 'Omes. We will pay anyzing for ze return." He also rose, moving in the direction of the doorway. "We 'ave ze suspicion zat Whistler's Mother may already 'ave been smuggled out of France, possibly 'ere to England."

"A natural conclusion," Homes agreed. "And where are you staying in London?"

"I do not stay. I return at once to Paris. I came only to ask your 'elp."

"And you shall have it! You may expect to hear from me quite soon, giving you my solution to this puzzle. I shall get right to it this very evening, my dear Septembre."

"But, 'Omes—I mean, Homes," I interrupted in disappointment. "You have forgotten. We have tickets for Albert Hall tonight. The Rome Flood-Control Chorus is doing 'Hold That Tiber.'"

He waved aside my objection almost impatiently. "Duty before pleasure, Watney," he replied a bit coldly. "Besides, I am not particularly interested in a programme consisting solely of popular tunes."

"But there is also classical music," I insisted, a bit stung by his tone. "Cyd Caesar is completing the programme by playing the 'Etude Brutus.'"

Homes thought a moment and then shook his head. "In that case it is a pity, but I have already given my word." He returned his attention to our guest. "One last question, Septembre," he said softly, staring at the other intently. "And once the return is effected——?"

"We shall 'ang 'er, of course," Duping replied simply, and closed the door behind him.

No sooner had our guest left than Homes flung himself back into his chair, tenting his fingers and staring across them towards me with a dark frown on his hawk-like features.

"A tragedy, is it not, Watney?"

"Indeed it is," I readily agreed. "An old woman kidnapped!"

"No, no!" He shook his head at me impatiently. "You missed the entire point! The tragedy is that a poor wine-stewardess in a night-club should face such a penalty for the mere pilfering of several bottles of wine. Particularly since the poor soul was under the influence at the time and scarcely liable for her actions."

"I beg your pardon?" I asked, bewildered. "I heard nothing today of night-clubs or wine-stewardesses. In fact, with the small amount of information Monsieur Duping furnished, I do not see how you can possibly hope to come up with any answer to the puzzle."

"Small amount of information? Really, Watney, at times I despair of you! Duping gave us more information than we really needed. For example, there was his description of the woman. Obviously, if she is five-foot-four by four-foot-nine, there was no need to inform us that she has a heavy frame. Similarly, if they plan to hang her when and if they get her back, it was scarcely necessary to tell us that her background was black. And being ninety-five years of age, one could automatically assume she would be gray. No, no, Watney! Duping gave us all we require. The real problem is how to handle it."

He swung about and stared fiercely into the flames of the fireplace, speaking almost as if to himself.

"There is a possibility, of course, that we can not only satisfy Duping but still save the poor old lady's life. If only——" He nodded to himself several times, and then turned around to face the room, glancing at his time-piece. "A bit early to make our move, though."

"Really, Homes," I said, deeply annoyed. "I honestly believe you are pulling my leg. That business before of wine-stewardesses and night-clubs! And now this mysterious muttering you are indulging in! What move, pray, is it too early to make?"

"Why," Homes replied, surprised, "to break into Professor Marty's digs, of course." He noted the expression on my face and suddenly smiled in a kindly fashion. "No, Watney, I am not teasing you. We have at least an hour to spare, so let me explain this sad case to you."

He leaned in my direction, ticking his points off methodically on his fingers.

"Let us start with Duping's description of the place where the old lady was last seen and from which she disappeared, this place called the Louvre – or, in English, The Louver. That the place is a night-club is instantly discernible: the fact that normally it was deserted between the hours of nine and ten, long before the most frivolous of French patrons would think of beginning their evening's entertainment, the presence of music in the form of this 'Hello, Dali' revue; and most important, the name, so typical, and so similar to The Venetian Blind or The Window or The Cellar or others which we know to be so popular in Soho today. I should not hesitate to predict that its decor consists of louvers painted in green against a puce background. But no matter – let us continue."

A second finger was bent over to join the first, while I listened in open-mouthed wonder to his brilliant deductions.

"Now, precisely what was this elderly lady doing in this night-club? Obviously, she was not merely an habituée. Duping's exact words were, 'Where she 'as been for years.' Had she been a client, even the most constant, he almost certainly would have worded it differently. He would have said, 'Where she 'as been in ze 'abit of dropping in for years,' or something of that nature. Therefore, not being a client, we are forced to the conclusion that she is – or was, rather – an employee of the establishment, and one of long standing, at that.

"But in what position?" He shrugged before continuing. "Well, considering her age and her measurements, I believe we can safely eliminate the positions of waitress and hat-check girl, both of which demand a certain degree of beauty. Matron in the Mesdames? Again, I believe we can disregard this possibility; her exact presence or absence at any particular hour would scarcely have been noted with the exactitude that Duping indicated. And the same holds true, of course, for any of the kitchen staff. Cashier? With her black background it is doubtful if the owners would permit her near the till. There is, therefore, only one position left: Mrs. Whistler could only have been the wine-stewardess!"

A third finger was depressed as I listened, amazed, to this startling demonstration of incontrovertible logic. Homes's eyes remained half-closed as he continued to clothe the thin facts given by his friend with the warm flesh of his impeccable analysis.

"Now, Watney, consider: How could an old lady like this manage to subject herself to a penalty as severe as hanging in the short period allowed her between the hours of nine and ten? Certainly her crime was not murder, for which the French still maintain the guillotine. It must therefore have been something equally severe in the eyes of her accusers, but short of murder. It must also, of necessity, be something within her power to perform. Recalling that her position was that of a wine-stewardess, and that she had no access to any of the funds of the club, we can only reach one conclusion: that her crime consisted of taking some of the wine stocks. Undoubtedly rare and precious, and therefore probably cognac."

"But, Homes!" I objected. "Hanging? Just for stealing a few bottles of wine?"

He smiled at me pityingly. "It is apparent you know little of human nature, Watney. In the American colonies, as I am sure you are aware, the penalty for stealing a horse is hanging. And not so long ago punishment even more severe was reserved for anyone taking the King's deer. Why should France, where their national pride in their liqueurs is paramount, feel any less strongly? No, no! It is the only conclusion consistent with all the facts, and therefore must be the correct one. You know my dictum: when all theories but one have been eliminated, that remaining theory, however improbable— indeed, however impossible—must be the truth—or words to that effect."

I nodded dumbly. "Now," Homes went on, "when Duping told us that she had been stolen, you assumed his poor English prevented him from using the word 'kidnapped.' Actually, his poor English prevented him from stating what he truly meant—not that she had been stolen, but that she herself had stolen something."

I could not help but accept the faultless conclusion. "But, Homes," I said hopefully, "you suggest there were mitigating circumstances?"

"Yes. As I have already said, the poor woman was obviously under the influence of alcohol. You may recall Duping stating that he hoped she would not be 'smashed' when apprehended. It is an American slang term apparently becoming popular even in France. In any event, his very fear of this indicates that she stole the bottles in order to drink them—proof positive that her excessive thirst caused her crime in the first place. That she chose a moment when everyone was concentrating on the revue is easily understood. Under normal conditions she would have been too busy serving customers to have succumbed to the temptation to imbibe."

"But you say you hope to be able not only to satisfy Duping but also save the old lady?"

"There is that possibility."

"And this somehow involves Professor Marty?"

"Exactly." He considered me sombrely. "It will mean a bit of risk tonight, but there is nothing else for it. If you do not care to join me in this venture, I shall not hold it against you. The Professor is undoubtedly the most dangerous man in all England."

"Nothing on earth could stop me from accompanying you, Homes!" I declared stoutly, and then frowned. "But where does Professor Marty come into this at all?"

He shook his head impatiently at my lack of perception. "Please, Watney! You may recall that when Duping suggested the old lady might even now be in England, I readily agreed. Why? Because the name Whistler is certainly not French, but rather British, and in times of trouble to whom would she turn, if not to her son in England? We can scarcely believe that with her black background her son is free of a taint of malfeasance, and no criminal in England is beyond the scope of knowledge of Professor Marty. No, no! If Whistler's mother is in England at the moment, you may be sure the Professor is well aware of it. By entering his rooms after he has left on his nightly foray against society, I hope to find proof of the fact. And possibly turn it to the advantage of the poor soul!"

"Bravo, Homes!" I cried, and could not help applauding both his motives and his infallible logic. Unfortunately, at the moment I was holding both a glass and a bottle, and while I shame-facedly hastened to clear up the débris, Homes disappeared into his room to change into more suitable raiment.

It was past the hour of ten when our hansom dropped us around the corner of Professor Marty's darkened rooms in Limehouse. The night had turned cold, which afforded us a good excuse to keep our collars high and our faces hidden from the denizens of the district, who slunk past us to fade into the growing miasma rising from the river beyond. With a glance in both directions, Homes chose a moment when a swirl of fog momentarily hid us from any passers-by to swiftly mount the steps and apply his skill to the lock. A moment later he was beckoning me to follow; scant seconds more and he had closed the door, and his bull's-eye lantern was casting its restricted beam about the empty room.

"Quickly, Watney!" he whispered urgently. "We have little time! You take the den and the bedroom, while I examine the kitchen and bath." He took one look at my opening lips and added coldly, "We are looking for anything that might indicate the presence of the old lady here."

I nodded and began to close my mouth when I remembered something else. "But I have no lantern, Homes."

"Use vestas, then, if need be, but hurry!"

He disappeared even as I was fumbling beneath my cape, and an eerie chill swept over me until I had the first one lit and spied a taper on the mantel-piece. A moment later I was shielding the flickering flame and studying the room in which I stood. To me it appeared as any other room, and my heart sank as I realized how ill-equipped I was for a search of this nature, and that I might very well fail my friend. To bolster my spirits I went to the liquor cabinet, and at that moment the beam of Homes's lantern joined my weaker candle as he returned to the den.

"There is nothing," he said in a dispirited voice, and then his tone sharpened. "Watney! What are you doing?"

"Nothing—" I began guiltily, but before I could offer my excuses he had dropped down beside me and was reaching past my arm for the contents of the cabinet. A moment later and he was pounding my back in congratulation.

"Watney, you have done it! Good man!"

I stared in bewilderment as he began withdrawing bottles and examining them, muttering half to himself as he did so. "Cordon Bleu, Remy Martin, Napoleon, Courvoisier – excellent! With any luck this should do it!"

"But, Homes!" I interjected. "I do not understand. Do what?"

He swung to me with a fierce light of triumph in his eyes. "My dear Watney! When Duping expressed fear that the old lady would be apprehended in an inebriated state, he was not worrying about *her*, since he gave no indication of reducing the penalty for her crime. No, he was fearful that the cognacs would be consumed, for they are his main interest. By returning these to him, it is well possible that he will allow the matter to drop, and stop his pursuit of the poor woman."

His eyes swung about the room. "Quickly! Find me something in which to package these bottles while I pen a brief note to Duping to enclose. The packet to Le Havre leaves on the midnight tide, and by hurrying we can just make it."

While he bent over the escritoire, I hastily searched the room for wrapping materials, but despite my efforts the best I could find was an old roll of canvas that had been shoved behind a bookcase. I brought it forward hesitatingly and showed it to Homes.

"Ah, well," he said, shrugging, "it is certainly not the cleanest, for somebody has smeared it with tar or something. However, we have no time for further delays – it will have to do. Help me roll these bottles in it and we will be on our way to the dock. With any luck these will be in Duping's hands tomorrow, and our problem will have been solved."

Our exertions of the previous evening kept us both late abed, and it was close to the hour of noon before I came into our breakfast room to find Homes already at the table. He nodded to me pleasantly and was about to speak when our page entered and handed Homes a telegraph form.

I seated myself, unfolded the afternoon journal, and was just reaching for the curried kidney when a sharp exclamation of dismay caused me to glance up. Homes, his face ashen, was staring in horror at the slip of paper in his hand.

"Homes!" I cried. "What is it?"

"I am an idiot!" he muttered bitterly. "An abysmal idiot! I should have anticipated this!"

"Anticipated what, Homes?" I inquired, and for an answer received the telegraph form flung across the table. I read it hastily; its message was succinct. HOMES, YOU HAVE DONE IT AGAIN. WHISTLER'S MOTHER IS ONCE AGAIN IN OUR HANDS AND HUNG, THANKS TO YOU.

"But, Homes!" I exclaimed. "I do not understand!"

"No?" he replied scathingly. "It is easily enough understood. I failed to take into account that the old lady might follow her booty back across the Channel and thus fall into their hands! I am a fool! Rather than save her, I actually led her to her death."

"You must not blame yourself, Homes," I said with warm sympathy. "You did your best, and no man can do more."

"I did far too well," he replied balefully. "Without my help Duping might have searched for the old woman and her cognac for years." He tried to shake off his black mood, shrugging. "Ah, well! It is too late now to cry over spilt milk. Tell me, Watney, is there anything of a criminal nature in today's journal to help take my mind from this terrible fiasco?"

I hastily abandoned my kidney, perusing the newspaper instead, running my eyes rapidly down one column after another, but without too much success. There was, however, one weak possibility, and in lieu of a more interesting case I offered it.

"There is this, Homes," I said, studying the article further. "It seems that a very valuable painting was stolen from the French National Gallery. But the dateline is several days old; it may very well be that by this time the trail is much too cold."

The renewed sparkle in Homes's eyes told me that he was already well on the road to recovery.

"The time element makes no difference, Watney! A crime is a crime, and the more difficult the case, the better I like it! Besides, we have one bit of information the Sûreté lacks: we know that Professor Marty could not have been involved, for we would have come upon some evidence of it during our search. And eliminating this adversary takes us quite a step forward! A telegram to the authorities offering my services, Watney, if you will!"

The Adventure of
The Dog in the Knight

IN glancing through my notebook delineating the many odd adventures which I was fortunate enough to share with my good friend Mr. Schlock Homes in the early months of the year '68, I find it difficult to select any single one as being truly indicative of his profound ability to apply his personal type of analytical *Verwirrung* which, taken at its ebb, so often led him on to success.

There was, of course, the case of the nefarious card-cheat whom Homes so cleverly unmasked in a young man's health organization in the small village of Downtree in Harts—a case I find noted in my journal as *The Adventure of the Y-Bridge*. It is also true that during this period he was of particular assistance to the British Association of Morticians in a case whose details are buried somewhere in my files but which resulted, as I recall, in a National Day being set aside in their honour. While it remains a relatively unimportant matter, the tale still is recorded in my case-book as *The Boxing-Day Affair*.

However, in general those early months were fruitless, and it was not until the second quarter of the year that a case of truly significant merit drew his attention. In my entry for the period of 15/16 April, '68, I find the case listed as *The Adventure of the Dog in the Knight*.

It had been an unpleasantly damp day with a drizzle compounded by a miasmic fog that kept us sequestered in our quarters at 221B Bagel Street; but evening brought relief in the form of a brisk breeze that quickly cleared the heavy air. "We have been in too long," Homes said, eyeing me queryingly. "I suggest a walk to clear away the cobwebs."

I was more than willing. Homes had spent his day at the laboratory bench, and between the stench of his chemicals and the acrid odour of the Pakistanis, the room fairly reeked. For several hours we roamed the by-ways of our beloved London, our coat-collars high against the evening chill, stopping on occasion at various pubs to ascertain the hour. It was eight o'clock exactly when we arrived back at our rooms, and it was to find a hansom cab standing at the kerb before our door.

"Ah," Homes observed, eyeing the conveyance sharply. "A visitor from Scotland Yard, I see!"

I was sufficiently conversant with Homes's methods by this time to readily follow his reasoning; for the crest of the Yard—three feet rampant on a field of corn—was emblazoned both on the door and on the rear panel of the coach, clearly visible under the gas-lamp before our house, and the jehu sitting patiently on the box was both uniformed and helmeted. With some curiosity as to the reason for this late visit I followed Homes up the stairs and into our quarters.

A familiar figure rose from a chair beside the unlit fireplace and turned to face us. It was none other than Inspector Balustrade, an old antagonist whose overbearing manner and pompous posturing had long grated upon both Homes's nerves and my own. Before we could even discard our outer garments he was speaking in his usual truculent manner.

"My advice to you, Homes," he said a bit threateningly, "is to keep your hands off the Caudal Hall affair. We have an open-and-shut case, and any interference on your part can only cause the luckless miscreant unwarranted and futile hope. In fact," he continued, looking fiercer than ever, "I believe I shall go so far as to *demand* that you leave the matter alone!"

Schlock Homes was quite the wrong person to address in such words and tones. "Inspector Balustrade, do not rail at me!" said he sharply. He doffed his coat and deerstalker, tossing them carelessly upon a chair, striding forward to face the Inspector. "I take those cases that interest me, and it is my decision alone that determines which they shall be."

"Ah!" Inspector Balustrade's tiny eyes lit up in self-congratulation. "I knew it — I knew it! I merely wished to confirm my suspicions. So they've been at you, eh? And, by the look of things, bought you! Lock, Stock, and Barrel!"

"Eh?"

"The lawyer chappies, that is," Balustrade continued. "Well, you're wasting your time listening to them, Mr. Homes. There is no doubt of the culprit's guilt." He smiled, a sneering smile. "Or do you honestly believe you have sufficient evidence to contradict that statement?"

"What I think is my affair," Homes said, eyeing the man distastefully. "You have delivered your message, Inspector, so I see little to be gained by your continued presence here."

"As you wish, Mr. Homes," Balustrade said with mock servility. He picked up his ulster, clamped his bowler firmly to his head, and moved to the door. "But Dr. Watney here can bear witness that I did my best to save you from making a fool of yourself!" And with a chuckle he disappeared down the stairs.

"Homes!" I said chidingly. "A new case and you did not inform me?"

"Believe me," he said sincerely, "I know nothing of this. I have no idea what the Inspector was talking of." He contemplated me with a frown. "Is it possible, Watney, that we have inadvertently missed some item of importance in the morning journal?"

"It would be most unusual, Homes," I began, and then suddenly remembered something. "I do recall, now, Mrs. Essex borrowing the front page of the *Globe* to wrap some boots for the cobbler's boy to pick up, but if I'm not mistaken, the lad failed to appear. Let me get it and see if it can cast any light on this mystery."

I hurried into the scullery, returning in moments with the missing sheet. I spread it open upon the table, pressing out the creases, while Homes came to stand at my side.

"Ah," said he, pointing triumphantly. "There it is!" He bent closer, reading the words half-aloud. "*Tragic Affair at Caudal Manor.* But where is the — ? Ah, here it is just beneath the headline." He smiled in satisfaction at his discovery, and read on:

"'Late last evening an unfortunate incident occurred at Caudal Manor, the country estate in Kent of Sir Francis Gibbon, the 62-year-old Knight of the Realm. A small dinner party was in progress, at which the only guests were Sir Francis' sister-in-law, Mrs. Gabriel Gibbon, who is married to Sir Francis' younger and only brother and who has often acted as hostess for her bachelor brother-in-law; and a Mr. John Wain, a young visitor from the Colony of California, a chemist by trade, who is staying with Mr. and Mrs. Gabriel Gibbon as a house-guest. Mr. Gabriel, two years younger than his illustrious brother, was absent, having claimed he preferred to see his romance at the theatre rather than at home, and for this reason was spending his evening at the latest Boucicault offering in Piccadilly. Readers of the society news may recall that the beauteous Mrs. Gibbon, like Mr. Wain, was also a colonial from California at the time of her marriage two years ago.

" 'The main course, chosen out of deference to their foreign guest, was frankfurters – called "hot dogs" abroad – which was also a favourite dish of his Lordship, Sir Francis. The course had already been consumed, washed down with ale, and a bitter-almond tart had also been eaten, when Sir Francis suddenly gasped, turned pale, and seemed to have difficulty in his breathing and his speech; then, in a high nasal voice, he apologized to his guests for suffering from a stomach indisposition and stumbled out of the room. As quickly as the other two could finish their dessert, coffee, and brandy, and avail themselves of the fingerbowls, they hurried into the drawing-room to offer succour; but Sir Francis was sprawled on the rug in a comatose state and died before medical assistance could be summoned.

" 'Mrs. Gabriel Gibbon was extremely distraught, and exclaimed, "I didn't think my brother-in-law looked well for some time, and I often warned him that bolting down hot-dogs was bad for his heart condition, so I really cannot claim to be surprised by this sudden cardiac seizure, although I am, of course, quite heart-broken."

" 'Her physician was called and offered her a sedative, but Mrs. Gibbon bravely insisted upon completing her duties as hostess, even demonstrating sufficient control to supervise the maids in the cleaning and thorough washing and drying of the dishes, as well as the incineration of all the left-overs.

" 'Students of Debrett will recall that the Gibbon family seat, Caudal Hall, was entailed for a period of ten generations by King George III, at the time the land, titles, and rights were bestowed on the first Gibbon to be knighted. The entailing of an estate, as we are sure our readers know, means that during this period the property must be passed on and cannot be sold or otherwise disposed of. With the death of Sir Francis, this condition has now ceased to be in effect, and Mr. Gabriel is now free to dispose of the estate as he chooses, or pass it on to his heirs in legal manner. Under the conditions of the original knighthood conferred on the first Gibbon, the title also continued for this period of ten generations, so Mr. Gabriel will only be entitled to be called Sir by his servants and those friends who dislike informality.' "

Homes paused a moment to remove a boot that blocked our vision of the balance of the article, and then leaned over further, staring in utter amazement at the portion of the column that had been revealed. In a startled tone of voice, he continued:

" 'STOP PRESS: The Police officials have just announced an arrest in the Caudal Hall affair, claiming that Sir Francis was the victim of none other than his guest, Mr. Wain, age 26, the American colonial. They point out that a chemist would have the necessary knowledge to administer a fatal potion in

Sir Francis' food, and that despite the knight's known heart condition as testified to by his sister-in-law, they believe there is more to the matter than meets the eye, and that the heart condition was at most only a contributory factor.

"'They note that Mr. Wain is left-handed and sat on Sir Francis's right, permitting his operative hand to constantly hover over his Lordship's food. They believe he took advantage of the fortuitous circumstance of a bitter-almond tart being served to pour oil of nutmeg, a high toxic abortifacient, either onto the tart itself, or more likely onto the "hot-dog" itself, in a dosage sufficient to cause Sir Francis his severe abdominal pain, and eventually his death. The police base their conclusion on the faint odour of nutmeg they discerned upon the lips of the deceased, although they admit it was difficult to detect because of the almost overpowering odour of the bitter-almond tart.

"'Whether Mr. Wain intended the dose to be fatal, the police say, is unimportant; he is nonetheless guilty of his victim's demise and shall pay the full penalty for his crime. They claim to have evidence that Mr. Wain is a revolutionary, propounding the theory that the American colonies are now independent, a viewpoint certain to have aroused the righteous wrath of so fine a patriot as Sir Francis Gibbon. Bad feelings could only have resulted, and it is the theory of the police that the dinner party developed into an argument which culminated in the tragic death of Sir Francis. Mrs. Gibbon's failure to remember any such quarrel is attributed to absent-mindedness, added to her concern over the success of the meal, which undoubtedly caused her to be inattentive. (Artist's sketches on Page 3).'

"Fools!" Homes exclaimed in disgust, replacing the boot and rewrapping the package. "Balustrade is an idiot!" He flung himself into a chair, looking up at me broodingly. "We must help this poor fellow Wat, Wainey—I mean, Wain, Watney!"

"But, Womes—I mean Homes," I said remonstratingly, "it appears to me that they have a strong case against the young man. As a medical practitioner I admit that stomach pain is often found to be related to heart seizure, but still, one cannot rule out the possibility of other agencies."

"Nonsense!" said Homes half-angrily. "I can understand a young man's reason for harming a complete stranger, and I can even understand a chemist carrying about a vial of oil of nutmeg on the offhand chance he might meet someone to whom he wished to give stomach indisposition. But what I cannot lead myself to believe is that a University graduate would be so ill-informed as to honestly believe the American colonies are independent!" He shook his head. "No, no, Watney, it is here that the police case falls down!"

He tented his fingers, staring fiercely and unseeingly over them through half-lidded eyes, his long legs sprawled before him. Minutes passed while I quietly sat down, remaining silent, respecting his concentration; then, of a sudden, our reveries were interrupted by the sound of footsteps running lightly up the stairs, and a moment later the door burst open to reveal a lovely young girl in her mid-twenties. She might have been truly beautiful had it not been for the tears in her eyes and the tortured expression on her face. Scarcely pausing for breath, she hurried across the room and knelt at Homes's side, grasping his two hands in hers.

"Oh, Mr. Homes," she cried beseechingly, "only you can save John Wain! In the first place, the scandal would be ruinous were a house-guest of mine to be found guilty of a crime; and besides, it would play havoc with the entire scheme!"

"You are Mrs. Gabriel Gibbon?"

"Yes. I will pay—" She paused, thunderstruck. "But how could you have possibly known my identity?"

Homes waved the question aside with his accustomed modesty, preferring to return to the problem at hand. "Pray be seated," said he, and waited until she was ensconced across from him. "I have read the account in the journal and I am also convinced that the police have made a grave error. Tell me," he continued, quite as if he were not changing the subject, "would I be correct in assuming that the cook at Caudal Manor is a fairly youngish woman? And unmarried, I should judge?"

"Indeed she is, but how you knew this I cannot imagine!"

"And did she recently have a quarrel with her fiancé?"

The young lady could only nod her head in stunned fashion.

"And one final question," Homes went on, eyeing her steadily. "By any chance did Mr. Wain complain at table because his ale was not iced, as he was accustomed to drinking it?"

"He did, but—" The girl stopped speaking, coming to her feet and staring down at Homes almost in fear. "Mr. Homes, your ability is more than uncanny—it borders on the supernatural!" Her eyes were wide. "How could you possibly have known—?"

"There is nothing mystical in it," Homes assured her gravely. "In any event, you may return home with an untroubled mind. I assure you that Mr. Wain will join you—a free man—before many hours."

"I cannot thank you enough, Mr. Homes! Everything I have heard and read about you is the truth!" Her lovely eyes welled with tears of gratitude as she left the room.

"Really, Homes," I said shortly, "I fail to understand any of this. What is this business of the unmarried cook and the warm ale?"

"Later, Watney!" Homes said, and picked up his greatcoat and deerstalker. "At the moment I must go out and verify a few facts, and then see to it that poor Mr. Wain is freed. These colonials suffer sufficiently from a feeling of inferiority; incarceration can only serve to aggravate it."

It was well past midnight before I heard Homes's key in the door below, but I had remained awake, a warmed kippered toddy prepared against my friend's return, my curiosity also waiting to be assuaged. He clumped up the stairs wearily, doffed his coat and hat, and fell into a chair, accepting the toddy with a nod. Then, after quaffing a goodly portion, he put the glass aside, leaned forward, and burst into loud laughter.

"It would have done you good, Watney, to see Balustrade's stare when he was forced to unlock Wain's cell and usher the young man to the street," he said with a grin. "I swear for a moment there I thought the Inspector was going to physically engage me in fisticuffs!" He chuckled at the memory and finished his kippered toddy, visibly relaxing. "And thank you, by the way, for your thoughtfulness in preparing this toddy for me. It was delicious."

"You can demonstrate your gratitude in far better manner," I said, possibly a trifle tartly, for it was well past my usual bedtime, "by explaining this entire complex, incomprehensible case to me, for none of it makes the slightest sense!"

"No?" he asked incredulously. "I am rather surprised. I should have thought the medical evidence would have pointed you in the right direction. However," he continued, seeing the look on my face and, as ever, properly interpreting it, "let us begin at the beginning." He lit a Pakistani.

"First, as you well know, Watney, I respect you quite highly as a medical man, but I have also made a study in depth of toxicology. You may recall my monograph on the Buster Ketones and the Halloids which had such a profound effect on early Hollywood comedies — but I digress. To me the evidence presented by the article in the morning journal was quite conclusive."

His fine eyes studied my face, as if testing me. "Tell me, Watney, what precise toxicity results in the symptoms so accurately described by the writer in the journal?" He listed them on his fingers as he continued, "One: stomach disorder. Two: dimness of vision — for you will remember that Sir Francis stumbled as he left the room, and yet, after living in Caudal Manor for all his sixty-two years, one must assume he could normally have made his way about blindfolded. Three: difficulty in speaking and breathing. And four: a nasal quality to his voice."

Homes looked at me inquiringly. "Well?"

"Botulism!" I said instantly, now wide-awake.

"Exactly! True, the symptoms are similar for hydro-cyanic poisoning, but with the knight consuming the frankfurter, botulism was clearly indicated. My questions to young Mrs. Gibbon regarding the ale and the cook merely confirmed it."

"I beg your pardon, Homes?" I asked, completely lost once again.

"Let us take the ale first," said he, his kindly glance forgiving my obtuseness. "Certainly Mrs. Gabriel Gibbon, herself a colonial, would be aware that icing of ale is almost compulsory in the colonies, and would therefore be expected by her compatriot. The failure to do so on the part of a dedicated hostess, therefore, could only have been caused by one thing — "

"The absent-mindedness which the reporter mentioned?" I asked, eager to be of help.

"No, Watney! *The lack of ice!* Now, in a household the size of Caudal Manor, who has the responsibility for seeing that the supply of ice is adequate? Naturally, the cook. But an elderly cook with years of experience would never forget a matter as important as ice, particularly with a foreign guest expected. Therefore, the conclusion is inevitable that the cook was not elderly, but rather, on the contrary, young. Still, even young cooks who manage to secure employment in an establishment as noted as Caudal Manor are not chosen unless they are well-qualified; therefore some problem must have been preying on the young cook's mind to make her forget the ice. Now, Watney, what problem could bother a young lady to this extent? Only one concerning a male friend; hence my conclusion that she had had a quarrel with her fiancé." He spread his hands.

"But, Homes," I asked, bewildered, "what made you think of ice in the first place? Or rather, the lack of it? Merely the floe of ideas?"

"The botulism, of course, Watney! Lack of proper refrigeration is one of the greatest causes for the rapid growth of the fatal bacteria, and both Mrs. Gibbon and her friend Mr. Wain may count themselves fortunate that the organism attacked only the one frankfurter, or they might well have both joined Sir Francis in death!"

For several moments I could only gaze at my friend Mr. Schlock Homes with the greatest admiration for his brilliant analysis and masterful deductions.

"Homes!" I cried. "You have done it again! Had it not been for your brilliant analysis and masterful deductions, an innocent colonial might have gone to the gallows for a crime due, in its entirety, to a hot-dog in the knight!" Then I paused as another thought struck me. "But one thing, Homes," I added, puzzled. "What of the oil of nutmeg that the police made such a matter of?"

Homes chuckled. "Oh, that? That was the easiest part of the entire problem, Watney. I stopped at the mortuary while I was out tonight and had a look at Sir Francis' cadaver. As I had anticipated, he had taken up a new after-shave lotion with a nutmeg bouquet, and as soon as I can determine its name, I believe I shall purchase it as well."

Due to the late hour when we finally retired that night, it was well past noon when I arose and made my way to the breakfast table. Homes had not arrived as yet, but I had no more than seated myself and reached for my first spoonful of chutneyed curry when he came into the room.

He greeted me genially and seated himself, drawing his napkin into his lap. In deference to his habits I put aside my spoon for the moment and picked up the morning journal, preparing to leaf through it in search of some tidbit of news that might serve Homes as a means to ward off ennui. But I did not need to turn the page. There, staring at me from scare headlines, was an announcement that made me catch my breath.

"Homes!" I cried, shocked to the core. "A terrible thing has happened!"

He paused in the act of buttering a kipper. "Oh?"

"Yes," I said sadly. "Tragedy seems to have struck poor Mrs. Gibbon again!"

He eyed me sharply, his fishknife poised. "You mean —?"

"Yes," I said unhappily, reading further into the article. "It seems that early this morning, while taking his constitutional along Edgeware Road, Gabriel Gibbon was struck and killed by a car recklessly driving on the wrong side of the road. The police surmise the culprit may have been from the Continent, where drivers are known to use the wrong side of the road; but this is mere theory and unsupported by fact, particularly since the driver escaped and the description of the few witnesses is considered useless."

"That poor girl!" said Homes, and sighed deeply.

"Yes," I agreed. "True, she will now inherit the Gibbon fortune, but this can scarcely compensate her for the loss of her loved one!"

"True," Homes said thoughtfully. Then a possible solution came to him and he nodded. "We can only hope that her friend Mr. Wain will stand by her in her hour of need, even as she stood by him in his! In fact, I believe he is enough in my debt for me to suggest it. A telegram form, if you please, Watney —"

The Adventure of
The Briary School

I HAD THOUGHT these memoirs to be ended for all time, for although my notebooks contained many as-yet-untold adventures which I had been fortunate enough to share with my good friend Mr. Schlock Homes, the fact was that after Homes's retirement to the Upson Downs for the purpose of bee-farming, he forbade me to release any further details of his many cases so long as he was no longer in the profession. It would bring him too much publicity, he feared, and would not permit him the seclusion he desired so fervently.

I was therefore quite surprised, one fine summer morning in the year '72, to hear a ring at the door and moments later to have my page usher in none other than Mr. Schlock Homes himself! I had retained our old rooms at 221B

Bagel Street, and at first I thought Homes had merely dropped in for a brief nostalgic visit while in town; but before I could even offer him a cold curry from the sideboard, he had called loudly down below and two large navvies came lumbering up the steps bearing his two trunks, his portmanteau, and a welter of boxes.

"Homes!" I cried in delight, coming to my feet, curry in hand. "You have come out of retirement!"

He put off answering until his gear had been placed down to his satisfaction, and then paying off the men, he closed the door behind them and fell into a chair.

"Would you mind, Watney," he inquired, "sharing your solitude after all these years?"

"Homes!" I exclaimed. "You must know better than that! It is a pleasure. But what happened to the bee-farming?"

He shook his head, a slightly puzzled frown upon his lean features.

"This bee-farming," said he, pinching his lip, "is far more difficult than one might imagine. Year after year I planted the little devils at exactly the proper depth according to my calculations, inserted what I still feel was the correct amount of fertilizer, tamped each little hill down securely, and watered them daily. Yet not one single crop did I get!"

"Possibly you used old bees?" I asked helpfully.

"No," said he, shaking his head, "nor could it have been the soil. My carrots were more than satisfactory, and my neighbour – with whom I have a slight altercation regarding boundaries – was decent enough to say that my cucumbers, which he claims are growing on his property, will end up giving me a fine pickle. Or something on that order." He sighed heavily. "No, Watney; I fear I was meant to be a private investigator and nothing more. It is a pity there is no case awaiting me. I may have merely exchanged the frustration of bee-farming for the ennui of the city."

"I doubt that, Homes," I said with a smile. "Only this morning a telegram arrived addressed to you. I was about to send the page around to return it to sender, as I have the many others, when you arrived. Here it is now."

He accepted the form from me with eager fingers, tore open the envelope, and perused its contents with his old concentration. I sat back, pleased to be once more back in harness with Homes, and watched his nostrils dilate in that fashion I recognized from the old days as indicating his allergy to cold curry.

"Ah," said he at last, a faint smile upon his face, "nothing of great merit, but still a welcome start after my years of inaction. It appears that a certain Mr. Silas Cornbuckle – a name, you note, of uncertain national origin – has asked for an appointment at ten, and" – he glanced at the mantel clock, just as the bell rang – "I shall be greatly surprised if this is not our Mr. Cornbuckle now!"

He leaned back comfortably as our page ushered in a stout young man of florid complexion, dressed in an atrociously striped garment, wearing a flaxen drooping moustache, and sporting a large chain across his weskit from which dangled a huge curved ornament. Homes nodded politely, but even before he could properly greet his visitor, I interrupted, a bit smugly, perhaps.

"Come, Homes," said I, smiling. "Let us see if your years of bee-farming have or have not dulled your talents. At one time you used to brag of your ability to discern a person's nationality or occupation from his mere appearance. What say you of this gentleman?"

Homes's eyes twinkled as he readily accepted the challenge. Our guest stood in puzzlement at our exchange as Homes considered the figure before him critically.

"You will note, Watney," he said at last, almost as if the years had not passed, or as if our guest were not in the room, "the clothing of our visitor is coloured in red and white stripes. Since only a patriot would wear such a garment, we can only conclude our guest is from Canada. A further proof of his nationality, if further proof were needed, is the ornament on his watch-chain, which I recognize as being an elk's tooth, since elk are native to Canada.

"As for his occupation, we must consider the fact that the elk is known for its ferocity when facing dentistry of any sort, so anyone removing a tooth must be someone familiar with the ways of the beast. When we add to this the sagging shoulders, the typical stance of one trained to follow a spoor, we can state with confidence that our guest is a professional—and obviously intrepid—hunter!"

The large man stared at Homes in amazement.

"I cannot fathom how you do it, Mr. Homes!" he exclaimed, his jaw agape. "You are absolutely right in stating that I am a patriot, and I truly meant to wear my blue weskit, but I seem to have misplaced it. Actually, I am from the Colony of New Jersey, although I have often visited Canada. I am also pleased that you recognize the courage of a member of the B.P.O.E. On the name, though, you were truly remarkable. Professional Hunter is my brother-in-law; I married his sister, Intrepid. As for the sagging shoulders, they come from carrying the luggage of ten young whippersnappers, and it is in connection with them that I find myself here."

Homes nodded genially and waved a hand.

"Have the basket chair, pray," he said, "and tell me your story. I shall be happy to assist you in any manner within my power."

Our guest sank gratefully into the indicated chair and reached into his pocket, withdrawing a bit of paper. He contemplated it in frowning silence for a moment or two and then looked up, speaking earnestly.

"Mr. Homes, I am the professor of spelling at the exclusive Briary School in Woodbine, New Jersey. Each year the staff draws straws, and the loser must accompany a group of students on the Grand Tour. This year I was the unfortunate one. I will not bore you with tales of my experiences to date, but will get directly to the point.

"This morning, Mr. Homes, I found the boys passing this note among them. Since in the past I have known to my sorrow that their boisterous spirits can become excessive at times, and since I could make neither head nor tail of the contents of the note, I hastened to make inquiries as to the best advice possible, and am now here."

He reached out and presented the paper to Homes. My friend took it and studied it intently as I came to stand behind him, reading it over his shoulder. As Mr. Cornbuckle had so truthfully stated, it seemed to be pure gibberish. It was scrawled in a childish copperplate and read as follows:

"*LSD party Savoy room 715. There will be lots of grass around as well, but NO heroin! We'll ship Papa Bear to the flicks.*"

There was no signature to this odd bit of nonsense. Mr. Silas Cornbuckle looked at Homes anxiously.

"I do pray, Mr. Homes," said he, "that you will be able to decipher this note and prove it merely to be the basis for some boyish prank and not, as I fear, something more serious."

Homes frowned at the small bit of paper in a manner which I knew indicated he had seen something in the weird phrases which had escaped both Mr. Cornbuckle and myself. When at last he raised his head his face was expressionless, but there was a fierce light hidden in his eye.

"I would hesitate to make judgment at first reading," said he, "but I fear you were quite right in seeking help in this matter. I seriously doubt if one might call this a boyish prank! May I ask a few questions?"

"Of course!"

"These boys—they were not chosen for this trip on the basis of scholastic merit, I gather?"

"I do not know how you do it, Mr. Homes!" Silas Cornbuckle exclaimed. "But the fact is they are far from our best students. However, since their parents were the only ones who could afford the voyage, they were chosen."

"Still," Homes said, his voice deceptively soft, "even though they are not particularly studious, and even though they tend towards pranks, at times they do show gentlemanly traits, do they not?"

"It is true."

"And to finish my questioning, the next stop on your Grand Tour, I imagine, would be France?"

"Amazing!" Cornbuckle murmured, his eyes wide. "But, yes. It is. We leave with the morning tide."

Homes paid no attention to the adulation in the man's eyes but nodded at him a bit abruptly.

"I suggest you remain in your quarters all day, for I hope to have an answer for you before the day is out. If you will leave your address with our page, I shall devote my entire efforts to a rapid solution of the problem!"

Once our visitor had left, Homes sprang to his feet, striding up and down the room in his old manner, his hands clasped behind his back, the note waving there from his long fingers. At last he fell into a chair, staring at the words fiercely, wriggling about in his chair in a manner I knew meant Mrs. Essex had put too much starch in his underwear.

"Homes," I asked, "can it be a code?"

"No, no!" said he, shaking his head impatiently. "It is far more intricate than that! It is quite obvious that the plan to kidnap the Chancellor is well advanced. The only problem is how to foil the dastardly plot!"

"Homes!" I exclaimed reproachfully. "Surely after all these years of absence you have not returned merely to pull my leg!"

He considered me for several moments coldly, and then answered my question with one of his own, an irritating habit he knew infuriated me.

"Have you nothing to do, Watney? Visit Albert Hall, or the British Museum? Enjoy the pleasant scenery of Putney? Or even see a patient?"

The years had not lessened my ability to read meaning into the slightest nuance in my friend's tone. I came instantly to my feet.

"As a matter of fact," I said coolly, "I have a cepillectomy scheduled, and should have been there before now."

But Homes had already forgotten my presence, and as I left the room he was reaching for a Vulgarian and a vesta, the paper still clutched fiercely in his fingers.

When I returned some two hours later, brushing hair from my lapel, it was to find the room full of smoke and Homes smiling quite genially at me from his chair. I recognized that he had discovered the solution to the problem.

"You must forgive me, Watney," he said, waving languidly towards the sideboard and the libation he had prepared there. "But by now you should be familiar with my humours, and time was of the essence. After all, the ides of July are almost upon us, and it would not do to allow this crime to be perpetrated without raising a finger!"

I poured myself a drink and turned to face him.

"Come, Homes," I said. "You cannot possibly mean you read some intelligent meaning into those few confused scrawls! After all, I saw the note as well as you, and I swear there was nothing there that lent itself to understanding!"

Homes shook his head in disappointment.

"Really, Watney! There was everything there. The meaning was quite clear. These young lads fully intend to kidnap one of Britain's leading statesmen and hold him, obviously for ransom, in the countryside of France, confident in their ignorance that they can fool the French police. The fact that they planned this wicked deed without involving young ladies is, of course, to their credit, but it still does not mitigate the seriousness of their intent."

I stared at Homes. He read the meaning in my frown and smiled.

"No, Watney," said he with a chuckle. "I am not mad, nor am I pulling your leg." His face straightened into seriousness as he reached over, taking up the note. "I have sent our page for Mr. Silas Cornbuckle, and until he arrives there should be ample time to explain this business to you."

He leaned over, placing the note on a table where we both might peruse it at the same time.

"It was really quite simple, Watney," he began. "Let us consider this note. It reads: '*LSD party Savoy room 715. There will be lots of grass around as well, but NO heroin! We'll ship Papa Bear to the flicks.*' As I had previously deduced from reading this, the boy writing these words was obviously a poor student. While I was too polite to mention the fact to Mr. Cornbuckle, since he is their professor, the spelling is atrocious."

His thin finger came out, pointing.

"For example, take the word 'Savvy,' a common colonial slang expression. And the word 'room' used as the abbreviation of the word Roman. Or 'flicks,' which is never spelled with a 'k.' Not to mention omitting the final 'e' from the word 'heroin.'" He shook his head. "Shocking!"

"But, Homes," I exclaimed a bit plaintively, "I still do not understand!"

Homes shook his head sadly at my ignorance.

"Really, Watney!" he said, and sighed. "Ah, well, let us start at the beginning, then. 'LSD' is obviously 'Pounds, Shillings, Pence.' Therefore the 'LSD party' can be nobody but the Chancellor of the Exchequer. The 'room 715'—or, more properly spelled, 'Rom. 715'—refers to the Roman calendar for the seventh month, the fifteenth day, or—as you may know—tomorrow's date. This afternoon I verified, as I had suspected, that the Chancellor travels tonight by the Channel steamer for a conference in Paris."

"But what made you suspect France in the first place?" I asked, amazed as always at the constant proof of Homes's brilliance.

"Note the last line, Watney." Homes pointed to the paper. "'We'll ship Papa Bear to the flicks.' In the colonies they have a mascot known as Smokey; it can only be he to whom 'Papa Bear' can refer. When we consider that the French police are known as 'flics,' the entire message becomes clear."

He leaned back, considering me gravely. "On the basis of our analysis, let us now re-read the note. It says: The Chancellor of the Exchequer, understand? Tomorrow July 15th. (We'll hide him) in the countryside—the reference to grass, of course. No girls will be allowed to participate. We'll put down a smoke-screen for the French police."

I brought my dazed eyes up from the slip of paper.

"Marvellous, Homes," I breathed worshipfully. Then I saw a problem. "But, Homes!" I cried. "At this late hour, how can this foul scheme be scotched?"

"Easily—" he began, and then paused as the sound of footsteps on our stairs could be heard. A moment later Mr. Silas Cornbuckle burst into our quarters.

"Mr. Homes!" he cried. "I pray you have the answer! What did the message intend to convey?"

"I cannot reveal that," Homes replied quietly. "It could do nothing but damage the already tenuous ties between the American colony and the mother country. However, I can tell you how to avoid any unpleasant consequences from your charges' intended deed."

"Of course, Mr. Homes," said Silas Cornbuckle. "What can I do?"

"You must cancel France from your tour," Homes said. "There is no other solution."

Mr. Silas Cornbuckle stared at my friend. "But the boys—"

"—will doubtless be disappointed," Homes said, concluding the other's sentence. "I am sure," he added dryly, and shrugged. "Well, one cannot have everything. However, if you wish a suggestion, you might consider giving the lads a special treat as compensation."

Mr. Cornbuckle grasped the recommendation eagerly. "Such as?"

"Well," Homes said, considering the matter, "I imagine an evening at one of our local hostelries might help them get over their disappointment. In fact," he added, "it might even be better if you left them to their own devices, thus indicating your faith in their ability to entertain themselves properly." He smiled at our guest genially. "To while away the hours while the lads are occupied, you might go to the cinema. I have never seen the Nickelodeon, but I understand it interests many."

"It shall be as you say," Mr. Cornbuckle said, and turned to the door. He paused and bowed. "Nor can I thank you enough, Mr. Homes."

"A pleasure," Homes said, and returned the bow, as we watched Homes's first client stumble through the doorway, overcome with gratitude.

The following morning I came into the dining-room to find Homes already before me, replacing the remnants of curry with stuffed chutneys, his own favourite. As he served himself and took his place at the table, I seated myself and opened the morning journal. Homes drew his napkin into his lap, speared his first chutney, and looked at me questioningly.

"Do you find anything in the paper to interest an up-coming, ambitious, and newly investitured private investigator this morning?" he inquired in a tone that was only half-joking.

"I am not sure, Homes," I said slowly, reading further into the article which had caught my attention. "It seems there was a narcotics raid at a hotel last night, but it appears the miscreants all managed to escape. The police are seeking whatever help they can obtain."

Homes sat erect.

"As you know, Watney," said he, "at one time I myself was the victim of the foul habit. There is no traffic I consider more reprehensible! A telegram to the authorities, offering my services, if you would!" He leaned back.

"Although," he added thoughtfully, "once the criminals hear that Schlock Homes is on the case, I should be gravely dubious if they do not flee the country by the first packet."

The Adventure of
The Hansom Ransom

IN considering the many adventures I have been fortunate enough to share with my good friend Mr. Schlock Homes, I am forced to the amazing conclusion that his activities following his return from retirement on the Upson Downs put any of his previous efforts to shame. The man seemed determined to make up for the years lost in bee-farming; his energies were prodigious. Nor had he lost any of his remarkable abilities; if anything, the results of his analysis and deductions were more startling than ever.

For example, in going over my notes for the balance of the year '72, I find reference to cases which not only furthered the incredible legend of Homes, but which also did much to strengthen the ties between our beloved Britain and many of our former colonies. In Tel Aviv, to mention one instance, Homes was able to capture the culprit who fed doped oats to the favourite in the tough Kosher Stakes, a horse noted for its ability on heavy and wet tracks. Readers of these memoirs may recall the affair as *The Adventure of the Jewish Mudder and Fodder*.

But not all of Homes's work took him abroad; in August of that year he was of singular service to the noted author, Mr. Stanley Yelling, who was plagiarized in his famous biography, *The Tome of the Unknown Soldier*. Still more interesting to me, however, was a case which Homes resolved while his mind was on other problems, an affair I find delineated in my journal as *The Adventure of the Hansom Ransom*.

I had finished my rounds that warm September afternoon and had returned to our quarters at No. 221B Bagel Street to find Homes hunched over his study table, the room full of smoke from the pipe upon which he was puffing furiously, and the floor littered with crumpled scraps of paper from his many calculations. As I entered the room, he turned to me a face pale with bafflement.

"Homes!" I cried, frightened at his wan complexion. I instantly put my bag aside and hurried to the sideboard, pouring a generous tot of brandy. "What is the matter?"

He flourished a sheet of note-paper in my face as I hastily swallowed my drink.

"As ingenious a code as ever I have faced!" said he, grimacing. "It was delivered several hours ago, but as yet I have been unable to decipher it."

I came to stand behind him and read the telegram over his shoulder. As Homes had so accurately stated, it was obviously in code and presented itself as unintellibible jargon. It read as follows:

"*Gotter see yer raht away. Hi'll stop rahnd yer flat fourish, abaht. 'Arry 'Iggins.*"

"Note the beastly cleverness of the writer," Homes said half-angrily, "intermixing real words with this other nonsense! The word 'see' and the word 'away,' the word 'stop' and the word 'flat.' I've tried 'see away stop flat,' 'see stop flat away,' 'away see flat stop,' 'flat stop see away.' " He paused as our doorbell suddenly rang. "But I'm afraid this puzzle must wait, for unless I am mistaken, we are about to have a visitor."

He hastily straightened his study table as our page boy ushered in a person who was pitiful in appearance. He cringed as he came to a shuffling stop before us, his head bent, his eyes cast down to his cracked shoes, his fingers nervously twisting a worn cap. He stood first on one foot and then on the other as if afraid to raise his head, until Homes took pity on the poor fellow.

"Here," he said in a kindly tone, "take that basket chair, and tell us your story. Other than the fact that by profession you are a hostler, I know nothing of your problem."

The man's face gaped in astonishment as he sank into the chair. Even I, familiar as I am with Homes's unusual powers, could not see the slightest basis for his deduction. Homes smiled at our confusion.

"It is really quite simple, Watney," said he, tenting his fingers. "The straight flat crease across the front of the trousers clearly indicates many hours of constant leaning over the edge of something approximately thirty inches from the floor. Since this is the height of a standard feeding bin, we can assume our visitor has something to do with stables. The chalk dust in the crease between the left thumb and forefinger looks suspiciously like Gentian Green, used as a germicide for cleansing saddles. Now, add to this the fact that even as our guest sits there, he unconsciously crooks the fingers of his left hand into the best position for holding reins, and there can be no doubt that for years he served as a hostler."

Our visitor gaped, his admiration for Homes's analysis visible on his face. Had he known Schlock Homes as long and as well as I have, he would not have been so surprised. " 'Ow yer does it I can't imagine, Guv'nor," he said, shaking his head, "but yer dead raht. Me name is 'Arry 'Iggins and I've been an 'ustler all me life, mostly down at the Spider and Fly Billiards Parlour. I been so upset by the loss of me boss's 'ansom I guess I forgot to wash me 'ands."

He hastily wiped the offending chalk from his fingers and sat more erect.

"What 'appened," said he, now visibly more at ease, "is some bloke I never seen afore in me life comes over to where I'm waitin' in front of me boss's 'ouse, see, an' me sittin' up atop the 'ansom like always, and tells me there's a sucker over at the Spider and Fly wiv more brass than skill, lookin' for a game. Well, I couldn't pass that up, could I? Course not, 'specially when the boss don't usually come down till eleven, so I asks the chap would 'e be so kind as to look arter me 'orse and buggy till I gets back, and off I goes to the Spider and Fly, but when I gets there, there's ain't no more mark than straight cues! So I 'urries back to me 'ansom an' me rig is gorn!"

He shook his head lugubriously.

"Can't trust a blinkin' soul these days," he said sadly. "Went rahnd t' the coppers and they wasn't no more 'elp than a bustid leg! And I'm scared t' tell me boss. 'E wasn't too 'appy wiv me before, and this ain't goin' t' make 'im love me no 'arder!"

Homes nodded sympathetically.

"Well," he said, smiling to make our guest comfortable, "consider me at your service. Tell me, was there anything special about this particular hansom that made it more worthy of stealing than any other? Plastic harness-breeching straps, perhaps? Imported check-reins? Gold-embossed hub-caps?"

"Naw!" said our guest disdainfully. "Can't imagine anyone floggin' that 'ansom wiv so many new ones practically askin' to be stole. This was mostly used for shoppin', this 'ansom was, only the big four-in-'and is in the shop wiv a sprung yoke, so me boss asks me to drive 'im abaht in this one. Matter of fact, I figures at first the chap just got tired of waitin' and went orf and me 'orse followed 'im, me 'orse bein' a friendly-type beast."

"A possibility," Homes conceded. "And may I ask who your employer might be?"

"Well," said the little man, " 'e might be the Queen o' the May, but 'e ain't. I 'eard that one on the telly," he added in hasty apology. "Actually, 'e's some big-wheel foreigner from be'ind the Iron Curtain. 'Eads up their Embassy 'ere in Lunnon. But we ain't supposed to mention no names."

"I see." Homes nodded. "And the man you left in charge of your hansom?"

"Never seen the bloke before," said our guest, "but 'e was a big one, 'e was! Seven foot tall at least, twenty stone of weight if an ounce, wiv a bad limp in one leg an' a big brush of orange 'air."

Homes shot erect in his chair, his nostrils flaring.

" 'Omes!" I cried. "I mean, Homes! What is it?"

"Later!" he said fiercely, and turned his attention back to our visitor. "Is there any other information you can furnish which might be of help?"

"That's abaht the lot, Guv'nor," the little man said, sad to be of such little use in his own behalf. He sounded wistful. "I don't suppose yer would consider takin' on a little no-account case like this, would yer, sir?"

"I would not miss it for the world!" Homes replied fervently, and came to his feet. "Well, since I imagine you can be reached at this Spider and Fly

Billiards Parlour at any time, it is needless for you to leave an address. Be assured I shall get right to it and advise you of the outcome of my investigation as soon as possible."

He waved aside the small man's profuse attempts to thank him, and was already pacing the floor, his brow furrowed in thought and his hands locked behind his back, even before our page had shown our guest to the street.

"Really, Homes," I said in mild surprise. "I have seldom seen you so wrought. And merely over a hansom whose horse has undoubtedly wandered away!"

"Are you deaf?" he inquired, swinging upon me suddenly. "Sometimes I fear for you, Watney! Did you not hear the description of the man with whom our small friend left his hansom? Think, Watney, think! Does it not strike a familiar chord?"

I considered the little man's description carefully: seven feet tall, twenty stone of weight, a bad limp in one leg, and a shock of orange hair. I was about to deny any recognition when I saw a faint chance. "You are thinking of Professor Marty, Homes?" I asked. "The one they call—with reason—The Butcher?"

"We cannot overlook the possibility, Watney!"

"True, Homes," I conceded, thinking about it. "Certainly Professor Marty never does anything on a small scale. Should he now be involved in a scheme to steal all means of transport, within a very short time he could bring all London to its feet!"

"I doubt that is his motive," said Homes, shaking his head. "With the shortage of parking space, such an effort would be doomed to failure. Where in all London would he find room for more than two or three?" He paced the floor in thought, seeking an answer. Suddenly his head came up. "Unless—"

"Yes, Homes?" I asked eagerly.

"Our client said the hansom was an old one, did he not?"

"He did."

"I believe I have it!" Homes exclaimed and fell into a chair, beginning to scribble on pieces of paper with pen and ink.

"Homes," I said reproachfully, "with a problem involving the Professor upon us, you have gone back to the puzzle of the note delivered this morning!"

"No, no," said he, continuing to scribble. "I should like to, for it bothers me to leave it unsolved, but what I am writing is for the Professor. If you would be so kind as to have our page round up the Bagel Street Regulars, I am sure we will be in position to scotch this nefarious scheme of the Professor's in a very short time!"

To this end I hastened to summon our page and give him proper instructions, while Homes—reminded by me, I am afraid—returned to the puzzle of the morning message, but before he could get much beyond "stop see flat away" and "stop see away flat," the Bagel Street Regulars came swarming up the stairs, under the leadership of a ragged small street Arab known, in the current fashion of name and initial, as Hasser I. Homes put aside the cryptic message, a bit reluctantly, I thought, and gave them their orders.

"A tall man, at least seven feet in height," said he sternly, while they hung on every word. "He weighs about twenty stone. He limps badly and has bright orange hair. I have identical notes for each of you; the one who locates him will give it to him. I suggest you split up, each taking a different billiard parlour, since these seem to be his usual base of operation. And tuppence-ha'penny extra for the brave lad who first locates him!"

I turned to him as the lads fled eagerly down the steps, each clutching his note tightly. "Your note to the Professor?" I asked, mystified.

"Merely an invitation to him for a chat," he said enigmatically, and returned at once to the crumpled sheet of paper upon his study table. And so passed the following hour, silent except for his occasional mutter, *sotto voce*, "'Flat see away stop'? 'Flat stop away see'? It is impossible! 'Away flat stop see'? 'See spot—I mean stop—' But here is one of our Regulars back already, I do believe."

It was Hasser I, and he catapulted into the room, panting.

"I have located him, Mr. Homes!" he said proudly, fighting for breath. "He is involved in a snooker game at a billiard parlour in Limehouse called The Quicksand Club."

"You gave him my note?" Homes demanded fiercely.

I did, indeed, sir. He was in the middle of a long run and said he would be along as soon as he finished."

"Good," Homes said, and reached for his purse. "Here is a shilling for each lad involved in the hunt, as well as the extra bonus I promised you. Well done, Hasser I!" Homes fell back into his chair as the lad went clattering down the steps. "Well, Watney," he continued, as the front door slammed, "I hope this affair with the Professor can soon be settled, for the matter of this infernal coded message is beginning to prey upon my mind."

"How do you plan on handling the Professor, Homes?" I asked curiously.

"Quite simply," he said, but before he could continue there was a loud sound in the passage and the door to our quarters burst open. Professor Marty brusquely brushed aside our page and came to stand above Homes, glaring down.

"Homes," he said gratingly, "what is the nonsense contained in this note?" He pulled a slip of paper from his pocket, dug about in his weskit for his spectacles, and read aloud in a sneering tone. "'Professor Marty, you will kindly forget about holding the foreign hansom for ransom and return it at once! Signed, Schlock Homes.'"

Homes nodded to him politely, but his face was expressionless and his voice cold.

"If you will take the large chair, Professor, I shall be pleased to explain." He waited until the Professor had sunk into the chair before continuing. "In the first place, there could never have been the slightest doubt as to why you stole that trap yesterday—"

"I needed something to run around in—"

Homes disregarded him. "Considering the age and lack of special features, the carriage undoubtedly falls into the category of an antique, and therefore must be quite valuable. As a valuable antique, it must therefore be worthy of a substantial ransom."

"I never thought of that," Professor Marty mumbled, shaking his head.

"However," Homes continued sternly, paying no attention to the man's mumbling, "it makes no difference as to its value. Since I am onto your scheme, there is nothing for you to do now but admit failure and return the carriage to its rightful owner."

Professor Marty started up, his face red. His voice was a growl.

"And what makes you think I'll do a fool thing like that?"

"Because, if you do not, I shall make London too hot to hold you," Homes returned, his eyes narrowed. He continued to hold the Professor in his steady gaze. "In addition to returning the hansom, you will write a note of apology to the owner. You will say you are sorry you took the hansom, and in compensation for the time you used it, you will send him some small present."

"You're mad!"

"You will send him some small present," Homes repeated firmly. "Let me see . . . Tomorrow being Thursday, the traditional day for English servants to enjoy their liberty, a thoughtful gesture would be some affair to save the mistress of the house the task of cooking their evening dinner. The Bow Street Banquet, for example, or comps to McDonalds—"

"Now you just wait a minute!" Professor Marty began in a roar, and then suddenly calmed down. He leaned forward in his chair, his tiny piggish eyes intent upon Homes's stern visage. "You say return the trap. You then suggest that tomorrow night—the servants' night out—I send these people tickets which will also take them from the home—to a banquet, that is, of course. Is that your suggestion?"

"It is not a suggestion," Homes said coldly. "It is a demand."

Professor Marty came to his feet with an effort.

"Homes," he said with deep feeling, "you are a find! I mean a fiend!" He shrugged hopelessly. "I have no choice. It shall be as you say." He sighed and limped from the room, a broken man.

"You have done it again, Homes!" I exclaimed in admiration, but my friend merely shrugged off the compliment and returned to his study table, glowering down at the sheet of note-paper which seemed intent upon perplexing him as no other problem had since I had known him.

I came to breakfast the following morning to find Homes dozing fitfully in his chair, the lamp still burning and the floor covered with the refuse of his calculations. Fearing for his well-being should he continue to concentrate on this one problem, I hastened to open the morning journal in search of some more interested divertissement, just as he stirred and sat up, stretching. I considered him anxiously.

"No luck, Homes?"

"None," he said glumly. "It is fiendish! And yet I am sure the answer is in those simple four words: 'see,' 'away,' 'stop,' and 'flat.' I have even tried the first letters in all combinations; they form 'sasf,' 'fass,' 'fsas,' 'assf,' 'ssaf'—"

"Come, Homes," I said soothingly, "let me have Mrs. Essex fix you a nice plate of creamed chutneys. You know how they always calm you."

He considered me balefully. "Do not commiserate with me, Watney! Nor treat me as an invalid!"

"Never, Homes," I said as I hurriedly turned the pages of the newspaper. Suddenly I sat erect, certain I had the solution to my friend's problem.

"Homes," I exclaimed, "here is a case which I am sure will interest you. Last evening the dwelling of Stannous Flouride, the Polish Ambassador, was burgled! It seems all the servants were out, and the Ambassador and his wife had accepted an invitation to dine at some banquet or other—"

"No, no, Watney," said he wearily. I should enjoy resolving the problem, since I feel strongly about treatment afforded guests of our Government, but I cannot give up so easily on this puzzle."

He returned to the crumpled paper before him, and then suddenly all trace of sleeplessness fled from his countenance.

"Watney!" he cried, excitement flushing his face. "I am a fool! The answer is simplicity itself!" He swung about, one finger still pointing to the sheet of paper on his study table. "My error was in discounting the writer's ability to misspell!"

"Homes," I exclaimed, "what do you mean?"

"I mean it was not the *word* 'see'—it is the *letter* 'C'! The message now becomes crystal-clear!" His thin finger pointed. "*C stop away flat.* It can only refer to the C-stop of the giant organ at Albert Hall, since it is the only organ I am familiar with! Fortunately, I am still in possession of the tuning fork I won at a bean-eating contest in my second year at public school. A note to the organist at the Hall, if you please, Watney, offering my services."

The Adventure of
The Great Train Robbery

IT was rare, indeed, for my good friend Mr. Schlock Homes and myself to disagree as to the merits of his ability in resolving a case, yet such a situation arose in regard to an affair which I find reference to in my notebook as *The Adventure of the Great Train Robbery*. In my estimation, the case allowed Homes as great a use of his exceptional powers as any I can recall, but the fact was that Homes himself was far from satisfied with his performance in the matter. I can but leave it to the reader to judge for himself.

It was upon a Wednesday, February 31st, that we first heard of Sir Lionel Train. Homes had been exceptionally busy those early months of '68, first with the problem of the championship kittens stolen just hours prior to an international show, a case I find referred to as *The Adventure of the Purloined Litter,* following which my friend went on to resolve the curious puzzle of a punch-drunk prize-fighter, a case I later chronicled as *The Adventure of the Rapped Expression*. It was not, therefore, until the final day of February that the matter of Sir Lionel came to our attention.

This particular Wednesday the weather had turned quite poor, with a night of fierce snow followed by dismal skies and a sharp drop in temperature. Homes, therefore, had given the day over to relaxation and was bent over his laboratory bench, with me in sharp attendance, studying some putty-like material called "Plastique" he had received without comment just that morning from his old friend M'sieu C. Septembre Duping in Paris. We had already noted its colour and odour, as well as its rubber-like consistency, and Homes was about to strike it with a hammer to test the resilience of the strange material when there came a sudden disturbance on the stairway, and a moment later Homes's brother Criscroft had burst in upon our scientific experiments.

It was extremely odd for Criscroft to appear at our quarters at 221B Bagel Street without prior notice, and even more unusual to see that normally most controlled of gentlemen gasping for breath. His clothing was awry, his gaiters unbuckled, and there was an air of urgency about him which communicated itself at once to Homes's razor-sharp instincts. Homes immediately replaced the putty-like substance in its wrapping, returned the hammer to its proper place in the tool rack, washed and dried his hands carefully, and, wasting no time, faced his brother.

"Well, Criscroft," said he, lighting a Vulgarian, "this is indeed a pleasure! But you appear disturbed—or have I misinterpreted the signs?"

Criscroft fell into a chair, still fighting for his composure.

"As usual you are correct, Schlock!" he exclaimed. "We may well be in deep trouble, indeed! I fear some grave misfortune may have befallen Sir Lionel Train."

Homes nodded in instant understanding. "Who?" he inquired.

"Sir Lionel Train, head of Q6–JB45–VX–2DD–T3, the most secret of our secret services. Other than the Yard and Special Services, no one has ever heard of the man."

"Ah! *That* Sir Lionel Train!" Homes said, and nodded. "Pray favour us with the details."

"Very well," Criscroft said. He sat a bit more erect, obviously relieved to have his brother's aid with the dire problem. "Well, then, the facts are these! Sir Lionel has his country estate at Much-Binding-in-the-Groyne, a typical English village near Tydin, Notts, where he spends his mid-weeks with his famous diamond collection. In any event, early this morning a neighbour of his, out to check the weather, happened to notice Sir Lionel struggling in hand-to-hand combat with an assailant in his bedroom. Not wishing to be hasty, this neighbour returned to his house and took up a pair of binoculars, with which he verified the sight he had seen. Satisfied he had not been incorrect—for through the binoculars he could see this unrecognizable assailant's hands around Sir Lionel's neck—he immediately sent his butler off to Scotland Yard with the information."

"He did not interfere directly?"

"Of course not. They had never been introduced."

"I understand. But he continued to watch?"

"He had come out without his slippers. No, once his butler had been sent off, this neighbour repaired to his basement, where he is building a bottle-in-a-ship."

"I see. And Scotland Yard—?"

"Aware of Sir Lionel's true status, the Yard instantly communicated with the Home Office, who in turn sent a messenger to advise me. When my man could not locate a cab, I hastily dressed and ran all the way. Schlock, you must go to Much-Binding-in-the-Groyne immediately and do everything in your power to save Sir Lionel!"

Homes considered his brother steadily behind tented fingers.

"At what hour did this neighbour note Sir Lionel struggling?"

"A bit before seven this morning."

"It is just after noontime. It is possible, of course, that I may arrive too late. However, we can but try. Tell me, where was Lady Train during all this?"

"Lady Train is visiting relatives."

"Sir Lionel has no staff?"

"Just a new maid he employed only yesterday, right after Lady Train left. Sir Lionel has an aversion to butlers."

"I see. But regarding your fears, surely Sir Lionel does not keep state secrets in his country home?"

Criscroft shook his head decisively.

"Sir Lionel commits nothing to paper. Still, under the duress of torture, who knows what secrets he might divulge?" Criscroft came to his feet. "It is in your hands, Schlock," he said. With an abrupt nod in our direction he stepped on a gaiter buckle and stumbled heavily down the stairs.

"Ah, well, Watney," said Homes with a sigh, "a pity our afternoon is to be compromised. They are playing the Hayden Go Seek concerto at Albert Hall and I had hoped to attend. However, duty before pleasure. You might bring along your medical bag, as it seems it might be useful. And you might also bring along Duping's gift. Studying it might help us while away an hour or so on the train."

The Nottingham Express dropped us off in Tydin, and a rented trap was easily arranged with the station-master. He also furnished us with directions to Sir Lionel's estate, and moments later we were driving smartly along the newly cleared road to Much-Binding-in-the-Groyne.

Here in Nottinghamshire the sun had wormed its way through the heavy overcast, a blanket of glistening snow stretched across the endless fields, and ice glittered on wires that hung between each house and a line of poles inexplicably planted in a row along the highway. Had our mission not been of such serious intent, we might well have enjoyed the brisk air and lovely scenery.

Sir Lionel's home lay around a curve beyond the quaint village. We passed the village green, crossed a small burn lightly crusted with ice, and slowed down as we approached the house. I was about to direct our trap down the carriage-way when Homes suddenly placed a hand upon my arm. I pulled our panting horse to a stop and looked at my friend inquiringly.

"From here on it would be best if we proceeded by foot," said he, his eyes sparkling with the excitement of the chase. "Note the unbroken expanse of snow. It would not do to disturb it without first seeing if it can answer any of our questions."

"True," I admitted, and looked about for a weight to throw down, but it seems our station-master had overlooked putting one into the carriage. Homes noted my search and shook his head.

"Block the wheels with Duping's package," said he impatiently. "Time may be of the essence."

Ashamed at not having thought of the simple solution myself, I dropped from the trap, propped the wheel against the horse's wandering, and turned to Homes, medical bag in hand. But Homes's attention was already directed towards the smooth snow that stretched on all sides of the manor house. A frown appeared on my friend's lean face, to be replaced almost at once by a look of determination.

"Come!" said he, and started off on a large circuit of the grounds with me close upon his heels. The snow lay unblemished in all directions. We passed the stables at the rear of the coach-house to one side, and at last came about our huge circle to our starting point. Suddenly my companion froze in his tracks.

"Homes!" I cried in alarm, since the temperature was not that low. "What is it?"

"Later," said he fiercely, and dropped to one knee to study intently two pairs of footprints beside our trap which I swear had not been there upon our arrival. I waited in silence as my companion checked them thoroughly, and then watched as he slowly rose to his feet with a frown, brushing the snow from his trousers.

"Two men," said he slowly. "One tall and thin, and from the angle of his prints, of rather intense nature. The other is short and walks with a slight limp. I should say without a doubt that the shorter of the two is a medical man by profession, and a bit absent-minded in the bargain."

"Really, Homes!" I exclaimed reproachfully. "I can understand that you might arrive at the relative heights of the men by the lengths of their stride, but surely you are pulling my leg when you claim one of them to be a medical man—and an absent-minded one, at that!"

"At times I wonder at you, Watney," said Homes impatiently. "You have forgotten that today is Wednesday, the traditional day for doctors to leave their practice to their nurse and take to the open air. You have also failed to properly examine the tracks this man left; had you done so you would have noted that the shorter of the two is wearing golfing shoes. Since the snow is too deep for playing the game, one can only assume he put them on automatically before leaving the house, an action which not only clearly indicates his absent-mindedness, but also serves as further proof of his profession, since on Wednesdays doctors don them from force of habit."

"He might have been a dentist," I hazarded a bit sullenly, although in truth I did not doubt the accuracy of Homes's masterful analysis.

"No, Watney," said he. "Dentists, from constant standing, develop much larger feet. But we are wasting time. The two men undoubtedly passed as we were in the rear near the stables. However, since their spoor does not approach the house, it is evident they have gone off about their business and have nothing to do with the case. Come!"

He turned and moved off towards the house, breaking trail through the snow, while I followed as quickly as my shorter legs would permit. A moment later and Homes was stamping the loose snow from his boots on the porch, while examining the lock on the main door with narrowed eyes.

"Homes!" I exclaimed as a sudden thought struck me. "I should have also brought my revolver! Surely if there are no footprints in the snow, the assailant must still be within the house, for there is no other exit."

"You forget the overhead wires leading to those poles in the road," he said, reaching into his pocket for his set of picklocks. "They have obviously been

placed on each house to afford an auxiliary means of exit from the upper
stories in case of emergencies; otherwise what purpose would be served by the
spikes in the poles, forming a ladder? No, Watney, our assailant would have
no problem leaving the house without leaving footprints, especially if he were
small."

I nodded in admiration for Homes's analysis, and then followed my friend
into the silent house as the door quickly succumbed to the magic of his touch.
We made our way through the main hall and up the steps of the grand
stairway. At its head an open door leading to the library revealed a large safe
standing ajar. Homes shook his head pityingly.

"Had the miscreant known, as we do, that Sir Lionel commits nothing to
paper, he might have saved himself the trouble of struggling with that heavy
safe," said he. "But let us continue our search."

We moved from the library, making our way along the balcony that
fronted the floor below across an ornate railing. As we reached the corner, a
sudden gutteral sound brought us up short, and a moment later Homes was
dashing down a hallway in the direction of the strangled noises. I followed in
all haste, my medical bag banging against my thigh. Homes threw open a
door and paused abruptly.

"It is Sir Lionel himself!" he said, turning to me. "Pray God we are not too
late. It is in your hands now, Watney."

I hastened to the side of the bed and bent over the man. He lay on his
back, one arm dangling helplessly over the side of the large mussed bed. Sir
Lionel was wearing his pajama bottoms, but his chest was bare, and even as I
watched, it rose and fell, accompanied by his stentorian breathing.

"Homes," I said in a low voice, "the poor man has been badly treated,
indeed. Note the scratches on his shoulders; note the puckered red blotches
on his cheeks and lips; smell the sweet odour similar to Chanel Number Five,
doubtless one of the new perfumed anaesthetics."

"But he put up a brave struggle from the appearance of the bedclothes,"
Holmes commented.

"Which probably saved his life," said I, and reached down and shook the
man gently. "Sir Lionel!"

"Not right now, darling," he muttered, and opened his eyes sleepily. They
widened incredulously at sight of my face. "Eh, what? Who? What, what?
What? Who, what, what?" He turned and saw my companion. "Schlock
Homes! How much did my wife pay—"

"The poor chap is completely incoherent, Homes," said I, and plunged the
needle of my hypodermic into his bare arm. "The shock of sudden rescue
often does this to people."

Sir Lionel's head fell back onto the pillow. I pulled his arm up to fold it
across his chest and then paused.

"Homes!" I ejaculated.

"Yes?" said he.

"Look here," I said, and pointed to a tattoo that ran across the biceps and which had been revealed as I drew up his arm. "What do you make of this?"

Homes moved swiftly to my side and read the tattoo over my shoulder.

" 'Left 36, Right 21, Left twice to 15, Right 9.' " My friend straightened up, staring at the mysterious symbols with a bitter look in his eyes. "Criscroft stated that Sir Lionel never committed secrets to paper, but he said nothing of a tattoo!"

"But surely those numbers can have but little significance, Homes," I said, hoping to soothe him. "They are probably merely the result of a boyish prank from his University days."

"I doubt it is that simple," Homes replied heavily. "They are obviously references to the political left and right. Undoubtedly the numbers delineate the code name of our secret agents in certain countries of both persuasions." He shook his head. "Come, Watney. If Sir Lionel is settled for the moment, let us continue our search of the house for more clues."

I hastily tucked a cover to Sir Lionel's chin and followed Homes as he moved from the room. Our search was more thorough this time, starting in the cellars, including the kitchens, and returning to the upper stories. At the far end of the final corridor we came upon a narrow set of steps leading to the attic rooms, and Homes took them evenly, with me upon his heels.

At the top a small landing beneath the eaves revealed a door set between dormers and partially open. Homes peered cautiously around the jamb and then stepped swiftly back, drawing me into the shadows. From my new vantage point I could see into the room; a young lady was bending over a small attaché-case, tucking a chamois bag into its depths. Homes gripped my arm painfully.

"Do you see that young lady?" he demanded in a taut whisper. "That, Watney, is none other than Miss Irene Addled, international jewel thief, and the only woman who ever bested me! And yet, see to what sad end she has come. Despite the proceeds of years of crime, see where she has ended—a maid of all work in a small country manor house! There is a lesson here for all of us, I am sure, but unfortunately, there is no time to explore it. Come!"

He pushed his way into the small room. The young lady looked up from closing her small case and then shrank back against the wall, aghast at sight of my companion.

"Mr. Schlock Homes!" she cried in terror. "What are you doing here?"

"It is all right, Miss Addled," Homes said gallantly. "I am not here in respect to you, nor am I one to bear a grudge, especially against one upon whom evil days have so obviously fallen. Still, I fear I have some bad news for you. Your master has been viciously attacked. However, thanks to Dr. Watney, he is resting comfortably. I suggest you go down and sit by his bedside. It will comfort him to see a friendly face upon awakening."

"And then may I leave?"

"As soon as the ambulance arrives. Dr. Watney and I shall go for one at once. I realize this means the end of your new-found employment, but if you stop by our quarters I shall do my best to see if I can arrange suitable employment in some other ménage."

"Some day, somehow, I shall find some means of thanking you!" she cried, and flung her arms about his neck, still holding her attaché-case. Homes reeled back, blushing, while Miss Addled hurried down the steps. Homes and I followed and watched as the thankful young lady moved towards the master bedroom with a remarkable sense of direction considering her few hours in the house. With the matter settled, Homes and I descended the main staircase and walked out onto the porch. Suddenly Homes stopped so abruptly that I ran into him from behind.

"Homes!" I said in a muffled voice. "What is it?"

"I am a fool!" he cried.

"But why?" I insisted.

His thin finger pointed dramatically. "We have been followed!"

I came from behind him and stared. It was true! The same two sets of footprints that had so mysteriously appeared beside our trap were now facing us again, leading directly to the house. There was no mistaking the long stride of the taller man, nor the spike-marks of the shorter.

"I am an idiot!" Homes cried. "I should have realized the only reason Sir Lionel was left alive was precisely because he had *not* revealed the secret of that tattoo, despite the terrible torture. Obviously, the smaller man left the house by means of the overhead wires for the purpose of bringing an accomplice, a larger person to exert greater pressure on Sir Lionel. And, locating the accomplice, the two returned to the house."

"But where are they now, Homes?" I cried.

"Obviously, they heard our sounds of search and have gone away. But these footprints are still quite fresh, Watney! They cannot have gotten very far. Come! After them!"

With a bound from the porch we dashed through the snow to our trap and scrambled inside, not even wasting time to unblock the wheels. I cracked the whip close beside our horse's ear, and with a convulsive leap he sprang forward. My last conscious memory as we rose in the air under the force of an explosion was of Homes's voice tinged with a bitterness I had seldom heard before.

"I am a *double* fool!" he cried. "Allowing them to booby-trap us!"

It was several weeks before we were released from St. Barts and allowed to return to the ministrations of Mrs. Essex. Sir Lionel Train, obviously unnerved by the events, had gone off to the Continent on a protracted holiday with a young nurse, and we had had no word from poor Miss Addled. But despite what I consider one of Homes's most brilliant successes, he continued to consider it a failure and to brood heavily upon it.

"Look, Homes," I said at breakfast the first day we were able to be up and about, "after all, Sir Lionel suffered no permanent harm, and that was your major assignment. Nor was the secret of the code numbers ever revealed, since the explosion apparently frightened the villains away. And as for poor Miss Addled, I am sure your paths will cross again one day. So how can you possibly consider this case a failure?"

"You do not understand, Watney," said he bitterly, reaching for a curried curry. "It is the fact that we had those nefarious criminals within our grasp and allowed them to escape! And not only to escape, but to hamper our pursuit by planting an explosive practically under our noses. How does one live down an insult of such dimensions? How, in addition, does one advise an old friend like M'sieu C. Septembre Duping that, due to my idiocy, his gift to me was destroyed? No, Watney, I shall not rest until I lay those two rascals by the heels!"

There being no arguing with Homes when he was in this mood, I turned to the morning *Times,* hoping to discover some interesting case which might take my friend's mind from his obsession. Suddenly, a new feature, imported from the American colonies, struck my eye.

"Homes!" I cried. "I do believe you will find this of interest."

He reached over and removed the journal from my hand. I watched his eyes narrow as he noted the design I had been studying. Suddenly he struck his fist upon the table, causing the chived chives to jump.

"There can be no doubt, Watney. It is they!" said he with deep satisfaction. "Note the silk topper worn by the shorter of the two—surely the sign of Harley Street affluence. And note the rather stupid expression on the face of his taller accomplice, for had he not been stupid he would never have crossed swords with Schlock Homes. A pity we should find them by pure chance, but better this way than not at all." He reached for his magnifying-glass. "What are their names again?"

I came to read over his shoulder. "Mutt and Jeff," I replied.

"Precisely! A letter to the editor of *The Times* at once, Watney, if you will!"

The Adventure of
Black, Peter

IT is some years since the events I am about to speak of occurred, mainly owing to our housekeeper Mrs. Essex's use of one of my journals as a doorstop; but it is still with admiration, after all this time, that I am able to report of the uncanny ability of my good friend Mr. Schlock Homes in

solving a problem that had baffled the best brains of Scotland Yard. Nor did
the case come at a bad time, for Homes was at a loose end, having just
resolved the singular affair of the circus performer who swallowed electric-
light bulbs for a living, a case my readers will recall as *The Adventure of the
Illustrious Client,* and was more than ready for a new challenge.

It was a stormy Wednesday morning in early March, with sheets of icy
rain beating our window panes, and the coal-fire in our quarters at 221B Bagel
Street a welcome buffer against the chill of the elements. Homes was curled
up in his easy chair, violin in hand, toying with the slow movement of
Copeland's Cymbal Concerto, while I was deep in research, studying a
treatise on digital serum injection, *Vaccinations on a Thumb,* by Hayden,
when there came a loud pounding on our street door, and a moment later our
page was announcing a visitor. Homes and I exchanged curious glances, since
neither of us was expecting company, but I dutifully dog-eared my page while
Homes laid aside his violin and came to his feet.

To our great surprise, the man who appeared dripping in the doorway was
none other than Inspector "Giant" Lestride, one of the original Bow Street
runners, and certainly not one of Homes's closest admirers. Homes frowned
but, in his hospitable manner, waved the man to enter.

"Come in, Inspector. Have a chair. Let me have your things."

The large man removed his bowler and macintosh and accepted a chair by
the fire, while Homes, after disposing of the garments, returned to his own
chair. There were several moments of silence before Lestride cleared his
throat and spoke.

"I may as well be blunt from the beginning, Mr. Homes," he said. "This
visit was none of my doing. But the Assistant Commissioner insisted that we
consult you on a rather interesting case that has come our way." He shrugged.
"I serious doubt you can be of any aid when the best brains of the Yard have
been unsuccessful, but the A.C.'s word is law."

"And precisely what is the case you refer to?" Homes inquired evenly.

Lestride withdrew his notecase, opened it to extract a folded slip of paper,
and handed it across to Homes. My friend accepted it and leaned back to
study it, his face expressionless. I stepped behind him to read it over his
shoulder. It had been typed on a standard telegraph form and read quite
simply:

BARCLAYS WEDNESDAY MIDNIGHT SOUP YOUR RESPONSIBILITY QUICK-
LOCK-TYPE VAULT

Homes fingered the note a moment and then looked up with a frown.
"Where did you obtain this, Inspector?"

"We found it on the person of a man named Peter Black, but known to his
intimates—for reasons we cannot fathom—as Peteman Black. He was picked
up this morning on a routine charge of mopery with intent to gawk, and in the

course of our regular search we discovered this telegram. Since our code experts could not make anything of it, we felt it highly suspicious. And, of course, unless a solution is discovered before eight o'clock this evening we shall be forced to release this man Black, since the maximum we can hold a person on his charge without additional evidence is twelve hours."

Homes nodded thoughtfully. "And this man Black, what does he do for a living?"

"Well," said Lestride, "he claims to work for Reuters, the news agency people, in some capacity that leaves him free evenings." He smiled a bit cruelly. "I can see you're stumped, Mr. Homes. Admit it."

"Since your people have had the message most of the morning, and I have just this moment been handed it, I think it only fair that you withhold your opinion until I have time to study the matter," Homes said with a cool smile. "Still, even at first glance certain things stand out."

Lestride frowned at him.

"Barclays," Homes continued evenly, " — if that is the one referred to — is, of course, one of London's leading restaurants, but I believe they normally close at ten, so bringing soup there at midnight seems a bit strange. As for the quicklock-type vault — "

He reached behind him for a reference book, opened it and studied a page for several moments, and then closed it, his finger marking the spot, while he looked at Lestride.

"Tell me," he said, "am I correct in assuming that this man Black is not a young man, but approximately my own age?"

"Why, yes, he is, Mr. Homes," Lestride answered, obviously taken aback.

"And did he serve, as did we all, in the Army during the Great War?"

Lestride's jaw dropped. "As a matter of fact, he did," he said, "although how you ever guessed it is beyond me!"

"It was not a guess, but a deduction," Homes replied coolly and came to his feet, closing the reference book and returning it to its proper place. He turned back to Lestride, who also had risen. "Well, Inspector, I suggest you return at six this evening. I should have some word for you on the matter at that time."

Lestride studied Homes with suspicion for several moments and then shrugged. "Well, you have been lucky on a few occasions," he said. "If you can solve that code by this evening, I shall only be too glad to let bygones be bygones." And picking up his mac and bowler, he quickly made his way down the stairs.

"'I shall only be too glad to let bygones be bygones'!" Homes quoted with a wry smile. "One would think I had not set him straight a dozen times in the past. Ah, well, I suppose I shall have to do it once more, for the Commissioner's sake, and still be forced to face Lestride's officiousness in the future."

"But, Homes," I cried, "how were you able to deduce the man's age and Army background from those few words?"

"Later, Watney," he said in kindly fashion. "At the moment there is much to do."

"And do you honestly feel you can solve a code that has stumped the experts at the Yard? I do not doubt your ability, Homes," I added, "but time is so limited."

"All the more reason not to waste it, then," he said, and started to undo the cord of his dressing-gown. "And now I must go out, much as I dislike to do so in this weather."

His final words were muffled as the door closed behind him. In mystified silence I awaited his reappearance, and when at last the door to his room opened, I fear my mouth fell open in astonishment, for Homes was dressed in the garb of a soldier. And since fully thirty years had passed since he last had occasion to wear it, it was necessarily short in the shank.

The campaign hat with the acorns fitted well enough, however, and the rolled puttees — other than being a bit faded — were not too bad. With the years his swagger stick had warped a bit but was still clearly usable. He walked to the doorway with an officer's strut that was characteristic of his great acting ability, swished his swagger stick against his leg, winced, and smiled painfully at me.

"I shall return," he said with a brave grimace that left me as puzzled as admiring, and limped down the steps.

Dusk had fallen and the cold rain continued to sweep the streets when Homes at last came back. He climbed the stairway in laboured fashion, flung the door shut behind him, and fell into a chair, immediately bending to loosen the tight puttees. I noted his scowling visage with concern.

"Homes," I asked anxiously, "are you all right?"

He did not answer but instead unwrapped the puttees and shook them violently. A torrent of water descended upon our rug, followed by several cigarette stubs and various other pieces of débris. "From the bottom up, not from the top down!" he muttered to himself in exasperation, and fell back into his chair. Suddenly he seemed to recall my question.

"Why, yes, Watney," he replied with a smile. "Other than being chilled and quite hungry, I am fine. What has Mrs. Essex prepared for our evening repast?"

"Pickled curries with buttered chutneys, your favourites," I replied. "But, Homes, what of the problem? What of those unintelligible words? Were you able to make any headway?"

"Of course," he said languidly, and reached behind him for a Venusian. He lit it and drew smoke into his lungs deeply, with a twinkle in his eye. I could see he was merely drawing out the suspense in that insufferable manner of his when he has finally brought some difficult problem to a successful conclusion.

"Really, Homes!" I said with a touch of asperity. "At times you are quite impossible!"

"No, no, Watney!" he said, holding up his hand. "Impossible is what you eliminate when you wish to remain with the improbable." He sighed. "All right, then, Watney, if you cannot await Lestride's arrival, I suppose I must satisfy your curiosity. The message was clarity itself, given the proper approach, and was quite natural to be on the person of Mr. Black, since he works for a news agency. It merely states that a romantic colonial with a rather odd appellation—apparently he drinks—has been fortunate enough to win a terpsichorean contest in one of our Commonwealth nations. Canada, to be precise. It was just that simple."

"Really, Homes," I said reproachfully. "You gain nothing by pulling my leg!"

"Oh, I am quite serious, believe me!" he replied. "But here, if I am not mistaken, is Lestride himself, and you shall hear the details as I give them to him."

The door opened to reveal the large police-officer, his bowler held tightly in his hand. He made no motion to relieve himself of his dripping macintosh but stood there like a rock, his normal superciliousness asserting itself as always.

"Well, Mr. Homes," he said with a sneer, and it was evident he was prepared to enjoy my friend's discomfiture, "I assume we shall be forced to allow Mr. Black his freedom simply because you were unable to break the code."

"Come in, Inspector," Homes said warmly. "Take off your coat and have a seat. You are quite correct in stating that you will have to free Mr. Black, not because I was unable to solve the riddle of those words, but precisely because they were so easily explained."

He smiled at the startled expression on the Inspector's face, waited until the still-suspicious police official had divested himself of his outer garments and was seated, and then withdrew the slip of paper from his pocket. He placed it on a table where we could all peruse it, and laid a thin finger upon it.

"Let us consider these words," he said calmly. "'BARCLAYS WEDNESDAY MIDNIGHT SOUP YOUR RESPONSIBILITY QUICKLOCK-TYPE VAULT.' Now, Watney, you asked me this afternoon how I was able to deduce the man's age and Army background from these few words. Well, you were in India at the time, I believe, and the Inspector, here, was too young to be involved; but in the extensive training we were put through to prepare us for the trenches of France, we were taught the quicklock-type vault as a means of leaping over enemy barbed wire. In fact, this type vault remained in Regs until it was pointed out that too many of our troops were suffering from hernias as a result of keeping the knees so tightly compressed during take-offs, after which the quicklock was replaced by the more sensible open-stance-type vault that I believe is in use to this day."

I stared in unashamed admiration at my friend, while even Inspector Lestride was forced to modify the frowning suspicion with which he had been attending Homes's words. Homes leaned back, tenting his fingers, and continued calmly.

"Now," said he, "knowing that this Peter – or Peteman – Black was familiar with the quicklock-type vault indicated to me he had been in the war; hence my deduction regarding his age and past Army experience." He untented his fingers long enough to raise one of them professorially. "However, it also indicated to me something far more important."

"And what is that, Homes?" I asked breathlessly.

He smiled at me. "Consider," he said. "Here we have a man who works for a wire service, an employment where information is often transmitted in code either for reasons of economy, or to prevent competitive services from stealing information. True, to us the information may not appear to be very significant, but undoubtedly it was to a born newsman."

"But what information?" Lestride asked, his attention now fully riveted upon my friend, and his sneering manner no longer in evidence. "And what possible code?"

"As to the information," Homes replied, "as I explained to Watney before your arrival, Inspector, it merely dealt with the winning of a dancing contest. And as for the code, it was the natural one for an ex-Army man to use. It was the standard military vocabulary – known, I believe, as the phonetic alphabet."

Lestride stared at him. "The *what?*"

"The phonetic alphabet," Homes repeated, and turned to me. "Did they not use it in India, Watney?"

"Of course," I said instantly and quoted from memory. "Able, Baker, Charley, Dog, Echo, Fox, and so on for A, B, C, D—"

Homes held up his hand. "Ah! I also thought so, but when I applied those letters to this message, I got no results. It then occurred to me that over the years the phonetic alphabet might well have been changed. In the proper raiment, I had no difficulty in gaining access to the local Army and Navy Store, and there I fell into conversation with a clerk who had served as signalman with General Rohr at Belleau Wood, and he gladly furnished me with the present version. Instead of Able, Baker, Charlie, Dog, and so forth, the phonetic alphabet in use in the Army today is now Alpha, Bravo, Charlie, Delta, Echo, and so forth."

Lestride shook his head. "I still fail to understand what that might possibly have to do with the message there on the table!"

"Let us consider that message, in view of what I have just revealed to you, Inspector," Homes said evenly. "'BARCLAYS WEDNESDAY MIDNIGHT SOUP YOUR RESPONSIBILITY QUICKLOCK-TYPE VAULT.' The words in themselves have no meaning, but were used merely to transmit the message by the use of the initial letter of each word. Let us take them, and we see we have B, W, M, S, Y, R, Q, T and V."

"So?" Lestride demanded, his old belligerence beginning to return.

"So let us see where these letters lead us when we apply them to the modern phonetic alphabet in use today, a copy of which I have here." Homes laid a second sheet beside the first one and pointed out the code words for each of the letters. With wonder we saw the message, which Homes wrote for us in his fine copperplate:

BRAVO! "WHISKY" MIKE SIERRA, YANKEE ROMEO, QUEBEC TANGO VICTOR!

"Homes!" I cried proudly. "You have done it again!"

"You mean—" Lestride faltered.

"Precisely," Homes said a bit severely. "Mr. Black was simply carrying this message, received, I have small doubt, from their Canadian correspondent. I do not claim the news is of world-shaking importance, but one thing is certain: delayed as it has been through the heavy-handed tactics of the police, it is undoubtedly no longer newsworthy, and Mr. Black has probably lost money because of you. You might consider this fact when you release him."

"I shall apologize to him most thoroughly as soon as I return to the Yard," Lestride said brokenly, and left our presence a more sober and, I hope, a more judicious man.

It was early morning and a strong wind during the night had cleared the heavy clouds, bringing us welcome relief from the poor weather that had plagued us. I was at the breakfast table shelling my first caper and attempting to peruse the morning journal at the same time, when Homes joined me. He looked pleased with himself, as well he might, having just saved a poor innocent from further incarceration. He seated himself across from me and drew his napkin into his lap.

"And have you found anything in the news of interest to a rather bored investigator, Watney?" he asked, reaching for the kippers and the marmalade.

"Well, Homes, there is this," I said, reading a front-page story. "It seems that last night one of the largest banks in London was burgled. The thieves managed to explode the safe and escape with several million pounds. Police have found some substance on the property which their chemists claim to be a combination of nitrate and glycerol."

"Nitrate, of course," Homes said thoughtfully, "is the reduced charge for telegrams after a certain hour, but glycerol?"

He eschewed his kipper for a few moments to go into his study and return with a reference volume from his vast library. He leafed through the pages, muttering to himself, and then suddenly stopped as he located the material he sought.

"Ah, here it is! Glycerol: '. . . used as a softener in pharmacy, as a preservative of food, as a moistener of tobacco and other materials, as an adulterant for wine, beer, etcetera'—"

His eyes came up to meet mine, horrified.

"As an *adulterant* for wine or beer? These miscreants must be brought to the bar of justice post-haste, Watney! A telegram to the authorities offering my services, if you will!"

The Adventure of
The Odd Lotteries

MY FRIEND, Mr. Schlock Homes, has often made the statement that in dealing with crime his gratification in clearing the innocent far exceeds any satisfaction to be gained in laying the guilty by the heels. His activities in the American Colonies in the year '74 give evidence of this. There was his handling of the affair concerning the death of a musician named Foster, for whose demise an innocent might well have suffered had not Homes suggested the possibility that the man had died from eating a poisonous concoction called grits—a case I find listed in my journal as *The Adventure of the Dixie Malady.*

Again, in the colony of California, he was able to prove that the actor Humphrey Beauregard had walked in the wet cement before Grauman's Chinese Theatre quite inadvertently, and therefore no charge of malicious intent could stand—a case I find noted in my records as *The Adventure of the Big Schlep.*

But no case exemplifies Homes's dedication to aiding the innocent as much as one which occurred in our own beloved England, and which I find annotated in my files as *The Adventure of the Odd Lotteries.*

It was a late evening in May and Homes and I had been at the theatre enjoying a wistful drama of old Genoa—*A Boy and His Doge*—and were strolling in leisurely fashion back to the quarters we shared at 221B Bagel Street. As we turned the corner and approached our door, Homes glanced at me with a faint frown.

"Are you expecting a patient at this hour, Watney?" he inquired.

"Why, no, Homes," I replied, mystified, and then saw the reason for his query. Before our house a hansom cab was stationed, its jehu nodding at the reins as if he might well have been waiting for hours.

We hurried our pace and with Homes in the lead rapidly mounted the stairs to our rooms. There, to our great surprise, ensconced on a comfortable chair before the empty fireplace and with a book in his lap was none other than Homes's old friend from Bloatings Castle in Scotland, Lord Epsworth. At our arrival his Lordship looked up in mild surprise, studying us curiously. Then a bright smile of recognition crossed his features.

"Homes!" he exclaimed in delight. "This *is* a pleasant surprise! What are *you* doing here?"

"I live here," Homes replied with a gentle smile. "What brings you to London, Lord Epsworth?"

"London?" Lord Epsworth looked about him a moment and then nodded. "You are absolutely right, Homes, but then you always are! This *is* London. I remember the sign at Kings Cross when I arrived, now that you mention it. What am I doing in London? Let me think. . ."

He frowned in concentration a moment and then brightened. "Of course! I came to see you, Homes. I need your help."

"To which you are always welcome," Homes said cordially, and lowered himself into the basket chair across from his old friend. He tilted his head in my direction. "You remember Watney, of course?"

"Whitney? Certainly. I knew his father, Eli. Eccentric. Tried to make gin out of cotton, I believe. But where was I?"

His Lordship worried his lower lip with thumb and forefinger a moment and then beamed as it came back to him.

"Of course! I need your help, Homes. Or, rather, I'm not sure I *do* need your help. Or even if help is needed, as far as that goes. But it is odd, you must admit. And what my brother-in-law would say—not to mention Lady Epsworth—if they were aware of it, Heaven only knows. *I* know, of course, which is the problem. Still, in the circumstances I felt it essential to speak with you. Surely you understand?"

"Of course," Homes said warmly. "But if you would care to elucidate?"

"Certainly," Lord Epsworth said and sat a bit more erect, his book sliding to the floor. "Lady Epsworth, my wife, I think—I mean, I know—has been insisting for some time that I do something more constructive than merely raising pigs, and since her brother is Commissioner of England Yard in Edinburgh she managed to get me appointed Chief Constable of our district. Ridiculous, isn't it?" He looked at us brightly.

We remained silent. He nodded in agreement and went on.

"Yes. In any event, about two months ago the famous cricketer, A. J. Lotteries, presented himself to me seeking employment. It was just after my appointment, my staff was short, and he came with an extremely high recommendation from none other than your cousin, Oliver Wendell—"

Homes interrupted, his eyebrows raised. "Oliver?"

"Yes. I said so, didn't I? Dear me, I'm sure I said—"

"The letter of recommendation was in Oliver's own hand?"

"Well, no," Lord Epsworth admitted. "As a matter of fact, now that I recall it, it had been produced on one of those new typing machines. But," he added, brightening, "it had clearly been signed with a large scrawled initial—R."

"But my cousin's initials are O.W."

"Ah!" said his Lordship with unaccustomed logic, "but you know how many poor unfortunates are cursed with forgetfulness."

"True," Homes conceded. "Pray continue."

"Yes. Well, with a recommendation that laudatory, I instantly hired the man as my personal assistant, and since we would be working closely together, I arranged his quarters at Bloatings Castle itself. And," Lord Epsworth added a bit defensively, "until quite recently I had no reason to doubt the wisdom of the move."

"Ah!" Homes considered Lord Epsworth gravely over tented fingers. "And now you do?"

"I am not sure, which is the reason for my visit," Lord Epsworth said, and stared contemplatively towards the sideboard. I took his hint and poured myself a drink as he continued: "As you know, Lady Epsworth as well as her brother are very demanding as far as the proprieties are concerned. Any odd behaviour, any variation from the norm on the part of a servant, public or private, would be cause for instant dismissal."

Homes nodded. "I am to understand, then, that this A. J. Lotteries has been acting strangely lately?"

"Yes," said his Lordship, "but I keep hoping there might be a good reason for his erratic behaviour. The thing is, Homes," Lord Epsworth added, looking a bit abashed at his defense of the man, "I like the chap. He's deuced valuable to me. You see, he's the only one who can open the safe. I keep forgetting the combination. Besides," his Lordship added apologetically, "we've been having quite a rash of burglaries in the neighbourhood lately, and it's no time for a Chief Constable to be without an assistant, what?"

"Quite," Homes said agreeably. "Well, of course I shall be only too pleased to help. Now, if your Lordship would care to tell me the exact form of this man's eccentricity?"

"His what?"

"The manner in which his odd behaviour expresses itself."

"Oh, that! What was it, now? Ah, yes! Well, the other night, when everyone was asleep, I was down in the library trying to remember what book I had come down for—or was I returning one?—when I heard a footstep upon the staircase and looked up to see Mr. Lotteries descending cautiously. It was quite dim where I was standing and I was able to observe him quite clearly without being seen in turn. And the chap had on the most outlandish costume! Really!"

Homes sprang to his feet and began to pace to and fro, his thin fingers clasped convulsively behind his back, his piercing eyes gleaming with interest. "Really?"

Lord Epsworth cast his eyes about. "You know, Homes, you *do* have a most annoying echo in here!"

"You were saying about his costume?"

"His what? Oh, you mean his dress! Well, the truth is the man was clothed from head to foot in black. It's the truth. He wore a black opera cloak, with black tennis shoes on his feet, black gloves on his hands, and to top off the wierd picture, he wore a black cap pulled low over his forehead, shadowing a black mask that completely covered his face. He—"

His Lordship seemed to note for the first time that Homes was on his feet. "You are leaving, Homes?" He saw the expression on my friend's face and hopped to his feet. "No, I suppose I'm the one who is leaving. Well, I knew it had to be one of us. I'll see you at Bloatings tomorrow, then. Good night, Homes. Good night, Mr. Watt. I knew your grandfather well—or was it Will? No, no, it was James! Had a thing about steam, as I recall. Well, ta!"

There was the clatter of his Lordship's boots on the stairs and a moment later we heard the crack of a whip followed by the diminishing rattle of carriage wheels in the roughly cobbled street below. Homes fell back into his chair, smiling broadly.

"Well, Watney," said he, "it seems we are off to Scotland in the morning. In the meanwhile, what do you make of the mysterious Mr. Lotteries and his odd habiliment?"

"Quite simple," I said easily, certain for once of the correctness of my analysis. "The man is plainly mad."

Homes's eyebrows quirked humorously. "Mad?"

"Come, Homes!" I said severely, although in truth I was a trifle pleased to get a bit of my own back with Homes in a matter of deduction. "Surely you heard his Lordship state that the man wore both an opera cloak and tennis shoes?"

"And?"

"Even you, Homes," I said pointedly, "must know that such footwear is strictly *de trop* at the opera! And a cap, rather than a topper!" I brought up my most devastating argument. "And gloves that were not white! Even for *Aïda!* Really, the fellow should be restrained!"

Homes nodded, his eyes sparkling with good humour. "Possibly," he agreed, "although probably not for the reasons you give. You seem to have forgotten certain facts."

"Such as?" I inquired coldly.

"Such as the fact that the man was masked. How do you account for that?"

For a moment I was nonplussed, but then I rose to the occasion.

"His Lordship's active imagination," I said loftily. "How else could it be explained, any more than his insistence that in the dim hallway he was able to determine that the man wore only black?"

"Oh, the wearing of the black is easily enough explained," Homes said quietly, and smiled at the puzzled expression on my face. "However, it is getting late and we have a long journey on the morrow. If you would please hand me the Bradshaw, Watney, we'll see if we can make some sense of it this time."

"The Bradshaw?" I asked, surprised. "I seem to recall that in the affair of the gentleman's gentleman who served the Yiddish quadruplets—you may remember my accounting it in *The Valet of Fir*—you made the statement that the vocabulary of Bradshaw is extremely limited."

"You do not understand," Homes said with a patience that showed signs of wearing thin. "It is precisely *because* Bradshaw is limited that I wish it. If you would look up the Highland Limited, please, Watney . . ."

It was nearing evening the following day when we stepped from our railway carriage at the little village of Rumen Turgid, the local stop for Bloatings. Homes had refused to discuss the case during our tedious ride, preferring to puff furiously upon his pipe and stare speculatively through the blue haze of our compartment out upon the dour landscape. Nor was it until our carriage had stopped at the platform that he put his pipe away and nodded his head in that gesture I knew so well that indicated he was approaching the solution to a problem, or developing palsy. Nor did he break his silence as we drove through the gathering dusk in our rented trap.

Bloatings Castle was a goodly distance from the station, and it was quite dark by the time we handed over the reins to a stableboy in the castle courtyard and made our way through the familiar passages to his Lordship's study. We came upon him in the midst of his cerebrations—he was toasting himself with some Saki at the time—but he quickly put the bottle away and motioned us to chairs.

"It's good to see you, Homes!" said he with warm hospitality. "And you, too, Walton. I knew your great-uncle, Izaak. Had a thing about fish, as I recall." He turned back to my friend, a puzzled frown upon his face. "But what brings you to Scotland, Homes?"

"The mysterious affair of your assistant's bizarre costume," Homes replied calmly.

"So you are aware of that!" said his Lordship, amazed. "Homes, you are amazing!"

Homes refused to respond to this flattery but continued to study his Lordship steadily. "Yes. In fact, I believe I am quite close to the answer to the riddle. Tell me, is Mr. A. J. Lotteries about?"

Lord Epsworth frowned. "I sent him out on some errand or other—I don't remember at the moment what it was——" His face suddenly cleared. "But, of course! He returned. He should be in his quarters at the moment, I believe. Would you wish me to ring for him?"

"No," Homes said quietly. "It would be best, I believe, if Dr. Watney and I were to speak with him alone. Could you tell me which room he occupies?"

"Let me see . . . It's the one at the top of the stairs—no, no, that's mine! The one next to it? Surely that's Lady Epsworth's? Or at least it was some years ago. And the next one's a closet—"

"We'll find it," Homes said bravely. "Come, Watney."

In mystified obedience I followed Homes into the hall, but before we could approach the staircase, Homes fell back and over his shoulder I saw, descending the steps, as odd an apparition as ever I have seen! Knowing Lord Epsworth as I did, I had put little true credence in his tale, but now I felt I owed him an apology, for coming down, cautiously but swiftly, was a figure dressed, indeed, entirely in black, garbed with gloves and mask.

Well could I imagine the natural abhorrence such abominable taste in clothing might arouse in one as sensitive to the mode as Lady Epsworth, but before I could pounce upon the creature to demand an explanation, the masked man had passed from the dim hallway and had closed the heavy door firmly behind him.

Homes came from his reverie with a start. "The clank!" he cried. "It is the final proof! Did you hear the clank?"

"The clank?" I asked, mystified.

"The clank!" he repeated fiercely. "After him before he can do harm!"

"You mean that little clinking sound when he walks?" I began curiously, but Homes was already through the doorway in hot pursuit of our prey. I followed instantly.

The moon was lost behind ruffled clouds, and the huge stands of ancient yew that made up the greater part of the castle grounds would have made following the man impossible, except that in the silence of the serene night we could hear the constant clashing of metal upon metal as the man strode confidently along, unaware of our pursuit. We might well have trailed him in this fashion to his destination, led by that clanking sound Homes had so cleverly perceived, had I not inadvertently fallen over a stump some careless gardener had failed to clear.

Our quarry turned instantly, prepared for immediate flight, but before he could make a move Homes was at his side, and a moment later I had joined the fray and had my hands about the miscreant's neck, bearing the scoundrel to the ground.

"I have the rascal, Homes!" I cried, and then could not help but add a bit triumphantly, "So you finally recognized that I was right, and that the man could do harm, eh?"

"Let him be, Watney!" Homes said sharply. He squatted down beside the fallen man, pushing me roughly to one side. "Are you all right, Mr. Lotteries?"

The masked figure sat up trembling, rubbing his throat. "What— what—?" He suddenly seemed to recognize his captor. "Schlock Homes! What did you do, get lucky for once?"

"Never lucky," Homes said, and shook his head sadly at the man before him. "It was the only solution possible." He reached for the man's cloak and removed the two sets of small tools whose clanking had led to the man's capture. "These tell the whole story. You are much better off without them. Go and try to forget what you had in mind for their use."

Lotteries stared at Homes in astonishment. "You mean I can go?"

"Of course," Homes said warmly. "It is not your fault."

"If you say so," Lotteries said, and stumbled away in the darkness, his shoulders heaving with what had to be sobs of gratitude for my companion's compassion.

"Homes!" I exclaimed. "This whole thing is a mystery to me! Why did you allow the man to escape? You, yourself, just stated that he could do harm!"

"Only to himself, Watney."

"You mean by demonstrating his execrable taste in clothing? Surely an enforced course in fashion at one of our leading boutiques would have been better for all concerned?"

"It would scarcely have cured the man's hypochondria," Homes said dryly, "for that, and that alone, is his problem."

"Hypochondria?" I exclaimed in astonishment.

"Of course! It was evident as soon as his Lordship described the man's costume yesterday evening in our quarters in London."

Homes took a deep breath and began his exposition in that pedantic manner which never failed to irritate me, tapping me upon the chest to emphasize each point.

"To begin with, let us take the gloves and the mask. As you should know, Watney, these are the most common precautions taken by anyone wishing to avoid contact with germs." He removed a finger from my chest to raise it for further emphasis. "*But* — in the pure clean air of Rumen Turgid, such a need must obviously only be imagined, and by definition, Watney, that is what is known as hypochondria!"

"But the tennis shoes, Homes?"

"Further proof if it were needed, Watney," Homes said, and thrust a bony finger against my fourth rib. "Tennis shoes are soft and are customarily used, when not on the sporting field, for feet that hurt. But aching feet on one of the leading cricketers of the world, whose feet are toughened by constantly being confined in heavy leather? Impossible! The need for soft shoes, therefore, again is to assuage an imaginary ailment, and again is hypochondria."

"But the black clothing, Homes? Surely," I said, drawing upon my medical background, "a person whose fear of microbes becomes so dominant would confine himself to clothing that is white?"

"Precisely!" Homes said, driving home his point with a further jab that almost took my attention from his argument. "And the fact that Mr. Lotteries did not, can only mean one thing: *that he did not know his clothing was black!* He is, therefore, colour-blind, and on top of his other troubles is therefore more to be pitied for it!"

I could but stand, rubbing my chest, lost in silent admiration for my friend's remarkable analytical ability. But then one disturbing question came to mind.

"But the tools, Homes!" I cried. "I can see no connection between them and the illness of that poor soul, and yet you stated that they were the final proof!"

"And so they were, Watney," Homes replied sadly, and stared down at the two small sets of tools. "Note them well—the miniature prizing levers, the tiny drills, the small sets of saws. Certainly you have seen their like before?"

"Of course, Homes!" I said, recognizing them at last. "In a hospital!"

"Exactly," Homes said soberly. "The poor fellow was prepared to perform surgery upon himself, surely the ultimate in hypochondria!"

There was no other answer! It was with the most profound admiration that I followed Homes back towards Bloatings Castle. Once again he had aided an innocent; through his masterful analysis he had saved a man from being condemned by society as a dilettante in fashion, surely a dreadful charge to follow a guiltless soul through life!

It was several mornings later that I entered our breakfast-room in our quarters in Bagel Street to find Homes before me. As he drew a curried haggis into his plate—a gift from Lord Epsworth we had forgotten to leave behind—I opened the morning journal and began to read an article which struck my eye.

"I hope, Watney," came the voice of my friend, not entirely in jest, "that you are perusing something which may be of interest to a pair of idle investigators!"

"On the contrary, Homes," I said, slowly reading further into the article which had caught my fancy. "It seems that the crime wave in Scotland has fallen off considerably in the past few days."

"We can only be happy for Lord Epsworth, then," Homes replied, "especially since he is now without an assistant." He suddenly frowned, and then his frown turned to a smile. "However," he added happily, "since the total is always equal to the sum of the parts, Scotland's loss in crime will undoubtedly be England's gain. A letter to the authorities of the northern counties offering my services, if you please, Watney!"

The Adventure of
The Elite Type

IN reviewing the many cases in which I was privileged to observe the analytical ability of my friend, Mr. Schlock Homes, in the year '74, I find several of ordinate interest. There was the matter, for example, of the young man accused of hanging awnings in a building where no canvassing was allowed, a case in which Homes easily proved the restriction was aimed at the sailsmen in the sail-loft on the second floor. There was also the mysterious affair of the chimney-sweep found dead on the pavement beneath his working place, a case Homes resolved in record time, and which I find in my notes as *The Adventure of the Purloined Ladder*. But no problem, I believe, better tested my friend's genius than the one I find annotated in my casebook as *The Adventure of the Elite Type*.

It was a pleasant Sunday morning in early June, and Homes and I were taking our ease in our quarters at 221B Bagel Street. Homes was toying with his violin, practising esoteric semibreve rests, while I was rereading all the works of a favourite author on a favourite subject of mine. I had completed *The Man Who Was Thirsty* and was just started on *The Keg of Notting Hill,* when our peace was disturbed by the urgent sound of pounding feet upon our staircase.

Both Homes and I looked at each other in surprise, as if silently questioning the other as to the identity of the unexpected visitor; but before either could voice his query, the door had burst open and a young man of dishevelled appearance had staggered into the room. In one hand he held a bit of paper which he continued to wave, almost in our faces, as he spoke with great agitation.

"Mr. Homes!" he cried, facing my companion. "You are the only one who can help me!"

Homes calmly set his instrument to one side and motioned our excited guest to the basket chair before the empty fireplace. It was only after the young man had finally seated himself and had rather brusquely refused a candied curry that Homes spoke.

"Now that you are in better control of yourself," he said in a kindly tone, "possibly you will favour us with your problem. You may speak quite freely in front of Dr. Watney as he seldom pays the slightest attention."

"I apologize for my melodramatic entrance," the young man said, although he did not appear particularly contrite, "but in my daily endeavour I face constant abuse, and when something of this nature comes along to further the degree of harassment, I find it difficult not to allow one's nerves to get the better of himself. Or, rather, misself. I mean, one's self, of course! Or is it myself? You see? Normally I would never be in the slightest doubt as to syntax or definition, but I must admit to being wrought. Or is it overwrought? It certainly isn't underwrought, is it?" Words seemed to fail him.

"Perhaps if you would begin at the beginning?" Homes suggested.

"The beginning? Oh, of course, the beginning!" The young man took a conscious grip upon himself. He leaned forward intently in the chair, fixing Homes with his eye. "Mr. Homes, my name is John Simple and I am the theatrical reviewer for *Old York Magazine*. In the course of my day's work I am frequently the target of jealous, malevolent missives from people whose insensitivities do not permit them to accept the fact that my reviews are not only accurate but brilliant, but that this brilliance and accuracy come to them couched in a purity of elitist language they frankly do not deserve. Normally, I am able to reply to these puerile critics with verbiage so devastating that they seldom attempt to face my virulent barbs a second time. But what can one do with something like this?"

In anguish he smote the paper he had been holding with the fingers of his other hand, as if for emphasis, while he turned a tortured visage to Homes.

"Mr. Homes," he cried, "what can one do when one is insulted in *cipher?* It should not be permitted! How can one answer an insult couched in language one cannot fathom?"

Homes shrugged and considered the young man with the faintest of smiles upon his face.

"If one cannot fathom a message," he suggested with his always-present indisputable logic, "can that message not contain a compliment rather than an insult?"

"Never!" said our visitor fiercely. "It has never occurred and I doubt it ever will. Nor," he added, thinking about it, "should I be particularly pleased if it did. No!" He stared at the bit of paper as if hypnotized by it. "It is an insult, Mr. Homes, but so devilishly clever as to be beyond my capacity to solve!"

Homes stretched out his hand. "If I may?"

"Certainly!" The young man handed over the paper he had been clutching so feverishly, and I came about Homes's chair to study the missive over his shoulder. It was, as the young man had so accurately stated, at least partially in cipher, but so complex that for once my great faith in Homes's ability to resolve a problem was shaken. It read, quite simply:

```
John Simple: I can only comment on your reviews
in comic-page language: !¢!!@!$(@!!#!@!%!#@@)!%!$(
@)%                              Signed J.L.
```

"Most interesting," Homes muttered, his eyes lighting up at the sight of the unintelligible gibberish. He brought his eyes from the intriguing bit of paper almost reluctantly. "If you leave your address with Dr. Watney, Mr. Simple, I shall get right to it, and hope to have a solution to your problem shortly."

"I pray you do," young Simple said, and came to his feet. "I am in the midst of composing a scathing reply to this J.L., whoever he is, and I should not like to waste my brilliant scurrility should the message be other than the usual. You see?" he said despondently. "I used the word 'brilliant' again! I should have said 'sagacious' or at the very least 'superlative'!"

"Quite," I said, holding my hand out for his card.

He disregarded my outstretched palm. "As for my whereabouts, I shall be in the wings of the Paladium Theatre, where a marvellous company is to perform one of the greatest works of the theatre in their superlative fashion this evening. You see? I said 'superlative' again!" And on this note our visitor wandered disconsolately from the room.

Homes paid his departure no attention, preferring instead to study the paper in his hand a moment, and then wriggled in his chair, a sure sign either of his delight in a new problem, or a recurrence of a broken spring I had thought long repaired. I sighed.

"Tell me, Homes," I said despairingly, "do you see the slightest possibility of solving a cipher so completely exotic?"

"The solution will undoubtedly be merely a matter of labour," Homes replied, pinching his lip as he continued to peruse the mysterious message. "The identity of the writer is less a problem. There can be little doubt that this J.L. is a vain young lady, rather near-sighted, quite careless, a scholar of the classics, but with a touch of genius to her make-up, as well. You agree, Watney?"

"Homes!" I exclaimed reprovingly. "It is not like you to make light of a matter that was of such import to your departing client! Why do you pull my leg at a time like this?"

"No, no, Watney," said he with more than a touch of his usual impatience. "I am quite serious." He picked up his Dr. Grabow and the shag and a moment later was sending clouds of acrid smoke ceilingwards as he tented his fingers and fell into a brown study, the note left in his lap for easy reference. Then, swinging about suddenly, he reached to a convenient shelf for a reference volume.

"Homes," I said reproachfully, "you are not going to tackle the problem at once, are you? We were supposed to go to the Zoo this afternoon, to watch the annual parade of the elk and the deer."

"I know, Watney," Homes said, and sighed. "You go alone. Much as I love to be around when the game is afoot, I'm afraid today it must be duty before pleasure!"

It was late afternoon when I returned. The room was filled with smoke and through the haze I was barely able to make out the form of Homes, bent over his desk, scribbling furiously. At his feet the numerous wads of crumpled paper testified to the intensity of his efforts during my absence.

Knowing his dislike of being disturbed when hard at work, I silently repaired to the sideboard and performed an experiment I had read about, the addition of gin to vermouth, an experiment first performed I believe by one of the early popes, Martin I. I scarcely had time to stir the concoction when there was a sudden exclamation from Homes.

"Of course, of course!" he exclaimed under his breath, and taking a fresh sheet of paper he quickly fell back to his calculations. I had been with Homes long enough to properly interpret his reactions. Pausing only long enough to test the new mixture, which was quite palatable, I hastened to his side.

"Homes," I said proudly, "you have solved it!"

But Homes brushed aside my interruption, continuing to transfer figures to the paper.

"Shall I take the answer to Mr. John Simple at the Paladium?" I asked, ready as always to serve.

But Homes did not hear me. He had completed his translation and was staring with ill-concealed horror at the very words he had just finished setting down. For a moment he appeared in a state of shock, but then he swiftly recovered.

"The Paladium, indeed!" he said heavily, and came to his feet. "There is not a moment to lose! Have our page take a message to Inspector LeStride at the Yard to take steps to see the Paladium is surrounded at once, and to wait for us there with sufficient men to make a complete search of the premises."

"But, Homes," I said in bewilderment. "I do not understand any of this. I am sure the doorman would be only too happy to locate John Simple for us, without the need for Scotland Yard. Or even a quiet announcement from the stage — ?"

But Homes was already urging me towards the door, and even as I sent our page off with the mysterious summons, Homes had hurried down the stairs and had joined me at the kerb, hastily pulling on his gaiters. A moment later he had waved down a passing hansom, sprung inside, and was dragging me in after him.

"The Paladium Theatre, driver!" he cried, "and tuppence-ha'penny extra if you get us there quickly!" He fell back into his seat as our cabbie cracked the whip and the hansom started up with a jerk. I turned to stare at my friend in astonishment.

"Really, Homes," I said reprovingly. "I realize our young visitor gave the performance at the Palladium an excellent recommendation, but the curtain does not go up for fifteen minutes. I see no necessity for this great urgency."

"No?" he said scathingly, a grim look on his face. "Tell me, Watney, would you consider the fact that an infernal machine has been placed at the Paladium Theatre reason enough for urgency?"

"Homes!" I exclaimed. "Are you certain?"

"Quite," said he, and reached into his pocket for the mysterious bit of paper. "We have ample time before we arrive at the theatre, so allow me to explain."

His thin finger traced the message as our coach swayed dangerously down Bagel Street before turning into Piccalilli, our horses' hooves clattering on the rough cobblestones, the whip cracking above us.

"You will note, Watney," Homes said, "the characters in which this message is printed. I have made a study of type faces, as you know, and I can assure you that this font comes from one of the new machines used to mechanically transfer individual characters to paper. These machines are called 'typewriters' and are not as rare as one might suppose. However, since the persons using these machines are almost invariably female, it was a fairly good guess that our mysterious J.L. is a woman."

I listened with widened eyes, as Homes continued.

"You may recall my mentioning the writer's expertise in the classics." His finger pointed. "Here, you see, she refers to a comic page. Who is the most famous comic page in all literature? Undoubtedly Sancho Panza in *Don Quixote,* who called himself 'Number Two' while he referred to his master as 'Number One'—or at least he did in the Swahili translation, a further proof, if need be, of the writer's classical background. Comic-page language, therefore, could only be language in *numbers.* But, if the message was meant to be in numbers, why do no numbers appear? *Because the writer inadvertently struck what is called a 'shift-key' on the machine, which causes, in place of numbers, these meaningless hieroglyphics to appear!"*

I stared at my companion in speechless amazement at the brilliance of his analysis, although in truth I had no idea what he was talking about. Homes smiled at me in his usual superior manner, and went on.

"We can therefore add to our growing picture of the writer the fact that she is careless and inattentive to details. Had she taken the trouble to check her message before sending it on, she would have seen at once her error. Even the simple chore of removing the sheet from the machine should have revealed it. Except, of course, to a person quite near-sighted."

"But you also said she is vain, Homes!" I exclaimed.

"Had she worn spectacles, she would have avoided the mistake."

"But—the touch of genius, Homes?"

His thin fingers tapped the message.

"Note, Watney, that despite the error of inadvertently striking this so-called 'shift-key,' the message is without a single mistake. Consider: here is a person who cannot clearly see the keys of the machine, yet she makes no mistakes. *She has memorized the position of each key and is therefore able to type-write without consulting the keyboard!* It must be a talent not one in a hundred thousand could master, and surely indicates a superior intelligence!"

As I marvelled at my friend's great perception, Homes waved away my congratulations and continued.

"However, the writer was not my concern. It was the message itself. By studying a diagram of the keyboard of one of these new machines in my reference file, I was easily able to determine which numerals the writer would have put down had she not carelessly struck this 'shift-key' first. They were as follows:

16112149211312151322015149205!"

I stared at my companion. "This was of help, Homes?"

He smiled grimly. "It was, indeed, Watney! By using the oldest transfer method known, where the numeral 1 equals the letter A, the numeral 2 the letter B, and so forth, I was able to come up with this." And he thrust a second sheet of paper into my hand. It read:

AFAABADIBAACABAEACBBOAEADIBOE

I frowned. "A bit cryptic, Homes, is it not?" A sudden thought struck me. "Or possibly in a foreign language?"

"At first I thought so, but I could find nothing in my file resembling it. It then occurred to me that the highest number, taken individually, was a 9, and it struck me as dubious that anyone would send a message to a person as literate as John Simple using only nine letters. It meant, therefore, that some of the 1's had to represent the first digit of a two-digit number—or a letter between J and S—while some of the 2's served the same purpose for the balance of the alphabet. After that, as I had suspected, it was merely a question of labour until I had the proper combinations."

"If you say so, Homes," I said dubiously, and wondered if my friend had been getting enough rest of late.

"I do say so," he replied shortly, and pointed to the paper again. "I now had this:

16 1 12 1 4 9 21 13 1 2 15 13 2 20 15 14 9 20 5!"

"And that was better, Homes?" I asked, worried whether Homes had been eating too many curried kippers of late.

"Quite," he said coldly. "Using the same transfer method, but with all twenty-six letters of the alphabet available, I now had the message." And he tapped the sheet significantly. I leaned over to read the last letters on the sheet. They read:

PALADIUM A BOMB TONITE

There was little I could say before this magnificent demonstration of analytical genius, but before I could even attempt to congratulate Homes on his remarkable achievement, our cab came rattling to a halt before the famous theatre, where we could see Inspector LeStride and a bevy of bobbies awaiting us. Homes hurried down, leaving me to pay our cabbie, as well as the exorbitant tip he had promised, and when at last I joined the others on the pavement, it was to hear the Inspector speaking.

"The theatre is crowded at the moment, Mr. Homes," he said respectfully, "and the performance is about to begin. To attempt to ferret out an infernal machine with that audience in the hall will only lead to panic."

Homes paused in thought.

"It would not be in the auditorium," he said at last. "It is difficult to imagine a miscreant who would destroy a beautiful edifice just to wreak revenge on one critic. Besides, were it planted in the auditorium, someone reaching beneath his seat to deposit his chewing gum might well discover the device. Add to this the fact that Mr. John Simple prefers to watch the performance from the wings, and the solution is obvious. The bomb will be on the stage. A search there before the curtain goes up is therefore indicated. Proceed!"

"It shall be done, Mr. Homes," the Inspector said, and instantly gave directions to his men. But when Homes moved forward, the Inspector put up his hand. "No, Mr. Homes, you must not risk joining in the search. You are too valuable to your country for me to permit you to face such danger needlessly. Go, for the sake of your nation and the world, and let us handle it!"

"If you insist," Homes said, and turned to me. "It will allow us to take some small advantage of the beautiful weather, Watney," he said, beginning to wave for a hansom. "We can go to Overton Stadium where they have sports under gaslight. Tonight they are featuring Nottingham versus Newcastle in the soccer matches."

"I should like that, Homes," I cried enthusiastically. "You know how much I love to be on hand when the game is afoot!"

The following morning I had preceded Homes into the breakfast room and was attempting to peel a curry and open the morning journal at the same time when Homes joined me. I already had time to have studied the headlines, and since there was no mention of an explosion in the theatrical district the evening before, it was evident that Inspector LeStride had done his job well and had been successful in discovering and disarming the infernal machine. But when I went to offer my congratulations to Homes on a job well done, he waved my felicitations aside.

"There is nothing as dead as yesterday's problem, Watney," said he, drawing a napkin into his lap and reaching for the kippered capers, "especially when it is solved. What can you find that might be of interest to an idle investigator today?"

"I'm afraid there is nothing," I said sheepishly, studying the front page once again, and then paused as I turned to an inside page and folded the journal back to read it better. My spirits lifted. "There is this, possibly, Homes, although why it should be in the entertainment section I cannot imagine! It is an article signed by one Judith Lord, which begins as follows:

"'If ever a crime was committed, it was committed last night when the curtain went up at the Paladium Theatre'."

"The Paladium Theatre!" Homes cried, flinging down his napkin. "It is too much for mere coincidence! A telegram to the management offering my services, if you will, Watney!"

The Adventure of
The Animal Fare

IT is a rather well-known fact that my friend, Mr. Schlock Homes, is the author of many scholarly monographs, covering subjects as diverse as the proper selective method for collecting cricket cards to the interpretation of instructions for the use of do-it-yourself kits. His erudition and inventiveness have often been demonstrated and given proper disclosure in connection with the many cases where his genius has revealed itself; his analytical ability and his musical talents have also long been recognized. But what is not so well known, possibly, is that in April of the year '76, on our visit to the colony of New York, he discovered the wireless—what the colonials call a radio.

It had been in his room for the length of our stay, but he had thought it a sewing machine, and it was only when he attempted to sew a button on his weskit and pressed the switch that he made his important discovery. And it was this most simple of accidents that led to our being involved in a case that, while it earned us the plaudits of the New York police-officers, was to Homes one of his greatest failures. In my notes I find the affair listed as *The Adventure of the Animal Fare.*

We had been brought to the colonies from our comfortable quarters at 221B Bagel Street in London by a most urgent appeal from Homes's old friend, Inspector Richard King of the New York bobbies. The Inspector had mentioned some problem of cigarette smuggling, but the details were unknown to us, nor were we better informed upon our arrival, as the Inspector was off on holiday. Rooms were at a premium at the moment because a circus was coming to town, but we were fortunate enough to find accommodations at Ill Manors, an old inn beside the local hospital, and it was there on the late afternoon of the day the Inspector was scheduled to return that Homes made his fateful discovery.

I was being served an early supper in the sitting-room of our suite when Homes burst into the room carrying this strange contraption. He brusquely pushed aside a plate of curried favour I had had to bribe the inn chef to prepare, set the box on the table in its stead, and glanced at me in triumph. Then, before either I or my youthful waiter could remonstrate with him for having moved the plate beyond my reach, he twisted the knob and the most frightful squeal issued from the box.

"Really, Homes," I said reprovingly. "An imprisoned cat? Beyond the cruelty of it, I consider it quite unsanitary to place animals on a table where someone is eating."

"No, no, Watney," said he impatiently, and sat down abruptly, drawing the box nearer him and adjusting the knob. "This is one of the newer inventions, known here as a 'radio,' I believe. I had heard of it, but I honestly did not believe it to more than an idle rumour. Now, however, I am forced to reconsider."

"But, Homes," I asked curiously, "what does it do?"

"I am not quite sure," he replied cautiously, pinching his lip. "I have been listening to it and apparently it is able to pick up and transmit conversations of people without their knowledge."

"Without their knowledge, Homes?" I asked, scandalized.

"Certainly nobody would discuss a ring of dirt about his collar, or the incontinent condition of his digestive tract, if he knew someone was listening," said he dryly.

"True," I conceded. "Is that all you heard, Homes?"

"Well, I did hear some woman speaking of frozen steaks—she referred to them as white tournedos—but I paid scant attention." His eyes shone as he studied the invention before him. "Just think, Watney. Consider the limitless possibilities of this machine. To be able to listen to criminals as they plot their nefarious schemes, all without their knowledge! Let us try the box again."

He pushed several buttons and twisted the dial. Almost instantly there was a response. The tone of voice speaking was lugubrious, tinged with tragedy. Homes instantly leaned closer to the machine, listening intently, his brilliant mind ready to record and analyze every word.

"I was doing a bounce-around from Shakyside," the voice said dolefully, "four days on the boulevard. I was just blowing the doors off a pregnant roller skate when I see I'm also skipping the chicken coop, but it was too late then. A bear in plain wrapper is waiting on the grass, and now I'm on my way to the zoo."

"Tough," said a second voice sympathetically. "Well, threes on you."

"Threes and eights," said the tragic voice, and the small box fell silent.

Homes turned the switch and leaned back, his eyes glistening with excitement. "Did you hear that, Watney?"

"Of course," I said a bit indignantly. My hearing has always been excellent, as Homes knows full well. "But what does it mean, Homes?"

"It means this machine has far greater range than I imagined," he replied thoughtfully. "What we have just heard is obviously in some foreign tongue."

My youthful waiter paused in his gathering of the dishes and allowed himself an indulgent chuckle.

"No, gentlemen," said he. "That is what is known as C.B. language and is quite American, I assure you. Those are merely two truck drivers conversing with each other. The first said that he was returning from California, four days on the highway. He was just passing a VW when he noticed he had inadvertently failed to notice a weigh-station. To his distress, a policeman in an unmarked car was lurking on the median strip and our driver is now following the policeman to the barracks. The second driver then commiserated with the first, after which they exchanged regards and fell silent."

Homes studied the youth thoughtfully for a moment, and then spoke. To my surprise he made no reference either to what we had heard on the radio, or to the young man's interpretation of it.

"Tell me," said Homes in a conversational tone of voice, "your name is Eric, is it not?"

"Why, yes," said the young man, obviously surprised.

"And am I correct in assuming that you wait tables, not as a vocation, but in order to work your way through University?"

"That is true," the young man stammered, "although how you knew is a mystery to me."

Homes pressed on, his eyes now half closed, his fingers tented.

"Would I also be correct to assume that it is your intention to major in mathematics?"

The young man turned pale. "That is also true, although how you could possibly know that is beyond me, as I had not made up my mind myself until just this morning. Until then I had hoped to be—"

"A veterinarian?" Homes interjected smoothly.

The look of pure terror in young Eric's eyes gave proof that Homes had again hit the mark. Without a backward glance the young waiter hastily shouldered his ladened tray and made his escape. Homes looked after him sympathetically.

"Poor misguided idealist," my friend murmured cryptically. "Still, the law is the law and since we are here under the aegis of an inspector of police, we can hardly allow it to be broken under our noses. Besides, how could we bear the burden of the unhappy children were we to do nothing?"

"Really, Homes!" I said, annoyed. "Where do children come into this? And how could you possibly have deduced all those facts about young Eric?"

"Later," replied Homes, but I was not to be put off.

"No, sir," said I. "I do not understand a bit of this! It is all gibberish to me, both what we heard on this—this radio object as well as the young man's explanation of it. I am aware of C. B. DeMille, but who is C. B. Language? What is a VW? And how does one pass it?"

Homes considered me sadly.

"I should have thought that after all these years you would have learned from my methods, Watney," said he. "Never complicate matters unnecessarily. VW is exactly what it appears to be—two adjoining letters in the alphabet. Doesn't that point you in the right direction?"

But before I could comment, he had tented his fingers again and fallen into a brown study. Several moments later he reached behind him for the one-inch scale map I had purchased to acquaint ourselves with the area, and fell to pondering it. A moment later he sat erect.

"Of course!" He looked up at me and chuckled, but there was little humour in it. "What a tissue of lies that young man fed us!"

"Homes!" I exclaimed reprovingly. "How can you doubt the word of an upstanding young man who would wait tables just to further his education!"

Homes smiled grimly.

"Surely you were not taken in, Watney?" said he. "His silly story of the colony of California being called Shakyside? Why would anyone call it that? Or his statement that the driver had inadvertently passed a way-station. Certainly after four days on the trip he must have been looking desperately for a way-station! No, no, Watney, it was all a fabrication."

"But for what purpose, Homes?"

His eyes narrowed. "To arrange a hijacking, of course, Watney!"

"But, Homes—!"

"Later," he said savagely and came to his feet, clutching the map. "Hurry, Watney! Arrange for a four-in-hand while I send a message for the Inspector to meet us." He paused as I started towards my room. "No, no, Watney! Not a cravat! A carriage!"

I shamefacedly descended the stairs and made the necessary arrangements, and moments later Homes joined me. Beneath his deerstalker he had concealed a dark-lantern, and a pistol peeped threateningly from his cape. Without the need for explanation he passed me the pistol, which I instantly hid beneath my shawl, and moments later we were in the carriage and Homes had given our jehu his directions. As we started off at a gallop, Homes fell back in his seat, turning to me.

"As we now have a few moments' time," said he with his usual insufferable air of superiority, "allow me to explain this simple affair to you. It was evident from the beginning that animals were involved, and that the young man named Eric – whose name I deduced from the tag on his lapel – was doing his best to lead us away from this track. Listen to the many references: 'Chicken coop'; 'bear'; 'zoo.' And have we heard anything recently connected with animals?"

"No," I said.

Homes shook his head despairingly. "Watney, at times I do not know what to do with you! Why are we incarcerated at an old broken-down inn such as Ill Manors?"

Suddenly I saw the light. "The circus!" I cried. "They are coming to town! And they have animals!"

"Exactly," he said with a sigh, and brought his eyes down from the ceiling. "You may also remember one of the lorry motorists saying 'threes,' which undoubtedly referred to the number of rings in the circus. But the important words spoken were the words: 'blow the doors off.' The plot, then, became evident – an attempt to rescue the animals from the lorries in which they are being transported.

"Certainly this can only be misguided idealism. When one thinks of animals being freed to suffer the environment of places like Times Square when they could be happily entertaining children, one is forced to call such motives misguided. But to a person who feels so strongly about animals being caged, it was also evident that a career as a veterinarian would be unthinkable for that young man."

"True," I said, admiring, as always, my friend's impeccable logic. Suddenly I saw a problem. "But, Homes, where is this villainous scheme to be attempted? How can we know?"

"You are not paying attention, Watney," he said chidingly. "I told you that VW were merely two letters. Between these two letters and the Z of the final word Zoo, we find the letters X and Y. What do these letters mean to you?"

"Unknown quantities," I said, sure of my ground. My mind began to fairly explode. "And the two letters *before* VW are TU! The two unknown drivers are trade unionists!"

"Possibly," Homes said through clenched teeth, "but that has nothing to do with the problem. X and Y are the standard references for map co-ordinates, the X co-ordinate being the horizontal, or east-west co-ordinate, while the Y is the vertical, or north-south co-ordinate. And locating the intersection of these co-ordinates on a standard one-inch map of New York, brings us *here*." His thin finger tapped the map in his hand. "This is where we are going!"

I leaned back, amazed as always at the ease with which Homes could bring clarity to a confused situation, although I would have been willing to wager that the two drivers we would shortly meet would have syndicate memberships in their possession when we searched them.

Moments later our driver tugged at his reins and drew in to the kerb, and we descended to find ourselves in a darkened alley. Night had fallen, and beyond the pale light cast by a flickering gas-lamp in the corner, we could hear the soft lapping of water against pilings, and smell the brackishness of the river. Homes slid a coin into our driver's hand, spoke a few words to him, and as the carriage faded into the night mist he drew me further into the shadows.

"Our cab will wait for us around the corner," said he in a subdued voice. "It would not do to advertise our presence." He dug his watch from his weskit pocket and consulted it by the light from the gas-lamp. "It will only be moments until they arrive," he said, and frowned darkly. "But where is the Inspector?"

"But how could you possibly know the time the attempt is to be made, Homes?" I asked.

"The 'threes and eights' mentioned by the first driver, Watney. They add up to elevens, which can only mean eleven minutes after eleven. As it is now nine minutes past that hour, they should be here shortly." He frowned again. "But where is the Inspector?"

Before I could assure him that I did not know, there was the sound of a lorry being driven slowly down the alley, and Homes drew me further back into the doorway. A moment later the lorry had cut its lights and drawn to a stop before a warehouse, after which the driver descended cautiously and began to fumble with the lock of the warehouse door.

"We cannot await the Inspector any longer," Homes whispered into my ear, and in the same motion he sprang from our cover and shone the light of the bull's-eye lantern full on the startled face of the driver. At the same moment I clapped the pistol to the man's head and minutes later we had him bound and at our mercy.

I wished to search him for his union membership card, but Homes would have none of it, and it was just as well, for no sooner had we regained the obscurity of the doorway when the second lorry arrived. Moments later we had the second driver bound as well, and Homes came to his feet and took a deep breath.

"And now to examine their cargo," he muttered, and clambered aboard the first lorry, pulling back the tarpaulin that concealed the contents. I waited as I heard him inside, but I was not prepared for the black look on his face when he emerged. A second later he had entered the rear of the second lorry, and if anything his scowl was intensified when he emerged.

"We are too late," he said heavily, and added harshly: "Murderers! And I thought they were merely misguided idealists, wishing to rescue the animals!"

"They did not, Homes?" I asked, surprised.

"Quite the contrary," he said blackly. "They wished to steal them for cat or dog food!"

"No!" I exclaimed, shocked.

"Yes," he replied, and swept the tarpaulin away. In the light of the bull's-eye lantern I could see the truth of Homes's statement, for not only had they slaughtered the animals, but they had already packaged them! On the case before me I could see, clearly marked: *Camels.*

With no appetite for further investigation in a colony where such cruelties could be perpetrated, Homes and I returned to the inn and packed our gear, and later that day we set sail for England, not wishing to hear the weeping of the children when they learned the fate of the circus animals. And it was there, back in our quarters in Bagel Street, that we heard from the Inspector.

CONGRATULATIONS, read his wire. YOUR MAGNIFICENT EFFORTS HAVE LED TO THE SUCCESS WE ANTICIPATED. WHEN CAN WE EXPECT ANOTHER VISIT FROM YOU? WE ARE HAVING TROUBLE WITH ANIMAL THIEVES.

Homes shook his head sadly.

"Those colonials!" said he. "They will never learn to speak our tongue properly. They clearly mean thieving animals, which is more in the line of a husbandry psychologist than in mine. A cable to the Inspector explaining this, if you will, Watney!"

The Adventure of
The Common Code

IT was rare, indeed, for my friend, Mr. Schlock Homes, to refer to his many adventures during the time he spent between the day he disappeared into that tavern in Switzerland and his return to London several years later. But on some occasions, when interesting cases were few, when his laboratory experiments resulted in undrinkable concoctions, or when the people in 221A would pound on their ceiling at his violin concerti, he would speak of those by-gone days.

I recall in particular one blustery morning in late February in the year '76. Homes had but lately returned from a trip to the Iberian Peninsula where, at the behest of a nagging wife, he had gone to delve into the mysterious disappearance of a Spanish fisherman—a case I find in my notes as *The Adventure of the Juan Who Got Away*—and he now found himself at loose ends. The snow was piled deep in the street below, the wind was bitter, and for once Homes was content to remain in our snug quarters at 221B Bagel Street and reminisce, rather than search out crime in the twisting warrens of Limehouse or Lincoln's Inn. With his dressing-gown wrapped around his gaunt figure, his chair drawn up before the blazing fireplace, and a Couffignal trailing smoke from between his stained fingers, he stared into the flames, while I hung on every word.

"It was a small coaster carrying soft drinks," he said, his voice low, his mind obviously reliving those harrowing days. "The *Glorious Cott*. It sank in Dire Straits, and the crew was fortunate enough to find several floats in the area, placed there without a doubt to mark the channel, and to which they clung in desperation. So tenaciously did they cling, in fact, that when we came to rescue them, we had a hard time separating the men from the buoys——"

It was at that moment, when I was intent upon hearing the end of his fascinating tale, that there came the sound of heavy footsteps upon the stairs, and a moment later the door opened to admit none other than Homes's brother, Criscroft. It was rare, indeed, for Criscroft Homes to appear at our quarters without prior notice, and rarer still when he forsook his niche at the Foreign Office in weather as beastly as we were suffering that day. He brushed aside our welcome, as well as the snow on his shoulders, and fell into the basket chair across from his brother.

"Schlock," he said heavily, "I fear the Government has need for your services again."

"I am, as always, at your service," replied Homes at once, his fine eyes alight at the thought of a new challenge. "Pray tell me the cause of your concern."

"Yes," said Criscroft, and frowned into the fire a moment, putting his thoughts in order. Then at last he sighed mightily and swung his chair to face his brother.

"Schlock," he said, his deep voice vibrant with emotion, "as you may or may not know, our Postal Service has been having its difficulties of late. Not only has its income failed to cover its expenses, but its deficit has been increasing. Add to this the fact that its losses have also been substantial, and you can begin to understand the problem. Or," he added ominously, "a portion of the problem."

Homes tented his fingers and observed Criscroft over them queryingly. Criscroft nodded, as if in recognition of his brother's attention, and continued.

"Now," he said, "as if this triple confoundment were not enough, we have come across a scheme we believe aimed at using the Postal Service without payment. It is our considered opinion that this dastardly plot must be nipped in the bud, or there is no telling where it might lead."

"Bankruptcy?" I hazarded.

Criscroft paid me no heed. He reached into his inner jacket pocket, bringing forth several envelopes. He studied them for a few moments, his face dark with emotion, and then handed them across to his brother as he went on.

"Those are standard envelopes, addressed to people in greater London from different locations throughout the world in the course of everyday business. Do not concern yourself either with the names or the street addresses; the people and their locations have been investigated in every detail — without their knowledge, of course — and have been found to be innocent of any involvement. The same is true of the senders of the letters. Yet, in every case someone has managed to use the envelopes to transmit a mysterious message in code, adding it blatantly to the cover after the legitimate postage has been paid, and in this manner saving himself monies which rightly belong to the Queen."

They both sprang instantly to their feet at mention of Her Majesty, but once they were re-seated, I came behind my friend's chair to study the envelopes in his hand over his shoulder. Surely enough, as Criscroft had stated, in each case someone had added a series of common but mysterious numbers and letters after the name of the city. The one on the first envelope, which I could not help but note had been sent from someone in Nottingham to someone in the City, had added to it the strange combination of: 2WC 6ST 3L. The second had been addressed to someone in St. Dunstans Hill, and in a handwriting remarkably similar to that of the letter-writer himself, someone had added the symbols: 2L 8FL 6G. The final envelope, which I noted had come from some place called Ohio in the colonies, had after the name of the city of London: 2J 4L 2W.

"Now," said Criscroft, while Homes continued to study the strange numbers and letters, "we in the Foreign Office have tried to consider all possible reasons why anyone would add such common numbers and letters to the envelopes. We have ruled out mere scribbling for the sake of mischief; we feel that not even miscreants who are thus using the Postal Service for their own ends would stoop to such malevolence. No, there is a purpose in this malfeasance, and we must know that purpose, as well as those responsible!"

Homes nodded. "One thing is certain," said he, pinching his lip and then rubbing it briskly in an effort to reduce the pain, "the symbols could not have been placed on the envelopes at the instigation of the Postal Service itself."

"Of course," Criscroft said, agreeing. "That was evident at once."

"I do not understand!" I cried. "How can you be so sure?"

The two men considered me pityingly.

"There are only two possible reasons why the Postal Service would ask people to add symbols of any nature to addresses on envelopes," Homes said in his insufferable, didactic manner. "Either to aid in making their deliveries more rapidly, or to make them more slowly. Agreed?"

"Agreed," I admitted a bit shamefacedly.

"But," he continued, one finger in the air — I assumed for emphasis — "to make the delivery faster cannot be in the best interest of the British Empire, or else it would have been done long since."

"And to use the mysterious code to make the service slower," said Criscroft, "would be in the nature of sending coals to Newcastle." He put me and my puerile comments out of mind and came to his feet, turning to his brother. "Schlock, I am sure you realize I would like to remain and solve this problem with you, but unfortunately today is Bingo at my club, and I have been honoured at being selected to call the numbers. I hope you understand."

"Of course!" said Homes warmly and also came to his feet, clasping his brother's hand. "I shall do my best to solve this code and be back to you as soon as possible."

Criscroft removed his watch from his weskit and consulted it. "But not before nine," he warned. "Our game does not end until then," and with a brief wave of his hand he clumped down the stairs and out into the snow.

Homes dropped back into his chair and placed the envelopes on the table before him, after which he tamped his pipe with Old Mephitis and lit up, sending clouds of smoke ceilingwards. He frowned down at the mysterious letters and numerals while I also studied them over his shoulder. Suddenly I had a thought.

"But, Homes," I said, "does not this seem a rather haphazard method of getting a message from one person to another? Would not a private messenger, or even the telegraph, be more reliable?"

"You do not understand," Homes said, shaking his head at me rather sadly. "The purpose of these rascals is to save money, not to spend it." He fell into a brown study, mumbling to himself, but audibly. "I should have suspected the finger in this pie of Professor Marty—the one they call, with reason, The Butcher—since I should have thought only his organization to be large enough to cover all corners of the globe. But I have been reliably assured by Inspector Lastride that the Professor is no longer on the run, but has gone straight. He is now in the realty business. A pity, in a way. He was a formidable opponent, and made life interesting. Ah, well..."

He reached behind him for a reference book and took it down, but it apparently did little to help him solve the puzzle, for a moment later he had returned the volume to its place and in its stead took another from the shelf. Since I know that Homes, when he is in this mood, is apt to be uncommunicative for hours, I repaired to the sideboard and was about to experiment with the addition of sweet Vermouth to colonial whisky—a concoction originally suggested, I believe, by a certain man, Hattan—when Homes looked up, the expression on his long face even colder than usual.

"Watney!" said he icily, his eyes boring into mine. "Why don't you go to your room? You know how I hate your fumbling around when I am trying to concentrate!"

"Fumbling?" I cried, hurt to the quick by the unfair accusation. "I picked out the Vermouth first shot!" But I had long since learned to read every nuance of Homes's tones, and felt it possible he wished me to leave him. Without another word I tucked the two required bottles under my arm and left the room.

It was late afternoon when I returned. The sun was beginning to hide its watery quality over the chimneypots of Bagel Street, and my experiments, while successful, required more material for the continuance. Homes was scribbling furiously on a bit of paper, and from the crumpled bits already littering the floor, and the acrid fumes that filled the room, it was evident he had not left his labours since my departure. As I entered he looked up, a faint smile on his face that indicated to me he had seen rift in the previously insoluble problem.

"Watney!" he exclaimed, his fine eyes begging my pardon. "You must forgive me! My very good and old friend, you should know me and my moods by now. When I am in the midst of a problem that threatens to best me, I'm afraid I am quite impossible."

"Agreed," said I cordially.

"Or, at least, difficult."

"Impossible was closer, I believe," said I, after giving the matter some thought.

"We shall not argue the matter," he said a bit savagely. But then he brightened again. "However, the important thing is that I believe I have a strong hint as to the meaning of those cryptic symbols. As well," he added, "as a possible means of resolving the problem they represent."

"Homes!" I cried. "Congratulations!"

"Not quite yet," he said, and came to his feet. "First I must go out and verify my suspicions, but when I return it is possible I shall have need of your services again, Watney. There could be a slight chance of danger."

"How slight?" I asked.

"I should have my revolver handy," he said, "as well as having the fireplace poker at hand, if I were you. One never can tell."

With this remark he disappeared into his room to return a few minutes later. He had exchanged his deerstalker for a ragged cap holding a jehu's badge, and was wearing a torn and wrinkled great-coat with patches on the elbows and held together at the front with large safety pins; while on his feet were a tattered and scuffed pair of brogans missing several buttons. As has often been said, when Homes chose detection as his career, the stage lost a great wardrobe mistress. He paused at the sideboard to stuff a chutney sandwich into the pocket of his disreputable coat, and then moved to the door.

"Ta," he said bravely, and disappeared down the steps.

It was after seven o'clock when Homes returned. He came up the stairs with so sprightly a tread that I was sure he had confirmed whatever suspicions had driven him out into the cold. He shook the snow from his outlandish costume and disappeared into his room, and when he came out, wrapped comfortably in his old dressing-gown, I charged him with the fact. He acknowledged the accuracy of my conclusion with a broad smile, but it did not remain for long.

"I believe we shall be having a visitor shortly," said he, "and one who may well prove to be dangerous. You have your revolver ready?"

"As always, Homes," I said, tugging the weapon with some difficulty from an inner pocket where it had snagged on the lining.

"Good! And I shall seat myself here, within reach of the poker."

I replaced the revolver in the inner pocket, again with a bit of difficulty. "And now, Homes," I said, once the weapon had again caught in the lining, "I would be most appreciative if you would be so kind as to elucidate this most mysterious affair. Just what did the code say? And who are we awaiting at the moment?"

Homes chuckled.

"You may recall," said he, "that I remarked on Inspector Lastride's running on about Professor Marty no longer being involved in crime, but instead being a legitimate businessman dealing in real-estate properties? Well, as he usually is, Lastride was only half right. It is true that the Professor is in real estate, but he is the same old Professor for all that. In addition to saving money by using the Postal Service without payment, as Criscroft so accurately deduced, Professor Marty deals in slum properties, as low a profession as can be imagined!"

"Slum properties?" I asked, amazed. "How were you able to deduce that, Homes?"

"From the envelopes, of course." He reached around him and brought the three envelopes from the table, handing them to me one at a time. "I should have solved the problem sooner, had I considered the Professor and his present endeavour, but once I suspected his involvement it was fairly simple. This one, for example, sent from Nottingham and to which one of the Professor's henchmen has added the notation: 2WC 6ST 3L. What do those strange numbers and letters suggest to you, Watney?"

"Nothing, I'm afraid, Homes," I replied honestly.

"Well," said he, "to be honest they meant little to me, as well, at first. But once I considered the possibility of Professor Marty's involvement, a brief trip to the location gave me the answer. It is a building in terrible shape. It has two water closets, is six storeys in height, and has exactly three lights—to wit, 2WC, 6ST, 3L. Most of the rooms are of the windowless type, long since outlawed by the Town Council, although such rules mean little to Professor Marty."

"But this second envelope, Homes?" I asked. "It says nothing that could be construed as meaning WCs, or storeys, or lights!"

"That also puzzled me at first, Watney," Homes admitted, "until I noted that it was addressed to St. Dunstans Hill, within a block of St. Mary's and the Bow Bells, and in the very heart of the Cockney district. In that neighbourhood they never refer to a water closet except as a loo; they also refer to floors rather than storeys, and glass for windows. That, incidentally," he added, "was one of the worst of the slums; only two sanitary facilities for eight storeys!"

"But the third, Homes?" I asked, perplexed. "From this place called Ohio, in the colonies, if such a name can be accredited?"

"That," Homes admitted, "took me the longest time and I was about to abandon my theory of the solution to the various codes as common when I was fortunate enough to refer to my dictionary of colonial argot. It seems in the colonies they call a water closet a john–the dictionary merely states it, it does not explain it–even as they call storeys levels, although they still refer to the glassed openings in a wall as a window."

"Masterful, Homes!" I said in admiration. Then I remembered something else, my memory prodded by the prodding I was receiving from my revolver. "But who is this dangerous visitor we are expecting? And what have you done to scotch his nefarious scheme?"

Homes's jaw tightened; his hand clutched the arm of his chair until the knuckles were white against the albescence of his skin.

"Watney, you should have seen the dismal hovels from which Professor Marty makes his living! Any step would be justified in protecting the Postal Service, as well as foiling the Professor, and I have taken those steps. In addition to my own activities at Professor Marty's home, it was necessary to have the Bagel Street Regulars do a bit of breaking and entering; but as you know, where justice is concerned I always believe the end justifies the means. The Regulars have been instructed to discover many of the letters giving information useful to the Professor and to change the conditions so that the properties will no longer appear so attractive to the fiendish Professor Marty!"

"Change the conditions?" I asked, confused.

"Exactly! If a building is described as having three water closets, in a total of eight storeys, say, and with only two windows–properties the Professor would be in a hurry to buy and rent at exorbitant rates to poor souls–the Regulars are instructed to change the code so that it appears the building has, say, twelve water closets, is only three storeys tall, and has, say, eighteen windows." He smiled, but there was little true humour in the smile. "No, Watney, the Professor will soon discover the source of his miserable rent gouging drying up!"

"But how are you certain it is the Professor who is involved in this scheme?" I asked. "Have you traced the ownership of any of these properties to him?"

Homes considered me with disappointment.

"Watney, Watney! Of course I did not; it would have been totally unnecessary, and would have wasted precious time! But who else has a world-wide organization and is also in real estate? It can only be Marty, and here, if I am not mistaken, is the Professor now!"

The door opened and as Homes had so accurately predicted, the huge figure with the orange-coloured hair filled the doorway, a frown upon his face. I instantly reached for my pistol, struggling to remove it from my jacket lining, and finally succeeded. I clapped the pistol to the Professor's head.

"Take heed!" I cried. "One move on your part and I shall fire!"

Professor Marty brushed me aside and turned to Homes.

"Homes," he said, and there seemed to be more sadness in his tone than the anger I had expected, "you have surpassed yourself! It seems you have finally gone over the edge! What on earth possessed you to do what you did at my home? And leaving your calling card, yet! You can expect a bill for repairs!"

Homes smiled coolly.

"I only hope you have learned your lesson from my symbolic action, Professor," he said. "I might also mention that since it was obvious that postmen had to be your accomplices, a message has gone up on the bulletin board of the Postal Workers Union Headquarters, advising against further coöperation in your scheme. Go, now, and gouge no more."

Professor Marty turned to me, taking the pistol from my hand and absent-mindedly tucking it back into my jacket lining.

"I would suggest you keep your friend indoors, Doctor," he said heavily. "I think he's playing pinochle with a bridge deck." And with no further ado he turned and left the room.

It was obvious the Professor was under some strain, since Homes was not playing cards at all, but was sitting quietly, smiling at the recently closed door.

"Homes!" I said. "What on earth did you do at the Professor's home that brought him here in this mood?"

Homes laughed aloud.

"What I did will make him think twice before he attempts any of his tricks on the Postal Service again," said he with a chuckle. "I poured glue in his letter-slot!"

It was the following morning and I was just pouring curried syrup over my chutney scones, when Homes appeared at the breakfast table. As he seated himself and began peeling a parsley, I hastily opened the morning journal and began searching for some possible case that might be of interest to my friend, for I knew his hatred of idleness. He looked at me queryingly across the table.

"There is this, Homes," I said, reading further into the article. "It seems that despite your excellent efforts of yesterday, the problems of the Postal Service appear still not to be completely resolved."

"No?" he inquired interestedly.

"Yes," I said. "It seems that the normal confusion of the postal system has somehow been compounded. Letters apparently destined for one postal zone are mysteriously being sent to another, and the result is havoc!"

"Then our job was only half done!" cried Homes, coming to his feet, his eyes flashing. "A letter to the authorities offering my services, if you will, Watney!"

The Adventure of

The Patient Resident

IT was when interesting cases were either rare or non-existent that my friend Mr. Schlock Homes found life most difficult to bear, nor was he loath to pass on his feelings of frustration to me. It made for uncomfortable moments for me, but at the same time the hiatus in work allowed me the necessary time to bring some order to my voluminous notes regarding the many cases I was privileged to share with the man a German acquaintance of ours called, in his delightful accent, the "vorld's vurst conzulting detectiff."

I recall in particular one warm sunny afternoon in June in the year '77, with the shadows just beginning to creep across the ceiling of our quarters at 221B Bagel Street. Homes and I had recently returned home from a visit to France. There, in the chief city of the *département* of the Rhone, my friend had successfully tracked down a miscreant using the sewers of the city to give the place a bad odour. I was in the process of putting my notes together under the tentative title of *The Adventure of the Lyons' Main*, while Homes, bored almost to distraction by not having a problem to occupy him, was slouched in the basket chair with his violin, playing what even to my untutored ear sounded like *An Err on the G-String*. I had just decided that some liquid refreshment might aid in my literary efforts, when there came a diffident knock on the door and a moment later our page had entered with the late afternoon post.

Homes quickly put aside his instrument, eagerly taking the packet from the boy and tearing the letters open in order, anxiously seeking some missive that might indicate a problem to test his enormous energies and massive brain. With a sigh I brought my attention from the sideboard to watch, wondering what new adventure for us might be concealed in the formidable pile of correspondence; but as Homes tossed aside piece after piece once he had perused it, and as the smiling look of anticipation on his lean face slowly turned to one of growing disappointment, I shook my head and returned to contemplating the sideboard. Suddenly there was a muffled exclamation from

my friend and I looked over at him once again to see Homes gripping an
envelope in his hand and staring at it with concentration.

"Homes!" I cried. "What is it?"

"Later, Watney," he said impatiently, and reached behind him for one of
his reference books. He brought it down, found the page he sought, and ran
his finger down a column; but instead of satisfying whatever curiosity had led
him to the book in the first place, the information he found seemed to puzzle
him further. With a frown he returned the book to its proper place on the
shelf and continued to finger the envelope as if intrigued by it.

"But, Homes," I repeated. "What *is* it?"

"A rather interesting problem," he replied, and tapped the envelope with
his finger. "To begin with, the letter appears to have been misdirected, for it is
not addressed to me, but rather to a certain 'The Resident.' I can only assume
the 'The' to be an abbreviation for the name 'Theodore,' but there is no
Theodore Resident in the London Directory. As a matter of fact, the
directory shows no person named Resident with any first name."

"How extremely odd, Homes!" I exclaimed.

"Yes," he replied. "Still, the address is quite clear – 221B Bagel Street – so I
can only assume the message was intended for me, although the false name,
I am sure, has some meaning for the writer."

With a shrug that indicated he was merely putting the matter of the name
aside for the moment and would return to it in time, he slit the envelope with
his pocket-knife and withdrew the contents, unfolding the single sheet the
envelope contained. I rose and came to stand at my friend's side, reading over
his shoulder. The sheet he had unfolded appeared to me to be nothing more
than an ordinary advertisement, and one which made little sense to me. Little
did I know that the words on that innocent-looking sheet of paper were to lead
to one of Homes's most interesting cases, and one which I now find in my
notes as *The Adventure of the Patient Resident.* At that moment I was only
puzzled at the strange words, which I reproduce below for the reader:

GRAND PREMIERE
NEW PANCRAS CINEMA
INTERNATIONAL WEEK

Sunday	DANDY IN ASPIC
Monday	UNDERCOVER
Tuesday	RULERS OF THE SEA
Wednesday	STROMBOLI
Thursday	ENCOUNTERS
Friday	MORT DU CYGNE
Saturday	RASHOMON

45 Lyme Street – Basement

"Homes," I cried, "what nonsense! Can you make the slightest sense of this gibberish?"

"Oh, I should hardly call it gibberish," Homes replied, with that insufferable air of superiority he always employed when explaining something which was clear as crystal to him, but which I found unfathomable. "It is, as you can see, an advertisement."

"I understand that, Homes," I said, hurt that he should think me that obtuse. "But for what?"

"Really, Watney," he said, frowning at me. "At times you try my patience. It is, obviously, an advertisement for a new restaurant. And," he added, wrinkling his nose, "an advertisement I find unbearably offensive in its attempt to be what the newer generation calls 'cute.' I am, as you know, Watney, a most patient man, but there are limits to that patience. I find as I grow older an increasing dislike for that childish attempt at cleverness as evidenced by this advertisement. The idiots," he added, "are also unable to spell!"

"Spell? Cute? A new restaurant, Homes?" I asked, mystified, and considered the advertisement again. "Is that what a 'cinema' is?"

"I have no idea what the derivation of the word might be," he replied. "It sounds like an Indian spice, possibly related to cinnamon, but definitely culinary. Still, to think of *any* spice, particularly cinnamon, being added to pancreas—which they have misspelled, and which we know as sweetbreads—is unthinkable!"

I stared in profound admiration as my friend ran his finger down the list and continued his discourse.

"Whatever they refer to in the argot as being 'dandy,' I cannot imagine it, or anything else, being smothered in aspic!

"Undercover!" said he with a snort. "Possibly pheasant, or more likely, simple chicken. And if pheasant, undoubtedly of poor quality or they would have identified more precisely what they are serving under cover!

"The rulers of the sea, of course, are shark, and while I have heard that some people consider the flesh of this predator to be palatable, I should not care for it myself."

I nodded in agreement. "And the stromboli?"

"An Italian pasta, obviously. You see, they advertise the cuisine as being of international character." He continued down the list. "And the fact that on Thursdays they openly admit they serve *en counters,* and not on the regular tables, undoubtedly to save napery, does not speak very highly of the establishment. Not to mention the fact that they wait until Saturday, when they have the leftovers of the entire week at their disposal, before they serve Japanese food!"

"The cygne I understand," I said, proud to be able to contribute. "That is the French word for swan, is it not?"

"Yes. Although," Homes added cynically, "in all probability they will merely serve pressed duck."

"But, Homes," I said as a thought struck me, "who could this Mort be?"

"Most probably a tailor in the neighbourhood who presses it, since I doubt a restaurant of this calibre would have a presser of their own." He shook his head. "No, Watney, I fear this is one eating establishment we shall not patronize!"

"A pity in a way, Homes," I remarked wistfully. "I have been tiring a bit of late of Mrs. Essex's fried chutneys."

"On the other hand," Homes pointed out, his eyes twinkling, "the advertisement speaks nothing of a lounge."

I looked over his shoulder and saw it was true. No refreshments!

"A place like that should be barred," I said with feeling, and was about to return in disgust to my labours when Homes suddenly frowned, his former good humour gone as quickly as it had come.

"What is it, Homes?" I inquired anxiously.

"Has it occurred to you, Watney," he said, staring at the sheet of paper in all seriousness, almost as if he were seeing it for the first time, "that it is exceedingly odd that this advertisement, intended to interest its readers in a new restaurant, should be sent to me? While I have no objection to a proper meal now and then, nobody, I warrant, would call me a gourmet."

"True, Homes," I said, thinking about it, and then recalled something else. "But the message was not sent to you, but to this Theodore Resident. Possibly he —"

"Come, come, Watney! At *my* address? Possibly, next to 10 Downing Street and the Lyons Corner House, the most famous address in all London?" He shook his head and reviewed the advertisement as he spoke. "No, Watney, there is something here that requires further study." He glanced up at me significantly. "I shall probably be busy attempting to make sense of this message for some time," he said. "Why don't you take the opportunity to verify the pub closing hours and see if they might have been changed in the past fortnight?"

"An excellent suggestion, Homes!" I cried, and then suddenly paused, eyeing him dubiously. "But will you not require my assistance?"

"I shall do my best to manage without you, Watney," said he, heavily.

"Very well, then," said I, and went down the steps, remarking to myself, as always, at the true unselfishness of my old friend.

It was just after eleven that evening that I returned to our rooms, having verified that not one of the pubs within a two-mile radius had changed their hours by so much as a minute. I went up the stairs, surprised to find them a bit steeper than usual, prepared to tell Homes about the closing hours and receive his congratulations on a job well done, but just as I was about to enter,

I heard a loud exclamation from within. Without further ado I burst through the door to find Homes staring at the advertisement in horror.

"Homes!" I cried. "What is it?"

"I am a fool!" he cried.

"Well, sometimes you do seem a bit—" I began, but before I could continue, Homes had come to his feet and was moving rapidly towards his rooms.

"Later, Watney," he said. "It is good you have come, and when you did! There is not a moment to lose! One second while I change into more suitable raiment and we shall be off."

"Off, Homes?" I asked, stifling a yawn, and moved towards the sideboard to see if possibly the liquid fare I had been subjected to in the course of my scientific experiment that evening had its equal in our more limited stock. But before I could check more than one or two mixtures, Homes had come hurrying from his room dressed for the street, and had grasped me by the arm.

"Be careful, Homes!" I cried. "You will spill it!"

He paid me no heed. "You have your pistol, Watney?"

"It's around somewhere, I believe, Homes," I replied, and tasted my drink. But before I even had a chance to make a decent judgment, Homes was joggling my arm again.

"Well, get it!" he said savagely. "I have my bull's-eye lantern under my Inverness, and my own revolver in my pocket. We must hurry if we are to prevent this foul crime from being consummated!"

"What foul crime, Homes?" I asked, and began looking about vaguely for my pistol.

"I will tell you on the way," he replied fiercely, and picked my pistol from its usual place on the desk and thrust it savagely into my pocket. I was about to remonstrate that I was wearing my best suit, but Homes had already plunged down the steps and I could hear him at the kerb calling feverishly at a passing carriage.

I barely had time to finish my drink when his voice came up the stairwell, demanding my presence. With a sigh I descended, finding the steps even steeper than before. Homes had managed a hansom and was already inside. He grasped my arm to drag me aboard, and I fell back into my seat, closing my eyes, as Homes called up loudly to our driver.

"45 Lyme Street, and a tanner extra if you get us there in five minutes, driver!"

Our jehu needed no further persuasion, and as he cracked his whip over his horse's head we took off with a bound over the rough cobblestones. Homes leaned over and shook me. I sighed.

"All right, Homes," I said, trying to sit a bit more erect. "What is this all about? Where are we going?"

"To that restaurant we saw advertised," he replied grimly.

"But, Homes," I said, surprised, "it has no bar! Besides, I thought you held the place in contempt. Also, to tell you the truth, I've been eating so many cashews tonight that I really have little appetite."

"You do not understand, Watney," he said fiercely, and reached for the advertisement in his pocket. He pulled it out but before he unfolded it, he looked at me. "Tell me, Watney, have you ever listed the days of the week in their alphabetical order?"

"Why, no, Homes," I said, thinking about it, and then added apologetically, "I've never really felt the need to, you see."

"Well," Homes said, heavily, "had you done so you would have noticed they come in the order of Friday, Monday, Saturday, Sunday, Thursday, Tuesday, and Wednesday."

"Really, Homes?" I murmured.

"Yes. And had you paid the slightest attention to the menus offered on this advertisement," said he coldly, unfolding the sheet and thrusting it under my nose as if expecting me to be able to read it by the intermittent light cast by the passing gas-lamps, "you might have noticed that the first letters of the various dishes for the week-days in alphabetical order, spell out a word!"

"How interesting, Homes," I said, yawning.

"Exactly! For the word is—murders!"

"Oh? But by what means will this foul scheme be perpetrated?" I asked, blinking rapidly to keep awake. "A tailor's awl in the pressed duck? Or from the natural declination of week-old leftovers in the Rashomon dish?" I immediately wished I had not mentioned the latter, and leaned further to get some fresh air.

"By nothing that simple," said Homes, his face a mask of sternness. "Once I had the basics of the scheme, it was easily supposed that if the first letter of the cuisine formed an anagram of the word 'murders,' then quite obviously the answer lay in an anagram of the final letters!"

"And did it, Homes?" I asked, yearning for my bed.

"It did, indeed. And the word was—arsenic!"

"What word was arsenic, Homes?" I began, but before he could answer we had come with a clatter into Lyme Street and had pulled up before Number 45, the hansom horse heaving and frothing. In a trice Homes was on the pavement, flinging our fare with the tip to our driver, and had pulled me from my comfortable place as our cab moved away in the night.

I looked about. The establishment before which we stood was dark, and I hoped that Homes would recognize the fact and allow us to return to Bagel Street and our comfortable beds. But Homes did not seem at all surprised by the darkness but moved instead stealthily in the direction of the rear of the building.

"Homes!" I said crossly. "What are we doing here at this hour? The place is obviously closed."

"Exactly, Watney," he said with a tinge of excitement in his voice. "Much better that we get into their kitchen when there are no chefs about with cleavers! And should they have left guards on the premises, we have our weapons! Come!"

"Come where, Homes?" I asked a bit petulantly.

"I said — but never mind! We are wasting time. Once we have located the kitchen and discovered the whereabouts of this arsenic and have removed it, I shall leave the proprietor a note telling him that all is known. I rather doubt they will attempt this malfeasance in the future."

As he had been speaking we had arrived at the rear of the building, and Homes immediately tackled the door-lock with his set of picks. A moment later and we could hear the click as the tumblers gave way to his skill. "Come, Watney," he said in a whisper, "and have your pistol ready!"

"Ready for what, Homes?" I began, but he had already turned the knob and was prepared to enter. With one last look over his shoulder to make sure I was with him, he took a deep breath and swung the door wide.

There was total silence for a moment, and then we seemed to hear a faint murmur of sound from somewhere below. Homes slid back the cover of his bull's-eye lantern and swung the steady beam about. We were in some sort of storehouse, it appeared, although in one corner we were able to see a set of steps leading downward.

"Of course," Homes whispered. "The advertisement said basement."

He withdrew his gun and with his weapon ready and his lantern beam on the stair steps, he led the way. Slowly we descended, and as we did so the strange sounds we had been hearing seemed to grow louder. At the bottom of the steps we saw a heavy velour curtain which seemed to contain a good portion of the strange sounds we had been hearing.

Homes instantly covered the lantern and in total darkness we groped our way to the curtain. A quick touch on my shoulder to assure me he was ready and to warn me to be prepared with my own weapon, and Homes in a sudden dramatic move swept aside the curtain.

It was close to his final move, for there before us, bearing down on us, was a huge locomotive. I at once recognized the sounds we had been hearing through the intervening curtain. The engine was getting closer as we stood, transfixed, while the great monster loomed nearer and nearer, its stack spewing black smoke, its wheels clattering over the rails, its whistle screaming its warning.

Suddenly Homes woke from his trance and had grasped me and dragged me back through the curtain, our weapons forgotten. We hurried up the steps and out into the evening air. Once clear, Homes leaned against the wall, wiping perspiration from his brow.

"A close call, that, Watney," said he and took a deep breath. "But at least we need not worry about the future of that murderous establishment."

"How is that, Homes?" I asked, awake at last from the terrible fright I had just suffered.

"The fools have located their restaurant on the tracks of the King's Cross railway tunnel," said he, and despite our close call he could not help but smile. "I doubt they will have any customers at all, with all that noise and smoke!"

And he walked calmly to the kerb to hail a cab.

I came to breakfast a bit late the following morning. For some unknown reason I had awakened with a headache and had remained abed a while to allow it to abate. Homes had already completed his repast and was seated at his desk, poring over the London Directory. I seated myself and had scarcely begun to butter a chutney, shuddering a bit as I did so, when suddenly Homes looked up with a loud exclamation.

"Not so loud, please, Homes," I said. "What is it?"

"I am a fool!" he cried.

"Could I answer that later, Homes?" I began. "At the moment I really am in no state —"

But he was paying me no attention. "The misdirected letter!" he cried, his finger pressed tightly to an entry in the directory. "I should have considered the possibility that the writer was dyslectic! Of course! The letter was meant to be addressed to Mr. Theodore Bagel at 221B Resident Street!"

He swung about, bringing down another volume, swiftly leafing through it to the entry he sought. He looked up, his face grim.

"As I suspected, Mr. Bagel is a chemist, undoubtedly with the ability to obtain arsenic at his convenience! And although his scheme may have failed in this one instance, there is no telling where and when he may try it in another place. A letter to this Mr. Bagel, if you will, Watney! Possibly once he knows that Schlock Homes is onto his murderous scheme, he will desist!"

The Adventure of

The Belles Letters

IT was a warm sunny day in late June in the year '79 and both my friend Mr. Schlock Homes and myself were taking our ease in our quarters at 221B Bagel Street, Homes softly humming the cannonade from the *1812 Overture,* while I cheerfully went over my financial statements for the Internal Revenue Service. Homes was entitled to his relaxation; he had just returned from a strenuous trip to the Malay Peninsula where he had gone at the behest of the Archipelago Administration to investigate the mysterious population explosion that had gripped one of the principal islands, a case I find delineated in my journal as *The Adventure of the Giant Rut of Sumatra.*

But little did we know, as we idly passed the time, that very shortly we would be engaged on a case that would make all of Homes's previous intricate analyses appear minor in comparison to the insulsity he was able to exhibit in the affair I find annotated in my casebook as *The Adventure of the Belles Letters.*

I had just moved a decimal point to the left in my INCOME column and was contemplating moving one to the right in my EXPENSES column in order to be fair about it, when there came the sound of footsteps upon the stairs, and a moment later our page had opened the door to admit none other than Inspector Lestoil of Scotland Yard. The Inspector stood without speaking, twisting his bowler in his hands, obviously perturbed to be forced once again to seek the help of a person the Yard considered more hebetudinous than fortuitous in his solution of problems. Homes smiled at Lestoil cordially.

"Pray take the basket chair, Inspector," said he, "and let me know what is on your mind. I see you have recently visited the Buddhist monastery in Jubblepore in India, since the mould on the left side of your brogan grows only on the northeast side of the temple there, to my knowledge."

"I had to stop at a pharmaceutical factory making some of those new so-called drugs the other day," Lestoil replied, seating himself. "You would think they would sweep the floor once in a while! But I am not here to discuss drugs this time, Mr. Homes. I am here because there has been a murder done, and murder most foul! And to be honest with you, we at the Yard are at a complete loss!"

"Ah," said Homes with a smile, rubbing his hands in a manner that indicated either his intense interest in a case of capital dimensions, or that Mrs. Essex had once again failed to furnish dry towels for the bathroom. "Pray give me the details."

"Yes. Well," the Inspector said, bringing forth his notebook and referring to it, "the victim was a Mrs. Janet Belles, who lived with her husband, Robert —a collector of coins and stamps—in one of those new high-rise apartment buildings in St. John's Wood, a place called Subterranean Towers. Mrs. Belles was found lying over one of those game boards that are so popular these days. Her head had been bludgeoned."

Homes was paying close attention. "I see. Was her husband present at the time?"

"Unfortunately no, and therefore can furnish us with no information of value. He was in a different part of the apartment and returned to the game room to find his wife dead, at which point he says he immediately notified the authorities."

"I see." Homes frowned. "But surely as the victim's husband he must have some opinion! What sort of man is he?"

Lestoil considered the question for several moments before answering. "A smallish man in size, and rather browbeaten by his wife, if the neighbours are to be believed. Still, there are people who stand for that, especially when the wife has all the money."

"I mean, what is he like?"

"Rather absent-minded, I should say," Lestoil replied with a frown on his face. "After calling us he immediately repaired to the basement of the building, where we found him stuffing his dressing-gown into the gas furnace which he had lit, completely forgetting that this is the month of June. And also," the Inspector added, recalling something else, "all during our interview he kept polishing the poker from their apartment fireplace, completely overlooking the fact that winter is still many months away."

"He could, of course, simply be a person who does not like to leave things to the last minute," Homes said thoughtfully, and shrugged. "However, let us forget the husband and continue. What else can you tell me of the case?"

Inspector Lestoil hesitated a moment and then sighed. He reached into his pocket and brought out three small squares of polished wood, each with a letter stamped on it. "These were found clutched in the hand of the victim. I'm sure they have nothing to do with the case," he said, "but I know your mania for having every little bit of possible evidence, so I brought them along." And he laid them upon the table. I came to stand beside Homes to stare at the tiny squares of polished wood. The letters that faced us were B, B, and O.

Homes frowned at the strange sight for a moment and then looked up at the Inspector curiously. "Were there any other bits of wood with letters on them in evidence?"

"Oh, yes! Many," the Inspector said. "It appears the game she was involved in at the time of her demise was concerned with the placing of letters on a board for the purpose of forming words. However," he added hastily, "the only letters she was clutching were these three." He leaned forward anxiously, gripping his bowler tightly, considering Homes earnestly. "Do you think they might possibly be a clue, Mr. Homes?"

"Quite possibly," Homes replied, and fell into a brown study, staring intently at the three letters, while Inspector Lestoil and I both wondered what possible conclusion Homes could hope to come to with those three simple letters as his only clue. At last Homes turned to his reference shelf to withdraw a heavy dictionary; a few moments of consulting with it and he returned it to the shelf, nodded his head, and spoke in a manner as if to himself. "There are possibilities. . . . They will require verification, of course. . . ."

"But, Homes!" I exclaimed. "What could you possibly see in those three little letters that could give a lead in this case?"

Homes smiled, but it was a cold, grim smile.

"Those letters say much," said he, and turned to Lestoil. "If I am not mistaken, Inspector, you will find your criminal to be a large man with flat feet, red cheeks, addicted to the wearing of ornate clothing, and with a penchant for blowing whistles. He also, of course," Homes added with the air of one wishing to be quite factual, "can obviously be vicious at times, as witness this murder he has committed."

Inspector Lestoil was staring at Homes with a look of incredulity on his face. I could see his mind beginning to come to the conclusion that Homes was making sport of him."

"Really, Homes!" I said chidingly. "It does nothing to play the fool in a case involving murder!"

"No, no, Watney," Homes said impatiently, coming to his feet. "I am quite serious. At the moment there is much to be done, or otherwise I would be happy to explain all to you." He turned to the Inspector. "If you will wait until I change to other raiment, I shall be pleased to return to the scene of the crime with you."

He moved in the direction of his room, beginning to remove his dressing-gown as he did so. When he reappeared a few minutes later, I stared. Homes was wearing an old overcoat held together with safety-pins over long underwear, leaving a goodly bit of thin cotton-covered shank visible; and on his head was a battered trilby.

"Homes!" I cried in delight. "What an original disguise! What are you supposed to be?"

"A man whose landlady sent all his suits to the cleaners at one time," he said sourly. "You might pick them up for me, since I understand you have arranged for tickets this evening at Albert Hall, and I could scarcely go in this guise."

"Ah, yes," I said. "I had forgotten. Dmitri Shostakovich."

"Dmitri Shostakovich?" Homes queried, frowning, and then shrugged. "In time I undoubtedly could solve that, but one case at a time," and he led the way down the steps with Inspector Lestoil at his heels.

I had had a busy afternoon, what with picking up Homes's clothing at the cleaners, and finishing not only one set of books for the Internal Revenue, but being thorough by nature, a second set as well. I was having a congratulatory drink when I heard Homes's footsteps on the stairs, and a moment later he appeared, but without the Inspector. Still, there was a look of satisfaction on his face.

"Homes!" I said. "You have solved the case! Here, let me pour you a drink. Where is the Inspector?"

Homes accepted my proffered drink with a brief nod of thanks, settled himself in his favourite chair, quaffed deeply, and set the glass aside, reaching for his Maiskolben, a gift from a grateful King of Prussia for his help in the matter of Irene Addled.

"We are to meet the Inspector later this evening," said he, puffing smoke. "The man we seek works at night, and we shall confront him with proof of his black deed when he appears. As I so accurately surmised, he is a large fellow, so in addition to your bull's-eye lantern, Watney, I suggest you bring your pistol, as well. If you care to join in the end of this affair, that is," he added with a faint smile.

"Of course, Homes!" I said instantly. "But —" I frowned. "In all truth I am unable to understand how you could possibly see light in a case whose only clue were those three letters. And two of them the same, which would seem to me to reduce the chances enormously!"

Homes glanced at the clock and nodded as he settled further into his chair.

"There is ample time before we must leave," said he. "Allow me to use some of that time to explain this case to you." He reached into a pocket of the overcoat and brought out the three small wooden tiles, placing them face up upon the table. "To begin with," he said, once the letters were arranged to his satisfaction, "it occurred to me at once that Mrs. Belles, in selecting these letters, was attempting to leave some clue as to the identity of her assailant, but did not have time to complete her task before she expired.

"Still, the woman had made a brave start, and it would not do for us to fail to heed the direction in which she pointed. However, I could not think of any word beginning with a double B, and a quick glance at my dictionary verified that fact. There was, of course, the use of the double B to designate small pellets for a child's gun, but since Mrs. Belles was bludgeoned and not shot, and also because I could see no use for the letter O in that case, I abandoned this line of thinking at once.

"So there I was with the letters BBO and making no progress until it occurred to me that possibly the clue lay, not in the letters in the order of B, B, and O, but rather in the reverse order of O, B, B."

He applied a match to his pipe which had gone out during his discourse, and puffed it back to life while I waited breathlessly for the continuation of his sensational ratiocination. When the Maiskolben was once again burning to his satisfaction, Homes went on.

"Once I considered the letters in this sequence, I had taken a huge step towards solving the problem. What had Mrs. Belles been trying to spell when she selected those particular letters? The first thought that came to mind was the word ROBBER which contains the selected letters in the proper order; but then I considered that the word ROBBER contains six letters, and I did not think a dying woman would have picked a longer word when a shorter word, the word THIEF, would have conveyed the same meaning. Therefore, Mrs. Belles was not attempting to spell the word ROBBER.

"Still, there was no doubt she was seeking as short a word as possible to give us some hint as to her assailant. I then carried my analysis a bit further. Since I could think of no word that *ends* with a double letter B any more than any word that begins with them, there had to be another letter Mrs. Belles would have selected to follow, had the poor woman had the time. And the letter that could follow a double B with the greatest of logic is simply the letter Y!"

"Wonderful, Homes!" I said, making no attempt to hide my profound admiration for his masterful analysis. Then I frowned. "But what does OBBY mean, Homes?"

"I am not through," he said a bit testily, and continued. "Obviously, Mrs. Belles was seeking the shortest word for her message, and there are only three likely words in English that have a single letter before the combination of O, B, B, Y. Those words are: Bobby, Lobby, and Hobby. I hated to think that a London bobby might be involved in a crime this despicable, but I had to admit it was a possibility. Lobby suggested a doorman. Since both a doorman and a bobby would be large men with flat feet, with red cheeks from being out of doors a good bit of the time, and since both wear ornate uniforms and are both addicted to whistle blowing, one in pursuit of evil-doers, the other in seeking cabbies for tenants, I felt safe in describing the assailant as I did."

"But what about Hobby, Homes?" I inquired.

Homes looked at me with disdain. "Two out of three isn't bad," he said, and glanced at the mantel clock once again. "In any event," he went on, "a trip to the scene of the crime settled everything, as I was sure it would. I spoke with Mr. Belles, the victim's husband, and he was quick to agree that the assailant was undoubtedly the doorman. It seems that Mr. Belles has small use for the doorman, who, it appears, in addition to constantly bragging he was once in the circus as a contortionist, prefers to stay in his cubicle and drink tea on rainy nights, rather than offer service to the tenants."

Homes came to his feet, adjusted his safety pins, and put aside his pipe. "Subterranean Towers operates on a rather odd basis," he went on. "For reasons of economy there is no doorman on duty during the day, but only at night when the security of the building is felt to be more greatly threatened.

For this reason the man we seek will appear at work at nine o'clock, and we shall be meeting Inspector Lestoil at nine thirty on the nearest corner, prepared to make the arrest."

"But, Shostakovich!" I cried.

"Bless you," Homes said absently, and repaired to the sideboard where Mrs. Essex had put out a cold meal of curried chives and herring omelet. He slipped several of each into the cavernous pocket of his coat and moved to the stairway. "The lantern and your pistol, Watney," said he remindingly, and started down the steps.

Inspector Lestoil was waiting for us under the gas-lamp on the street corner closest the building; once we had seen to our weapons we advanced upon the building, ready to take the murderous doorman into custody. But to our surprise the lobby appeared to be deserted. The door to the cubicle where the doorman was accustomed to take his tea stood ajar, and the interior was empty.

Inspector Lestoil removed his bowler and scratched his head. "I cannot understand it," said he in a puzzled tone. "I saw the man enter this lobby a good half hour ago, yet he is nowhere in evidence at the moment!" He shrugged. "Possibly he is on an errand for one of the tenants."

"Possibly," Homes agreed, and leaned against the wall, prepared to wait, and to spend the time as he often did in mentally solving some problem or other. But I was more restless, and opened the door leading below, propping it open against my return. I raised my bull's-eye lantern and went down the steps. Once there, I called out.

"I say, Homes —"

"Later, Watney," said Homes in his usual insufferable tone.

"No, really, Homes —"

"I said later, Watney!"

"But quite seriously, Homes —"

My friend appeared in the door opening, glowering down at me. "Really, Watney! A few moments of silence given over to contemplation would do you no harm, you know!"

"Oh, I agree, I agree!" I said hastily. "Couldn't really do anyone any harm, I suppose. But still —"

Homes sighed, a martyr's sigh. "All right, Watney. What is it?"

"I just wished to inquire – this doorman, did he have a sort of a reddish uniform with buff piping?"

"I'm sure I have no idea. Why?"

"Well," I said apologetically, "there is this rather largish man with a reddish sort of uniform, with this buff – or possibly ecru – piping, and his head is in the gas furnace with the gas on. But no fire," I added, wishing to be accurate. I reached over and felt for the pulse; there was none. "He has no pulse," I added.

Homes sighed and came down the steps followed by Inspector Lestoil. The three of us managed to pull the man out and place his body on the floor. Homes contemplated the man with bitterness.

"So he cheated the hangman by committing suicide!" he said half-angrily.

"He has also been bludgeoned, Homes," I pointed out.

"No great trick for a man who was a circus contortionist," Homes said, and gave me a look that put my puerile comment in its place. He turned to Inspector Lestoil. "Well, Inspector, there's your case!"

"Thanks to you, Mr. Homes, only thanks to you!" said Inspector Lestoil with shining eyes, and gripped my friend's hand firmly in profound gratitude.

It was late the following morning when Homes put in his appearance at the breakfast table. By the time he had unfolded his serviette and had reached for his first buttered clove, I had almost finished perusing the morning journal.

"Well, Watney," said Homes with a faint smile, "from the look of dejection on your face I gather there are no interesting cases to be gleaned from the morning paper?"

"I'm afraid not, Homes," I said with a sigh, and then noticed a small article. "This has nothing to do with crime, I'm afraid, Homes, but it does mention a familiar name."

"Oh?" Homes said and waited for me to continue.

"Yes," I said. "It seems that Mr. Robert Belles is engaged to be married again, this time to the rich widow of a financier. She is quite a bit older than he is, but Mr. Belles claims it is true love."

"There are people like that, who are so enamoured of the married state that even a few hours or days away from it are too much," Homes said philosophically. "Fortunately, I am not one of them." He thought for a moment. "Still, after the help Mr. Belles gave me in pinning the murder of his wife on the doorman, the least I can do is congratulate him. A letter to Mr. Belles, if you please, Watney, and let us not make it impersonal. Address him 'My dear Bob...'"

The Adventure of
The Short Fuse

IT should not be thought that only cases involving either capital crimes or international intrigue earned the attention of my friend, Mr. Schlock Homes. At times, when there were no other problems upon which he could expend his particular talents, Homes was known to take on the most minor of commissions, although even to these he brought his own expertise in a manner it is doubtful any other could hope to emulate. This was particularly true in any case that evoked either his own personal sympathy to one party of a dispute, or his anger with the other, as was evidenced in the affair I find delineated in my notebook as *The Adventure of the Short Fuse.*

It was close upon noon one sunny day in late April of the year '78 when Homes made his appearance at the breakfast table of our quarters at 221B Bagel Street. I had long since finished my own repast of buttered chutneys, had searched the morning journals for some report of crime that might be of interest to Homes and myself—unfortunately finding nothing—and at the moment was just relaxing and enjoying a quiet pipe, when Homes entered the room, yawning. His sleeping late, however, was readily forgivable; he had arrived from the North of England but late the night before, where he had resolved the mysterious affair concerning young Rudolph Staine, Junior, a case I find outlined in my notes as *The Adventure of the Second Staine.*

Homes seated himself at the table, studied the cold remains of the buttered chutneys, now admittedly slightly rancid, made a grimace of distaste, and came to his feet, wandering to the window to stare down into the street, a frown upon his forehead.

"Homes," I said reprovingly. "You are not eating."

He turned to look at me, a faint smile replacing the frown on his saturnine features. "You are improving, Watney," said he. "You are beginning to note the obvious."

"Thank you, Homes," I said appreciatively.

"You are quite welcome," he replied, and once again turned to stare into the street. Wondering what could possibly attract Homes's attention to the extent of disregarding Mrs. Essex's rancid buttered chutneys, I came to stand beside him and looked down. But all I could see were a young man and a girl kissing each other passionately on the other side of the road. It was certainly no unusual sight in London in these dissolute days, yet it was precisely this sight which seemed to be the focus of my friend's attention. But before I could question him on the matter, Homes spoke over his shoulder.

"Osculation upon the pavement, Watney," said he, "always means an *affaire du coeur.*" He frowned slightly. "In fact," he added, "I believe we shall shortly be involved in the matter, for here to visit us, if I am not mistaken, comes one of the pair of lovers."

I glanced down again. Surely enough, the two had parted, the girl walking quickly down Bagel Street in the direction of the horse-cars, while the young man dodged several hansoms and was making his way to our very door. A moment later there was the sound of footsteps upon the stairs and our page was ushering into our presence the young man we had been observing. He stood in the opening, looking a trifle embarrassed, and holding tightly to a small box in his hands.

"Mr. Homes?" he said, and looked about. "I'm afraid I am disturbing you at your meal."

"It is nothing," Homes assured him in kindly tones as he glanced back at the chutneys. "It is *really* nothing. Pray take the basket chair, there, and tell me what brings you here. Other than the fact that you are a sapper by trade, come from the Cotswolds, and have a sweet tooth, I am afraid I know nothing of your problem."

The young man's mouth fell open in astonishment. Even I, who pride myself on being almost as astute as Homes from my many years of observing him, was completely taken aback. "Really, Homes!" I said chidingly. "Surely you are merely guessing!"

"Not at all," Homes said languidly. "The fact that the young man is a sapper is easily discerned; the marks of maple syrup upon his cravat is a common sign of those who tap the maple trees for the juice. Since maple trees grow principally in the Cotswolds, the area from which he has journeyed to visit us is just as easily deduced. And only a person with a sweet tooth for maple syrup would remain in the trade, since with today's growing industrialization there are many more lucrative positions to be had."

"It is truly amazing!" the young man exclaimed, hastily wiping off his cravat. "While I come from the Isle of Wight rather than the Cotswolds, and while I like sweets as much as the next man, I suppose, it is true that I am a sapper—or was until my recent discharge from Her Majesty's Fourteenth Demolition Division. I can see, Mr. Homes," he continued earnestly, "that what I have heard of you is the truth and that you are, indeed, the man to resolve my problem. I apologize for my carelessness with my pancakes at breakfast this morning, but the plain truth is I have been so upset of late that I scarcely know what I am doing, let alone what I am eating!"

Homes nodded and waited while our visitor adjusted himself to the basket chair. Then, seating himself across from the young man, Homes smiled at him. "Pray tell me your problem. You may speak quite openly before Dr. Watney, whose attention wanders freely."

"Yes, sir. Well, Mr. Homes," said the young man, "my name is Hosmer Angle, and I am on the horns of a dilemma. On the one hand, my religion forbids me to hate a person, but on the other hand, with this particular man, I cannot help myself!"

Homes raised an eyebrow at this strange and contradictory statement. The young man edged closer to the end of this chair, holding his small box tightly in his hands as he continued.

"Mr. Homes, let me explain. I am deeply in love, a love I am happy to say is returned, but unfortunately Marie, the girl I love, is already married to a person named Alex Northerland. Northerland is much older than she, probably by as much as three or four years. He was an old friend of Marie's family to whom she turned in desperation when her parents died, and who took advantage of her youth and innocence to force marriage upon her when she was, in all truth, too immature to be aware that true love could exist and should not be confused with gratitude, particularly gratitude ill-placed."

Young Hosmer Angle paused, breathless, as if wondering exactly which words to choose to continue. Homes waited patiently, smiling at the young man encouragingly. Thus heartened, young Mr. Angle went on, leaning forward, his eyes boring into Homes's.

"Mr. Homes, this Alex Northerland to whom Marie is wed, is a fiend incarnate!"

Homes frowned and raised a hand, interrupting. "He treats her poorly?"

"Oh, no, the miscreant is far too clever for that! He disguises his true baseness by treating her at all times with the utmost kindness and respect!"

"This Marie—is she at times detained? Held a prisoner in her own home?"

"Would that she were, for then I could rescue her!" the young man cried. "No, no! The rascal is far too artful to be caught out like that! He allows her every freedom and is so devilishly Machiavellian as to never ask her where she has been when she returns."

"Does he restrict her, then, in the matter of money?"

"Oh, no. The archfiend gives her more than ample allowance. But then, he is so filthy rich that in all probability he does not even miss it. Besides, it will all be Marie's money when—" He apparently felt he was wandering from the point and fell silent.

"A worthy opponent, it appears," Homes observed, and studied the young man over tented fingers. "And where does your dilemma come in?"

"Well, Mr. Homes," the young man said earnestly, "as I stated before, my religion does not permit me to hate a person, yet I find it hard in my heart to forgive Northerland his inhuman behaviour. I thought, therefore, that the least I could do as a sop to my conscience would be to present him with a gift of some sort. Unfortunately, I am not permitted on the premises of Northerland Manor. I was hoping, therefore, that you might be so kind as to deliver it for me." And he held out the small box he had been clutching so tightly. "If you could do it tomorrow, say, at exactly two o'clock in the afternoon? Marie will be with me then in my rooms in Albemarle Street."

"A pleasure," Homes assured him warmly, and picked up the box. "And just what gift do you feel a man of this terrible disposition is worthy of, even as a sop to your conscience?"

"Not a very fancy one, I'm afraid," young Mr. Angle said a bit ruefully. "I'm far from rich, at least not yet, although one always has hopes. It is merely an alarm clock, although not a cheap one. Still," he added, brightening, "if you will remember to push this button just before you deliver it, at least Northerland will have an operating mechanism when thirty minutes pass."

"This button? Of course," Homes said, and came to his feet. "If you will leave the number in Albemarle Street with Dr. Watney, I shall be pleased to advise you when this minor commission is executed. And may I wish you the best of luck in the matter of your Marie."

"It is number 16 Albemarle Street," the young man said, and added a bit absently, "although I should imagine I'll know from the journals..." He seemed to realize that Homes was already afoot and came to his own feet hurriedly. "I shall never be able to thank you enough, Mr. Homes," he said sincerely, and hurried from the room.

Homes waited until the door had closed upon our visitor and then reseated himself, turning to the shelf behind him, taking down one of his reference volumes, and leafing through it.

"Ah! Here we are," he said with satisfaction. "Sir Alex Northerland, DSC, OBE, BPOE. Member of the stock exchange, has a box at Ascot and another at Earl's Court for the yearly trap-show. Considered one of the wealthiest men in the Empire, a great donor to charities, founder of the Putney troop of the Boy Scouts, and chief financial supporter for the Home of the Blind." He closed the volume and returned it to its place on the shelf. "A worthy opponent, indeed," he repeated softly. "And if young Hosmer Angle's story contains even the slightest seeds of truth, a devilishly cunning one at that! See how this hypocrite has covered his true character with charity donations and the sponsoring of Boy Scout troops!"

"Reprehensible," I agreed. "But still, what can you do, Homes? After all, you merely agreed to deliver a package to the man."

"Ah!" Homes said sagaciously. "Young Mr. Angle may feel that a gift of a valuable alarm clock is a sop to *his* conscience for hating Northerland, but I am under no such compulsion. As one dedicated to the ferreting out of malfeasors, the least I can do is to investigate this miscreant, Sir Alex Northerland!"

He came to his feet and disappeared into his rooms, removing his dressing-gown as he did so. When he returned a few minutes later, I was surprised to see that Homes was dressed in the costume of a butler, and with his unsurpassed artistry, even managed to look a bit like one.

"I shall appear at Northerland Manor in the guise of a servant seeking work," said he, adjusting his dickey. "In the servant's quarters there is always a wealth of gossip and I shall shortly know exactly to what depths this fiend

Northerland has sunk!" He picked up the small box that Hosmer Angle had left and moved towards the door. "I shall be back soon."

"But, Homes!" I cried. "What if they offer you employment?"

"Then I may be a bit longer," he said thoughtfully, and went down the stairs.

It was late that afternoon when Homes returned, no longer carrying the small box with the alarm clock. I had been at the sideboard, attempting, by adding Jamaican rum to a soft-drink imported from the colony of Georgia, to make it palatable, when Homes came into the room and fell into a chair, shaking his head direly.

"Homes!" I cried. "What is it?"

He looked up at me broodingly. "To call this man a fiend incarnate is to flatter him!" he said heavily.

"But—what happened?" I insisted.

Homes took a deep breath. "I appeared at the rear door of the manor, at the servant's quarters," he said, "and I spoke first to the cook, a pleasant person who not only offered tea, but a plate of properly fresh buttered chutneys. As I ate I queried her.

"'How does your master treat the staff?' I asked. 'I should not care to work in a place where the staff are treated poorly.'

"'"Oh, you need have no fears on that score," she replied reassuringly. "Although the mistress can be a bit trying at times, being no better than she should be! But the master is a real gentleman, a wonderful person!"'" She leaned towards me confidentially. "'"When I first came to work here as cook, I was also worried about how the staff might be treated, so I spoke with Michael, the first footman. "'"'Michael,' I said, 'How are the staff treated here?'"'"

"'"'"Fine!" he replied. "I had the same question when I first arrived, as well, so I asked John, the butler. "'"'"'John,' I said, 'how are the staff treated?'"'"'"

"'"'"'"Never a problem with that," John replied. "When—"'"'"'"

"'"'"'"Homes!" I cried, interrupting. "I mean, Homes! I'm completely at sea. Exactly what did you discover?"

"I was just coming to that," Homes said a bit testily. "Well, the upshot of the whole thing was that this Alex Northerland has completely fooled his own staff, principally by making conditions at Northerland Manor so good that they do not even suspect his true colours; they believe him to be the finest of men."

"And their feelings towards their mistress?"

"Ah! Here the attitude is quite different. The entire staff are under the impression that their mistress, Marie, is flighty, selfish, and even a bit interfering at times."

"Interfering?"

"Yes. The cook claims she found Marie putting some strange white powder in the master's soup, when she should have known how upset Cook gets with anyone else in the kitchen. The chauffeur, who I only had a minute to speak to, claims he found the mistress filing the brake cable on the master's car one day, although the chauffeur says she should know how much it upsets him to have anyone else use his tools, which he has laid out to his satisfaction. Neither the cook nor the chauffeur seem to realize the poor girl was merely attempting to see that everything was proper for her lord and master."

"And the butler?"

"Oh, his story was of the time he found Marie tying a stout cord across the top of the steps that lead from the master's bedroom; his complaint seemed to be that she had used a granny knot rather than a square knot. It seems he is the actual scoutmaster of the Putney troop."

"It strikes me as a poor reason to be down on the poor girl," I exclaimed. "In fact, it almost seems as if the servants were in a conspiracy against the poor lass," I added, "undoubtedly fed by the lies of the despicable cad who is her husband! It seems a pity that a bounder like that should be the recipient of that fine alarm clock young Hosmer Angle was kind enough to send him."

"I agree completely," Homes said. "So much so, in fact, that I did not leave the alarm clock at Northerland Manor. It struck me as far too expensive a gift, especially coming from a poor lad such as young Mr. Angle."

"But the poor lad's conscience?" I cried.

"Oh, I left something, of course. My old stem-winder. It hasn't been working well of late, so it is a small loss. A contribution, let us say, for a lad whose heart is in the right place."

"And the alarm clock? Surely you did not keep it?"

"Of course not! I dropped it off at 16 Albemarle Street. Not wishing to disturb the lovers, I left a note explaining my actions. I even remembered to press the small button, wishing your Hosmer Angle to have the mechanism in operating condition when he discovers it." Homes's geniality disappeared. "I only wish I could have done something to punish this Sir Alex Northerland properly. Ah, well, in time I am sure his sins will catch up with him, as they will with all sinners!"

"Amen to that, Homes," I said, and reached for the bit more of rum that the Georgian soft-drink seemed to require.

I had completed my share of the kippered curries which Mrs. Essex had deigned to prepare for our breakfast and was well into the morning journal the following day when Homes came into the room and dropped into his chair, drawing his napkin from its ring.

"Ah, Watney," said he, watching me turn pages, "I will even accept another minor commission such as the one of yesterday, rather than face the ennui of another problemless day!"

"Possibly you shall not have to, Homes," I said, reading further into the article that had suddenly claimed my attention. "It seems there was a major explosion in Albemarle Street yesterday evening, with several victims. The authorities are convinced it was caused by an infernal device."

"Albemarle Street, eh? Quite a coincidence," said Homes, and his appetite whetted by the possibility of a major problem, he reached for the kippered curries. "An infernal device, eh? Dastardly things! A letter to the authorities offering my services, if you will, Watney!"

The Adventure of
The Ukrainian Foundling Orphans

IT was a fine warm morning in June of the year '79 and my friend Mr. Schlock Homes and myself were taking our ease after breakfast in our quarters at 221B Bagel Street. I was perusing the daily journal in search of some bit of crime news that might be of interest to my friend, while Homes was practising sudden stops on his fiddle—*stringhalt* as it is known both in musical and veterinarian circles—when a certain article caught my attention.

"Homes," I asked curiously, glancing up from the paper, "what is a U.F.O.?"

"U.F.O.?" Homes replied, frowning in my general direction. "I honestly cannot say, Watney." He put aside his fiddle for the moment and turned to pull down one of his many reference volumes from the shelf behind him, leafing through the pages. He paused at last, nodding. "Ah! Here we are," said he with satisfaction. "Ukrainian Foundling Orphans." He returned the volume to its proper place and was about to attend to his fiddle once again, when I held up my hand.

"Homes," I asked, "are you quite sure you are in possession of the latest in that reference series?"

He turned to check and then nodded. "Of course. 1897. Have there been any more recent?"

"Probably not," I admitted, and returned to my article. "I was merely wondering. It is simply that it says here that these U.F.O.'s have just recently been sighted in London, and I cannot see the connection."

"That is because you do not use the analytical method," Homes replied.

"Actually, the matter is obviously more in your field than in mine. Blind before, the poor orphans undoubtedly have finally, through some miracle operation, probably at St. Bart's here in London, been given the gift of vision."

"Of course!" I said, ashamed of myself for my obtuseness, and was about to turn the page of the journal and continue my search for something more of a criminal nature, when there came the sound of footsteps on the stairs. A moment later our page had ushered into our presence none other than Criscroft Homes, Schlock's brother. It was rare, indeed, for Criscroft to leave his desk at the Foreign Office to pay us a visit during his office hours, and rarer still for him to do so without first telegraphing his intentions.

Recognizing the urgency of the matter, Homes instantly finished the page he had been practising, put his fiddle back in its case, clipped the bow in place, placed his handkerchief across the strings to protect them, closed the case, stood it in the corner behind him, and then came to his feet at once, his hand extended.

"Criscroft! Your problem must be grave, indeed, to bring you unheralded here at this hour! Pray tell me what it is."

Criscroft Homes barely touched his brother's outstretched hand before falling heavily into the basket chair before the cold fireplace and looking up at his brother broodingly.

"Schlock," he said, and the very lack of emotion in his voice made it even more imperspicacious than usual, "I'm afraid Her Majesty's Government once again has need of your services."

Homes instantly sat down across from his brother while I repaired to the sideboard for a better view of the two. "Of course!" Homes said warmly. "Pray tell me all."

"Yes," Criscroft said heavily, while I poured some whisky into a glass in order to lower the level and permit me to observe them better through the bottle. "Well, there have been reports of late of unidentified flying objects having been seen in England."

"Unidentified flying objects?" Homes cried, appalled, and then paused, frowning. "What are they?"

"That is precisely the problem," Criscroft replied in a worried tone. "If we knew what they were they would not be unidentified."

"You may have a point there," Homes said thoughtfully, while I could only stand and drink with admiration as two of the finest minds in all the Empire wrestled with the complex problem. "Odd, though," Homes added, "that there has been no mention of this in the newspapers."

"If not, there soon will be," Criscroft said, and continued. "Our best brains in the department have studied the matter and have come to the conclusion that these objects are either extra-terrestrial, or that they are not."

"A reasonable assumption," Homes remarked, nodding, "and one with which I should tend to agree."

"Quite. On the one hand, if they are extra-terrestrial, we should like to know if they pose a threat of any sort to our beloved England. If they are not, of course, we should like to know if they pose a threat of any sort to our beloved England."

"Ah! I see the problem," Homes said, peering at his brother over tented fingers. "My suggestion would be that the first step should be an attempt to identify these flying objects."

"Precisely!" Criscroft said, and came to his feet, looking relieved. "I was sure you would see right to the heart of the matter, Schlock. I assume you are free to accept this commission?"

"Of course! I would not miss it for the world, or even for the *Daily Express!* If you will leave your address with Dr. Watney here—I mean, I shall get back to you either at the Foreign Office or at your club as soon as I have some definite information for you."

"Her Majesty shall be most appreciative," Criscroft said with gratitude and was about to take his departure when Homes held him back.

"One thing," Homes inquired. "Exactly where have these unidentified flying objects been seen?"

"Anywhere and everywhere," Criscroft said heavily, and stamped from the room.

"Anywhere and Everywhere, eh?" Homes murmured and repaired to his atlas. "Ah! Anywhere is a small village in Surrey, while Everywhere is a hamlet in Sussex. It will mean a bit of travelling, but no matter. Your Bradshaw, if you will, Watney, while I don more suitable raiment, and we shall be off—the game's afoot!"

Our first stop was at the little village of Anywhere, in Surrey, and as we climbed down from the train I was pleased to see Homes had that look of fierce concentration, the pursed forehead, the wrinkled nose, the general look of distaste that he often assumed when he was either faced with a hot scent or an unpleasant one. I was about to comment on it, but Homes had already pushed his way through the barrier and was speaking to the attendant.

"Flyin' objects?" that worthy was replying to Homes's query. "We got bats, o' course, but them ain't unidentified. Them got wings attached to they bodies. You can tell 'em right away. And we got birds, o' course, but while most o' them's unidentified as far as I'm concerned, old Mrs. Broome can identify 'em in a hurry. And you'm don't need no identification for our'm mosquitoes, you can tell 'em in a second."

"Little help there," Homes observed as we walked away, leaving the man staring after us and scratching his head. "Still, there must have been something in common between this town and Everywhere, in Sussex, to have made them the common target of these unidentified flying objects. Let us take a walk and make a study of this pleasant little village, after which we can repair to Everywhere and make a comparison to see what they have in common."

I could see very little in Anywhere different from any other village its size I had been unfortunate enough to have visited in the past. There was, of course, the village pub, but as I headed towards it to see if it might conform to any pubs we might later discover in Everywhere, Homes had taken my arm and was piloting me down the street in the opposite direction. We passed the mandatory post office, the village green, the police station, the cinema, the greengrocer's, the church with its rectory, the stationer's shop that undoubtedly sold stamps and journals; they were all standard establishments in almost every village in England.

Homes's efforts to elicit information on the strange objects from the taciturn natives we met led to no more success than we had encountered with the station attendant. Still, when we had completed our excursion and had returned to the railway platform to continue our journey, I was surprised to see a faint look of satisfaction on Homes's saturnine features.

"Homes!" I said, properly interpreting that self-satisfied expression. "What have you seen here that could possibly lead you to a solution to this case?"

"It is too early to say," said he in his usual insufferable manner when he has noted something that has clearly passed me by. "Possibly after our visit to Everywhere we shall be in a position to draw some definite conclusions."

We sat in silence in the train going to Sussex, Homes wreathed in smoke from his briar which he had packed with Rasura de Lápiz, a new mixture sent him by a former client in Spain in appreciation of my friend's efforts on his behalf, while I sat and stared from the car window, unaware of the passing villages, all undoubtedly with police station, church, rectory, and all the other accoutrements of English country living. I wondered exactly what Homes had seen in Anywhere that I had failed to see, what there might possibly have been to see that anyone else could have failed to see. It was quite frustrating, and it was in that same frustrating silence that we descended at Everywhere and proceeded to duplicate our previous actions at Anywhere, in Surrey.

There was the same greengrocer's as I had known there would be, the same cinema with what seemed to be the same advert outside, the same village green, the same church with what appeared to be the same rectory, the same stationer's, the same police station, even the same village pub from which Homes steered me in precisely the same way.

"Homes," I said, "we have come in a circle and are in the same village."

"No, no, Watney!" said he. "This is quite another place in another shire."

"Then we would have best remained in Anywhere and seen everything twice. In that way we would have saved ourselves the journey here."

"Oh, I don't know, Watney," Homes replied, his eyes twinkling. "I feel our visit here may, in the end, prove the basis for the solution to this problem."

"Homes!" I said reproachfully. "You know something I do not know!"

"Probably several things," he remarked with a smile. "Even some pertaining to this case."

"But what, Homes?" I cried.

He paused to look at his pocket watch and then spoke quietly, quite as if he were answering my question. "I suggest we return to London, Watney. With any luck we shall wrap this matter up tonight. Tell me, did you put this morning's journal in the trash before we left?"

"No, Homes," I said, and then added curiously, "but what difference would it make? There was nothing in this morning's paper regarding unidentified flying objects."

"There are more things in heaven and earth, Horatio, than are dreamt of in your philosophy," was Homes's strange reply.

"Homes," I said, hurt to the quick at his poor memory. "My name is John. Horatio is my cousin. Are you feeling well?"

"Never better," said he, his eyes twinkling once again, and would say no more as we rode back to London, preferring to stare from the train window pursuing his own thoughts, while I wondered how Homes had managed to confuse me with my cousin.

Arriving at Victoria, Homes hailed a hansom and minutes later we were once again within the confines of our quarters. There he instantly picked up the morning journal I had discarded at Criscroft's arrival, and began to turn the pages feverishly. At last he paused and I heard him give a satisfied sigh.

"Homes!" I cried. "What is it?"

He looked at me, his expression a subtle cross between the enigmatic and the arcane. "Tell me, Watney," said he. "How would you like to take in the cinema tonight?"

"Homes!" I said reproachfully. "Her Majesty is undoubtedly awaiting with anxiety your report. Your brother Criscroft may even have foregone his weekly Bingo in order to remain available for your answer to this grave problem. How can you think of visiting the cinema at a time like this?"

"Easily," he replied, no muscle on his face moving. "Will you join me or not?"

"Will there be a Tom and Jerry?" I asked.

"It is a possibility."

"Then I shall come," I said, for it had occurred to me that Homes might have some purpose other than pure entertainment for his decision to attend the cinema.

The cinema Homes had chosen to visit was in the neighbourhood and within minutes we found ourselves seated in the darkness and watching the announcement of the programme. I was pleased to see that after we had suffered the main feature there would be, indeed, a Tom and Jerry, but before I could comment the feature film had begun. As I watched my eyes widened.

"Homes!" I whispered. "The unidentified flying objects!"

"Precisely," he replied, and came to his feet. "Come, we have seen all we need to see."

"But, Homes," I objected as quietly as I could, "what about the Tom and Jerry?"

"They will have to do without us," he said abruptly, and was already pushing his way through to the aisle. There was nothing I could do but follow. At the front of the cinema Homes paused and studied the sheet that advertised the film—the same sheet, I now recalled, that had graced the cinemas in both Anywhere and Everywhere, and which Homes had noted and which I had not.

I was on the verge of congratulating him on his perspicacity when he stepped into the street and hailed a hansom. Thoroughly confused at this point, I could only follow him into the cab and listen to him give our jehu an address I did not recognize.

"Homes," I said as he sat back, his expression unfathomable, "I do not understand any of this. Where are we going? What were those flying objects we have just seen? And why are they unidentified?"

"They shall not be unidentified for long," he replied grimly. "This business shall end tonight, Watney." Nor would he say any more until we had drawn up before a building I had never seen before. As we got down I saw a sign over the entrance. I read *UKRAINIAN LODGE*. More puzzled than ever, I followed Homes inside and waited as he asked for a name I had never heard before. There was a brief delay and then we found ourselves in the presence of a man who looked faintly familiar. Suddenly I recognized him as one of the faces I had just seen on the cinema screen.

"Is there some place we can speak in private?" Homes asked the man.

The man nodded and led us into a small cubicle. Once there he waited until we were seated, then seated himself, and stared at my friend with a worried expression on his face.

"What can I do for you, gentlemen?" he asked.

Homes came right to the point. "My name is Schlock Homes," he said, "and you are one of the Flying Waluskis, are you not?"

The man paled. "How did you know?" he whispered.

"You gave me trapeze lessons at one time, but no matter. You have been acting in pictures lately, have you not? Together with some of the younger members of your troupe?"

Waluski could only nod miserably. "We did it for charity. The money all went to help orphans. We did not keep a penny."

"I am aware of that, and you deserve full credit for it. But my question is quite another. Why did you do it without having your name on the programme?"

Waluski looked about, even though we were alone, and unconsciously lowered his voice.

"Mr. Homes," he said earnestly, "myself and the other members of my family are in this country without permission. Were you to denounce us to the authorities, we should be deported to the Ukraine. Were that to happen we should be doomed to do our act in circuses, and nothing more. Mr. Homes, two of my sons are allergic to bears..." He allowed his words to trail to significant silence.

Homes came to his feet and placed a sympathetic hand on the man's shoulder.

"Worry not, Mr. Waluski," he said, his tone warm with understanding. "I shall say nothing of the matter. I only hope the time comes when you can be given the credit you deserve both for your kind deeds and your remarkable acrobatic skills. However," he added, his voice becoming a trifle stern, "I must ask you to refrain from any future flying until your position in this country becomes legalized, as your performance has led to unneeded perturbation among certain Government agencies in our beloved England."

"I promise," Waluski said brokenly, and he would have kissed Homes's two hands had we not already been on our way down the stairs.

As we stood at the kerb trying to wave down a hansom, Homes turned to me.

"I would appreciate your advising Criscroft that there is no threat at all in the unidentified flying objects, Watney, and that I consider the matter closed."

"I shall do so as soon as we are in our quarters," I promised. "But tell me, Homes, what led you to the solution of this complex affair in the first place?"

"The posters before the cinema in both Anywhere and Everywhere," he replied. "It has been many years since I have seen *Peter Pan,* and then just on the stage, but the memory of that fine bit of work has always remained."

Our activities of the previous evening having kept us from our beds to a rather late hour, it was past ten when Homes made his appearance at the breakfast table. He sat down, helped himself to a large portion of the grilled curries, and looked at me inquiringly across the table.

"I see you have your nose in the morning journal as usual, Watney," said he. "I hope you are able to unearth some small bit of malfeasance upon which we might practice our rusting skills."

"I'm afraid not, Homes," I replied, reading further into the article that had caught my attention. "However, there is this: it says here that U.F.O.'s have also been sighted in the former colony of New York."

"It is truly wonderful what those Ukrainians are doing for their orphans!" Homes said warmly. "A telegram to the New York chapter of their lodge offering our congratulations, if you will, Watney!"

The Adventure of

The Pie-Eyed Piper

IT was rare, indeed, for my friend, Mr. Schlock Homes, to indulge himself excessively in spirits; but the one time I recall when he might have been said to have had one over the eight, he still proved himself capable of resolving a situation that another might well have handled in an entirely different fashion, and almost certainly with completely different results.

I had come into the breakfast room of our quarters at 221B Bagel Street one fine morning in June of the year '79, to find Homes quite neatly fettered in a maze of rope. The chair to which he was bound had fallen to its side, carrying Homes with it, but still, in his indomitable manner, he was struggling to reach a book above him on the edge of the table.

"I should think that a most uncomfortable position in which to read, Homes," I said, and then added, ever considerate, "However, I can see you are tied up. I can return for my repast at a later hour, if that should be more convenient."

"No, no, Watney!" said he, a trifle impatiently. "It is simply that I suppose I should have read a bit further into Sir Baden-Powell's book on scouting knots before I attempted to solve them. However, if you would kindly tug on this exposed portion of the cord—"

A moment later Homes was free and upon his feet, and after righting the chair and placing Sir Baden-Powell's book in the dustbin, he seated himself across from me and reached for the parslied chutneys that Mrs. Essex had generously provided for our morning meal. As I drew my napkin into my lap, Homes began to eat while at the same time spreading the morning journal open upon the table and perusing the headlines. Suddenly he made a sound deep in his throat and looked up, considering me with a black frown upon his face.

"Tell me, Watney," said he in dire tones, "what do you think of gifted children?"

I paused in reaching for a chutney to consider the question carefully, determined to be as analytical in my attention to the matter as Homes, himself, would have been. "Why," I said at last, "it sounds rather onerous. Slavery has been abolished for some years now, and the giving of children, particularly as gifts, strikes me as being quite reprehensible, to say the least."

"I should tend to agree," said he, and continued to read further in the newspaper article that had claimed his attention. As I watched I could see the frown deepen upon his saturnine features. "Watney!" he exclaimed after a moment, looking up in horror, "this is infamous! Something must be done about it!"

"But what is it, Homes?" I cried.

"These gifted children," he said darkly, "all of whom have in their time won medals for their musical ability, are being sent abroad! It says here 'as a reward,' but to whom they are being given, or what that person has done to deserve these talented children as a reward, the article does not say."

He pushed his plate away, cast the journal to one side, and came to his feet heavily.

"We cannot stand idly by and see these poor children enslaved against their will!"

"But where are they being sent, Homes?" I inquired anxiously. "And why, if they must be enslaved, are not Englishmen at least given first occasion for their services?"

"Precisely my query!" he replied. "The children are being sent to Germany, to a small town there called Hamelin, on the banks of the Weser. But whoever arranged this fiendish mission has overlooked Schlock Homes!"

He began to undo the cord of his dressing-gown, but he had tied it in accordance with the strictures of Sir Baden-Powell and I was forced to come from my place and tug the end of the cord to free him.

"Thank you," he said graciously. "Now, a moment for me to change to more suitable raiment, and we shall be off to scotch this nefarious scheme in the bud!"

"Scotch?" I said wonderingly, for in truth I had not been paying close attention. "And Budd? For a chaser? At this hour — ?"

But Homes had already disappeared into his room, and I was left to reflect on the poor state of his memory, for he had not even attempted to pause at the sideboard on his way.

And so began the case which I find annotated in my daybook as *The Adventure of the Pie-Eyed Piper,* and most welcome it was. Homes had spent much of the previous fortnight at Loose Ends, the country estate of a banker friend of his, resolving the delicate matter of the huge sums that had been embezzled from the Chase Madly Bank, a case I find delineated in my notes as *The Adventure of the Veiled Ledger;* and now that the affair had been brought to its aoristic conclusion, he was once again restless and searching for any matter that might occupy his ever-active mind. The situation in which he had discovered the poor children was to bring his ennui to an end, as well as to bring him, I was pleased to see, the consideration his results in the case so richly deserved.

Our Bradshaw indicated there was a steamer from Callooh to Calais which we were fortunate enough to book. Since Homes's beloved violin was out to have the frets tranquilized, and since my friend never travelled without a musical instrument of some sort to while away his unoccupied moments, he carried with him a penny-whistle, an instrument to which he had recently become introduced and which he played with considerable skill.

With it he was able to provide entertainment for our fellow passengers on the ship; nor were his efforts unappreciated, for we were regaled with coins presented, without doubt, by those in his audience familiar with the fact that Homes was an ardent numismatist. Thus occupied, my friend did not discuss the case at all during the voyage, nor did he deign to refer to it while we were on the Hamelin Express, preferring instead to softly play the Aria Coda from the Bell song on his whistle, as he undoubtedly planned his strategy.

We stepped from the train at the quaint station of Hamelin and were soon comfortably settled in at the Unterirdisch Heights Hotel, in connecting rooms. Travelling on the Continent has always been a challenge to me, since the pub hours of each country are so much at variance with our own, and I was about to knock up Homes and suggest we investigate Hamelin's particular schedule, when there was a rap on our connecting door and I opened it to find myself staring in astonishment at Homes in the most outlandish garments.

At sight of the figure he cut all other thoughts were banished from my mind, at least temporarily, for Homes had chosen to dress in the fashion of a schoolboy. I knew he had not brought along the accoutrements necessary for any of his spectacular disguises; but then I saw he had merely cut a pair of his trousers off at the knees, had rolled down his socks, and had clipped the brim of a derby and painted stripes on it to make a fair imitation of a schoolboy's cap. With his tremendous histrionic ability he undoubtedly felt sure he could easily pass off as a lad from a public school, albeit one who was six foot three inches in height with unusually hairy legs, in need of a facial shave, and with a penny-whistle tucked in one pocket.

"Homes!" I cried in bewilderment. "What is the meaning of this absurd costume?"

"You recognized me?" he asked in evident disappointment. "Ah, well, I suppose it was only to be expected, after the years of training I have afforded you. The costume will not be so readily penetrated by the uninitiate, however, and it will enable me to merge without suspicion with the poor enslaved children. The whistle, of course, will also give me *entrée* into their ranks, since they are all musicians. I shall be back as soon as possible."

"But, Homes," I cried. "Supposing you are also enslaved, since you will appear so much like the others?"

"Then, of course, one can only hope for a reasonable master," he replied with a brave attempt at a schoolboy grin, and was off down the stairs.

While it was true that the public-house hours in Hamelin were, indeed, quite different from the outmoded practice still in force in our otherwise-enlightened Britain, the prices were also quite different, and I found myself returning to our rooms at the Unterirdisch Heights with six bottles of the local alcoholic endeavour, determined not to waste the currency of our beloved but admittedly financially distressed kingdom needlessly. I had sampled four of these liquid refreshments without determining if the savings were worthwhile, when Homes came up the stairs to my room and fell into a chair, staring at me morosely. I instantly offered him a drink which he downed in one draught, a clear indication that his mind was on other matters, or that he was thirsty. As I hurriedly refilled his glass, he sighed mightily.

"The condition of servitude of these children, Watney," said he heavily, "is far more subtle than one might imagine. Ostensibly they are being given a modicum of freedom, but obviously only to lull them into a false sense of security before being sent to their eventual masters."

"A modicum of freedom, Homes?" I inquired curiously.

He absent-mindedly drank off his drink and handed me the glass.

"Freedom of shorts," he said.

I stared at him in horror. "They have deprived the children of their underwear?" I asked, aghast.

"Freedom of sorts, I meant," said he, and took down his drink in one gulp, his mind on the problem of the children. He held out his glass. "Unforshunate for these mishcreans, they did not figure on the intervasion — intertasion — "

"The meddling of Schlock Homes?" I suggested helpfully.

"Profusely," he said. "I mean, precisely."

"But you do have a plan to aid these poor souls, Homes?" I asked anxiously.

"Of a certainly." He leaned forward a bit, weaving slightly in his chair. "These chillruns, Watley, have formed theirselves into a orshester, and I have been electric loader."

"I beg your pardon, Homes?" I said, puzzled.

"I said, I have been electered lader. I mean, leader." He beamed at me proudly a moment, but then his face fell slightly. "Prollaly because I was the only one tall enough to be sheen from all parts of the orshester."

"It's still an honour, Homes," I said soothingly. "But what has this to do with your plan to rescue the poor youngsters?"

"Ah! My plan!" He frowned a moment and then his frown disappeared as he remembered. "I shall need your help, Whitley, but I am sure I can deepen on that."

"Of course, Homes!" I said warmly. "And your plan?"

"Ah, the plan! Tonight, Whitney, I have arrange for the orshester to parade through the streets of — where are we?"

"Hamelin."

"Hamelin, then. There is a broadridge that crosses the river Weser — "

"A what, Homes?"

"A broadridge!" Homes said impatiently, and glared at me for my stupidity. "A ridge that goes up and down to let the chips go through!"

"Oh! You mean a drawbridge!"

"Thass what I said! Anyway, you shall be in the control room of the broadridge. At precisely eight o'clock I shall lead the orshester over the ridge. At profusely eight-oh-two the lass man will have cross. At exactful eight-oh-three you will open the ridge so nobody can follow. Do you understand?"

"But what of the regular operator?" I asked nervously. "Might he not take exception to my presence?"

"Play him with wicksy. I mean, ply him with whisky." Homes pointed to a bottle. He came to his feet and then stumbled slightly. He stared at me in horror. "Witby! They are on to us!"

"What do you mean, Homes?" I cried in alarm.

"They have dragged my drunk!"

"You mean, they have drugged your drink?" I looked into his eyes, standing on tiptoe to do so. "You are right, Homes! Here, a hair of the dog and I am sure you will be fine in time for the rescue tonight!"

"Thank you," Homes said gratefully, and then collapsed gently to the floor. "A shore nap before our work tonight . . ." And he relaxed to allow my cure to take effect.

It was seven in the evening when Homes awoke. The effects of the drug our vile opponents had been clever enough to serve him without his knowledge were still slightly evident, for he grimaced with headache; nor did another drink seem to help. He glanced at his timepiece and came to his feet.

"It is time to leave, Watney," said he, feeling about for his penny-whistle.

It was with relief that he found it and played a few notes, nodding at the purity of their tone. "The night dampness," he explained, and led the way from the room.

The members of the orchestra were awaiting their leader on the village green, and came to their feet as Homes approached, lining up in marching formation. Homes glanced at his timepiece and nodded to me to get moving on my assignment, while he raised his penny-whistle to gain the attention of his musicians. As the first notes of his concert began, I hurried down the street to the bridge and made my way to the room where the controls for raising and lowering the structure were located. Following Homes's advice, I had brought with me a bottle of the strongest whisky I had purchased that afternoon. The bridge-tender frowned darkly when I made my appearance.

"Sir," he said, "visitors are not allowed."

"Not even when they bring drinks?" I asked coyly, holding out the bottle of whisky.

He raised his eyebrows. "Sir! I am the president of the Hamelin

Temperance Society!" he said. "Whisky has never passed my lips, nor shall it! I must ask you to leave at once!"

I stood nonplussed, for the music of Homes and his orchestra was gaining in volume as they approached the bridge that could lead them to the other side of the river and to freedom, but only if I were successful in my mission.

"Not even a short one?" I asked pleadingly, and found myself on the street, with the imprint of the bridge-tender's foot undoubtedly necessitating a visit in the near future to my dry-cleaner's. I hurried down the street, coming to Homes as he marched at the head of his band. He frowned darkly to see me.

"The bridge-tender is a teetotaler," I explained quickly.

Homes wasted not a moment, but his mammoth intellect instantly understood and concocted an alternate scheme in a moment. He signalled a player in the front row of the marchers to take his place, and hurried me along on our way back to the bridge.

"I shall ask the bridge-tender for a match to light my calabash," he explained. "As he reaches into his pocket for a vesta, you will strike him unconscious. Do it posthaste, for time is running out!"

He swung open the door to the control room without awaiting my comments, and a moment later found himself facing an irate bridge-tender. Homes smiled at the man in his most charming manner. "I wonder if I might bother you for a match to light my calabash," he asked ingratiatingly.

The man scowled at him. "You are asking me to encourage the foul habit of smoking?" he demanded. "You, a schoolboy too young for such a vice?" He turned away in disdain. "D' you want to stunt your growth?"

"Hurry, Watney!" Homes exclaimed.

"But he didn't give you a match yet!" I objected.

"Oh, for heaven's sake!" Homes said in disgust, and struck the man on the head with the blunt end of his penny-whistle. Even as the bridge-tender collapsed to the floor, Homes reached for the lever that opened the bridge. As the sounds of the creaking cables came to us, indicating the bridge was opening, Homes had me by the arm and was hurrying me from the room.

"And now we had best escape ourselves, while the time is ripe," he said. "I investigated this bridge thoroughly in formulating my plan, and there is an old passage here which will lead us safely a distance from the bridge itself. But wait!" He paused and looked at me. "Did you hear something?"

"A splash and then someone saying 'Glug,' I thought," I said. "Or possibly a whole number of people saying 'Glug'."

Homes looked at me almost pityingly.

"Your ignorance is monumental, Watney," he said with scorn. "It is undoubtedly the bridge-tender saying 'Gluck,' meaning 'luck' in German. He is undoubtedly congratulating himself on not having been more seriously injured!"

And Homes led me out upon a path far from the bridge that would take us eventually to our hotel and thence to the railway station.

Having returned late at night from our journey to Hamelin, it was close upon noon when we came into the breakfast room the following morning and seated ourselves to a repast of Mrs. Essex's curried oreganos. Feeling that possibly my contribution to the previous evening's success had been minimal, I hastened to open the morning journal and search for some case that might keep Homes and myself occupied.

"Is there anything at all?" Homes inquired, looking at me queryingly across the table.

"Nothing new," I said. "But there is a reference here to those lads we rescued last evening. It states and I quote: 'The gifted young musicians that had gone to Hamelin are still missing.'"

Homes laughed in pure delight.

"Ah, youth! So pleased by their unexpected freedom that they are undoubtedly celebrating with a holiday in the country, without a thought to their worried parents! A letter of reassurance to the editor of the journal, if you would, Watney!"

Bibliography

All the stories in this volume were originally published in
Ellery Queen's Mystery Magazine

Collected as ***The Incredible Schlock Homes*** (1966)

The Adventure of the Ascot Tie February 1960
The Adventure of the Printer's Inc. May 1960
The Adventure of the Adam Bomb September 1960
The Adventure of the Spectacled Band November 1960
The Adventure of the Stockbroker's Clark March 1961
The Adventure of the Missing Cheyne-Stroke August 1961
The Adventure of the Artist's Mottle November 1961
The Adventure of the Double-Bogey Man February 1962
The Adventure of the Lost Prince July 1962
The Adventure of the Counterfeit Sovereign June 1963
The Adventure of the Snared Drummer September 1963
The Adventure of the Final Problem February 1964
(Entitled "The Final Adventure" in *The Incredible Schlock Homes*)

Collected as ***The Memoirs of Schlock Homes*** (1974)

The Return of Schlock Homes June 1964
The Adventure of the Big Plunger February 1965
The Adventure of the Widow's Weeds August 1966
The Adventure of the Perforated Ulster February 1967
The Adventure of the Missing Three-Quarters September 1967
The Adventure of the Disappearance of Whistler's Mother February 1968
The Adventure of the Dog in the Knight February 1970
The Adventure of the Briary School February 1973
The Adventure of the Hansom Ransom May 1973
The Adventure of the Great Train Robbery April 1974
The Adventure of Black, Peter July 1974

Previously uncollected

The Adventure of the Odd Lotteries July 1975
The Adventure of the Elite Type July 1977
The Adventure of the Animal Fare October 1977
The Adventure of the Common Code September 1979
The Adventure of the Patient Resident February 11, 1980
The Adventure of the Belles Letters June 30, 1980
The Adventure of the Short Fuse August 18, 1980
The Adventure of the Ukrainian Foundling Orphans January 28, 1981
The Adventure of the Pie-Eyed Piper June 17, 1981